BEN<s></s>DICT KIELY

Benedict Kiely, novelist, short-story writer, journalist, broadcaster and lecturer, was born in Dromore, County Tyrone in 1919 and raised in Omagh. After graduating from University College Dublin in 1943, Kiely settled in Dublin and began what was to be a long and prolific writing career. By 1945 he was a full-time critic for the *Irish Independent* and had also published his first book, *Counties of Contention*, a non-fiction account of the partition of Ireland. His first novel, *Land Without Stars*, was published shortly afterwards and was followed by a steady flow of highly praised novels and short-story collections including *The Cards of the Gambler* (1953), *There Was an Ancient House* (1955), *The Captain with the Whiskers* (1960), *A Journey to the Seven Streams* (1963), *A Ball of Malt and Madame Butterfly* (1973), *Proxpera* (1977), *A Cow in the House* (1978), *The State of Ireland* (1985) and *God's Own Country* (1993), as well as numerous works of non-fiction and two volumes of memoirs, *Drink to the Bird* (1991) and *The Waves Behind Us* (1999).

Having lectured and taught widely across Ireland and the United States, Kiely was Literary Editor of the *Irish Press*, and a regular contributor to the *New Yorker* and *The Irish Times*. A recipient of the Award for Literature from the Irish Academy of Letters and a Saoi of Aosdána, he passed away in 2007.

Ben Forkner recently retired as Professor of English at the University of Angers in France where he founded the *Journal of the Short Story* thirty years ago. He has written many essays on writers from Ireland and the American South, and has edited a dozen anthologies, including *Modern Irish Short Stories* (Penguin), *A New Book of Dubliners* (Methuen), *Stories of the Modern South* (Penguin) and *Louisiana Stories* (Pelican). His most recent books include *Cajun* (a study of the Louisiana photographer Fonville Winans), and a new edition of John James Audubon's journals, *Selected Journals and Other Writings*, for Penguin Nature Classics. His afterword, 'The Long Way Round', for this selection of Benedict Kiely's stories was first presented as a talk at the Benedict Kiely Literary Weekend in Omagh in 2008.

First published in 2011 by
Liberties Press
Guinness Enterprise Centre | Taylor's Lane | Dublin 8
Tel: +353 (1) 415 1224
www.libertiespress.com | info@libertiespress.com

Trade enquiries to Gill & Macmillan Distribution
Hume Avenue | Park West | Dublin 12
Tel: +353 (1) 500 9534 | Fax: +353 (1) 500 9595
sales@gillmacmillan.ie

Distributed in the United States by
Dufour Editions | PO Box 7 | Chester Springs | Pennsylvania 19425

Cover design by Sin É Design
Internal design by Liberties Press
Printed and bound in the UK by CPI Antony Rowe, Chippenham and Eastbourne

The publishers gratefully acknowledge
financial assistance from the Arts Council.

BENEDICT KIELY

Selected Stories

*Edited and with an Afterword
by Ben Forkner*

Contents

The Heroes in the Dark House

'They were gone in the morning,' the old man said. His name was Arthur Broderick, and the young folk-tale scholar sat quietly, listening for the story that had been promised him.

'Lock, stock and barrel,' said the old man. 'The whole U.S. garrison, off for the far fields of France. Jeeps, guns, and gun-carriers. In the dump behind the big camp at Knocknashee Castle the handful of caretakers they left behind slung radio sets and bicycles and ran a gun-carrier with caterpillar wheels over the lot, and as good as made mash of them. Very wasteful. War's all waste. Those bicycles would have kept every young boy in the county spinning for the next five years.'

Like the plain girl that nobody wanted Mr Broderick's nine-times rejected manuscript-folk-tales set down with such love and care in highspined script lay between them on an antique drawing-room table. The table's top, solid oak and two inches thick, was shaped like a huge teardrop pearl with the tip abruptly nipped off.

'Oak,' Mr Broderick said through the smoke. 'Solid oak and two centuries old. In 1798, in the year of the Rising, it was the top of a bellows in a smithy. Look here where the British yeomanry sawed the tip off it so that the rebels could no longer use it for the forging of the pikes. When I was the age of yourself I converted it into a table. Sixty years ago last July.'

Around them in the ancient, musty, tapestried room the wreathing smoke might have come from the fires of 1798. Birdsong outside, sun-shine, wind in the creepers were as far away as Florida. The greedy, nesting jackdaws held the flues as firmly as ever at Thermopylae or the Alamo or Athlone, or a score of other places all around the battered globe, unforgotten heroes had held passes, bridgeheads or gun-burned walls. And unforgotten heroes had marched through the smoke in this room: Strong Shawn, the son of the fisherman of Kinsale, triumphant, with the aid of white magic, crossed the seven-mile strand of steel spikes, the seven-mile-high mountain of flames, the seven miles of treacherous sea, and came gloriously to win his love in a castle court-yard crowded with champions and heroes from the four sides of the world; the valiant son of the King of Antua fought with Macan Mor, son of the King of Soracha, in the way that they made rocks of water and water of rocks, and if the birds came from the lower to the upper world to see wonders it was to see these two they came.

Mr Broderick went on with his tale. All night long through the village below the old, dark, smoky house that had once been a rectory the lorries had throbbed and thundered on the narrow, twisted street and above, in the upper air, the waves of planes had swept east towards Europe.

'They were gone in the morning,' he said. 'Lock, stock and barrel. There was never a departure like it since the world was made. For quick packing, I heard afterwards, they drove the jeeps up the steep steps of the courthouse below. It reminded me of the poem about the three jolly gentlemen in coats of red who rode their horses up to bed.'

'They were gone,' he said, 'like snow off a ditch.'

It was as much as the young scholar could do to see him for smoke.

But with an effort that would have done credit to Macan Mor or Shawn of Kinsale he managed to control his coughing.

In the old dizzy chimney the jackdaws were so solidly entrenched that at times Mr Broderick had found it hard to see the paper he tran-scribed the folk-tales on. The smoke no longer made him cough, but at eighty-five his eyes were not as keen as they had been when he was in his prime and from the saddle of a galloping hunter could spot, in passing, a bird's nest in a leafy hedgerow. Lovingly he transcribed the tales in the high, spidery handwriting that – like himself, like his work for Sir Horace Plunkett in the co-operative creameries, his friendship with Thomas Andrews who had built the *Titanic* and gone bravely with it to Wordsworth's incommunicable sleep – belonged to a past, forgotten time. For years of his life he had followed these tales, the people who told them, the heroes who lived in them, over miles of lonely heather-mountain, up boreens that in rain became rivulets, to crouch in mountain cabins by the red hearth-glow and listen to the meditative voices of people for whom there was only the past.

Peadar Haughey of Creggan Cross had sat on the long, oaken settle with his wife and three daughters and dictated to him the adventures of the son of the King of Antua, as well as the story of the giant of Reibhlean who had abducted from Ireland a married princess. Giants as a rule preferred unmarried princesses. Peadar told the story in Irish and English. His wife and daughters understood only English but together they rocked in unison on the settle and sang macaronic songs in a mixture of both languages. That simple world had its own confusions. At times in his smoky house he found it hard to separate the people in the tales from the people who told them.

Bed-ridden Owen Roe Ward, in a garret in a back-lane in the garrison town ten miles away, had told him the story of the King of Green Island and other stories that were all about journeys to the end of the earth in search of elixirs that could only be won by herculean labours. Hewing trees for hire in a tangled plantation whose wood had once paid for the travels and other activities of D'Orsay and Lady Blessington, Owen had brought down on his hapless spine a ton-weight of timber. Paralysed in his garret he travelled as he talked to find life-giving water in the well at the world's end.

A woman of eighty by the name of Maire John (she still sang with the sweet voice she had at twenty and displayed the fondness for embracing men that, according to tradition, had then characterised her) had told him of the three princesses who sat in the wishing chair. One wished to marry a husband more beautiful than the sun. The second wished to marry a husband more beautiful than the moon. The third stated her honest but eccentric preference for the White Hound of the Mountain. It was a local heather-flavoured version of the marriage of Cupid and Psyche, and Maire John herself was a randy old lady who would, in the days of silver Latin, have delighted Apuleius.

The stories had come like genii, living, wreathing from holes in the wall behind smoky hearths, or from the dusty tops of dressers, or from farmhouse lofts where ancient, yellow manuscripts were stored. By Bloody Bridge on the Camowen River (called so because of no battle, but because of the number of fine trout killed there) he had heard from Pat Moses Gavigan a completely new version of the story of Fionn MacCumhail and the enchanted Salmon of Wisdom.

Plain and mountain and river-valley, the places he knew were sombre with the sense of family, and folk-tales grew as naturally there as grass. Heroes, princesses, enchanters good and bad, he had marshalled them all, called them to order in his own smoky room, numbered them off right to left, made his roll-call, described them in that high-spined handwriting he had studied so laboriously in the old manuscripts. Properly thus caparisoned they would go out into the twentieth century. He made his own of them. He called them his children. He sent them out to the ends of the earth, to magazine editors and publishing houses. They came back rejected to him, as if being his children they could have no life when torn away from him. Then one day in the smoky room under the power of the squabbling enchanters of jackdaws he had the bitterness of discovering that his children had betrayed him. In a Dublin newspaper he read the review of the young scholar's book:

'The scholar who has compiled, translated and edited these folk-tales has a wise head on young shoulders. Careful research and a wide knowledge of comparative folklore have gone into his work. He has gleaned carefully in the mountainous area ten miles north of the town where he was born. He presents his findings with an erudite introduction and in an impeccable style . . .'

The smoke wreathed around him. The reviewer's weary sentences went on like the repetition of a death-knell:

'His name is worthy to rank with that of such folklorists as Jeremiah Curtin. Particularly notable is his handling of the remarkable quest tale of the King of Green Island . . .'

Mr Broderick couldn't blame the three princesses for leaving the wishing chair and making off with a younger man. That scholar, wise head on young shoulders, could be Cupid, more beautiful than the sun and the moon: he might even be that enigmatic character, The White Hound of the Mountain. But Shawn of Kinsale could have been kinder to old age, and so could all those battling heroes or venturesome boys who crossed perilous seas, burning mountains and spiked strands.

He wrote to the young scholar at the publisher's address: 'While I am loath to trade on your time, I have, it would seem, been working or wandering about in the same field and in the same part of the country. We may share the acquaintanceship of some of the living sources of these old tales. We certainly have friends in common in the realms of mythology. Perhaps my own humble gatherings might supplement your store. So far I have failed to find a publisher for them. If you are ever visiting your home town you may care to add a few miles to the journey to call on me. My congratulations on your achievement. It gratifies me to see a young man from this part of the country doing so well.'

A week later he took up his stick one day and walked down the winding, grass-grown avenue. An ancestor was rector here long years ago, he thought, as in the case of William Yeats, the poet, who died in France on the eve of this war and who had an ancestor a rector long years ago in Drumcliffe by the faraway Sligo sea. Mr Broderick's house had been the rectory. When the church authorities judged it a crumbling, decaying property they had given it to Mr Broderick for a token sum – a small gesture of regard for all that in an active manhood he had done for the village. Crumbling and decaying it was, but peace, undisturbed, remained around the boles of the trees, the tall gables and old tottering chimneys, the shadowy bird-rustling walks. Now, as he walked, yews gone wild and reckless made a tangled pattern above his head.

Weeks before, from the garrison town in the valley, war had spilled its gathering troops over into this little village. Three deep, burdened with guns and accoutrements, they slouched past Mr Broderick on the way down the hill to their courthouse billet. Dust rose around them. They sang. They were three to six thousand miles from home, facing an uncertain future, and in reasonably good humour. A dozen or so who knew Mr Broderick from the tottering house as the old guy who made souvenirs out of blackthorn and bog oak, waved casual, friendly hands. Beyond and behind them as they descended was the blue cone of Knocknashee Hill where the castle was commandeered and where a landlord had once stocked a lake with rainbow trout that like these troops had been carried across the wide Atlantic. The soldiers' dust settling around him in wreaths and rings, Mr Broderick went down the road to collect his mail at the post-office. There had been no troops in this village since 1798 when the bellows had been mutilated and the soldiers then, according to the history books, had been anything but friendly.

The long red-tiled roofs and white walls of the co-operative creamery, the sheen of glasshouses from the slopes of the model farm were a reminder to Mr Broderick of the enthusiasms of an active past. People had, in his boyhood, been evicted for poverty in that village. Now every year the co-operative grain store handled one hundred and fifty thousand tons of grain. An energetic young man could take forty tons of tomatoes out of an acre and a quarter of glasshouses, and on a day of strong sunshine the gleam of the glasshouses would blind you. Crops burst over the hedges as nowhere else in that part of the country. It was good, high, dry land that took less harm than most places from wet seasons and flooding, and the cattle were as heavy and content as creamy oxen in French vineyards.

Over the hedge and railings by the parish church the statue of the old Canon, not of Mr Broderick's persuasion, raised a strong Roman right arm. The pedestal described the Canon as a saintly priest and sterling patriot and to anybody, except Mr Broderick, that raised right arm might have been minatory. To Arthur Broderick it was a kind memory of hero and co-worker, it was an eternal greeting in stone.

'Arthur,' the statue said, 'yourself and myself built this place. There was a time when you'd have clambered to the top of a telegraph pole if somebody'd told you there was a shilling there would help to make the village live. You did everything but say mass and I did that. You got little out of it yourself. But you saw they were happy and strong. Look around you. Be proud and glad. Enjoy your dreams of lost heroes in the mist. No young man can steal from you what you want to give away.'

High above the dead stone Canon the Angelus bell rang. Before him, down the cobbled foot walk, so steep that at times it eased itself out with a sigh into flat, flagged steps, went a tall soldier and a small young woman. Mr Broderick knew her. She was one of the eighteen Banty Mullans, nine male, nine female, all strawheaded and five feet high, the males all roughs, and the females, to put it politely, taking in washing for the Irish Fusiliers in the town below. She was ill-dressed, coarse-tongued and vicious. She carried in her left hand a shiny gallon buttermilk-can. Stooping low, the tall warrior eased the handle of the can from the stumpy, stubborn fingers and, surprised at a gentlemanly gesture that could never have come from a pre-war fusilier trained in the old Prussian school and compelled in public to walk like clock-work, she asked with awe, 'Aren't you feared the sergeant will see you?'

'In this man's army,' he said.

He could be a Texan. It was diverting to study their accents and guess at States.

'In this man's army, sister, we don't keep sergeants.'

Suddenly happy, Arthur Broderick tripped along behind them, kicked at a stray pebble, sniffed at the good air until his way was blocked by the frail, discontented figure of Patrick who kept the public house beside the post-office and opposite the courthouse, and who sold the bog oak and blackthorn souvenirs to thirsty, sentimental soldiers.

'Lord God, Mr Broderick,' said Patrick. 'Do you see that for discipline? Carrying a tin can like an errand boy.'

'But Patrick, child, it's idyllic. Deirdre in the hero tale couldn't have been more nobly treated by the three Ulster brothers, the sons of Uisneach. Hitler and Hirohito had to bring the doughboys over here before one of the Banty Mullans was handled like a lady.'

'Mr Bee,' said Patrick, 'we all know you have odd ideas on what's what. But Mr Bee, there must be a line of demarcation. Would you look across the street at that for soldiering?'

In sunshine that struggled hard, but failed, to brighten the old granite walls and Ionic columns of the courthouse the huge, coloured sentry had happily accepted the idea that for that day and in that village he did not have to deal with the Wehrmacht. Unlike the court-house he looked as if he had been specially made by the sun. He sat relaxed on a chair, legs crossed, sharing a parcel of sandwiches with a trio of village children. Behind him on a stone ledge, his weapon of war was a votive offering at the feet of a bronze statue of a famous hanging judge who, irritated by the eczema of the droppings of lawless, irreverent birds, scowled like the Monster from Thirty Thousand Fathoms. Then clattering down the courthouse steps came fifty young men, very much at ease. Falling into loose formation they went jauntily down the hilly street to the cookhouse at the bottom of the village. To the rhythm of their feet they played tunes with trays and table utensils.

'Their morale is high,' said Mr Broderick.

Dark, hollow-cheeked, always complaining, persecuted by a corpulent wife, Patrick resented the young warriors with every bone in his small body. Some local wit had once said that he was a man constitutionally incapable of filling a glass to the brim.

'Those fellows, Mr Bee, are better fed than yourself or myself.'

'They're young and growing, Patrick. They need it more. Besides, doesn't the best authority tell us an army marches on its belly?'

'They're pampered. Starve the Irish, Lord Kitchener said, and you'll have an army.'

'Ah, but Patrick the times have changed. I had the pleasure of serving under Lord Kitchener. But he never impressed me as a dietician.'

'Soft soles on their boots,' said Patrick, 'and their teeth glued together with chewing gum and all the girls in the country running wild since they came.'

'Life,' said Mr Broderick, 'we can't suppress. Every woman worth breathing loves a warrior who's facing death.'

'Once upon a time,' Patrick said, 'your old friend, the Canon, made a rake of a fellow kneel at the church gate with a horse collar round his neck to do public penance for his rascalities with the girls.'

'Lothario in a leather frame, Patrick.'

Mr Broderick laughed until his eyes were moist, at the memory and at the unquenchable misery in the diminutive, unloved, unloving heart of hen-pecked Patrick.

'Today, Patrick, there wouldn't be enough horse collars to go round. The horse isn't as plentiful as it was. The Canon had his foibles. He objected also to tam o'shanters and women riding bicycles. That was so long ago, Patrick. We'll drink to his memory.'

Everything, he thought as he left the public house and stepped on to the post-office, was so long ago. Patrick could hardly be described as part of the present. His lament was for days when heroes went hungry, when the fusiliers in the town below were forbidden by rule to stand chatting on the public street, were compelled to step rigidly, gloves like this, cane like that under the oxter – like a stick trussing a plucked chicken in a poulterer's shop. Patrick in his cave of a pub was a comic, melancholy, legendary dwarf. His one daring relaxation was to brighten the walls of his cave with coloured calendars of pretty girls caught with arms full of parcels and, by the snapping of some elastic or the betrayal of some hook or button, in mildly embarrassing situations. With startled but nevertheless smiling eyes they appealed to Patrick's customers.

'Your souvenirs sell well, Mr Bee,' Patrick said. 'The pipes especially. But the sloe-stone rosary beads too. Although it puzzles me to make out what these wild fellows want with rosary beads.'

'They may have mothers at home, Patrick, who like keep-sakes. They're far from home. They're even headed the other way.'

At the post-office the girl behind the brass grille said, 'Two letters, Mr Broderick.'

He read the first one. The young scholar said that he had read with great interest of Mr Broderick's interest in and his collection of folktales. He realised that folk-tales were often, curiously enough, not popular fare but he still considered that the publishers lacked vision and enterprise. He had only had his own book published because of the fortunate chance of his meeting a publisher who thought that he, the young scholar, might some day write a book that would be a moneymaker. The young scholar would also in the near future be visiting his native place. He thanked Mr Broderick for his kind invitation and would take the liberty of calling on him.

The second letter came from an old colleague in the city of Belfast. It said: 'Arthur, old friend, yesterday I met a Major Michael F. X. Devaney – it would seem he has Irish ancestry – who has something or other to do with cultural relations between the U.S. troops and ourselves. He's hunting for folk-tales, local lore, to publish in book-form for the army. I thought of you. I took the liberty of arranging an appointment and of loaning him a copy of some of the stories you once loaned me.'

Mr Broderick went to Belfast a few days later to keep the appointment. From the window of the major's office the vast, smoky bulk of the domed City Hall was visible. He turned from its impressive Victorian gloom to study the major, splendidly caparisoned as any hero who had ever lived in coloured tales told by country hearths.

'Mr Broderick,' said the major, 'this is real contemporary.'

'Old tales, major, like old soldiers.'

'This spiked strand and burning mountain. I was in the Pacific, Mr Broderick. This seven miles of treacherous sea. A few pages of glossary, Mr Broderick. A few explanatory footnotes. How long would that take you?'

'A month, major. Say a month.'

'We'll settle for a month. Then we'll clinch the deal. These tales are exactly what we want, Mr Broderick. Tell the boys something about the traditions of the place.'

He took the train home from the tense, overcrowded city to the garrison town in the valley. The market-day bus brought him up over the ridge to his own village. All that warm night the lorries on the steep street robbed him of his sparse, aged sleep as the troops moved; and they were gone in the morning, lock, stock and barrel, and on the far French coast the sons of the Kings of Antua and Soracha grappled until they made rocks of water and water of rocks, and the waves of the great metal birds of the air screamed over them.

High in the sky beyond Knocknashee one lone plane droned like a bee some cruel boy had imprisoned in a bottle to prevent it from joining the swarm. At his hushed doorway sad Patrick the publican looked aghast at the newspaper headlines and more aghast at the cold, empty courthouse that once had housed such thirsty young men.

'You'd swear to God,' he said, 'they were never here at all.'

Arthur Broderick left him to his confusion. He walked home under twisted yews, up the grass-grown avenue to his own smoky house. The heroes had gone, but the heroes would stay with him for ever. His children would stay with him for ever, but, in a way, it was a pity that he could never give his stories to all those fine young men.

'Come in,' Mr Broderick said to the young scholar, 'you're welcome. There's nothing I'm prouder of than to see a young man from these parts doing well. And we know the same people. We have many friends in common.'

'Shawn of Kinsale,' the young scholar said, 'and the son of the King of Antua.'

'The three princesses,' said Mr Broderick, 'and the White Hound of the Mountain.'

He reached out the hand of welcome to the young scholar. 'Publishing is slow,' the young man stammered. 'They have little vision . . .'

'Vision reminds me,' Mr Broderick said. 'Do you mind smoke?' He opened the drawing-room door. Smoke billowed out to the musty hallway.

'My poor stories,' he said. 'My poor heroes. They went away to the well at the world's end but they always came back. Once they came very close to enlisting in the U.S. army. That's a story I must tell you sometime.'

The manuscript of his tales lay between them on the table that had once been part of the rebel's bellows. Around them in the smoke were the grey shadows of heroic eighteenth-century men who, to fight tyranny, had forged steel pikes. And eastwards the heroes had swept that earth-shaking summer, over the treacherous mined sea, over the seven miles of spiked strand, over the seven and seventy miles of burning mountain.

Soldier, Red Soldier

For Padraic Colum
whose poem provided the title

Nobody could ever have imagined that awkward John, the milkman, was the sort to come between a husband and his wife. There was no badness in him and he was anything but handsome. To think of John was to think of easy, slow-moving, red-faced good nature, of the jingle of harness bells and the clip clop of hooves in the morning, of the warm breath of milk fresh from the udder in the byres of Joe Sutton's place out in Coolnagarde. John was one of Sutton's several hired men.

He would enter singing with his morning delivery into our informal town. He was the harbinger of day, as punctual as an alarm clock but by no means as minatory. He was closer to the birds than to any time-machine because he came, simple and melodious, from fresh, awakening fields and warm byres to arouse and refresh the leaden mechanical streets. This was long before bottling and pasteurisation took the flavour of life, and the cream, out of the milk; and the vehicle that John drove, and the well-combed, long-tailed, grey pony pulled, was as splendid as a chariot; and no dull array of shelves stacked with squat bottles. Heavy on his heels, leaning slightly backwards, managing the pony with the gentlest touches of finger-tips on the strap-reins, the huge, crimson, flaxen-haired, innocent youth stood up as high as a statue. There were two large silvery milk-cans to his right and two to his left. The pint and half-pint measures dangled and rattled on hooks in front of him. The taps of the cans were gleaming brass. You turned a lever and the milk flowed out. If you were up early enough in the morning, and if you were young and a favourite of his, you could fill your own measure. It was nearly as good as milking a cow.

And he was fond of the young and the young fond of him, so that in school-holiday time it was a common sight to see two or three boys travelling with him as volunteer assistants, and a hilarious flight of six or seven racing behind the cart to snatch a quick mouthful of milk from the brass taps. John, laughing loudly and not bothering to look back, would scatter them by flicking his whip over their heads, harmlessly, but with a crack that could be heard all over the town. He was a star performer with that whip.

As I said, it was an informal town. In High Street and Market Street where the rich shopkeepers lived, and in Campsie Avenue where the doctors and professional people lived, a white-aproned maid might, in some of the more staid houses, meet John at the side-door and present a jug for the milk. More often, he whistled his way affably into the kitchen, found the jug himself, filled it, made a harmless glawm at the maid, and went on his way contentedly.

But every door was open to him in the working-class kitchen houses that stood in parallel rows on Gallows Hill. The kitchen houses indeed, were brown brick ramparts against any sort of formality. The architectural pattern came over to us from the industrial areas of Scotland and Northern England: an entrance hall, about five feet square, opening into a kitchen-cum-living-room; a steep twisted stairway ascending from the kitchen; two doors opening from the far end of the kitchen, one via a pantry and scullery to the backyard, the other into a diminutive parlour or drawing-room or what you will – it was never described as anything grander than The Wee Room. They were small intimate, cosy nests of houses and, if the next-door neighbour had a row you could, if you were curious, learn all about it and, in exceptional circumstances even offer your services as arbitrator.

It was an honest town and nobody bothered much to bolt doors so that in the mornings Awkward John was king of the kitchen houses. He might waken the family with a healthy shout up the crooked stairs. Or he might quietly put a match to the ready-laid fire in the range and proceed to the cooking of breakfast for the family and himself. The sleepers would be aroused not by sound but by the wispy, drifting odour of rashers and eggs on the pan and, dressing and descending the stairs, would find the fire blazing, the food cooking, and John at his ease in a chair, reading the paper – which he did with difficulty, big, blunt forefinger following the line of print – or chanting a fragment of a song he had picked up from Joe Sutton who was a great traditional man. (His favourite fragment went something like this: 'I wonder how you could love a sailor. I wonder how you could love a slave. He might be dead or he might be married or the ocean wave might be his grave.') It was reckoned that, on an average, John ate three full English breakfasts a morning, discounting casual collations and cups of tea or, in the more select houses, coffee, to show that he had nothing against continental customs. But he was a big, healthy, amiable youth, slightly stooped in the shoulders because he was too tall and heavy to carry himself straight, and nobody grudged him his excessive provender.

He also seemed as happy in his way of life as the lark in the clear air. That was why my mother was so startled when he told her one morning over his rashers, 'Missus, I'm thinking of 'listing in the British Army.'

'God look to your wit,' she said. 'Are you an Irishman at all?'

'The barracks is full of Irishmen,' he said. 'Some of them from as far away as Wexford. The two full-backs on the depot team are from Sligo.'

'More shame for them,' she said. 'They worked to earn it. The army's a place for disobedient boys. They wouldn't obey their mother at home so God punished them by delivering them into the hands of the sergeant major.'

'Wasn't your own husband, missus, a soldier?'

'He was,' she said. 'And he rued the day he 'listed. And he'd be the last man to encourage you to follow in his foolish footsteps. You're not cut out for the army.'

'Amn't I as strong as any sergeant in the barracks?'

''Tisn't strength, but rascality, counts in the army, boy. You're too soft, John, too used to easy ways. The good life you had of it with Joe Sutton.

'My own girlhood,' she said, 'was spent in Coolnagarde.'

'That I know. Mr Sutton often mentions your name.'

'I had the greatest regard for his lately deceased mother. A lady if ever there was one. In that great place of Sutton's the servant-boys led the lives of princes. I'm sure her son treats them no differently.'

'He's easy on us, true enough.'

'The long warm evenings at the hay,' she said. 'The taste of strong tea in the bog at the saving of the turf. Tea anywhere else never tasted like that. And the boys on their hunkers in the heather or stretched chewing among the bilberry bushes. And always a bit of music and a song. The heavenly taste of the bilberries and the lovely wine you could make from them. And the wicked bites of the grey midges as the evening came on.'

'True enough, missus, the little cannibals would stand on their heads to get a better bite at you.'

'You've thick, healthy skin, John, that they'd never puncture. 'Twas different for soft young girls. And at Ballydun Foresters' Hall the dances.'

'Mostly poker or pitch-and-toss nowadays, missus. Times must be changed. There's no life in the country for the young people. And little money or adventure.'

'You'll have adventure in the army. Up at dawn to scrub out the latrines.'

But there was another, different prospect before John's big, blank, blue eyes: He saw a vision that altered, dissolved, reshaped itself, was now an eastern palace with towers like twisted, beckoning fingers, now a half-circle of laughing girls, and now a field of sport or of battle where Awkward John was transformed into the lithe, powerful hero. The warnings of an old woman, or her rhapsodies about the simple joys of her girlhood when, it seemed, every day had been summer, had no power against that compelling dream.

The tall talk of Yellow Willy Mullan who was a storyteller, or a liar, of the first order had brought the vision to John all the way from the garrisons of India. Twelve to fifteen years previously Yellow Willy, a pale-faced Irish boy, brown scapular and a chain of holy medals round his neck, had marched away with the Inniskilling Fusiliers. Six months previously he had marched home again: a gaunt, sallow-faced, sinful-looking man who had been but once to confession all the time he was in the East, and only then because he was ambushed, as he put it, by an aggressive Irish padre in Bombay. Seeing him in the home-coming parade, his aged mother burst into tears: weeping, perhaps, for the boy who had marched away for ever or, as the gossip of the kitchen houses cynically said, judging from the lean, lined face and wolfish eyes of him, how much it would take to feed him. At Kane's public house corner he was king of the Indian Army reservists, the toughest old sweats the Empire had, and his tales, lies or truth, of brothels in Bombay or bullets on the Khyber Pass made the story of the lives of the Bengal Lancer read like a white paper on social welfare. For John, the whirling words of Yellow Willy gave life and truth and all the needed corroborative detail to the coloured recruiting posters outside the courthouse and the post office, and all along the grey stone wall in Barrack Lane where he drove to deliver milk to the married quarters. On some of the posters a fine, brown-faced fellow in white knickers and red jersey leaped up to head a flying football, or came running in first at the end of a race, or went diving and swimming – ringed with the faces of admiring girls. Another poster showed a smiling soldier pointing to the Taj Mahal as if he had just bought it at a sacrifice price from an estate agent who was retiring from the business.

John could never grow weary of listening to Yellow Willy telling how he had actually seen the Taj Mahal.

'It was big, John, and shining. Six times as big as the courthouse and the town hall together. As big nearly as the mental hospital. Palaces, John. India's full of them. But you'd soon be fed up looking at palaces. Give me the brown girls and the wiggles of them, and the perfume – I can smell it still.'

To captivate John's ears, by bringing girls and palaces into the same tale, Yellow Willy told how he had spent a holiday with a prince who was a friend of his and how the prince, squatting, like Paddy MacBride the tailor, on a pile of silken cushions, waved his beringed, bejewelled hand at the glittering dancing-girls and said, 'Fusilier Mullan, pick the six you fancy and keep them for a week.'

Later, a tender affection developed between Yellow Willy and the prince's daughter who wanted to elope with him, but Willy, treating her as he'd wish another man to treat his own young sister, dissuaded her. 'She wasn't a Catholic, John, you see. And what life would it be in a kitchen house on Gallows Hill for a girl was used to palaces and plenty.'

After all that romancing, it was little use to talk to John about the good life at Coolnagarde, or about the kind heart and sweet songs of Joe Sutton; or for my mother to point out that Yellow Willy was just the biggest boaster in an unemployable group of misfits who never stirred their arses from Kane's Corner except to go to bed at night, or to go into Tom Kane's to get drunk on stout and cheap red wine – Red Biddy – when the army reserve money came up once a month.

My mother said, 'John, what did Joe Sutton say when you told him you'd 'list?'

'He said nothing, missus. He said a verse of poetry: "And soldiers, red soldiers! You've seen many lands. But you walk two and two and by captain's commands".'

'Very true,' said my mother. 'He has a verse to meet every need.' But no verse had Joe Sutton to halt John in his career. The day he headed up Barrack Lane, not to deliver milk but to offer his services to the King of England, Yellow Willy made the nasty joke, 'They'll never take him, not with the crouch he has in his shoulders. Men for India they want, not camels for Egypt.'

Yellow Willy was wrong, and all through the houses on the hill mornings were not real mornings any more. No other milkman could be found to equal Awkward John.

Sergeant Cooper, at that time, was the brutal, blackavised, tyrannical ruler of the barracks gymnasium. We knew that, to our cost, because our own school had no gymnasium and, by arrangement between the commanding officer and the superior of the school, the boys who played football went twice a week to the barracks to be put through their paces. That could have been fun if it hadn't been for Sergeant Cooper.

He was a man, not heavily or largely built but perfectly proportioned, with chest muscles that extended to the limits of endurance the fabric of the red-and-black barred football jersey he wore in the gymnasium. In tight serge trousers and slippers he was as light on his feet, on the polished wooden floor of his athletic torture-chamber, as the most sylph-like of ballet dancers. He had dark hair cropped to stubble, a Roman nose, a full mouth, a mole to the left of his chin, and grey, quite motionless eyes. To anyone except ourselves, the schoolboys, and the raw recruits, the rookies, in the barracks he would have been a mighty handsome man particularly when, in dress uniform, he stepped out with his olive-skinned, opulent, brunette wife. She was taller and heavier than her husband and a sight, fore and aft, to observe when she walked the town.

'By Mahomet,' said Yellow Willy, 'she's something to think about. There's Indian blood in her. Such a woman to be wasted on the like of that man.'

Yellow Willy, to do his line of talk justice, had a lot more remarks, highly technical and speculative, to make about the scandalous squandering of such material.

But to the schoolboys and still more to the rookies – those shapeless youths from barns and back-streets who had to be licked into the semblance of soldiers – the sergeant was a monster. At least he couldn't assault us with the sweat-hardened flat palm of a boxing glove as he could and did assault, or discipline, the rookies. We weren't in the army – not yet. We hadn't, according to my mother's fatalistic morality, advanced far enough in disobedience to our parents to be doomed by avenging heaven to the mercy of Sergeant Cooper. What morbid cul-de-sac in North London had reared him? From what sulphurous Rillington Place, with the corpses of unfortunate women decaying in every alcove, had he paced forth to work off his venom on things green and fresh, things young and happy? Everything and everybody who looked rustic – that word was his favourite abusive adjective, and his sharp London voice could make it sound viler than sin – were anathema to him: grass, blue skies, birds on the bushes, clean water flowing otherwise than through pipes, unsurfaced, dusty side-roads, and unspoiled children of nature like Awkward John.

Twice a week, then, forty or fifty of us would troop apprehensively up Barrack Lane, under the long grey wall and the radiance of the same recruiting posters that had enticed and deluded John, to keep our assignment with the satanic sergeant. Some boys take better than others to the challenge of the horse, the wall-bars and the parallel-bars. Some men like war and climbing Everest. But even those of us who might have loved the gymnasium machines and rituals were put off by the sergeant's manners. For he had a way of making horse and bars and punch-balls, mats, skipping ropes, clubs and boxing gloves, his allies against the crowd of us. They were all civilised Londoners together and we were the benighted children of brambles and hayseed.

'Up, up, up boys,' he would snap – prancing east to west and west to east like something made out of steel springs.

'Up, up, up. You're not just going to market and you haven't all day.'

Like a flight of demented bats we would go at the wall, clamber up the bars with varying degrees of speed, skill and grace, swing face outwards at the crack of command and at the grave risk of losing both arms at the shoulders, and descend, like birds to a mesmerising bird-catcher, in obedience to that prancing man, 'Down, down, down boys. Back to good old Mother Earth. Back to the friendly soil of Mother Erin.'

To welcome us back to the friendly soil of Mother Erin there stood the sergeant's most obedient servant: the monstrous, headless, legless, tailless horse, an insult and a blasphemy against the beauty and goodness of living horses. One look at it, with the sergeant by its side, and you could think of nothing but of strong men being held face down, legs and arms straddle across its smelly leather padding, and flogged to the drumbeat until they broke down and yelled. We suffered so much from our compulsory assaults on its slothlike obscenity, and Cooper obviously enjoyed himself so much as he impelled us on, that we suspected some unholy compact between them; and one sour wit went so far as to say that in the dead of night the master of the gymnasium came out, bucket in hand, to talk to the brute, stroke it down, and feed it oats. For over and above all things, he believed in the horse, and his greatest joy in life – if the name of joy could for anything be applied to him – was to see its ravenous appetite fed by a flying file of boys.

'On the toes. Off we go. Hit the board. On your toes. Up. Touch. Splits over. Hit the mat. Fast out of the way, boy. This isn't the place to say your prayers. Up and Out. Keep the line revolving. On the toes. Hit the board. Splits over.'

Fear of the mockery of that voice, in the case of clumsiness or failure, made antelopes out of boys who, under normal circumstances, wouldn't have moved so fast or jumped so high to save their lives. Through desperation we all became masters of the horse. There are scientific experiments in which caged rats are set running up tiny circular flights of steps which descend as the rats attempt to ascend. The creatures just keep turning wheels until they drop from exhaustion. Cooper's stage-army of half-terrified boys had its cheerful resemblance to that rat race, and perhaps, in moments of a special cold frenzy, he may really have been trying to discover the secret of perpetual motion. Round and round we went and over and over, and the process more closely resembled an eternity of punishment because there was no clock visible in the gymnasium. It was only when he pulled one dried-up boxing glove onto his left hand that we knew for us the respite had come and a deeper, hotter hell was about to commence for the rookies. By the barrack timetable the sad souls who wouldn't do what their mothers told them were doomed, immediately after the sergeant had disposed of us, to an hour's instruction in some elementary methods of defence and offence. For most of that hour they were very much on the defensive. He was a boxer and wrestler of some note, that sergeant.

From the dressing-room as we steamed with perspiration and sighed with relief we could study in awe what was liable to happen to us if we showed an habitual disregard for the fourth commandment. High in his pride, that arrogant son of Greater London was master of thirty or so pairs of simultaneously performing game-cocks and, down there on the sand of the bloody pit, it must have grieved him to think that he couldn't fit them out with flesh-rending spurs. He set them hammering each other, or throwing each other, and egged them on until he brought out the bestial or the demoniacal, or both, in every one of them.

'Put your heart in it, hayseed. Hit him. Think it's a bloody Boche you've got, if you can think.'

The blows, the grunts, the sound of falling bodies resounded, punctuated by the steel-like crack of the dry, open glove on the head of some recalcitrant performer. It was hammer your opponent or be lacerated by the glove.

Cooper was the emperor, and reserved the gladiatorial contests all for his own cruel delight. He rested his dulcet voice more with the rookies than with us, and let his viper of a left hand, fanged by the glove, supply the word of command: bull-whips were frowned on in the British Army.

'Give me any day the galleys in *Ben Hur*,' said the voice of that sour wit.

And so pitifully unprotected the rookies were – in black shorts, sleeveless green singlets, slippers and short socks. Chain mail would not have been excessive for what they were called upon to encounter.

To demonstrate the more delicate points of throwing or buffeting he'd pick on one guinea pig; and, in some black book in the lowest caverns of Gehenna, it was written in pitch that five times out of ten Awkward John should be his choice. The size and shape, or lack of shape, of John would have aggravated any well-formed soldier. The width of John's stooping shoulders stretched the green singlet to the transparency of sheer nylon. The seeming nakedness of his torso was made more provokingly pitiful by the real nakedness of his white-blond head, as good as scalped by the barracks barber. His slow-moving body was the focal point of all confusion, and in three minutes he could have transformed a dress-parade of the Irish Guards into Keystone Comedy: turning left when the rest went right, by-the-left-quick-marching a half minute too late and halting a half minute too early, affronting even those military virtues which the sergeant undeniably possessed, making to his vices the perverted appeal helpless innocence makes to the heart of corruption. A perfect sawdust-stuffed dummy was John for the expert application of the subtleties of wrestling: Chancery back heel, cross buttock and waist hold, the half Nelson, quarter Nelson, full Nelson; and not Milo of Croton, supreme among the Greeks, nor the deified Sukune of Japan, nor the Great Danno Mahony of Ballydehob in the County Cork, was more adept than Sergeant Cooper. Patiently, John accepted every shattering fall. Ox-like he waited, for the next experiment, resigned, it would seem, to the misery and humiliation, if others could by his tumbles learn how to keep their feet.

'There's styles and styles of wrestling,' the sergeant would say. 'Cumberland and West Country, and catch-as-catch-can as is practised in Lancashire and many foreign parts. But take it from me, if you go on a man, disregarding styles, and squeeze his kidneys down he has to go.'

Panting, and clearly in some pain, down John went. When he was bent enough and low enough, the sergeant rested his right leg over the bowed neck and shoulders – a gallant captain and his heathen slave – and, for one fatal moment, relaxed as he explained the technicalities of his triumph to the gaping, breathless throng. At the same moment, possibly without any malice in the world, John decided to straighten up, and the loudest noise heard that day was the clump of the sergeant's head on the gymnasium floor. There was no laughter. One does not laugh when the lightning strikes and the earth opens. He didn't curse or shout or call names as a normal man might have done. He sat on the floor and shook his head once, twice, thrice – methodically. It almost seemed as if we could hear his brain tick, not like a clock but a time bomb. Spluttering apologies, John stepped forward and stooped to pick him up, when with the force and exactitude of a skilled dirty fighter, Cooper shattered the big fellow's mouth with a foul blow of the right elbow.

As he staggered back, spitting out and swallowing blood and teeth, John, I'd say, abandoned without regret his dream of ever seeing the Taj Mahal.

For myself and the other observers in the dressing-room that blow was the end of boyhood, of mornings chiming with harness bells and flowing with creamy milk. John was lost for ever to us in a heartless world where, with the regularity of monastic bells and the viciousness of dropping guillotine blades, strident bugles dismembered the day. What happened about a month after that was, to begin with, a slightly altered version of the hoary story of the sergeant who asked for four volunteers who knew something about music and, when four innocents had stepped out, roared at them to carry a grand piano four hundred yards from the O.C.'s residence to the officers' mess.

Cooper never roared. His voice was sharp, level, penetrating and exact as a chisel, and his face was never flushed. He surveyed twenty or thirty possible victims. He said, 'You're all experts on hay. Reared on grass by the look of you. Your fathers kept the sons at home and sent the donkeys to the army.'

A little, fearful laughter acknowledged his traditional army witticism.

'But which of you is the best hand with the scythe, the bleeding scythe – you know, favourite weapon of Old Father Time. One pace forward. Four men or what passes for men in this 'ere barracks.'

Awkward John was out in front before Cooper had finished speaking.

Every man has his moments of power and poetry, and it was common knowledge out in Coolnagarde that with a scythe in his hand and his feet well-spread to balance his great body on Antaean earth, and the razor-sharp blade shearing the roots of good meadow-grass and, in delicate curves, shaving the ground, Awkward John was no longer awkward.

Reluctantly, and fearing the worst, three other martyrs stepped out beside him.

'By the left quick march,' the sergeant said. 'Shoulder scythes. Step forward the merry farmers' boys. To the swamp. Left. Right. Left.'

The laughter of the fortunate ones who had escaped that fatigue followed the four victims as he herded them across the interminable barrack square. It was a hot sultry day in late summer and the black flies and horse flies in the swamp were a bloody torment. The barracks stood on a high hill with the town to the south and a river running northwards from the town below the eastern wall of the barracks, then faltering in its course and looping, first west, then south, before turning again to the north. The wide acres that the looping river enclosed were known as The Soldiers' Holm, and held playing-fields, firing ranges and jumps for exercising horses. Lovely green land that Holm was, except for one scabrous spot of sour marsh where the river made its final northward turn. There, rushes and brambles grew in unholy profusion and, at intervals, an attack had to be made on the swamp to preserve a pathway leading to an iron foot-bridge. Half-eaten alive by the pestering flies and attempting to swing jagged-edged scythes that no stone could sharpen or no skill balance, John and the other hapless three suffered under the sergeant's flinty, unrelaxing eye. He wore his tight serge trousers, his black-and-red jersey and a pair of running shoes. He left the four labourers at intervals and coursed like a thoroughbred over the velvet levels of the Holm and thus evaded the torment of the flies.

The sweat blinding him, soaking his yellow canvas fatigue suit, making puddles in his army boots, the black flies crawling all over him, the horse flies drawing blood, John swung the wobbly scythe at rasping brambles and leathery rushes that lay down and then stood up again to mock the blunt, hacked blade. He saw the sweet, scented meadow-grass of Coolnagarde. He heard the singing of good well-sharpened blades. He saw the servant girls carrying food and strong tea across the mown land. Then with one last swing he sent the hopeless scythe spinning to the deep middle of the river. The sergeant, raising his knees high like a runner in track-training, was half a mile away across the Holm. But he turned, when he heard the clang of nailed boots on the metal bridge, to see the big youth cross the river and head north for open country, freedom and the haven of Coolnagarde. Like the wind he crossed the Holm and started in pursuit. Happy at any excuse to escape from the flies the three mowers downed tools and followed them – a good ways behind and steadily losing distance, for John was a good runner even if he was ungraceful and the sergeant had style and could travel like a springbok.

John was a better jumper than he was a runner. It was a wonder to the world at jumping contests at rural sports how high he could ascend before gravity claimed him and he began to come down again.

'Well I knew,' he said long afterwards, 'the hoor would be too fast for me on the flat. But I could beat him at the jumps. So I steeple-chased him over bog-holes and ditches until there wasn't a puff of wind left in his body.'

He echoed an old racing-song from Joe Sutton's repertoire, 'Over hedges and ditches and bogs I was bound.'

'I drew the map of Ireland for him,' he said, 'around three swampy, low-lying townlands.'

It was the season of the year when the flax-crop had been pulled by hand and lay retting in the water of the dams, the softening fibres stinking to the sky above.

A week previously a doctor's wife out riding in all her grandeur had been thrown and badly injured when her horse shied at the stench of a flax-dam near a crossroads a mile outside the town; and, to anyone who has ever given the matter thought, it is quite miraculous that decaying vegetable matter, breathing out from filthy water an almost visible smell, should ever have been part of a process leading to beautiful table-cloths or to gentlemen in Cuba dressing themselves in gleaming suits of Irish linen.

Panting heavily, and with the inexorable pursuit closing in on him, Awkward John, running like a gingered mule, came to a wide flax-dam and crossed it with a tremendous leap, then on the far side of the scummy vaporous water he stood at bay.

Afterwards, as he told the tale, he said, 'I waited for him with my fist in a ball.'

He struck a pose like Cúchullain at the ford. An enormous ball of a fist it was.

'I could never face him in the ring, but thon slippy mucky bank was no ring. And I swung when he jumped, and struck when he touched the ground and he went down like a duck. The gas and the dirty water came up like steam.'

Then with an élan, and a brutality, that he had never before displayed and with the massive hitting power of his heavy boots, John jumped on the fallen man's stomach, recrossed the dam, and headed off at a canter across country to Coolnargarde. Doubled in agony, waterlogged and stinking, the sergeant, after several efforts, crawled out of the mire and made, back to the barracks, the broken-backed movement of a man disgraced for ever.

No more than a month later the long yellow Rolls-Royce took to calling to the sergeant's house, in a quiet road on the fringe of the town, at times when even the nuns in the convent knew that the sergeant, by duty, was confined to the barracks. That splendid woman would emerge dressed in the best, and while a uniformed chauffeur held the door of the car would survey the small street and the mean houses with their twitching window-blinds half-concealing curious eyes. Then she would wave the daintiest of white handkerchiefs to the watchers, and step in and be driven away. The owner of the Rolls – the watchers at the windows soon found out – was the son of a family who lived in a town ten miles away and out of sawmills in World War One had made a fortune which the son was scattering as a gentleman should. In later years he was to be seen through a hole in the hedge, in the park before his house, being supported by two male nurses while he restudied the art of walking. Brandy had made him bowlegged and reduced him to a curious staccato movement.

Yellow Willy, who always defended her, implied that she had fallen on reckless ways because she could not stand the odour of ridicule and retting flax.

In the evening when the Rolls-Royce had delivered her back to her door she would stand on the sidewalk until it had driven away, then wave that tiny handkerchief to the eyes behind the twitching curtains and say with great gaiety, 'You can go to bed now. He's gone away. Sleep tight.'

She seemed to know that she was talking to people who had nothing to do but peep out from their own lives: they possessed no big rooms that could engage their attention.

There were other whisperings about her. There were tales of muffled tappings and visits by night and, as Kipling said, knocks and whistles round the house, footsteps after dark, and a legend of one greyheaded, dignified solicitor whose sprained ankle, which kept him from taking his usual place in the Corpus Christi procession, was the result of the nocturnal necessity of making a hasty departure over the back-garden wall.

So in the end off she went one day in the Rolls and didn't come back, and the watchers behind the window-curtains waited in vain, and the sergeant took to living a lonely life in the barracks until he got the transfer he applied for – back to the part of England to which the false one had flown.

'What else could you expect,' said Yellow Willy, 'if you let the like of Awkward John into the army.'

In an abandoned chest of drawers in the house she left behind her the new inhabitants found bundles of letters, each bundle tied in differently coloured ribbon, addressed to her by her many admirers. A fine, poetic anthology, it was circulated for many a day among the town's careful readers: and wry humour was added to the glowing sentiments by the fact that one of the contributing authors was a highly respectable and wealthy member of the urban district council. It could at least be said of her as Yellow Willy, who to the end admired her from afar, said, that she didn't go in for blackmail. But since one graphologist said that some of the letters were in her own handwriting her purpose may even have been more humorous and subtle.

In the Second World War, we heard, the sergeant distinguished himself by many wounds and much promotion and his wife rejoined him, turning the blades of her shapely shoulders on the liquefying sawmills.

The day that John, like the hare whom hounds and horn pursue, panted home to Coolnagarde, Joe Sutton, a man of persuasion and influence, went to the barracks and saw the commanding officer, a man of humanity and understanding. For thirty pounds Joe bought the runaway soldier back from the King of England who probably never missed him anyway. The Commanding Officer may also have considered that in those halcyon days of peace the Army was better off without Awkward John. And when John had his false teeth – paid for by Joe Sutton – he was able to sing as well as ever and recount his army experiences like a veteran of the field. The milk trade and the early mornings were the better of it all, and the Taj Mahal remained as far away as India.

The Dogs in the Great Glen

The professor had come over from America to search out his origins and I met him in Dublin on the way to Kerry where his grandfather had come from and where he had relations, including a grand-uncle still living.

'But the trouble is,' he said, 'that I've lost the address my mother gave me. She wrote to tell them I was coming to Europe. That's all they know. All I remember is a name out of my dead father's memories: the great Glen of Kanareen.'

'You could write to your mother.'

'That would take time. She'd be slow to answer. And I feel impelled right away to find the place my grandfather told my father about.

'You wouldn't understand,' he said. 'Your origins are all around you.'

'You can say that again, professor. My origins crop up like the bones of rock in thin sour soil. They come unwanted like the mushroom of *merulius lacrimans* on the walls of a decaying house.'

'It's no laughing matter,' he said.

'It isn't for me. This island's too small to afford a place in which to hide from one's origins. Or from anything else. During the war a young fellow in Dublin said to me: "Mister, even if I ran away to sea I wouldn't get beyond the three-mile limit".'

He said, 'But it's large enough to lose a valley in. I couldn't find the valley of Kanareen marked on any map or mentioned in any directory.'

'I have a middling knowledge of the Kerry mountains' I said. 'I could join you in the search.'

'It's not marked on the half-inch Ordnance Survey map.'

'There are more things in Kerry than were ever dreamt of by the Ordnance Survey. The place could have another official name. At the back of my head I feel that once in the town of Kenmare in Kerry I heard a man mention the name of Kanareen.'

We set off two days later in a battered, rattly Ford Prefect. Haste, he said, would be dangerous because Kanareen might not be there at all but if we idled from place to place in the lackadaisical Irish summer we might, when the sentries were sleeping and the glen unguarded, slip secretly as thieves into the land whose legends were part of his rearing.

'Until I met you,' the professor said, 'I was afraid the valley might have been a dream world my grandfather imagined to dull the edge of the first nights in a new land. I could see how he might have come to believe in it himself and told my father – and then, of course, my father told me.'

One of his grandfather's relatives had been a Cistercian monk in Mount Melleray, and we went there hoping to see the evidence of a name in a book and to kneel, perhaps, under the high arched roof of the chapel close to where that monk had knelt. But when we had traversed the corkscrew road over the purple Knockmealdowns and gone up to the mountain monastery through the forest the monks had made in the wilderness, it was late evening and the doors were closed. The birds sang vespers. The great silence affected us with something between awe and a painful, intolerable shyness. We hadn't the heart to ring a doorbell or to promise ourselves to return in the morning. Not speaking to each other we retreated, the rattle of the Ford Prefect as irreverent as dicing on the altar-steps. Half a mile down the road the mute, single-file procession of a group of women exercitants walking back to the female guest-house underlined the holy, unreal, unanswering stillness that had closed us out. It could easily have been that his grandfather never had a relative a monk in Mount Melleray.

A cousin of his mother's mother had, he had been told, been a cooper in Lady Gregory's Gort in the County Galway. But when we crossed the country westwards to Gort, it produced nothing except the information that, apart from the big breweries, where they survived like birds or bison in a sanctuary, the coopers had gone, leaving behind them not a hoop or a stave. So we visited the woods of Coole, close to Gort, where Lady Gregory's house had once stood, and on the brimming lake-water among the stones, we saw by a happy poetic accident the number of swans the poet had seen.

Afterwards in Galway City there was, as there always is in Galway City, a night's hard drinking that was like a fit of jovial hysteria, and a giggling ninny of a woman in the bar who kept saying, 'You're the nicest American I ever met. You don't look like an American. You don't even carry a camera. You look like a Kerryman.'

And in the end, we came to Kenmare in Kerry, and in another bar we met a talkative Kerryman who could tell us all about the prowess of the Kerry team, about the heroic feats of John Joe Sheehy or Paddy Bawn Brosnan. He knew so much, that man, yet he couldn't tell us where in the wilderness of mountains we might find the Glen of Kanareen. Nor could anybody else in the bar be of the least help to us, not even the postman who could only say that wherever it was, that is if it was at all, it wasn't in his district.

'It could of course,' he said, 'be east over the mountain.'

Murmuring sympathetically, the entire bar assented. The rest of the world was east over the mountain.

With the resigned air of men washing their hands of a helpless, hopeless case, the postman and the football savant directed us to a roadside post office twelve miles away where, in a high-hedged garden before an old grey-stone house with latticed windows and an incongruous, green, official post office sign, there was a child, quite naked, playing with a coloured, musical spinning-top as big as itself, and an old half-deaf man sunning himself and swaying in a rocking-chair, a straw hat tilted forwards to shade his eyes. Like Oisin remembering the Fenians, he told us he had known once of a young woman who married a man from a place called Kanareen, but there had been contention about the match and her people had kept up no correspondence with her. But the day she left home with her husband that was the way she went. He pointed. The way went inland and up and up. We followed it.

'That young woman could have been a relation of mine,' the professor said.

On a rock-strewn slope, and silhouetted on a saw-toothed ridge where you'd think only a chamois could get by without broken legs, small black cows, accurate and active as goats, rasped good milk from the grass between the stones. His grandfather had told his father about those athletic, legendary cows and about the proverb that said: Kerry cows know Sunday. For in famine times, a century since, mountain people bled the cows once a week to mix the blood into yellow maize meal and provide a meat dish, a special Sunday dinner.

The road twisted on across moorland that on our left sloped dizzily to the sea, as if the solid ground might easily slip and slide into the depths. Mountain shadows melted like purple dust into a green bay. Across a ravine set quite alone on a long, slanting, brown knife blade of a mountain, was a white house with a red door. The rattle of our pathetic little car affronted the vast stillness. We were free to moralise on the extent of all space in relation to the trivial area that limited our ordinary daily lives.

The two old druids of men resting from work on the leeward side of a turf-bank listened to our enquiry with the same attentive half-conscious patience they gave to bird-cries or the sound of wind in the heather. Then they waved us ahead towards a narrow cleft in the distant wall of mountains as if they doubted the ability of ourselves and our conveyance to negotiate the Gap and find the Glen. They offered us strong tea and a drop out of a bottle. They watched us with kind irony as we drove away. Until the Gap swallowed us and the hazardous, twisting track absorbed all our attention we could look back and still see them, motionless, waiting with indifference for the landslide that would end it all.

By a roadside pool where water-beetles lived their vicious secretive lives, we sat and rested, with the pass and the cliffs, overhung with heather, behind us and another ridge ahead. Brazenly the sheer rocks reflected the sun and semaphored at us. Below us, in the dry summer, the bed of a stream held only a trickle of water twisting painfully around piles of round black stones. Touch a beetle with a stalk of dry grass and the creature either dived like a shot or, angry at invasion, savagely grappled with the stalk.

'That silly woman in Galway,' the professor said.

He dropped a stone into the pool and the beetles submerged to weather the storm.

'That day by the lake at Lady Gregory's Coole. The exact number of swans Yeats saw when the poem came to him. Upon the brimming water among the stones are nine and fifty swans. Since I don't carry a camera nobody will ever believe me. But you saw them. You counted them.'

'Now that I am so far,' he said, 'I'm half-afraid to finish the journey. What will they be like? What will they think of me? Will I go over that ridge there to find my grandfather's brother living in a cave?'

Poking at and tormenting the beetles on the black mirror of the pool, I told him, 'Once I went from Dublin to near Shannon Pot, where the river rises, to help an American woman find the house where her dead woman friend had been reared. On her deathbed the friend had written it all out on a sheet of notepaper: "Cross the river at Battle Bridge. Go straight through the village with the ruined castle on the right. Go on a mile to the crossroads and the labourer's cottage with the lovely snapdragons in the flower garden. Take the road to the right there, and then the second boreen on the left beyond the schoolhouse. Then stop at the third house on that boreen. You can see the river from the flagstone at the door."'

'Apart from the snapdragons it was exactly as she had written it down. The dead woman had walked that boreen as a barefooted schoolgirl. Not able to revisit it herself, she entrusted the mission as her dying wish to her dearest friend. We found the house. Her people were long gone from it but the new tenants remembered them. They welcomed us with melodeon and fiddle and all the neighbours came in and collated the long memories of the townland. They feasted us with cold ham and chicken, porter and whiskey, until I had cramps for a week.'

'My only grip on identity,' he said, 'is that a silly woman told me I looked like a Kerryman. My grandfather was a Kerryman. What do Kerrymen look like?'

'Big,' I said.

'And this is the heart of Kerry. And what my grandfather said about the black cows was true. With a camera I could have taken a picture of those climbing cows. And up that hill trail and over that ridge is Kanareen.'

'We hope,' I said.

The tired cooling engine coughed apologetically when we abandoned it and put city-shod feet to the last ascent.

'If that was the mountain my grandfather walked over in the naked dawn coming home from an all-night card-playing, then, by God, he was a better man than me,' said the professor.

He folded his arms and looked hard at the razor-cut edges of stone on the side of the mountain.

'Short of too much drink and the danger of mugging,' he said, 'getting home at night in New York is a simpler operation than crawling over that hunk of miniature Mount Everest. Like walking up the side of a house.'

He was as proud as Punch of the climbing prowess of his grandfather.

'My father told me,' he said, 'that one night coming home from the card-playing my grandfather slipped down fifteen feet of rock and the only damage done was the ruin of one of two bottles of whiskey he had in the tail-pockets of his greatcoat. The second bottle was unharmed.'

The men who surfaced the track we were walking on had been catering for horses and narrow iron-hooped wheels. After five minutes of agonised slipping and sliding, wisdom came to us and we took to the cushioned grass and heather. As we ascended, the professor told me what his grandfather had told his father about the market town he used to go to when he was a boy. It was a small town where even on market days the dogs would sit nowhere except exactly in the middle of the street. They were lazy town dogs, not active, loyal and intelligent like the dogs the grandfather had known in the great glen. The way the old

man had described it, the town's five streets grasped the ground of
Ireland as the hand of a strong swimmer might grasp a ledge of rock to
hoist himself out of the water. On one side was the sea. On the other
side a shoulder of mountain rose so steeply that the Gaelic name of it
meant the gable of the house.

When the old man went as a boy to the town on a market day it
was his custom to climb that mountain, up through furze and following goat tracks, leaving his shiny boots that he only put on, anyway,
when he entered the town, securely in hiding behind a furze bush. The
way he remembered that mountain it would seem that twenty minutes
active climbing brought him halfways to heaven. The little town was
far below him, and the bay and the islands. The unkempt coastline
tumbled and sprawled to left and right, and westwards the ocean went
on for ever. The sounds of market-day, voices, carts, dogs barking,
musicians on the streets, came up to him as faint, silvery whispers. On
the tip of one island two tall aerials marked the place where, he was
told, messages went down into the sea to travel all the way to America
by cable. That was a great marvel for a boy from the mountains to hear
about: the ghostly, shrill, undersea voices; the words of people in every
tongue of Europe far down among monstrous fish and shapeless sea-
serpents that never saw the light of the sun. He closed his eyes one day
and it seemed to him that the sounds of the little town were the voices
of Europe setting out on their submarine travels. That was the time he
knew that when he was old enough he would leave the Glen of
Kanareen and go with the voices westwards to America.

'Or so he said. Or so he told my father,' said the professor.

Another fifty yards and we would be on top of the ridge. We kept
our eyes on the ground, fearful of the moment of vision and, for good
or ill, revelation. Beyond the ridge there might be nothing but a void
to prove that his grandfather had been a dreamer or a liar. Rapidly,
nervously, he tried to talk down his fears.

'He would tell stories for ever, my father said, about ghosts and the
good people. There was one case of an old woman whose people
buried her – when she died, of course – against her will, across the
water, which meant on the far side of the lake in the glen. Her dying
wish was to be buried in another graveyard, nearer home. And there

she was, sitting in her own chair in the chimney corner, waiting for them, when they came home from the funeral. To ease her spirit they replanted her.'

To ease the nervous moment I said, 'There was a poltergeist once in a farmhouse in these mountains, and the police decided to investigate the queer happenings, and didn't an ass's collar come flying across the room to settle around the sergeant's neck. Owing to subsequent ridicule the poor man had to be transferred to Dublin.'

Laughing, we looked at the brown infant runnel that went parallel to the path. It flowed with us: we were over the watershed. So we raised our heads slowly and saw the great Glen of Kanareen. It was what Cortez saw, and all the rest of it. It was a discovery. It was a new world. It gathered the sunshine into a gigantic coloured bowl. We accepted it detail by detail.

'It was there all the time,' he said. 'It was no dream. It was no lie.' The first thing we realised was the lake. The runnel leaped down to join the lake, and we looked down on it through ash trees regularly spaced on a steep, smooth, green slope. Grasping from tree to tree you could descend to the pebbled, lapping edge of the water.

'That was the way,' the professor said, 'the boys in his time climbed down to fish or swim. Black, bull-headed mountain trout. Cannibal trout. There was one place where they could dive off sheer rock into seventy feet of water. Rolling like a gentle sea: that was how he described it. They gathered kindling, too, on the slopes under the ash trees.'

Then, after the lake, we realised the guardian mountain; not rigidly chiselled into ridges of rock like the mountain behind us but soft and gently curving, protective and, above all, noble, a monarch of mountains, an antlered stag holding a proud horned head up to the highest point of the blue sky. Green fields swathed its base. Sharp lines of stone walls, dividing wide areas of moorland sheep-grazing, marked man's grip for a thousand feet or so above sea-level then gave up the struggle and left the mountain alone and untainted. Halfway up one snow-white cloud rested as if it had hooked itself on a snagged rock and there it stayed, motionless, as step by step we went down into the Glen. Below the cloud a long cataract made a thin, white, forked-lightning line, and, in the heart of the glen, the river that the cataract became, sprawled on a brown and green and golden patchwork bed.

'It must be some one of those houses,' he said, pointing ahead and down to the white houses of Kanareen.

'Take a blind pick,' I said. 'I see at least fifty.'

They were scattered over the glen in five or six clusters.

'From what I heard it should be over in that direction,' he said.

Small rich fields were ripe in the sun. This was a glen of plenty, a gold-field in the middle of a desert, a happy laughing mockery of the arid surrounding moors and mountains. Five hundred yards away a dozen people were working at the hay. They didn't look up or give any sign that they had seen two strangers cross the high threshold of their kingdom but, as we went down, stepping like grenadier guards, the black-and-white sheepdogs detached themselves from the haymaking and moved silently across to intercept our path. Five of them I counted. My step faltered.

'This could be it,' I suggested with hollow joviality. 'I feel a little like an early Christian.'

The professor said nothing. We went on down, deserting the comfort of the grass and heather at the side of the track. It seemed to me that our feet on the loose pebbles made a tearing, crackling, grinding noise that shook echoes even out of the imperturbable mountain. The white cloud had not moved. The haymakers had not honoured us with a glance.

'We could,' I said, 'make ourselves known to them in a civil fashion. We could ask the way to your grand-uncle's house. We could have a formal introduction to those slinking beasts.'

'No, let me,' he said. 'Give me my head. Let me try to remember what I was told.'

'The hearts of these highland people, I've heard, are made of pure gold,' I said. 'But they're inclined to be the tiniest bit suspicious of town-dressed strangers. As sure as God made smells and shotguns, they think we're inspectors from some government department: weeds, or warble-fly, or, horror of horrors, rates and taxes. With equanimity they'd see us eaten.'

He laughed. His stride had a new elasticity in it. He was another man. The melancholy of the monastic summer dusk at Mount Melleray was gone. He was somebody else coming home. The white cloud had not moved. The silent dogs came closer. The unheeding people went on with their work.

'The office of rates collector is not sought after in these parts,' I said. 'Shotguns are still used to settle vexed questions of land title. Only a general threat of excommunication can settle a major feud.'

'This was the way he'd come home from the gambling cabin,' the professor said, 'his pockets clinking with winnings. That night he fell he'd won the two bottles of whiskey. He was only eighteen when he went away. But he was the tallest man in the glen. So he said. And lucky at cards.'

The dogs were twenty yards away, silent, fanning out like soldiers cautiously circling a point of attack.

'He was an infant prodigy,' I said. 'He was a peerless grandfather for a man to have. He also had one great advantage over us – he knew the names of these taciturn dogs and they knew his smell.'

He took off his white hat and waved at the workers. One man at a haycock raised a pitchfork – in salute or in threat? Nobody else paid the least attention. The dogs were now at our heels, suiting their pace politely to ours. They didn't even sniff. They had impeccable manners.

'This sure is the right glen,' he said. 'The old man was never done talking about the dogs. They were all black-and-white in his day, too.'

He stopped to look at them. They stopped. They didn't look up at us. They didn't snarl. They had broad shaggy backs. Even for their breed they were big dogs. Their long tails were rigid. Fixing my eyes on the white cloud I walked on.

'Let's establish contact,' I said, 'before we're casually eaten. All I ever heard about the dogs in these mountains is that their family tree is as old as the Red Branch Knights. That they're the best sheepdogs in Ireland and better than anything in the Highlands of Scotland. They also savage you first and bark afterwards.'

Noses down, they padded along behind us. Their quiet breath was hot on my calves. High up and far away the nesting white cloud had the security of heaven.

'Only strangers who act suspiciously,' the professor said.

'What else are we? I'd say we smell bad to them.'

'Not me,' he said. 'Not me. The old man told a story about a stranger who came to Kanareen when most of the people were away at the market. The house he came to visit was empty except for two dogs. So he sat all day at the door of the house and the dogs lay and watched him and said and did nothing. Only once, he felt thirsty and went into the kitchen of the house and lifted a bowl to go to the well for water. Then there was a low duet of a snarl that froze his blood. So he went thirsty and the dogs lay quiet.'

'Hospitable people.'

'The secret is touch nothing, lay no hand on property and you're safe.'

'So help me God,' I said, 'I wouldn't deprive them of a bone or a blade of grass.'

Twice in my life I had been bitten by dogs. Once, walking to school along a sidestreet on a sunny morning and simultaneously reading in *The Boy's Magazine* about a soccer centre forward, the flower of the flock, called Fiery Cross the Shooting Star – he was redheaded and his surname was Cross – I had stepped on a sleeping Irish terrier. In retaliation, the startled brute had bitten me. Nor could I find it in my heart to blame him, so that, in my subconscious, dogs took on the awful heaven-appointed dignity of avenging angels. The other time – and this was an even more disquieting experience – a mongrel dog had come up softly behind me while I was walking on the fairgreen in the town I was reared in and bitten the calf of my leg so as to draw spurts of blood. I kicked him but not resenting the kick, he had walked away as if it was the most natural, legitimate thing in heaven and earth for a dog to bite me and be kicked in return. Third time, I thought, it will be rabies. So as we walked and the silent watchers of the valley padded at our heels, I enlivened the way with brave and trivial chatter. I recited my story of the four wild brothers of Adrigole.

'Once upon a time,' I said, 'there lived four brothers in a rocky corner of Adrigole in West Cork, under the mountain called Hungry Hill. Daphne du Maurier wrote a book called after the mountain, but divil a word in it about the four brothers of Adrigole. They lived, I heard tell, according to instinct and never laced their boots and came out only once a year to visit the nearest town which was Castletownberehaven on the side of Bantry Bay. They'd stand there, backs to the wall, smoking, saying nothing, contemplating the giddy market-day throng. One day they ran out of tobacco and went into the local branch of the Bank of Ireland to buy it and raised havoc because the teller refused to satisfy their needs. To pacify them, the manager and the teller had to disgorge their own supplies. So they went back to Adrigole to live happily without lacing their boots, and ever after they thought that in towns and cities the bank was the place where you bought tobacco.

'That,' said I with a hollow laugh, 'is my moral tale about the four brothers of Adrigole.'

On a level with the stream that came from the lake and went down to join the valley's main river, we walked towards a group of four whitewashed, thatched farmhouses that were shining and scrupulously clean. The track looped to the left. Through a small triangular meadow a short-cut went straight towards the houses. In the heart of the meadow, by the side of the short-cut, there was a spring well of clear water, the stones that lined its sides and the roof cupped over it all white and cleansed with lime. He went down three stone steps and looked at the water. For good luck there was a tiny brown trout imprisoned in the well. He said quietly, 'That was the way my grandfather described it. But it could hardly be the self-same fish.'

He stooped to the clear water. He filled his cupped hands and drank.

He stooped again, and again filled his cupped hands and slowly, carefully, not spilling a drop, came up the moist, cool steps. Then, with the air of a priest, scattering hyssop, he sprinkled the five dogs with the spring-water. They backed away from him, thoughtfully. They didn't snarl or show teeth. He had them puzzled. He laughed with warm good nature at their obvious perplexity. He was making his own of them. He licked his wet hands. Like good pupils attentively studying a teacher, the dogs watched him.

'Elixir,' he said. 'He told my father that the sweetest drink he ever had was out of this well when he was on his way back from a drag hunt in the next glen. He was a great hunter.'

'He was Nimrod,' I said. 'He was everything. He was the universal Kerryman.'

'No kidding,' he said. 'Through a thorn hedge six feet thick and down a precipice and across a stream to make sure of a wounded bird. Or all night long waist-deep in an icy swamp waiting for the wild geese. And the day of this drag hunt. What he most remembered about it was the way they sold the porter to the hunting crowd in the pub at the crossroads. To meet the huntsmen halfways they moved the bar out to the farmyard. With hounds and cows and geese and chickens it was like having a drink in Noah's Ark. The pint tumblers were set on doors lifted off their hinges and laid flat on hurdles. The beer was in wooden tubs and all the barmaids had to do was dip and there was the pint. They didn't bother to rinse the tumblers. He said it was the quickest-served and the flattest pint of porter he ever saw or tasted. Bitter and black as bog water. Completely devoid of the creamy clerical collar that should grace a good pint. On the way home he spent an hour here rinsing his mouth and the well-water tasted as sweet, he said, as silver.'

The white cloud was gone from the mountain.

'Where did it go?' I said. 'Where could it vanish to?'

In all the wide sky there wasn't a speck of cloud. The mountain was changing colour, deepening to purple with the approaching evening.

He grasped me by the elbow, urging me forwards. He said, 'Step on it. We're almost home.'

We crossed a crude wooden stile and followed the short-cut through a walled garden of bright-green heads of cabbage and black and red currant bushes. Startled, fruit-thieving birds rustled away from us and on a rowan tree a sated, impudent blackbird opened his throat and sang.

'Don't touch a currant,' I said, 'or a head of cabbage. Don't ride your luck too hard.'

He laughed like a boy half hysterical with happiness. He said, 'Luck. Me and these dogs, we know each other. We've been formally introduced.

'Glad to know you, dogs,' he said to them over his shoulder.

They trotted behind us. We crossed a second stile and followed the short-cut through a haggard, and underfoot the ground was velvety with chipped straw. We opened a five-barred iron gate, and to me it seemed that the noise of its creaking hinges must be audible from end to end of the glen. While I paused to rebolt it he and the dogs had gone on, the dogs trotting in the lead. I ran after them. I was the stranger who had once been the guide. We passed three houses as if they didn't exist. They were empty. The people who lived in them were above at the hay.

Towards the fourth thatched house of the group we walked along a green boreen, lined with hazels and an occasional mountain ash. The guardian mountain was by now so purple that the sky behind it seemed, by contrast, as silvery as the scales of a fish. From unknown lands behind the lines of hazels two more black-and-white dogs ran, barking with excitement, to join our escort. Where the hazels ended there was a house fronted by a low stone wall and a profusion of fuchsia. An old man sat on the wall and around him clustered the children of the four houses. He was a tall, broad-shouldered old man with copious white hair and dark side whiskers and a clear prominent profile. He was dressed in good grey with long, old-fashioned skirts to his coat – formally dressed as if for some formal event – and his wide-brimmed black hat rested on the wall beside him, and his joined hands rested on the curved handle of a strong ash plant. He stood up as we approached. The stick fell to the ground. He stepped over it and came towards us. He was as tall or, without the slight stoop of age, taller than the professor. He put out his two hands and rested them on the professor's shoulders. It wasn't an embrace. It was an appraisal, a salute, a sign of recognition.

He said, 'Kevin, well and truly we knew you'd come if you were in the neighbourhood at all. I watched you walking down. I knew you from the top of the Glen. You have the same gait my brother had, the heavens be his bed. My brother that was your grandfather.'

'They say a grandson often walks like the grandfather,' said the professor.

His voice was shaken and there were tears on his face. So, a stranger in the place myself, I walked away a bit and looked back up the Glen. The sunlight was slanting now and shadows were lengthening on mountain slopes and across the small fields. From where I stood the lake was invisible, but the ashwood on the slope above it was dark as ink. Through sunlight and shadow the happy haymakers came running down towards us; and barking, playing, frisking over each other, the seven black-and-white dogs, messengers of good news, ran to meet them. The great Glen, all happy echoes, was opening out and singing to welcome its true son.

Under the hazels, as I watched the running haymakers, the children came shyly around me to show me that I also was welcome. Beyond the high ridge, the hard mountain the card-players used to cross to the cabin of the gambling stood up gaunt and arrogant and leaned over towards us as if it were listening.

It was moonlight, I thought, not sunlight, over the great Glen. From house to house, the dogs were barking, not baying the moon, but to welcome home the young men from the card-playing over the mountain. The edges of rock glistened like quartz. The tall young gambler came laughing down the Glen, greatcoat swinging open, waving in his hand the one bottle of whiskey that hadn't been broken when he tumbled down the spink. The ghosts of his own dogs laughed and leaped and frolicked at his heels.

The Shortest Way Home

The first school I ever went or was sent to was full of girls and that wasn't the worst of it. We were taught by big black nuns who had no legs or feet but who moved about as if, like the antediluvian chest of drawers in my mother's bedroom, they went on concealed casters. They used to haunt my dreams, moving uncannily about in thousands, their courses criss-crossing like the navigational lines on the maps on the classroom walls, bouncing off each other and spinning around like bumper cars at a fancy fair, holding aloft white canes like witch's wands. They didn't teach us much. All I remember is making chains by tearing up and intertwining thin strips of coloured paper, and rolling plasticine which we called plaster seed, into sticky balls. I can smell the turpentiny smell of it still.

At any rate the wells on my path to learning in that harem of a school were poisoned by the affair of the school-reader and by the blow Sister Enda caught me on the knuckles with her cane when I was absorbed drawing funny faces, with spittle and finger-tip, on the glossy brown wooden desk.

'Wipe the desk clean this instant,' she said. 'You naughty little boy.'

The offending funny faces – they were a first effort at recapturing the fine careless rapture observed, in a newspaper strip, on the faces of Mutt and Jeff – I wiped out or dried off with my handkerchief fastened with a safety pin to my white woollen gansey. That was a precautionary measure taken against loss of linen by my mother who for years preserved a snapshot of me pennant-cum-nosebag flying, a surly freckled boy with uncontrollable hair who looked as if he had just murdered nine reverend mothers. In more select schools, I've heard tell, they had in those days an inhuman device by which gloves too were ensured against loss. An elastic string passed around the back of the young victim's neck and then down the insides of the sleeves and from each extremity of the string a glove depended: so that when not in use, the gloves retreated up the sleeves like mice into holes. Fortunately, we were never grand enough for gloves. The worst we had was this pinned-on wiper with which I extinguished Mutt and Jeff, and I looked for sympathy towards Big May, and hated Sister Enda, as the long Act of Charity said, with my whole heart and soul and above all things.

At that time Big May was the only woman I loved and, great-hearted queen that she was, it wasn't Big May betrayed to the nun that I already had at home a duplicate copy of the coloured school reader, the first book that I, a born collector of books, ever possessed. She was nine and a half, four years older than me, her protégé, and big even then so that she might, in the words of the poet, with her great shapely knees and the long flowing line, have walked to the altar through the holy images at Pallas Athene's side, or been fit spoil for a centaur drunk with the unmixed wine. She was big and wild and lovely and never could take the straight road to school nor the straight road home, so that to be in her company was always an unguessable adventure. She ran messages for my mother and undertook to chaperone me to school when my sister, who was thirteen and a half, was too busy and superior and too absorbed in her own companions to be pestered with the care-taking of a toddler of a brother. May was lithe, laughing-eyed and dark-headed and could box better than most boys and climb trees like a monkey. She was an adorable woman and a born mother, so with my knuckles smarting, I turned my moistening eyes towards her for sympathy.

But the morning that martinet, Sister Enda, tried to commandeer my second copy of the school reader, Low Babies Edition, I wasn't looking for any woman's sympathy. Sister Enda said precisely, 'Your sister tells me you have one of these at home.'

It was a lovely reading-book: sixteen pages of simple sentences, big print, coloured pictures. It told the most entrancing stories. This one, for instance: My dog Rags has a house. He has a little house of his own. See, his name is over the door.

Or this one: Mum has made buns for tea. She has made nice hot buns.

Or yet another: When the children went to the zoo they liked the elephant best of all. Here is the elephant with happy children on his back.

Or breaking into verse: When the old owl lived in the oak never a word at all he spoke.

To have one copy, which my mother had bought me, at home, and another copy, supplied by regulations, in school, gave that miracle of coloured picture and succinct narrative the added wonder of twins or of having two of anything. So when Sister Enda, soaring to the top of her flight in the realms of wit, said one reader should be enough for such a little boy, and when all the girls except May giggled I saw red and grabbed, leaving Sister Enda momentarily quite speechless with shock and turning over and over in her hand a leaf that said on one side: Here comes the aeroplane, says Tom; and on the other: When the children came home from town they had much to tell Mum.

Gripping the rest of the reader I glared at the nun who was white in the face with something – fright or fury – at this abrupt confrontation with the male forces of violence and evil. She looked at me long and thoughtfully. Fortunately for me she was perambulating without benefit of cane. She said, 'You naughty boy. Now your poor mother will have to pay for the book you destroyed. Stand in the corner under the clock with your face to the wall until home-time.'

Which I did: tearless, my face feverish with victory, because that onset with Sister Enda had taught me things about women that some men never learn and, staring at the brown varnished wainscotting in the corner of the room, I made my resolve. On the homeward journey I told May all about it.

I said, 'As long as I live I'm not going back to that school. It's all women.'

'Not till tomorrow morning.'

'Never. Never, if I die.'

'Where will you go?'

'To the Brothers with the big boys.'

'You're too little.'

'I'll go all the same.'

'They mightn't take you.'

'They'll take me.'

'What will your mother say?'

'I don't care what she says.'

Which was true, because I knew if I could best Sister Enda I could best my mother. It was a man's world.

'You're a terrible boy,' May said. 'But I'll miss you.'

She believed me, I felt, and knew in her heart that that was our last day at school together, and she was proud of me. So with my hand in hers we went on the last detour of my career at the female academy, leaving Brook Street and Castle Street, our proper route, and wandering into the cosy smelly crowded world of the gridiron of lanes of one-storeyed whitewashed houses below and at the back of the towering double-spired Catholic Church; Fountain Lane, Brook Lane, The Gusset, St. Kevin's Lane, Potato Lane, and the narrowest of all, which was a cul-de-sac called the Rat's Pad. Previously we had prudently passed it by because even to May, the narrow roofed-over entry opening out into a small close that held only four houses was a little daunting. Besides, you could not go through it and come out the other end and, as May saw things, a place of that sort did not constitute a classical diversion.

It was a dog's walk, she said. You came back the way you went.

But on this day the Rat's Pad attracted us because a woman in one of its four houses was shouting her head off and outside her half-door a dozen or so people had gathered to find out what all the noise was about. Skilfully May worked her way in to a point of vantage, carrying me pick-a-back, both to save space and to give me enough altitude to study the domestic interior. The woman, in blouse and spotted apron, was gesticulating with a long knife. Of all the words or sentences only one remained with me, 'I'll cut the head off you, you lazy gazebo.'

The man saying nothing, his head bowed as if meekly to accept the blade, sat on a low stool by an open, old-fashioned grate. The fire burned brightly.

'May,' I whispered, 'will she really and truly cut the head off him?' I wasn't sure whether I did or did not want to witness the spectacle.

'From what they say,' said May, 'she couldn't cut a slice of bread.'

So since there was nothing happening but shouting, we rejoined our main route homewards and May bought for me, as a special treat to mark the ending of the first phase of my scholastic career, a toffee apple in Katy McElhatton's huckster shop in Castle Street. Those toffee apples were a noted home-made delicacy, and Katy was a woman as old as the Hag of Beare, who lived in the end to be one hundred and eight and only died of a stomach disorder that came on her when she mistook a bottle of Jeyes fluid for a bottle of stout she kept always on a shelf behind the counter. But her toffee apples were something to savour and remember, and the flavour of thick golden syrup toffee and roasted green apple was still in my mouth when I fell asleep that night to dream of a severed head held aloft by the hair in the hand of an irate wife. There was no blood neither from stump nor severed neck, nor any jagged dangling sinews. When, for purposes of demonstration, the vengeful spouse turned the head and neck around and around, the cross-section of the neck was solid and shiny like the corned beef when it had been subjected to the slicer in James Campbell's big shop. That was the way you were when your head was cut off. It was also true that husbands and wives could work themselves into such a state that they threatened each other with knives and decapitation. My last day at the school for girls had taught me a lot and I owed it all not to any organised institutional education but to my own assertion of manly independence and to the divagations of my amazonian love and protectress, that queen among women, Big May. Henceforth I would be a man and would bear my expanding satchel into the world of the big boys. Farewell, farewell for ever to first love and all it had given me.

'The only Brother I'll go to,' I dictated to my mother, 'is the Wee Brother.'

Having won my battle against any return to the monstrous regiment of women, I was advancing to invest new positions.

The six black Brothers of the Christian Schools emerged from their monastery every morning to kneel in the top pew, to the left of the nave and under the marble pulpit, at eight o'clock mass. A wide-eyed study of their movements, kneeling, sitting, standing, praying, yawning, genuflecting, reading missals, blowing noses, had for some time been for me a substitute for any form of worship: latria or dulia.

The Grey Brother, whose place was on the extreme right of their pew, was Brother Superior. His bush of grey hair was clipped and shaved in an exact straight line dead level with the tops of his ears. He had a fine Roman nose and a trumpet style of blowing it that never since have I seen or heard surpassed. His production of handkerchief from a slit in his black habit, his preliminary flourish of white linen, added up to a ritual fascinating to watch. He never produced the handkerchief with his right hand. He always flourished before he trumpeted and, when he blew, even the two old voteens, one man and one woman, who prayed out loud and talked over their affairs with God for all to hear, were momentarily startled out of the balance and rhythm of their recitative.

To the left of the Grey Brother stood or knelt or sat, according to the stage of the celebration, Brother Busto and Brother Lanko, for even then I knew them according to the nicknames the boys bestowed on them, and had to that extent my instruction in the lingua franca of the world of men. They had the same soothering Munster accents and the same surnames and were distinguished from each other only, as the nicknames so subtly indicated, by the robust girth of one and the handsome height of the other. The Beardy Brother was unusual because beards were rare among Brothers, but the phenomenon was satisfactorily explained by the boys saying that the Beardy Brother had been in China, and later in life it came as a shock to me to find that beards were comparatively as rare among Chinamen as among Brothers. The Red Brother, true to the colour of his hair and the close, disciplined army cut of it, was the terror of the school and the legend went so far as to say that on one of his punitive forays he had trapped the shoulders of a delinquent boy under a window sash and thumped him on the buttocks with a hurling stick. To my extreme relief he had withdrawn from the religious life, possibly to devote more time to hurling, before I had advanced as far as the grade he so robustly instructed.

But it would have been clear to me, even if the opinion of the grown up people had not already been there to confirm my intuitive judgement that the Wee Brother was an angel descended from above. The children adored him. They ran messages for him, swept the schoolrooms and the schoolyard for him, and in the season, under his direction, shook the trees and picked up the fallen apples in the monastery orchard. They banded themselves at his behest into groups of all sorts, from paper and comb orchestras to football teams, or went walking with him in crowds in the country learning the names of birds and trees, and not too often wandering off in small foraging parties to rob orchards or egghouses. In spite of the vow of poverty he always clinked with small coins to reward them for their more meritorious efforts. He was good to the poor and his favourite pupil was Packy Noble, a shuffling albino boy too big for his grade and mentally incapable of advancing further or of mastering more than the alphabet. Grown men admired the Wee Brother because he had been a famous amateur horse jockey before religion claimed him, and – although this was something I did not then understand – the girls, looking at him, sighed heartbroken resignation to the inscrutable ways of the Lord who claimed such a paragon for the cloister.

It was his waving fair hair and the way the light reflected on his pince-nez that caused me first to worship him, and shining pince-nez seemed to me the clearest of all marks of the angelic nature manifesting itself in mortal shape. Even still I'm inclined to think that the world is the way it is because not half enough people wear pince-nez.

So I said to my mother, 'The only Brother I'll go to is the Wee Brother.'

It was autumn, and the schoolyard was the best place in our world for horse-chestnuts. The yard was triangular with the apex pointing up a slope towards the schoolhouse, an oblong cut-stone building of two storeys. Access to the second storey, because of the oversight of the builder who forgot the stairs originally planned for, was by an iron outside stairway. The long branches of the chestnut trees overhung the walls of the yard and with a little encouragement from sticks and stones readily dropped their thorny green fruit. Wonder was all around my mother and myself as we ascended towards the school. Ten million boys, it seemed to me, were playing conkers, swinging the seasoned chestnuts scientifically on lengths of string, slashing at and bashing their opponents' chestnuts. Fragments of the casualties of myriad battles crackled under our feet like cinders. Surrounded by an excited crowd a tiny fellow called Tall Jimmy Clarke was bending down with his hands behind his back and picking ha'pence off the ground with his teeth. He did it for the price of the ha'pence he picked up and prospered by it because the fascination of what's difficult always proved overpowering, even for boys who had seen and paid for the trick a dozen times over. In a corner by the concrete lavatories and washrooms a crowd of hydro maniacs were having the time of their lives pumping the handles of the drinking fountains and covering each other and the ground around them with water. This was life, this was a battlefield, this was the wonderful world of school and apart from my mother, there wasn't a petticoat to be seen.

Then a whistle blew and in shuffling hordes the boys ascended, to be swallowed up by the old stone building. The slamming of doors, the clatter of iron-tipped heels on the iron stairway were wonderful to hear; then we were alone, my mother and I. Dust still rose from the yard. It steamed in the sun on the damp patch left by the water-sprites. Beyond a row of chestnut trees the gardens kept by the Brothers were well-ordered and radiant. Variously-regulated chants arose from various classrooms and we listened to them, my hand in hers, until the Grey Brother came to us from the monastery beside the schoolhouse and said, 'So this is the little man who doesn't like the girls.'

The Grey Brother I took to from the start for he was a fellowman and he saw my point.

'And what book shall we put him into,' he said. 'He's so far under the admittance age.'

Book, I thought, I have my own books. In the satchel on my back there was one jotter, slightly scribbled on, one pencil, two school readers even if one of them, owing to the villainy of woman, was lacking a leaf. There was also my lunch of bread and butter sandwiches, a small bottle of milk, two biscuits and one piece of cake.

'He wants nobody but the Wee Brother,' my mother said. 'Then the Wee Brother it shall be.'

He waved his arm at a window on the second storey and on the landing of the stairway at the corner of the building the vision appeared, fair hair like a halo blowing around its head, the sunlight shining through the halo, the sun beaming out of its glass eyes, truly an angel descending to walk with us. He took me up the stairs again with him and that was how I came to meet the Four Horsemen of the Apocalypse who, after Big May and the Wee Brother, were the greatest teachers I ever had.

Sometimes the Wee Brother called them the Twelve Apostles because he said any one man of them was as good as three. Other times he called them simply the Four Just Men. But mostly, and I think merely because they ran most of his messages for him – carrying dispatches all over the town, from errands of charity to admonitory notes to parents who weren't sending their boys to school – he called them the Four Horsemen of the Apocalypse. They sat, or knelt at prayer time, on the bench nearest to the door, making sure in winter that the door was securely closed against draughts, enjoying in summer a high green view of the neighbouring convent field where the nuns, for some symbolic devotional purpose, grazed a small black donkey; the happiest laziest donkey in the world, the Wee Brother said. That big bench by the door was the highest and oldest in the classroom. Even by the standards of those days it was a museum piece. It had survived several changes of school furniture. It was battle-scarred with the names of boys now grown to be men. It towered over the other desks like a Spanish galleon over the dogged little ships of Elizabeth's gunners. It creaked with age every time one of its occupants moved. It had space, the Wee Brother said, for four and a quarter men, so he lifted me up, seated me at one end of it, my legs dangling, beside Packy Noble, told me I was the image of an artistic mantelpiece ornament in a modern house, and placed me thus under the Tutelage of the Four Horsemen, Packy himself, Tall Jimmy Clarke, Jinkins Creery and Tosh Mullan, who later in life was to become a boxer and to acquire by a painful accident the pseudonym of Kluterbuck.

My two school readers opened before me, I studied the pictures and listened to the drone of learning all around me and sometime in the afternoon fell asleep. For no lullaby ever sung soothingly by loving peasant mother could equal the power of the simple addition table to induce slumber: One and one are two, one and two are three, one and three are four. Before my eyes radiant woolly balls rolled up and down hills and I slept and, as I learned afterwards, was gently lifted by the snowheaded Packy and, under the direction of the Wee Brother, laid to rest on the broad bottom shelf of a brown press used as a wardrobe on dry days for the scholars' coats and caps. Comfortably cushioned, I slumbered until it was time for the litany of the Blessed Virgin and the journey home and then, thumbing the sleep out of my eyes, I boarded the galleon again and balanced on my knees for a prayer so soothing that I would have fallen asleep again except that, just as the Wee Brother said Tower of Ivory and we sang out Pray for Us, the old desk gave up the ghost and collapsed with a crash, and the litany dissolved in the laughter of boys and when the Wee Brother saw that nobody was hurt he laughed too. That was a day's learning I'll remember when I've forgotten – as I have already – sines, cosines and declensions and the fine poem about the Latin prepositions that govern the accusative case.

The Four Horsemen, taking the place of Big May, conducted me home. Tall Jimmy Clarke, by stooping and lifting, acquired on the way four halfpennies and bought sweets and shared them out. Jinkins Creery held me up on the parapet of the bridge over the Strule and showed me where he had caught a river lamprey a mile long and promised to show me the seven baby lampreys he had in a glass jar at home. He explained to me how he had caught them by holding a tennis-ball in among a maze of them in a foot of water in the Killyclogher Burn and how the stupid, vicious creatures had clung on to it so tightly with the suckers they had instead of mouths that he was able to lift seven of them out of the water. Packy, who was Master of All, and Tosh Mullan put on, for my instruction, a display of the noble art of self-defence which was great fun because Packy was huge and white-headed and his battered boots were too big for him and his toes turned up and he could imitate a dancing bear he had once seen in John Duffy's travelling circus.

Packy's greatest weakness was that he could never be in time for school in the morning. His mother or, to be more charitable his aunt, went by the strange name of Pola and was the proprietress of what we knew bluntly as a tramp lodging-house where, it was rumoured, the itinerant patrons cooked over candles and slept on their feet, elbows hooked on a common rope, so that inexorably they were all roused together when the rope was slackened at reveille. Cooking conditions may not have been so primitive or sleeping conditions so arbitrary in Pola's caravanserai, but certain it was that the mixed clientele of sallow-faced oriental bagmen, pedlars, vagrant musicians, buskers and down-right beggars who patronised it did not go to bed until the small hours and then only to the accompaniment of a pretty consistent bedlam. So, shuffling in late, morning after morning, Packy would wearily rub red eyes that had around them rims of sleep, like grey mud around a weep-ing flowering marsh; and the back of his white poll was never devoid of a tiny pillow-feather or two. Every morning the prolegomena to his day's study followed the same pattern.

'He who rises late must gallop all day. Do you know what that means, Packy?'

'Yes, sir.'

'What, Packy?'

'It's in the headline copy, sir.'

The headline copy, with its incomprehensible maxims in stiff old-fashioned copperplate, in elegant lines and curves that no young inex-perienced hands could ever imitate, was the master-work on which we were supposed to model our handwriting.

'Packy, you're right. I suppose one way or another the sum total of wisdom is in the headline copy.'

'Yes, sir.'

'Packy, I must buy you an alarm clock.'

'Yes, sir.'

'Diluculo surgere saluberrimum est, Packy. To rise early is most healthful.'

Tenderly, with his fingertips, the Wee Brother would pick the feath-ers of the night before from the close-cropped white head.

'Yes, sir,' said Packy.

'Early to bed and early to rise makes a man healthy, wealthy and wise, Packy.'

With those gentle fingertips he would drum out on Packy's shoulder rhythm to go with the words.

'That's in the headline copy too, Packy.'

'Yes, sir.'

The early bird catches the worm was also in the headline copy and it struck me as a brutal saying because the early worm was the head of a fool to be out at that hour. The only saying I liked at all in the headline copy was about violets: I would give you some violets but they withered when my father died. Not one of us, not even John MacBride, a clean boy who was clever and was taught by his musical mother to sing Moore's melodies at parochial concerts, knew what it meant or who said it or who died or who wanted to give violets to whom. But, regardless, we copied out the words painfully and with all the intensity of faith: slope lightly up, slope heavily down, curve at the top and curve at the bottom, Packy peering so closely at the page that his nose was as good as in the inkwell, the tip of Tall Jimmy Clarke's tongue peeping out like a moist pink rodent.

Packy, being as he was and doomed to an early grave, could only in some heavenly fields ever have discovered the coy beauty of the modest flower. Here on this earth his peering eyes discovered more about nettles than violets, for Pola was a great believer in the health-giving powers of nettle tea, nettle soup or nettles as a vegetable and it was Packy's task to gather, in the spring, the soft succulent young nettles before age had soured them and forced them to show their stings. The other three horsemen went along to help and I went with them.

Because of the four oblong fields that belonged to Big James Campbell, the butcher, and the engine shed and Spyglass Hill and the grass wigwam and the cave at the spot where four hedgerows joined and the Ali Baba's treasure house of a town dump and the roaring bull in Mackenna's meadow, gathering the nettles was not as prosaic a business as you might readily imagine. Three of the fields were gently rising slopes and the fourth was a dome of a hill overlooking the bull's deep meadow, and the four of them lay just beyond the straggling fingers of houses at the edge of the town.

You crossed the town dump, a grey-black wasteland, smoking with an occasional volcano where discarded cinders had refused to die. There were always a few old people, sacks in hands, shoulders hunched and eyes on the ground, wandering slowly about, gathering the makings of a fire and hoping for treasures of scrap. Since the most extraordinary relics of careless housekeeping came to that island of lost ships the aged searchers were quite frequently rewarded and the curious schoolboy could find there, too, objects to delight the heart: shining biscuit tins, discarded motor wheels and tyres, bicycle frames that could be refurbished and made useful. Tosh Mullan, who was lucky at finding things, had once come upon a handsome point-twenty-two rifle that would do everything but shoot.

The best nettles were always found on the fringe of the dump just before you ascended the slope, climbed a fence and crossed the railway line to the turntable and the engine shed.

'Nettles for measles and pimples,' Packy would say. 'That's what my aunt Pola says.'

In the murk of the one-night lodging house for wandering men who had no parish of their own, Pola managed to maintain a flawless olive complexion.

'Boil them in water, she says, and drink the tea. She says if you drink nettle tea you'll always have a clear skin.'

'Tosh could do with it,' said Tall Jimmy Clarke.

For Tosh, with a hanging lower lip and a squint and a recurring rash of pimples was not the most beautiful of boys. Yet even then he had in his social relations the tolerant mildness of the natural professional fighter who never, outside the ring, feels called upon to prove his prowess; and the pummellings with which he responded to Tall Jimmy's witticisms were perfectly good-natured.

One day – if I can distinguish one day from another over a period of years – Tosh flourished in his hand a full-grown dead lamprey that Jinkins had caught and given to him. He carried it as proudly as if it had been a policeman's truncheon, until the stench became too much. Waving it in his hand he pursued Jimmy with warlike whoops towards the railway line and the engine shed. Jinkins, carrying his fishing rod, ran after them and I ran after Jinkins because, bright ferret-eyes glistening in his turnip of a head, he had promised to show me how he caught fish and how, incidentally, he had acquired the nickname we called him by. I never knew his Christian name.

From the fence on top of the railway embankment we looked back at Packy the Herbalist on hands and knees among the rank green growth at the fringe of the wasteland. Even if he was never to know much about violets it could just be part of the irony of living that he knew more than any of us about the meaning of growing things. He was so close to them because, being half-blind, he had to kneel to see them, their shapes and colours, and when the rare flowering nettle showed its fragile white bloom through the red mist of his eyes it must have meant something miraculous to him. He was the herbalist gathering plants from the ground to make messes and potions to keep blood pure and a woman beautiful.

'Come on Packy,' Tosh called. 'We have nettles enough to sink a battleship.'

Packy rose, clutching his herbs, and to excite our laughter, did his bear's gallop towards us.

'We'll cross over the engine shed and grease our boots.'

'We'll wait for the goods first. We always wait for the goods.'

Swinging on the wire fence we watched with a wonder that never lessened the variety of cargo on the interminable lumbering goods train. We counted the trucks. Cattle on their last sad journey looked out at us morosely. The wind blew towards us smells of dung and good timber, the sour smell of scrap metal, the wet milky smell of farm produce. The tick-tock of wheels over joints and fish-plates was delightfully soothing. We cheered the guard in his van at the end of the train as a crowd in a theatre might cheer the author. He waved his flag to us, as he always did before the embankment, and the round mouth of a bridge devoured him.

'Big Mick O'Neill, the railway porter, can turn the turntable with one hand and an engine and a coal-wagon on it.'

'He's farandaway the strongest man in this town.'

'He's the strongest man in Ireland.'

We had never you see, heard of the bragging man who said: 'Give me a lever and I'll move the world.'

'There was a stronger man in Dublin once,' said Tall Jimmy Clarke. 'My father told me about him.'

Tall Jimmy's father, a roadworker, was admittedly a man of great knowledge as all makers and menders of roads come, by dint of their occupation, to be. All day long they watch the world, unaware of their observation, passing them by.

'He was a policeman. His name was Patrick Sheehan. He caught a mad bull by the horns once and when people asked him was he afraid he said he was only afraid the horns would break.'

In the middle of the railway track we stopped and listened, each one of us thinking that far away across the four fields we could hear our own private bull roaring in Mackenna's meadow.

'He went down a manhole once,' said Tall Jimmy, 'to rescue a work-man was stuck in a pipe and he rescued the workman and he was smothered dead by the gas. He was so strong that was the only way he could be killed. My da says there's a monument to him in Dublin.'

'We'll grease our boots,' said Packy.

It was a thick yellow suet-like grease kept in little iron boxes on the sides of the freight trucks. It was meant to soothe and cool the friction of axles and wheels and not to be applied to any leather ever hammered out of an animal's hide. But in ritual fashion, like savages daubing on war paint, we greased our boots with it before we entered the four fields. Its one beneficial quality was that it could withstand moisture and, if the grass was wet, the beads of rain or dew danced like jewels on the dulled leather. Leather treated with that yellow grease could defy for ever all shine and polish and cause quarrels between mystified parents and indignant bootsellers about the quality of the material they put in footwear nowadays.

With our feet anointed we slipped through a well-worn hole in a high hawthorn hedge and trod the holy grass of the first field. Tall Jimmy was in the lead, dancing a dance that was halfway between his idea of an Indian war-dance and his slightly more accurate idea of a sailor's horn-pipe. Packy came in the rear, beaming like a bride over his bouquet of nettles. Pola, who never had had a wedding, white or coloured, or a groom from whose arm she could dangle, was an assiduous spectator at every wedding in the parish church, and Packy could simper like any lace-clad virgin just as well as he could prance like a circus bear.

In the middle of a clump of rushes a tall unheeded wooden pole carried a notice saying trespassers would be prosecuted. We regarded it as the dissolute members of an aristocratic family would regard a family ghost who had become an old-fashioned bore. No longer even did we use it as a cockshot for cinders carried from the engine shed.

'Tony,' Tall Jimmy shouted, 'Tony.'

Running away from us he called back, 'Watch me. I'm Tom Mix.'

For the old horse grazed or wearily sucked the grass in the first field. Nothing less like the renowned Tony ever shuffled along on four shaky feet. He was an old saddle-backed bay left out there to die in peace. There were white spots of age on his hide like stabs of lichen on old stone. He was just about able, and no more, to bear the featherweight of agile Jimmy and it was Jimmy's delight to straddle on the sunken back that seemed almost to creak like a worn iron bedstead, to hammer his heels as if they were spurred against the withered flagging flanks, to hang from the scraggy neck as if he was a Red Indian, to wind up the exhausted slack-springed body to a trot in which every leg seemed to limp away in a different direction.

'Look at him now. Hasn't he the lovely smile.'

He pulled the lips apart to show great green and yellow teeth lazily floating in saliva. They weren't bright or beautiful, yet the expression was more like a smile than it was like anything else.

He was an amiable old animal and to him and Tall Jimmy I owe it that I was never afraid of the long heads of horses, and that, later in life I was able to find myself in agreement with the Tipperary trainer who at the Curragh of Kildare races smacked the tight-skirted titled lady on her prancing buttocks and cried out for all to hear, 'Women, the best things God made – after horses.'

Tall Jimmy on horseback leading us, we went in procession through the gapped hedge and up the slope to the grass wigwam on Spyglass Hill. From the Wee Brother's public readings we knew about Long John Silver, Jim Hawkins and the fifteen men on a dead man's chest so, although the dome-shaped hill that was the highest of the four fields offered no view of the blue Pacific, that was still the only name we could give it. From the wigwam that Tosh and Tall Jimmy had lovingly plaited from branches, rushes and long grass you could see the traffic on the road to Clanabogan, the long scimitar-shaped meadow where our bull fed, Pigeon Top Mountain where the sportsmen went for grouse, the town's three steeples, the deep Drumragh River where Jinkins fished and the clanking metal structure called the Lynn Bridge which carried the railway over the river. So we called the place Spyglass Hill. The wigwam was a magic restful place. Green light filtered down into it. The air was sweet with the smell of warm grass. The parti-coloured branches, peeled in strips by Tosh who had a clasp-knife as long as a sabre, seemed, if you lay flat on your back and looked up at them long enough, to move and writhe like serpents. Although that big man James Campbell who owned the fields went to the trouble of putting up notices banning trespassers, neither he nor his foreman nor working men ever tampered with the grass wigwam and, when Tosh had built around it a circular palisade of strong sticks to protect it from the curiosity of cows, it lasted for a whole summer.

All together we lay in the green light and Tall Jimmy's exhausted discarded mount lay thinking the thoughts of age on the grass outside the palisade. From the tired horse to the roaring bull was no distance at all because the wigwam was our halfway house to the cave that wasn't a cave. It was a sort of unfinished tunnel that cattle seeking shade from the sun had made under branches at the meeting place of four hedgerows. Smaller than the cattle, we could penetrate further into gloom and then, parting a few branches, peer down into the meadow where the big red bull grazed. The game was to roar at him until he roared back. He never failed to oblige us. He would delight us still further by rooting at the ground with his homed head and some-times even drive us into sheer ecstasy by racing around in circles and kicking his hind legs in the air as a horse would. He was a fine per-former. He was our own menagerie: a giant red bull alone like a king in his private park.

'They'll kill him some day,' Jimmy said sadly. 'They'll kill him and make Bovril out of him. That's what they do with bulls.'

Our roaring done – Packy who could dance like a bear was also the best of us to roar like a bull – we wandered aimlessly across the grass thinking sadly of all the noble roaring bulls, black and red, who had gone down to the doom of being melted to fill small bottles with meat extract. To brighten our mood Tall Jimmy seized one of a pair of pitchforks, left stuck in a hedge by some of Campbell's men, and shouted, 'We'll play "Ninety-Eight".'

It wasn't a card game. It was a by-product of the Wee Brother's fervent lecturing on the long sad history of Irish Rebellion. The pitchforks, one in the hands of Packy and one in the hands of Tall Jimmy, became the pikes the boys of Wexford carried in 1798. Before their glistening points hordes of redcoats fell back at Camolin, Enniscorthy, Tubberneering, and Tosh with the dead lamprey was beating an invisible big drum and Jinkins with his fishing rod was a galloping lancer, and the high town of New Ross and Three Bullet Gate were about to be stormed and taken when Big James and his foreman appeared through a gap in a hedge and roared at us and we ran.

'They'll prosecute us, sure as God,' said Jinkins, who had a natural horror of the law.

So we ran faster and the two men for the hell of it ran after us. For my age and the length of my legs I could run well but the Four Horsemen were bigger and better athletes and I was losing ground badly: confused, too, with the awesome thought that I was a trespasser, one of a group referred to specifically in the Lord's Prayer. Staggering under the weight of that thought, I stumbled and fell and was resigning myself to prosecution and prison when I was picked up by Packy and carried through a narrow gap between two trees to the covert of a terraced whindotted slope above the river. Concealed by green thorn and yellow blossom we sat whispering for half an hour and looking at, and listening to, the water. It came rattling down over the shallows, curved and spread out to make a deep pool that went on under the railway and the girders of the Lynn Bridge.

'That's where I catch my fish,' Jinkins said.

'Where you catch the jinkins you should throw back,' said Tall Jimmy. 'Some day Robert McCaslan, the water bailiff, will get you.'

On our river the salmon fry and the tiny trout were called jinkins and our friend, the great hunter, had earned his name from his passion for catching, cooking and eating them against all the laws ever made for the conserving of game fish.

Packy held his nose. He said, 'Jinkins always stinks like a fish.'

'No. It's this,' said Tosh.

He dangled the hideous, headless, mouthless lamprey under Packy's nose.

'Come and watch me catch them,' Jinkins said to me.

So when we thought the coast was clear and our pursuers gone, Jinkins mounted his rod and readied his dry flies and in single file we marched out from the shelter of the whins, to be greeted with gales of friendly laughter from Big James and his foreman. They waved at us through our escape gap between the two trees.

'They were only fooling all the time,' said Packy.

'They're funny men,' said Tall Jimmy with scorn.

'Don't kill all the fish in the river,' the foreman shouted.

And when Tall Jimmy, never at a loss for an answer, cried back that we'd cut them up and use them for bait, they laughed even louder and went back laughing towards Spyglass Hill.

Far away our lonely doomed bull roared on his own demesne.

With a light breeze at his back Jinkins let the long line float out easily. Packy, on his bended knees peering at the earth, might have been the image of the ancient herbalist half-blind from searching the fields and from concocting in his magic cellar, but Jinkins by the river bank was for sure the natural hunter. The stiff hair stood up on him like the bristles on a hedgehog. His ferret eyes pierced the water for the first white flash of soft under-belly. The small hook struck with deadly accuracy and Jinkins chuckled to himself as he unhooked the tiny, silvery, fluttering bodies and strung them through the gills on a looped, peeled ash-twig. It was methodical massacre; and if the salmon are not in that water as they were of old, then the cause of their absence, under God and new land-drainage systems, is the Herod-complex that impelled Jinkins Creery to his slaughter of the innocents. As Tall Jimmy taught me never to fear horses, so the sight of Jinkins at work taught me to pity fish: fish on the hook, fish in aquariums gazing sadly through the frustrating glass, pinkeens imprisoned in jam jars, fish sacrificed on slabs in shops and doomed to the fire and the knife and fork.

When the killing was all done we walked the railway line to the middle of the Lynn Bridge, opened a metal trap door between the rails

and descended a ladder to a plank walk that workmen used when
inspecting or painting the girders. The deep water was quite still below
us. Packy held me by the shoulders but, in spite of his protection, I
had, that night, my first falling nightmare.

'Long Alex Nixon,' Tosh said, 'drowned himself in that pool.'

'He didn't drown himself,' said Packy. 'He just sank.'

'He couldn't sink.'

'He wasn't cork, was he?'

'I saw them dragging the river for his body,' Tall Jimmy said. 'There
was a man diving all the time from a boat looking for him.'

'We all saw that,' Jinkins said. 'They were at it for days.'

'He was the best swimmer in the world,' Tosh said. 'He just held
his nose and sank and drowned himself. He was always fighting with
his wife.'

'That doesn't prove he drowned himself,' Packy said. 'You couldn't
drown yourself just by holding your nose.'

He released my shoulder and, holding his nose with his left hand,
did, on the swaying plank a few steps of his bear's shuffle. But our
laughter between the unanswering black water and the metal girders
were hollow. Awed by the sound of it we climbed back up the ladder
and gratefully closed the clanking door on the mystery of Long Alex
Nixon.

The possibility or otherwise of drowning by holding the nose was
a topic that kept us talking all the way back along the rusted branch-
line to the town's auxiliary goods station, where the coal-wagons were
lined up with the supplies for the lunatic asylum, and halfway up the
town's main street where shops were closed and the tea-time hush
had descended. Thought and remembrance came with the hush and
we heard the agonised voice of Packy, 'Mother of God, I've lost my
nettles.'

Red and blue shop-blinds carefully drawn made the town look like
a place of the dead. Not a nettle grew on the cruel pavement. With
guilt I remembered that I had seen Packy's nettles fall to the grass when
he redeemed me, the trespasser. With the folly of youth I said, 'We'll
go back for more.'

'We wouldn't have time. We're late already. She'll murder me.'

Generously Jinkins the hunter said, 'Give her a couple of fish.'

'She never eats fish. She says they're greasy.'

'Give her my ampor eel,' said Tosh.

Ampor eel was our mispronunciation for lamprey.

But sick to the soul, we all knew that this was no joke for Pola put great faith in nettles.

Then as we stood sadly thinking, the angel came to our rescue. She came tall wild-haired and ragged. She came as she always came, from a side street of shabby, brown-and-yellow brick houses. She bore in her arms a jungle profusion of wild nettles and, bending her ear to the sorrowful tale, she said simply to Packy, 'One of the women I work for is mad about nettles. But take half of mine. I have enough to physic the town let alone one old woman.'

She patted my head. She said, 'How do you like the big boys?'

She took the lead as if she was the biggest boy of all and we followed her up the street for fifty yards until, being Big May, she left us to make her own detour along another side street.

The day the Wee Brother would no longer close me in the press to slumber my way to learning on the piled coats and caps I knew sorrowfully that life had begun. What happened was that one of the scholars, for reasons known only to himself and which he was never sufficiently articulate to explain, had a pocket of his coat full of broken glass. Turning over in my slumber I lacerated my left hand – I still have a faint scar. I emerged, when awakened, dripping blood. The Wee Brother looked as if he and the class were guilty of murder. He staunched the flow, sent Jinkins to buy me a bag of hard sweets, then sent me home in the company of shambling Packy. It wasn't a serious wound but it was the beginning of the end. Thereafter there was nothing for me but the common lot, the hard reality of wooden desks and, as I mentioned – Life; and Life remorselessly was to take me away from Big May and the Wee Brother and the Four Horsemen, my six favourite teachers.

The Wee Brother is with the Saints and Packy is more than likely his favourite pupil still, for Packy died young. Short of dancing like a bear and roaring like a bull, being late for school and being kind to me, and gathering nettles to preserve Pola from pimples, he never accomplished much in life that I ever heard of. But he had a splendid funeral paid for by the subscriptions of the Wee Brother's numerous clients and led by Pola and the Wee Brother as chief mourners.

Tosh took to boxing and retained his professional amiability except for one unfortunate moment when he was engaged in conflict with a fighter who had the provoking name of Kluterbuck. Every just man loses his composure at least once and Tosh struck Kluterbuck very much and very severely below the belt, lost the fight and gained a new name. Never afterwards was he known as Tosh. The change of name may have altered his character. He gave up boxing. He left the town and never came back. He was last heard of just before the war, working in a bicycle factory in Coventry. In occasional dreams I see him grown larger but otherwise unchanged, swinging a bicycle tyre around his head as once he swung the dead and odorous ampor eel.

Jinkins had a mental breakdown and went for treatment to the asylum whose coal supply we walked past the day Packy lost the nettles. He remained there as a trusted patient, working around the grounds and fishing in the river that flows just outside the walls.

Tall Jimmy Clarke became a jockey but took to drink, put on weight, descended to truck-driving and became a wealthy owner of trucks. No longer as supple or as close to the ground as he was that day under the chestnut branches, he makes no money by picking ha'pence up with his teeth. But then, as he told me himself, he now has other ways of earning his living.

Big May went off to London and, if you could believe on their Bible oaths the people in the town I came from, went on thinking the longest way round was the shortest way home. Her thick dark hair, the outline of her strong jawbone is still visible to me. She holds me pick-a-back. Together we peer at the flashing knife and the raving woman and the slave of a man in the dim kitchen, and May says, 'From what they say she couldn't cut a slice of bread.'

By the tone of her voice then, she never put much weight on what people said. She gave generously. What violets she had she shared them with Packy.

A Journey to the Seven Streams

My father, the heavens be his bed, was a terrible man for telling you
about the places he had been and for bringing you there if he could
and displaying them to you with a mild and gentle air of proprietor-
ship. He couldn't do the showmanship so well in the case of Spion Kop
where he and the fortunate ones who hadn't been ordered up the hill
in the ignorant night had spent a sad morning crouching on African
earth and listening to the deadly Boer guns that, high above the plain,
slaughtered their hapless comrades. Nor yet in the case of Halifax nor
the Barbadoes where he had heard words of Gaelic from coloured girls
who were, he claimed, descended from the Irish transported into
slavery in the days of Cromwell. The great glen of Aherlow, too, which
he had helped to chain for His Majesty's Ordnance Survey was placed
inconveniently far to the South in the mystic land of Tipperary, and
Cratloe Wood, where the fourth Earl of Leitrim was assassinated,
was sixty miles away on the winding Donegal fjord called Mulroy
Bay. But townlands like Corraheskin, Drumlish, Cornavara, Dooish,
The Minnieburns and Claramore, and small towns like Drumquin and
Dromore were all within a ten-mile radius of our town and something
of moment or something amusing had happened in every one of them.

The reiterated music of their names worked on him like a charm.
They would, he said, take faery tunes out of the stone fiddle of Castle
Caldwell; and indeed it was the night he told us the story of the stone
fiddle and the drowned fiddler, and recited for us the inscription

carved on the fiddle in memory of the fiddler, that he decided to hire a hackney car, a rare and daring thing to do in those days, and bring us out to see in one round trip those most adjacent places of his memories and dreams.

'In the year 1770 it happened,' he said. 'The landlord at the time was Sir James Caldwell, Baronet. He was also called the Count of Milan, why, I never found anybody to tell me. The fiddler's name was Dennis McCabe and by tradition the McCabes were always musicians and jesters to the Caldwells. There was festivity at the Big House by Lough Erne Shore and gentry there from near and far, and out they went to drink and dance on a raft on the lake, and wasn't the poor fiddler so drunk he fiddled himself into the water and drowned.'

'Couldn't somebody have pulled him out, Da?'

'They were all as drunk as he was. The story was that he was still sawing away with the bow when he came up for the third time. The party cheered him until every island in Lough Erne echoed and it was only when they sobered up they realised they had lost the fiddler. So the baronet and Count of Milan had a stone fiddle taller than a man made to stand at the estate gate as a monument to Dennis McCabe and as a warning for ever to fiddlers either to stay sober or to stay on dry land.

'Ye fiddlers beware, ye fiddler's fate,' my father recited. 'Don't attempt the deep lest ye repent too late. Keep to the land when wind and storm blow, but scorn the deep if it with whiskey flow. On firm land only exercise your skill; there you may play and safely drink your fill.'

Travelling by train from our town to the seaside you went for miles along the green and glistening Erne shore but the train didn't stop by the stone fiddle nor yet at the Boa island for the cross-roads' dances. Always when my father told us about those dances, his right foot rhythmically tapped and took music out of the polished steel fireside fender that had Home Sweet Home lettered out on an oval central panel. Only the magic motor, bound to no tracks, compelled to no fixed stopping places, could bring us to the fiddle or the crowded cross-roads.

'Next Sunday then,' he said, 'as certain as the sun sets and rises, we'll hire Hookey and Peter and the machine and head for Lough Erne.'

'Will it hold us all,' said my mother. 'Seven of us and Peter's big feet and the length of the driver's legs.'

'That machine,' he said, 'would hold the twelve apostles, the Connaught Rangers and the man who broke the bank at Monte Carlo. It's the size of a hearse.'

'Which is just what it looks like,' said the youngest of my three sisters who had a name for the tartness of her tongue.

She was a thin dark girl.

'Regardless of appearance,' he said, 'it'll carry us to the stone fiddle and on the way we'll circumnavigate the globe: Clanabogan, and Cavanacaw, Pigeon Top Mountain and Corraduine, where the bare-footed priest said Mass at the Rock in the penal days and Corraheskin where the Muldoons live . . .'

'Them,' said the third sister.

She had had little time for the Muldoons since the day their lack of savoir faire cost her a box of chocolates. A male member, flaxen-haired, pink-cheeked, aged sixteen, of those multitudinous Muldoons had come by horse and cart on a market day from his rural fastnesses to pay us a visit. Pitying his gaucherie, his shy animal-in-a-thicket appearance, his outback ways and gestures, she had grandly reached him a box of chocolates so as to sweeten his bitter lot with one honeyed morsel or two or, at the outside three; but unaccustomed to towny ways and the mores of built-up areas the rural swain had appropriated the whole box.

'He thought,' she said, 'I was a paleface offering gifts to a Comanche.'

'But by their own hearth,' said my father, 'they're simple hospitable people.

'And Comavara,' he said, 'and Dooish and Carrick Valley and your uncle Owen, and the two McCannys the pipers, and Claramore where there are so many Gormleys every family has to have its own nick-name, and Drumquin where I met your mother, and Dromore where you' (pointing to me) 'were born and where the mail train was held up by the IRA and where the three poor lads were murdered by the

Specials when you' (again indicating me) 'were a year old, and the Minnieburns where the seven streams meet to make the head waters of the big river. Hookey and Peter and the machine will take us to all those places.'

'Like a magic carpet,' said my mother – with just a little dusting of the iron filings of doubt in her voice.

Those were the days, and not so long ago, when cars were rare and every car, not just every make of car, had a personality of its own. In our town with its population of five thousand, not counting the soldiers in the barracks, there were only three cars for hire and one of them was the love-child of the pioneer passion of Hookey Baxter for the machine. He was a long hangle of a young fellow, two-thirds of him made up of legs, and night and day he was whistling. He was as forward-looking as Lindbergh and he dressed like Lindbergh, for the air, in goggles, leather jacket and helmet; an appropriate costume, possibly, considering Hookey's own height and the altitude of the driver's seat in his machine. The one real love of his young heart was the love of the born tinkerer, the instinctive mechanic, for that hybrid car: the child of his frenzy, the fruit of days spent deep in grease giving new life and shape to a wreck he had bought at a sale in Belfast. The original manufacturers, whoever they had been, would have been hard put to it to recognise their altered offspring.

'She's chuman,' Peter Keown would say as he patted the sensitive quivering bonnet.

Peter meant human. In years to come his sole recorded comment on the antics of Adolf Hitler was that the man wasn't chuman.

'She's as nervous,' he would say, 'as a thoroughbred.'

The truth was that Peter, Hookey's stoker, grease-monkey and errand boy, was somewhat in awe of the tall rangy metal animal yet wherever the car went, with the tall goggled pilot at the wheel, there the pilot's diminutive mate was also sure to go. What living Peter earned he earned by digging holes in the street as a labouring man for the town council's official plumber so that, except on Sundays and when he motored with Hookey, nobody in the town ever saw much of him but the top of his cloth cap or his upturned face when he'd look up from the hole in the ground to ask a passer-by the time of day.

Regularly once a year he spent a corrective month in Derry Jail, because his opportunities as a municipal employee and his weakness as a kleptomaniac meant that good boards, lengths of piping, coils of electric wire, monkey wrenches, spades, and other movable properties faded too frequently into thin air.

'A wonderful man, poor Peter,' my father would say. 'That cloth cap with the turned up peak. And the thick-lensed, thin-rimmed spectacles – he's half-blind – and the old tweed jacket too tight for him, and the old Oxford-bag trousers too big for him, and his shrill voice and his waddle of a walk that makes him look always like a duck about to apologise for laying a hen-egg. How he survives is a miracle of God's grace. He can resist the appeal of nothing that's portable.'

'He's a dream,' said the third sister. 'And the feet are the biggest part of him.'

'The last time he went to Derry,' said my brother, 'all the old women from Brook Street and the lanes were at the top of the Courthouse Hill to cheer him as he passed.'

'And why not,' said my mother. 'They're fond of him and they say he's well-liked in the jail. His heart's as big as his feet. Everything he steals he gives away.'

'Robin Hood,' said the third sister. 'Robbing the town council to pay Brook Street.'

'The Council wouldn't sack him,' said my eldest sister, 'if he stole the town.'

'At the ready,' roared my father. 'Prepare to receive cavalry.'

In the street below the house there was a clanking, puffing, grinding tumult.

'God bless us, look at Peter,' said my father. 'Aloft with Hookey like a crown prince beside a king. Are we all ready? Annie, Ita, May, George, yourself ma'am, and you the youngest of us all. Have we the sandwiches and the flasks of tea and the lemonade? Forward.'

A lovelier Sunday morning never shone. With the hood down and the high body glistening after its Saturday wash and polish, the radiator gently steaming, the car stood at the foot of the seven steps that led down from our door. The stragglers coming home from early mass, and the devout setting off early for late mass had gathered in groups to

witness our embarkation. Led by my father and in single file, we
descended the steps and ascended nearly as high again to take our lofty
places in the machine.

There was something of the Citroën in the quivering mongrel, in
the yellow canvas hood now reclining in voluminous ballooning folds,
in the broad back-seat that could hold five fair-sized people. But to
judge by the radiator, the absence of gears, and the high fragile-spoked
wheels, Citroën blood had been crossed with that of the Model T. After
that, any efforts to spot family traits would have brought confusion on
the thought of the greatest living authorities. The thick slanting glass
windscreen could have been wrenched from a limousine designed to
divert bullets from Balkan princelings. The general colour-scheme,
considerably chipped and cracked, was canary yellow. And there was
Hookey at the wheel, then my brother and father, and Peter on the
outside left where he could leap in and out to perform the menial
duties of assistant engineer; and in the wide and windy acres of the
back seat, my mother, myself and my three sisters.

High above the town the church bell rang. It was the bell to warn
the worshippers still on their way that in ten minutes the vested priest
would be on the altar but, as it coincided with our setting out, it could
have been a quayside bell ringing farewell to a ship nosing out across
the water towards the rim of vision.

Peter leaped to the ground, removed the two stones that, blocked
before the front wheels, acted as auxiliaries for the hand brake. Hookey
released the brake. The car was gathering speed when Peter scrambled
aboard, settled himself and slammed the yellow door behind him.
Sparing fuel, we glided down the slope, back-fired twice loudly enough
to drown the sound of the church bell, swung left along John Street
and cleared the town without incident. Hands waved from watching
groups of people but because this was no trivial event there were no
laughs, no wanton cheers. The sound of the bell died away behind us.
My mother expressed the hope that the priest would remember us at
the offertory. Peter assured her that we were all as safe as if we were at
home in bed. God's good green Sunday countryside was softly all
around us.

Squat to the earth and travelling at seventy you see nothing from cars nowadays, but to go with Hookey was to be above all but the highest walls and hedges, to be among the morning birds.

'Twenty-seven em pee haitch,' said Hookey.

'Four miles covered already,' said Peter.

'The Gortin Mountains over there,' said my father. 'And the two mountains to the north are Bessy Bell and Mary Grey, so named by the Hamiltons of Baronscourt, the Duke of Abercorn's people, after a fancied resemblance to two hills in Stirlingshire, Scotland. The two hills in Stirlingshire are so called after two ladies of the Scottish court who fled the plague and built their hut in the wild wood and thatched it o'er with rushes. They are mentioned by Thomas Carlyle in his book on the French Revolution. The dark green on the hills by Gortin Gap is the new government forestry. And in Gortin village Paddy Ford the contractor hasn't gone to mass since, fifteen years ago, the parish priest gave another man the job of painting the inside of the sacristy.'

'No paint no prayers,' said the third sister.

'They're strange people in Gortin,' my mother said.

'It's proverbial,' said my father, 'that they're to be distinguished anywhere by the bigness of their backsides.'

'Five miles,' said Peter. 'They're spinning past.'

'Running sweet as honey,' said Hookey.

He adjusted his goggles and whistled back to the Sunday birds.

'Jamie Magee's of the Flush,' said my father.

He pointed to a long white house on a hill slope and close to a waterfalling stream.

'Rich as Rockefeller and too damned mean to marry.'

'Who in heaven would have him?' said the third sister.

'Six miles,' said Peter.

Then, with a blast of backfiring that rose my mother a foot in the air, the wobbling yellow conveyance came to a coughing miserable halt. The air was suddenly grey and poisoned with fumes.

'It's her big end, Hookey,' said Peter.

'She's from Gortin so,' said the third sister.

The other two sisters, tall and long-haired and normally quiet girls, went off at the deep end into the giggles.

'Isn't it providential,' said my mother, 'that the cowslips are a glory this year? We'll have something to do, Henry, while you're fixing it.'

Hookey had been christened Henry, and my mother would never descend to nicknames. She felt that to make use of a nickname was to remind a deformed person of his deformity. Nor would she say even of the town's chief inebriate that he was ever drunk: he was either under the influence or he had a drop too many taken. She was, my mother, the last great Victorian euphemiser.

'We won't be a jiffy, ma'am,' said Hookey. 'It's nothing so serious as a big end.'

The three sisters were convulsed.

The fields and the roadside margins were bright yellow with blossom.

'Gather ye cowslips while you may,' said my father.

He handed the ladies down from the dizzy heights. Peter had already disembarked. Submitting to an impulse that had gnawed at me since we set sail, I dived forwards, my head under Hookey's left elbow, and butted with both fists the black, rubber, punch-ball horn; and out over the fields to startle birds and grazing cattle went the dying groan of a pained diseased ox.

'Mother of God,' said my father, 'that's a noise and no mistake. Here boy, go off and pick flowers.'

He lifted me down to the ground.

'Screw off the radiator cap, Peter,' said Hookey.

'It's scalding hot, Hookey.'

'Take these gauntlet gloves, manalive. And stand clear when you screw it off.'

A geyser of steam and dirty hot water went heavenwards as Peter and my brother, who was always curious about engines, leaped to safety.

'Wonderful,' said my father to my brother, 'the age we live in. They say that over in England they're queued up steaming by the roadsides, like Iceland or the Yellowstone Park.'

'Just a bit overheated,' said Hookey. 'We won't be a jiffy.'

'Does it happen often?' said my father.

Ignoring the question, descending and opening the bonnet to peer and poke and tinker, Hookey said, 'Do you know a funny thing about this car?'

'She's chuman,' said Peter.

'You know the cross-roads at Clanabogan churchyard gate,' Hookey said. 'The story about it.'

'It's haunted,' said my father.

'Only at midnight,' said Peter.

As was his right and custom, my father stepped into the role of raconteur, 'Do you know that no horse ever passed there at midnight that didn't stop – shivering with fear. The fact is well attested. Something comes down that side road out of the heart of the wood.'

Hookey closed over the bonnet, screwed back the radiator cap and climbed again to the throne. He wiped his hands on a bunch of grass pulled for him and handed to him by Peter. Slowly he drew on again his gauntlet gloves. Bedecked with cowslips and dragging me along with them the ladies rejoined the gentlemen.

'Well, would you credit this now,' Hookey said. 'Peter and myself were coming from Dromore one wet night last week.'

'Pouring rain from the heavens,' said Peter, 'and the hood was leaking.'

'A temporary defect,' said Hookey. 'I mended it. Jack up the back axle, Peter, and give her a swing. And would you credit it, exactly at twelve o'clock midnight she stopped dead at the gate of Clanabogan churchyard?'

With an irony that was lost on Hookey my mother said, 'I could well believe it.'

'She's chuman,' said Peter.

'One good push now and we're away,' said Hookey. 'The slight gradient is in our favour.'

'Maybe,' he said to my father and brother, 'you'd lend Peter a hand.'

Twenty yards ahead he waited for the dusty pushers to climb aboard, the engine chug-chugging, little puffs of steam escaping like baby genii from the right-hand side of the bonnet. My father was thoughtful. He could have been considering the responsibilities of the machine age particularly because when it came to team pushing Peter was more of a cheer leader, an exhorter, a counter of one two three, than an actual motive force.

'Contact,' said Hookey.

'Dawn patrol away,' said Peter. 'Squadron Leader Baxter at the joy-stick.'

He mimicked what he supposed to be the noises of an aeroplane engine and, with every evidence of jubilation, we were once again under way; and a day it was, made by the good God for jubilation. The fields, all the colours of all the crops, danced towards us and away from us and around us; and the lambs on the green hills, my father sang, were gazing at me and many a strawberry grows by the salt sea, and many a ship sails the ocean. The roadside trees bowed down and then gracefully swung their arms up and made music over our heads and there were more birds and white cottages and fuchsia hedges in the world than you would readily imagine.

'The bride and bride's party,' sang my father, 'to church they did go. The bride she goes foremost, she bears the best show . . .'

'They're having sports today at Tattysallagh,' said Hookey.

'But I followed after my heart full of woe, for to see my love wed to another.'

We swept by a cross-roads where people and horses and traps were congregated after the last mass. In a field beside the road a few tall ash plants bore fluttering pennants in token of the sports to be.

'Proceed to Banteer,' sang my father, 'to the athletic sporting and hand in your name to the club comm-i-tee.'

'That was a favourite song of Pat O'Leary the Corkman,' he said, 'who was killed at Spion Kop.'

Small country boys in big boots, knickerbockers, stiff celluloid collars that could be cleaned for Sunday by a rub of a wet cloth, and close-cropped heads with fringes like scalping locks above the foreheads, scattered before us to the hedges and the grass margins, then closed again like water divided and rejoining, and pursued us, cheering, for a hundred yards. One of them, frantic with enthusiasm, sent sailing after us a half-grown turnip, which bounced along the road for a bit, then sought rest in a roadside drain. Looking backwards I pulled my best or worst faces at the rustic throng of runners.

'In Tattysallagh,' said my father, 'they were always an uncivilised crowd of gulpins.'

He had three terms of contempt: Gulpin, Yob and, when things became very bad he became Swiftian, and described all offenders as Yahoos.

'Cavanacaw,' he said, 'and that lovely trout stream, the Creevan Burn. It joins the big river at Blacksessiagh. That there's the road up to Pigeon Top Mountain and the mass rock at Corraduine, but we'll come back that way when we've circumnavigated Dooish and Comavara.'

We came to Clanabogan.

'Clanabogan planting,' he said.

The tall trees came around us and sunlight and shadow flickered so that you could feel them across eyes and hands and face.

'Martin Murphy the postman,' he said, 'who was in the survey with me in Virginia, County Cavan, by Lough Ramor, and in the Glen of Aherlow, worked for a while at the building of Clanabogan Church. One day the vicar said to him: "What height do you think the steeple should be?" "The height of nonsense like your sermons," said Martin, and got the sack for his wit. In frosty weather he used to seal the cracks in his boots with butter and although he was an abrupt man he seldom used an impolite word. Once when he was aggravated by the bad play of his wife who was partnering him at whist he said: "Maria, dearly as I love you, there are yet moments when you'd incline a man to kick his own posterior".'

'There's the church,' my father said, 'and the churchyard and the haunted gate and the cross-roads.'

We held our breath but, with honeyed summer all around us and bees in the tender limes, it was no day for ghosts, and in glory we sailed by. 'She didn't hesitate,' said Peter.

'Wonderful,' said the third sister.

It was more wonderful than she imagined for, as the Lord would have it, the haunted gate and cross-roads of Clanabogan was one of the few places that day that Hookey's motor machine did not honour with at least some brief delay.

'I'd love to drive,' said my brother. 'How did you learn to drive, Hookey?'

'I never did. I just sat in and drove. I learned the basic principles on the county council steamroller in Watson's quarries. Forward and reverse.'

'You have to have the natural knack,' Peter explained. 'What's the cut potato for, Hookey?' asked my brother.

'For the rainy day. Rub it on the windscreen and the water runs off the glass.'

'It's oily you see,' said Peter.

'Like a duck's back,' said the third sister.

'Where,' said my father – sniffing, 'do you keep the petrol?'

'Reserve in the tins clipped on the running board. Current supply, six gallons. You're sitting on it. In a tank under the front seat.'

'Twenty miles to the gallon,' said Peter. 'We're good for more than a hundred miles.'

'God almighty,' said my father. 'Provided it isn't a hundred miles straight up. 'Twould be sad to survive a war that was the end of better men and to be blown up between Clanabogan and Comavara. On a quiet Sunday morning.'

'Never worry,' said Hookey. 'It's outside the bounds of possibility.'

'You reassure me,' said my father. 'Twenty miles to the gallon in any direction. What care we? At least we'll all go up together. No survivors to mourn in misery.

'And turn right here,' he said, 'for Comavara. You'll soon see the hills and the high waterfalls.'

We left the tarred road. White dust rose around us like smoke. We advanced half a mile on the flat, attempted the first steep hill and gently, wearily, without angry fumes or backfiring protests, the tremulous chuman car, lying down like a tired child, came to rest.

'We'll hold what we have,' said Hookey. 'Peter . . . pronto. Get the stones behind the back wheels.'

'Think of a new pastime,' said the third sister. 'We have enough cowslips to decorate the town for a procession.'

With the sweet face of girlish simplicity she asked, 'Do you buy the stones with the car?'

'We'd be worse off without them,' Hookey muttered.

Disguised as he was in helmet and goggles, it was impossible to tell exactly if his creative soul was or was not wounded by her hint of mockery, but my mother must have considered that his voice betrayed pain for she looked reprovingly at the third sister and at the other two who were again impaled by giggles, and withdrew them out of sight down a boreen towards the sound of a small stream, to – as she put it – freshen up.

'Without these stones,' Peter panted, 'we could be as badly off as John MacKenna and look what happened to him.'

'They're necessary precautions,' said Hookey. 'Poor John would never use stones. He said the brakes on his car would hold a Zeppelin.'

The bonnet was open again and the radiator cap unscrewed but there was no steam and no geyser, only a cold sad silence, and Hookey bending and peering and probing with pincers.

'She's a bit exhausted,' Peter said.

'It's simple,' Hookey said. 'She'll be right as rain in a jiffy. Going at the hill with a full load overstrained her.'

'We should walk the bad hills,' Peter explained.

'Poor John MacKenna,' Hookey said, 'was making four fortunes drawing crowds to the Passionist monastery at Enniskillen to see the monk that cures the people. But he would never use the stones, and the only parking place at the monastery is on a sharp slope. And one evening when they were all at devotions doesn't she run backways and ruin all the flower-beds in the place and knock down a statue of Our Lord.'

'One of the monks attacked him,' said Peter, 'as a heathen that would knock the Lord down.'

'Ruined the trade for all,' said Hookey. 'The monks now won't let a car within a mile of the place.'

'Can't say as I blame them,' said my father.

'Poor John took it bad,' said Hookey. 'The lecture he got and all. He was always a religious man They say he raises his hat now every time he passes any statue: even the Boer War one in front of the court-house.'

'So well he might,' said my father.

Suddenly, mysteriously responding to Hookey's probing pincers, the very soul of the machine was again chug-chugging. But with or without cargo she could not or, being weary and chuman, would not assault even the first bastion of Cornavara.

'She won't take off,' said Hookey. 'That run to Belfast and back took the wind out of her.'

'You never made Belfast,' said my father, 'in this.'

'We did, Tommy,' said Peter apologetically.

'Seventy miles there and seventy back,' said my father incredulously.

'Bringing a greyhound bitch to running trials for Tommy Mullan the postman,' said Hookey.

'The man who fishes for pearls in the Drumragh river,' said Peter.

They were talking hard to cover their humiliation.

'If she won't go at the hills,' my father said, 'go back to the main road and we'll go on and picnic at the seven streams at the Minnieburns. It's mostly on the flat.'

So we reversed slowly the dusty half-mile to the main road.

'One night in John Street,' Peter said, 'she started going backways and wouldn't go forwards.'

'A simple defect,' Hookey said. 'I remedied it.'

'Did you turn the other way?' asked the third sister.

Artlessly, Peter confessed, 'She stopped when she knocked down the schoolchildren-crossing sign at the bottom of Church Hill. Nipped it off an inch from the ground, as neat as you ever saw. We hid it up a laneway and it was gone in the morning.'

My father looked doubtfully at Peter. He said, 'One of those nice shiny enamelled pictures of two children crossing the road would go well as an overmantel. And the wood of the post would always make firewood.'

Peter agreed, 'You can trust nobody.'

Hurriedly trying to cut in on Peter's eloquence, Hookey said, 'In fact the name of Tommy Mullan's bitch was Drumragh Pearl. Not that that did her any good at the trials.'

'She came a bad last,' burst out the irrepressible Peter.

'And to make it worse we lost her on the way back from Belfast.'

'You what?' said my father.

'Lost her in the dark where the road twists around Ballymacilroy Mountain.'

My mother was awed, 'You lost the man's greyhound. You're a right pair of boys to send on an errand.'

''Twas the way we stepped out of the car to take the air,' said Hookey.

By the husky note in his voice you could guess how his soul suffered at Peter's shameless confessions.

'And Peter looked at the animal, ma'am, and said maybe she'd like a turn in the air too. So we took her out and tied her lead to the left front wheel. And while we were standing there talking didn't the biggest brute of a hare you ever saw sit out as cool as sixpence in the light of the car. Off like a shot with the bitch.'

'If the lead hadn't snapped,' Peter said, 'she'd have taken the wheel off the car or the car off the road.'

'That would have been no great exertion,' said my father. 'We should have brought a greyhound along with us to pull.'

'We whistled and called for hours but all in vain,' said Peter.

'The hare ate her,' said the third sister.

'Left up the slope there,' said my father, 'is the belt of trees I planted in my spare time to act as a wind-breaker for Drumlish schoolhouse. Paddy Hamish, the labouring man, gave me a hand. He died last year in Canada.'

'You'd have pitied the children on a winter's day,' my mother said, 'standing in the playground at lunchtime taking the fresh air in a hill-top wind that would sift and cut corn. Eating soda bread and washing it down with buttermilk. On a rough day the wind from Lough Erne would break the panes of the windows.'

'As a matter of curiosity,' my father said, 'what did Tommy Mullan say?'

'At two in the morning in Bridge Lane,' said Peter, 'he was waiting for us. We weren't too happy about it. But when we told him she was last in the trials he said the bloody bitch could stay in Ballymacilroy.'

'Hasn't he always the pearls in the river,' my mother said.

So we came to have tea and sandwiches and lemonade in a meadow by the cross-roads in the exact centre of the wide saucer of land where seven streams from the surrounding hills came down to meet. The grass was polished with sunshine. The perfume of the meadowsweet is with me still. That plain seemed to me then as vast as the prairies, or Siberia. White cottages far away on the lower slopes of Dooish could have been in another country. The chief stream came for a long way through soft deep meadowland. It was slow, quiet, unobtrusive, per-turbed only by the movements of water fowl or trout. Two streams met, wonder of wonders, under the arch of a bridge and you could go out under the bridge along a sandy promontory to paddle in clear water on a bottom as smooth as Bundoran strand. Three streams came together in a magic hazel wood where the tiny green unripe nuts were already clustered on the branches. Then the seven made into one, went away from us with a shout and a song towards Shaneragh, Blacksessiagh, Drumragh and Crevenagh, under the humpy crooked King's Bridge where James Stuart had passed on his way from Derry to the fatal brackish Boyne, and on through the town we came from.

'All the things we could see,' said my father, 'if this spavined brute of a so-called automobile could only be persuaded to climb the high hills. The deep lakes of Claramore. The far view of Mount Errigal, the Cock of the North, by the Donegal sea. If you were up on the top of Errigal you could damn' near see, on a clear day, the skyscrapers of New York.'

In his poetic imagination the towers of Atlantis rose glimmering from the deep.

'What matter,' said my mother. 'The peace of heaven is here.'

For that day that was the last peace we were to experience. The energy the machine didn't have or wouldn't use to climb hills or to keep in motion for more than two miles at a stretch, she expended in thunder-ous staccato bursts of backfiring. In slanting evening sunlight people at the doors of distant farmhouses shaded their eyes to look towards the travelling commotion, or ran up whinny hills for a better view, and horses and cattle raced madly around pastures, and my mother said the country would never be the same again, that the shock of the noise would turn the milk in the udders of the cows. When we came again to the cross-roads of Tattysallagh the majority of the spectators, standing on the road to look over the hedge and thus save the admission fee, lost all interest in the sports, such as they were, and came around us. To oblige them the right rear tyre went flat.

'Peter,' said Hookey, 'jack it up and change it on.'

We mingled unobtrusively with the gulpins.

'A neat round hole,' said Peter.

'Paste a patch on it.'

The patch was deftly pasted on.

'Take the foot pump and blow her up,' said Hookey.

There was a long silence while Peter, lines of worry on his little puckered face, inspected the tube. Then he said. 'I can't find the valve.'

'Show it to me,' said Hookey.

He ungoggled himself, descended and surveyed the ailing member. 'Peter,' he said, 'you're a prize. The valve's gone and you put a patch on the hole it left behind it.'

The crowd around us was increasing and highly appreciative.

'Borrow a bicycle, Peter,' said Hookey, 'cycle to the town and ask John MacKenna for the loan of a tube.'

'To pass the time,' said my mother, 'we'll look at the sports.'

So we left Hookey to mind his car and, being practically gentry as compared with the rustic throng around us, we walked to the gateway that led into the sportsfield where my mother civilly enquired of two men, who stood behind a wooden table, the price of admission.

'Five shillings a skull, missus, barring the cub,' said the younger of the two. 'And half a crown for the cub.'

'For the what?' said my mother.

'For the little boy, ma'am,' said the elder of the two.

'It seems expensive,' said my mother.

'I'd see them all in hell first – let alone in Tattysallagh,' my father said. 'One pound, twelve shillings and sixpence to look at six sally rods stuck in a field and four yahoos running round in rings in their sock soles.'

We took our places on the roadside with the few who, faithful to athletics and undistracted by the novelty of the machine, were still looking over the hedge. Four lean youths and one stout one in Sunday shirts and long trousers with the ends tucked into their socks were pushing high-framed bicycles round and round the field. My father recalled the occasion in Virginia, County Cavan, when Martin Murphy was to run at sports and his wife Maria stiffened his shirt so much with starch it wouldn't go inside his trousers, and when he protested she said, 'Martin, leave it outside and you will be able to fly.'

We saw two bicycle races and a tug-of-war.

'Hallions and clifts,' he said.

Those were two words he seldom used.

'Yobs and sons of yobs,' he said.

He led us back to the car. Peter soaked in perspiration had the new tube on and the wheel ready.

'Leave the jack in and swing her,' Hookey said. 'She's cold by now.'

There was a series of explosions that sent gulpins, yobs and yahoos reeling backwards in alarm. Peter screwed out the jack. We scrambled aboard, a few of the braver among the decent people, rushing into the line of fire to lend a hand to the ladies. Exploding, we departed, and when we were a safe distance away the watchers raised a dubious cheer.

'In God's name, Henry,' said my father, 'get close to the town before you blow us all up. I wouldn't want our neighbours to have to travel as far as Tattysallagh to pick up the bits. And the yobs and yahoos here don't know us well enough to be able to piece us together.'

Three miles further on Peter blushingly confessed that in the frantic haste of embarkation he had left the jack on the road.

'I'll buy you a new one, Henry,' my father said. 'Or perhaps Peter here could procure one on the side. By now at any rate, they're shoeing jackasses with it in Tattysallagh.

'A pity in a way,' he said, 'we didn't make as far as the stone fiddle. We might have heard good music. It's a curious thing that in the townlands around that place the people have always been famed for music and singing. The Tunneys of Castle Caldwell now are noted. It could be that the magic of the stone fiddle has something to do with it.

'Some day,' he said, 'we'll head for Donegal. When the cars, Henry, are a bit improved.'

He told us about the long windings of Mulroy Bay. He explained exactly how and why and in what year the fourth Earl of Leitrim had been assassinated in Cratloe Wood. He spoke as rapidly and distinctly as he could in the lulls of the backfiring.

Then our town was below us in the hollow and the Gortin mountains, deep purple with evening, away behind it.

'Here we'll part company, Henry boy,' said my father. ''Tisn't that I doubt the ability of Peter and yourself to navigate the iron horse down the hill. But I won't have the town blaming me and my family for having hand, act or part in the waking of the dead in Drumragh graveyard.'

Sedately we walked down the slope into the town and talked with the neighbours we met and asked them had they heard Hookey and Peter passing and told them of the sports and of the heavenly day it had been out at the seven streams.

My father died in a seaside town in the County Donegal – forty miles from the town I was reared in. The road his funeral followed back to the home places led along the Erne shore by the stone fiddle and the glistening water, across the Boa Island where there are no longer crossroads dances. Every roadside house has a television aerial. It led by the meadowland saucer of the Minnieburns where the river still springs from seven magic sources. That brooding place is still much as it was but no longer did it seem to me to be as vast as Siberia. To the left was the low sullen outline of Carnavara and Pigeon Top, the hurdle that our Bucephalus refused to take. To the right was Drumlish. The old schoolhouse was gone and in its place a white building, ten times as large, with drying rooms for wet coats, fine warm lunches for children and even a gymnasium. But the belt of trees that he and Paddy Hamish planted to break the wind and shelter the children is still there.

Somebody tells me, too, that the engine of Hookey Baxter's car is still with us, turning a circular saw for a farmer in the vicinity of Clanabogan.

As the Irish proverb says: It's a little thing doesn't last longer than a man.

A Great God's Angel Standing

Pascal Stakelum, the notorious rural rake, and Father Paul, the ageing Catholic curate of Lislap, met the two soldiers from Devon by the bridge over the Camowen River and right beside the lunatic asylum. It was a day of splitting sunshine in the year of the Battle of Dunkirk. Pascal and the priest were going to visit the lunatic asylum, Father Paul to hear confessions, Pascal to bear him company and to sit at a sealed distance while the inmates cudgelled what wits they had and told their sins. The two soldiers, in battledress and with heavy packs on their backs, were on their way home from Dunkirk, not home to Devon exactly but to Sixmilecross, to the house of two sisters they had married in a hurry before they set off for France. It was, as you may have guessed, six miles from our garrison town of Lislap to the crossroads village where the two sisters lived, and it was a very warm day. So every one of the four, two in thick khaki, two in dull black, was glad to stop and stand at ease and look at the smooth gliding of the cool Camowen.

The bridge they rested on was of a brownish grey stone, three full sweeping arches and, to the sides, two tiny niggardly arches. In a blue sky a few white clouds idled before a light wind, and beyond a wood at an upstream bend of the river a two-horse mowing-machine ripped and rattled in meadow grass. The stone of the bridge was cut from the same quarry as the stone in the high long wall that circled the lunatic asylum and went for a good half-mile parallel with the right bank of the river.

—In France it was hot, said the first soldier.

—He means the weather was hot, said the second soldier.

The four men, priest and rake and soldiers two, laughed at that: not, Pascal says, much of a laugh, not sincere, no heartiness in it.

—Hot as hell, said the second soldier. Even the rivers was hot.

—Boiling, said the first soldier. That canal at Lille was as hot as a hot bath.

—Ruddy mix-up, said the second soldier. The Guards, they fired at the Fusiliers, and the Fusiliers, they fired at the Guards. Nobody knew who was what. Ruddy mix-up.

They took the cigarettes Pascal offered.

—Boiling hot and thirsty, said the second soldier. Never knew such thirst.

Father Paul said: You could have done with some Devon cider.

—Zider, said the first soldier. There were zomething.

—Zomerzet you are, said the second soldier.

They all laughed again. This time it was a real laugh.

The Camowen water where it widened over gravel to go under the five stone arches was clear and cool as a mountain rockspring. Upstream, trout rings came as regularly as the ticks of a clock.

The two soldiers accepted two more cigarettes. They tucked them into the breast-pockets of their battledress. They hitched their packs, shook hands several times and knelt on the motorless roadway for Father Paul's blessing. They were not themselves Arcees, they said, but in camp in Aldershot in England they had been matey with an Arcee padre, and they knew the drill. Blessed after battle, they stood up, dusted their knees as carefully as if they'd never heard of mud or blood and, turning often to wave back, walked on towards the two sisters of Sixmilecross.

—Virginia, Father Paul said, was the best place I ever saw for cider. Just to annoy him, Pascal said: Virginia, County Cavan, Ireland. They were walking together on a narrow footwalk in the shadow of the asylum wall.

—Virginia, USA, Paul said. The Old Dominion. Very well you know what Virginia I mean. They had great apple orchards there, and fine cider presses, around a little town called Fincastle under the shadow of the Blue Ridge Mountains. That was great country, and pleasant people and fine horses, when I was a young man on the American mission.

It was a period out of his lost youth that Paul frequently talked about.

In those days of his strange friendship with Pascal he was thin and long-faced and stoop-shouldered with the straining indignant stoop that is forced on tall people when the years challenge the power to hold the head so high. That day the sun had sucked a little moisture out of his pale cheeks. He had taken off his heavy black hat to give the light breeze a chance to ruffle and cool his thin grey hair, but the red line the hat rim had made was still to be seen and, above the red line, a sullen concentration of drops of sweat. He was though, as Pascal so often said, the remains of a mighty handsome man and with such dignity, too, and stern faith and such an eloquent way in the pulpit that it was a mystery to all of us what the bishop of the diocese had against him that he had never given him the honour, glory and profit of a parish of his own.

—In the mood those two boyos are in, Pascal said, it will take them no time at all walking to the sisters at Sixmilecross.

That was the way Pascal, in accordance with his animal nature, thought; and Sixmilecross was a village in which, as in every other village in our parts, Pascal had had some of the rural adventures that got him his dubious reputation, and that made us all marvel when we'd see a character like him walking in the company of a priest. In Burma, I once heard an old sweat say, adulterers kill a pig to atone for their crime, so it was only apt and proper, and even meet and just, that Pascal should be a pork butcher. When he went a-wooing in country places he'd never walk too far from his rattly old Morris Cowley without bringing with him a tyre lever or starting handle, for country girls were hell for having truculent brothers and if they didn't have brothers they had worse and far and away worse, male cousins, and neither brothers nor male cousins, least of all the male cousins, had any fancy for Pascal rooting and snorting about on the fringes of the family. That's Pascal, for you. But at the moment, Paul is speaking.

—A man hungers to get home, he said. The men from Devon won't count the time or the number of paces. Time, what's time? They've come a long walk from the dreadful gates of eternity. Once I told you, Pascal boy, you were such a rake and run-the-roads you'd have to live to be ninety, to expiate here on this earth and so dodge the devil.

Complacently Pascal said: The good die young.

—Ninety's a long time, Father Paul said. But what's time? Here in this part of my parish . . .

They were walking in at the wide gateway. He waved his black wide-brimmed hat in a circle comprehending the whole place, as big almost as the garrison town itself, for all the crazy people of two counties, or those of them that had been detected and diagnosed, were housed there.

—This part of my parish, he said. As much happiness or unhappiness as in any other part of the parish. But one thing that doesn't matter here is time. As far as most of them know, time and eternity are the same thing.

They walked along a serpentine avenue, up sloping lawns to the main door. The stone in the walls of the high building was cut from the same quarry as the stone that bridged the river, as the stone in the encircling wall. The stone floor in the long cool corridor rang under their feet. They followed a porter along that corridor to a wide bright hospital ward. Unshaven men in grey shirts sat up in bed and looked at them with quick bright questioning eyes. The shining nervous curiosity of the ones who sat up disturbed Pascal. He preferred to look at the others who lay quietly in bed and stared steadily at points on the ceiling or on the opposite wall, stared steadily but seemed to see neither the ceiling nor the opposite wall, and sometimes mumbled to nobody words that had no meaning. A few men in grey suits moved aimlessly about the floor or sat to talk with some of the bright curious men in the beds. Beside the doorway a keeper in blue uniform dotted with brass buttons sat and smoked and read a newspaper, raised his head and nodded to the priest, then returned to his pipe and his newspaper.

Father Paul moved from bed to bed, his purple stole about his neck. The murmur of his voice, particularly when he was at the Latin, was distinctly audible. His raised hand sawed the air in absolution and blessing. Once in a while he said something in English in a louder voice and then the man he was with would laugh, and the priest would laugh, and the man in the next bed, if he was a bright-eyed man, would laugh, and another bright-eyed man several beds away would start laughing and be unable to stop, and a ripple of laughter would run around the room touching everybody except the staring mumbling men and the keeper who sat by the door.

Pascal sat beside an empty bed and read a paperbacked book about a doctor in Germany who was, or said he thought he was, two men, and had murdered his wife, who had been a showgirl, by bathing her beautiful body in nitric acid. That sinful crazy waste of good material swamped Pascal in an absorbing melancholy so that he didn't for a few moments even notice the thin hand gripping his thigh. There, kneeling at his feet, was a man in grey clothes, misled into thinking Pascal was a priest because Pascal wore, as did the gay young men of that place and period, a black suit with, though, extremely wide and unclerical trousers. Pascal studied, with recognition, the inmate's grey jacket, the scarce grey hair, the spotted dirty scalp. The kneeling man said: Bless me, father, for I have sinned.

—Get up to hell, Jock Sharkey, Pascal said. I'm no priest. You're crazy. He was, he says, crimson in the face with embarrassment. The keeper was peeking over his newspaper, laughing, saying Jock sure was crazy and that, in fact, was why he was where he was. The keeper also blew smoke-rings from thick laughing lips, an irritating fellow. He said: Fire away, Pascal. It'll keep him quiet. I hear him two or three times a week.

—It wouldn't be right, Pascal said. He had theological scruples, the only kind he could afford.

Only once in my life, he was to say afterwards, did a man ever ask me to listen to him confessing his sins and, fair enough, the place should be a lunatic asylum and the man, poor Jock Sharkey, that was put away for chasing women, not that he ever overtook them or did anybody any harm. They walked quick, he walked quick. They walked slow, he walked slow. He was just simply fascinated, the poor gormless bastard, by the sound of their feet, the hobbled trot, the high heels, you know, clickety-click, thigh brushing thigh. Poor Jock.

—What he'll tell you, said the keeper, is neither right nor wrong.

Who'd anyway be better judge than yourself, Pascal? Even Father Paul doesn't know one half of what you know. You, now, would know about things Paul never heard tell of.

The man on his knees said: I suppose you'll put me out of the confession box, father. I'm a terrible sinner. I wasn't at mass or meeting since the last mission.

—Why was that? said Pascal the priest.

—The place I'm working in, they won't let me go to mass.

—Then it's not your fault, said Pascal. No sin. Grievous matter, perfect knowledge, full consent.

He did, he said afterwards, remember from his schooldays that impressive fragment of the penny catechism of Christian doctrine: the stud-book, the form-book, the rules for the big race from here to eternity.

—But when I go to confession, father, I've a bad memory for my sins. Will you curse me, father, if I forget some of them?

—By no means, Jock. Just recite what you remember.

The keeper, more offensive as his enjoyment increased, said that Pascal wouldn't know how to curse, that he didn't know the language. The head of the kneeling man nodded backwards and forwards while he mumbled the rhythmical words of some prayer or prayers of his childhood. Now and again the names of saints came clearly out of the confused unintelligible mumble, like bubbles rising from a marshy bottom to the surface of a slow stream. Then he repeated carefully, like a child reciting, these words from an old rebel song: I cursed three times since last Easter Day. At mass-time once I went to play.

Pascal was seldom given to visions except in one particular direction, yet he says that at that moment he did see, from his memory of school historical pageants, the rebel Irish boy, kneeling in all innocence or ignorance at the feet of the brutal red-coated captain whose red coat was, for the occasion, covered by the soutane of the murdered rebel priest.

The keeper said: You should sing that, Jock.

—I passed the churchyard one day in haste, Jock said, and forgot to pray for my mother's rest.

—You're sure of heaven, said the keeper, if that's the sum total of your sins. The Reverend Stakelum himself, or even Father Paul, won't get off so easy.

The penitent looked up at Pascal and Pascal looked down at stubbly chin, hollow jaws, sorrowful brown eyes. Poor Jock, Pascal thought, they put you away just for doing what I spend all my spare time, and more besides, at: to wit, chasing the girls. Only you never even seemed to want to catch up with them.

For poor Jock was never more than what we called a sort of a mystery man, terrifying the girls, or so they claimed, by his nightly wanderings along dark roads, his sudden sprints that ended as sharply and pointlessly as they began, his shouted meaningless words provoked perhaps by a whiff of perfume in his nostrils or by that provocative tap-tippity-tap of high hard heels on the metalled surface of the road. A child might awaken in the night and cry that there was a man's face at the window. A girl might run home breathless and say that Jock had followed her for half a mile, suiting his pace to hers, like a ghost or a madman. He couldn't be a ghost, although he was as thin and as harmless as any ghost. So we put him away for a madman.

He stared long and hard at Pascal. His thin right hand tightly grasped Pascal's knee.

—David Stakelum's son, he said. I'd know you anywhere on your father. Thank God to see you in the black clothes. Your father was a decent man and you'll give me the blessing of a decent man's son.

He bowed his head and joined his hands. Behind the newspaper the keeper was gurgling. Pascal said afterwards that his father wouldn't be too pleased to think that his hell's own special hell-raker of a son bore him such a resemblance that even a crazy man could see it. But if his blessing would help to make Jock content, then Jock was welcome to it. So he cut the sign of the cross over the old crazy dirty head. He touched with the tips of the fingers of both hands the bald patch on the dome. He held out those fingers to be kissed. The most fervent young priest fresh from the holy oil couldn't have done a better job. Pascal had so often studied the simple style of Father Paul. The keeper was so impressed that he folded the newspaper and sat serious and quiet.

Father Paul walked slowly towards them, along the narrow passage between the two rows of beds. Walking with him came a fat red-faced grey-headed inmate. The fat inmate talked solemnly, gestured stiffly with his right hand. The priest listened, or pretended to listen, turning his head sideways, stretching his neck, emphasising the stoop in his shoulders. He said: Mr Simon, you haven't met my young friend, Pascal.

The fat man smiled benevolently at Pascal but went on talking to the priest. As you know, sir, I am not of the Roman Catholic persuasion, yet I have always been intrigued by the theory and practice of auricular confession. The soul of man, being walled around and shut in as it is, demands some outlet for the thoughts and desires that accumulate therein.

He had, Pascal says, a fruity pansy voice.

—The child, he said, runs to its mother with its little tale of sorrow. Friend seeks out friend. In silence and secrecy souls are interchanged.

It was exactly, Pascal was to say, as if the sentences had been written on the air in the loops and lines of copper-plate. You could not only hear but see the man's talk: A Wesleyan I was born, sir, and so remain. But always have I envied you Roman Catholics the benefits of the confessional, the ease that open confession brings to the soul. What is the Latin phrase, sir?

Paul said: *Ad quietam conscientiam.*

—*Ad quietam conscientiam,* Simon repeated. There is peace in every single syllable. There is much wisdom in your creed, sir. Wesley knew that. You have observed the spiritual similarity between Wesley and Ignatius of Loyola.

The keeper said: Simon, Doctor Murdy's looking for you. Where in hell were you?

—He asks me where I have been, sir. Where in hell.

Father Paul said: He means no harm, Simon. Just his manner of speaking.

Simon was still smiling. From elbow to bent wrist and dangling hand, his right arm was up like a question mark. He said to Father Paul: Surveillance, sir, is a stupid thing. It can accomplish nothing, discover nothing. If I were to tell this fellow where I had been, how could he understand? On this earth I have been, and beyond this earth.

He shook hands with the priest but not with Pascal nor the keeper nor Jock Sharkey. He walked with dignity past the keeper and back down the ward.

—There goes a travelled man, Pascal said.

Father Paul was folding his purple stole. He said: There are times when religion can be a straitjacket.

—It's not Simon's time yet for the straitjacket, the keeper said. When the fit takes him he'll brain the nearest neighbour with the first handy weapon.

At the far end of the ward where Simon had paused for a moment, there was a sudden noise and a scuffling. The keeper said: Too much learning is the divil.

He thumped down the passage between the beds.

—Now for the ladies, Father Paul said. You'll be at home there, Pascal. They say all over the town that no man living has an easier way with the ladies.

Pascal was to report to myself and a few others that if Paul had wanted to preach him a sermon to make his blood run cold and to put him off the women for the rest of his life, he couldn't have gone about it in a better way.

Is it true that, as the poet said, you never knew a holy man but had a wicked man for his comrade and heart's darling? Was it part of Paul's plan to pick Pascal as his escort and so to make an honest boy out of him or, at least, to cut in on the time that he would otherwise spend rummaging and ruining the girls of town and country? The thing about Pascal was that, away from the companionship of Paul, he thought of nothing but women when, of course, he wasn't butchering pork, and perhaps he thought of women even then. Like many another who is that way afflicted, he wasn't big, violent, handsome, red-faced or blustering. No, he went about his business in a quiet way. His hair was sparse, of a nondescript colour, flatly combed and showing specks of dandruff. He wore horn-rimmed spectacles. He was one of those white-faced fellows who would, softly and secretly and saying nothing about it to their best friends, take advantage of their own grandmothers. The women were mad about him. They must have been. He kept himself in fettle and trim for his chosen vocation. When the two soldiers and Paul were, in the sunshine on the Camowen Bridge, talking of Devon cider, Pascal was thinking, he says, of sherry and raw eggs, and oysters, porter and paprika pepper.

On the day of Paul's funeral he said to me: A decent man and I liked him. But, my God, he had a deplorable set against the women or anybody that fancied the women.

—Except myself, he said. For some reason or other he put up with me.

—That day at the female ward, he said, at the geriatrics you call 'em, I cheated him, right under his nose, God forgive me. And may Paul himself forgive me, since he knows it all now.

Pascal stood at the threshold of this female ward while Father Paul, purple stole again around his neck, moved, listening and forgiving with God's forgiveness, from bed to bed. Pascal wasn't much of a theologian, yet looking at the females in that female ward he reckoned that it was God, not the females, who needed forgiveness. They were all old females, very old females, and as such didn't interest Pascal. He had nothing, though, against old age as long as it left him alone. His father's mother was an attractive, chubby, silver-haired female, sweet as an apple forgotten and left behind on a rack in a pantry, wrinkled, going dry, yet still sweet beyond description. But these sad old females, a whole wardful of them, were also mad and misshapen, some babbling like raucous birds, some silently slavering.

He couldn't make up his mind whether to enter the ward and sit down or to walk up and down the cool echoing corridor. He always felt a fool when walking up and down like a sentry, but then he also felt a fool when standing or sitting still. He was just a little afraid of those caricatures of women. This was the first time he had ever been afraid of women, and afraid to admit to himself that these creatures were made in exactly the same way as women he had known. He was afraid that if he went into the ward and sat down he would see them in even greater detail than he now did from the threshold. He was young. Outside the sun was shining, the Camowen sparkling under the sun, the meadow grass falling like green silk to make beds for country lovers. But here all flesh was grass and favour was deceitful and beauty was vain. It was bad enough looking at the men. To think what the mind could do to the body. But it was hell upon earth looking at the women. Jock Sharkey, like a million lovers and a thousand poets, had gone mad for beauty. This, in the ward before him, was what could happen to beauty.

He stepped, shuddering, back into the corridor and collided with a tall nurse. He apologised. He smelled freshly ironed, starched linen and disinfectant, a provoking smell. A quick flurried glance showed him a strong handsome face, rather boyish, brick-red hair bursting out over the forehead where the nurse's veil had failed to restrain it. He apologised. He was still rattled by his vision in the ward. Contrary to his opportunist instinct he was even about to step out of the way. But the nurse didn't pass. She said: It is you, Pascal Stakelum, isn't it? Did they lock you up at last? A hundred thousand welcomes.

He had to do some rapid thinking before he remembered. There were so many faces in his memory and he was still confused, still a little frightened, by those faces in the ward. She didn't try to help. She stood, feet apart and solidly planted, and grinned at him, too boyish for a young woman but still fetching. She was, if anything, taller than he was. Her brother, then he remembered, had gone to school with us, a big fellow, as dark as she was red, very clever but capricious, making a mockery of things that he alone, perhaps, of all of us could understand and, in the end, throwing the whole thing up and running away and joining the Royal Air Force. So the first thing Pascal said, to show that he knew who she was, was to ask about the brother, and when would he be coming home. She said: He won't be coming home.

—Why for not?

She said he had been killed at Dunkirk.

Coming right after the prospect of the mad old women, that was a bit of a blow in the face, but at least, he told himself, clean death in battle was not madness, deformity, decay; and the moment gave Pascal the chance to sympathise, to get closer to her. He held her hands. He said he was sorry. He said he had always liked her brother. He had, too. They had, indeed, been quite friendly.

She said: It's war. He would always do things his own way.

She seemed proud of her brother, or just proud of having a brother dead at Dunkirk.

—This is no place to talk, Pascal said. And I'm with Father Paul. Meet me this evening at the Crevenagh Bridge.

That was the old humpy seventeenth-century bridge on the way to a leafy network of lovers' lanes and deep secret bushy ditches.

—Not this evening, she said. I'm on duty. But tomorrow.

—Eight o'clock on the dot, said Pascal.

That was his usual time during the summer months and the long warm evenings. And he was very punctual.

She walked away from him and towards Father Paul. He looked after her, no longer seeing the rest of the ward. She was a tall strong girl, stepping with decision and a great swing. Jock Sharkey would have followed her to the moon.

Father Paul, the shriving done, was again folding his stole. He joked with a group of old ladies. He told one of them that on his next visit he would bring her a skipping rope. He told another one he would bring her a powderpuff. He distributed handfuls of caramels to the whole crew. They cackled with merriment. They loved him. That was one bond between Pascal and himself. The women loved them both.

—But if he meant to preach to me that time, Pascal said to us, by bringing me to that chamber of horrors, I had the laugh on him.

In the sunshine on the lawn outside, the superintending doctor stood with his wife and his dogs, three Irish setters, one male, two female. The doctor and his wife stood, that is, and the setters ran round and round in erratic widening circles.

Those smart-stepping Devon men were by now approaching Sixmilecross, and the two sisters, and rest after battle and port after stormy seas.

The doctor was a handsome cheery fellow, even if he was bald. He wore bright yellow, hand-made shoes, Harris tweed trousers and a high-necked Aran sweater. The wife was small and dainty and crisp as a nut, and a new wife; and the two of them, not to speak of the three setters, were as happy as children. They talked – the doctor, the woman, Paul and Pascal – about the war, and about the two soldiers

from Devon and their two women in Sixmilecross. Then Father Paul
wished the doctor and his wife many happy days, and he and Pascal
stepped off towards the town. At the gateway they met a group of
thirty or forty uniformed inmates returning, under supervision, from
a country walk. One of them was gnawing a raw turnip with which,
ceasing to gnaw, he took aim at Pascal and let fly. Pascal fielded the
missile expertly – in his schooldays he had been a sound midfield man
– and restored it to the inmate who was still chewing and looking quite
amazed at his own deed. All this, to the great amusement of the whole
party, inmates and three keepers. But, oddly enough, Paul didn't join
in the merriment. He stood, silent and abstracted, on the grass at the
side of the driveway. He looked at the sky. His lips moved as though
he were praying, or talking to himself.

Pascal gave away what cigarettes he had left to the hiking party and
he and the priest walked on, Paul very silent, over the Camowen.
When they were halfways to the town, Paul said: Some men can't live
long without a woman.

Pascal said nothing. He remembered that there was a story that
Paul had once beaten a loving couple out of the hedge with a blackthorn stick. He remembered that Paul came from a stern mountainy
part of the country where there had been a priest in every generation
in every family for three hundred years. He thought of the red nurse
and the hedge ahead of her. So he said nothing.

—That new wife of his, Paul said, was American. Did you notice?

—She dressed American, Pascal said. But she had no accent.

—She comes from a part of the States and from a class in society
where they don't much have an accent, Paul said. At least not what you
in your ignorance would call an American accent.

Pascal said: The Old Dominion.

—You're learning fast, Paul said.

The town was before them.

—Three wives he had, Paul said. One dead. Irish. One divorced.
English. And now a brand new one from Virginia. Some men can't go
without.

Pascal made no comment. He contented himself with envying the
bald doctor his international experience. He resolved to travel.

—Most men, said Paul, aren't happy unless they're tangled up with a woman. The impure touch. But the French are the worst. Their blood boiling with wine. From childhood. How could they keep pure?

Pascal hadn't the remotest idea. So he made no comment. He didn't know much about the French but he reckoned that just at that moment in history they had enough and to spare on their plates without also having to worry about purity.

—But pleasures are like poppies spread, Paul said,

He was a great man always to quote the more moralising portions of Robert Burns. Pascal heard him out: You seize the flower, its bloom is shed. Or like the snow falls in the river – a moment white, then melts forever. Or like the borealis race, that flit ere you can point their place. Or like the rainbow's lovely form, evanishing amid the storm.

—Burns, said Father Paul, well knew what he was talking about. Those, Pascal, are the words of wisdom gained through sad and sordid experience.

Pascal agreed. He was remembering the nurse's dead brother who had been a genius at poetry. He could write parodies on anything that any poet had ever written.

When Pascal met the nurse at the Crevenagh Bridge on the following evening she was, of course, in mourning. But the black cloth went very well with that brilliant red hair. Or like the rainbow's lovely form. There was something about it, too, that was odd and exciting, like being out, he said, with a young nun. Yet, apart from the colour of her clothes, she was no nun. Although, come to think of it, who except God knows what nuns are really like?

Pascal, as we know, was also in black but he had no reason to be in mourning. It had rained, just enough to wet the pitch. Otherwise the evening went according to Operation Pascal. When he had first attacked with the knee for the warming-up process, he then withdrew the knee and substituted the hand, lowering it through the band of her skirt, allowing it to linger for a playful moment at the bunker of the belly button. Thereafter he seemed to be hours, like fishermen hauling a net, pulling a silky slip out of the way before the rummaging hand, now living a life of its own, could negotiate the passage into her warm drawers. Pascal didn't know why he hadn't made the easier and more orthodox approach by laying the girl low to begin with and then raising skirt and slip, except it was that they were standing up at the time, leaning against a sycamore tree. The rain had passed but the ground was wet, and to begin his wooing by spreading his trenchcoat (Many's the fine rump, he boasted, that trenchcoat had kept dry, even when the snow was on the ground) on the grass, seemed much too formal. Pascal Stakelum's days, or evenings or nights, were complex with such problems.

Later came the formal ceremonious spreading of the trenchcoat on a protective mattress of old newspapers, and the assuming by both parties of the horizontal. By that time the big red girl was so lively that he swore she'd have shaken Gordon Richards, the King of them All, out of the saddle. She kept laughing and talking, too, so as to be audible, he reckoned, thirty yards away but fortunately he had chosen for the grand manoeuvre a secluded corner of the network of lanes and ditches. He had a veteran's knowledge of the terrain and he was nothing if not discreet.

He was not unmindful of the brother dead in faraway France. But then the brother had been such an odd fellow that even in Pascal's tusselling with his strong red sister he might have found matter for amusement and mockery. As Pascal bounced on top of her, gradually subduing her wildness to the rhythmic control of bridle and straddle and, in the end, to the britchen of his hands under her buttocks, he could hear her brother's voice beginning the schoolboy mockery of Shelley's soaring skylark: Hell to thee, blithe spirit. Pascal and the splendid panting red girl moved together to the poet's metre.

That was one brother Pascal did not have to guard against with starting handle or tyre lever. Working like a galley slave under the dripping sycamore he was in no fear of ambush.

Paul got his parish in the end, the reward of a well-spent life, he said wryly. He died suddenly in it before he was there for six months. That parish was sixty miles away from Lislap, in sleepy grass-meadow country where the slow River Bann drifts northwards out of the great lake. Pascal missed Paul's constant companionship more than he or anybody else would have believed possible and began, particularly after Paul's sudden death, to drink more than he had ever done before, and went less with the girls, which puzzled him as much as it did us. It worried him, too: for in the house of parliament or public house that we specially favoured, he asked me one day was he growing old before his time because he was growing fonder of drink and could now pass a strange woman on the street without wondering who and what she was.

—You're better off, Pascal, I said. What were you ever doing anyway but breaking them in for other men? You never stayed long enough with any one woman to be able in the long run to tell her apart from any other woman.

He was more hurt than I had imagined he would be. But he sadly agreed with me, and said that some day he hoped to find one real true woman with whom he could settle down.

—Like with poor Paul that's gone, he said. Some one woman that a man could remember to the last moment of his life.

—No, I'm not crazy, he said. Two days before his death I was with Paul in his parish, as you know. We went walking this evening after rain, by the banks of a small river in that heavy-grass country. That was the last walk we had together. The boreen we were on went parallel with the river bank. We met an old man, an old bewhiskered codger, hobbling on a stick. So Paul introduced us and said to Methuselah: What now do you think of my young friend from the big garrison town of Lislap?

—The old fellow, said Pascal, looked me up and looked me down. Real cunning country eyes. Dare say he could see through me as if I was a sheet of thin cellophane. But he lied. He said: Your reverence, he looks to me like a fine clean young man.

—That was an accurate description of me, Pascal Stakelum, known far and wide.

Pascal brooded. He said: A fine clean young man.

—Then that evening, he said, we sat for ages after dinner, before we knelt down to say the holy rosary with those two dry sticks of female cousins that did the housekeeping for him. One quick look at either of them would put you off women for time and eternity. There's an unnerving silence in the houses that priests live in: the little altar on the landing, you know, where they keep the sacrament for sick calls at night. Imagine, if you can, the likes of me on my bended knees before it, wondering would I ever remember the words when it came my turn to lead the prayers. But I staggered it. Closed my eyes, you might say, and took a run and jump at it, and landed on the other side word perfect. It would have been embarrassing for Paul if I hadn't been able to remember the words of the Paterandave in the presence of those two stern cousins. One evening one of them sat down opposite me in a low armchair and crossed her legs, poor thing, and before I could look elsewhere I had a view of a pair of long bloomers, passion-killers, that were a holy fright. You wouldn't see the equal of them in the chamber of horrors. Six feet long and coloured grey and elastic below the knee. But when the two cousins were off to bed, and good luck to them, we sat and talked until all hours, and out came the bottle of Jameson, and Paul's tongue loosened. It could be that he said more than he meant to say: oh, mostly about Virginia and the Blue Ridge Mountains and the lovely people who always asked the departing stranger to come back again. Cider presses near Fincastle. Apple orchards. Dogwood trees in blossom. He went on like that for a long time. Then he got up, rooted among his books, came back with this one book covered in a sort of soft brown velvet with gold lettering and designs on the cover and, inside, coloured pictures and the fanciest printing you ever saw in red and in black. He said to me: Here's a book, Pascal, you might keep as a memory of me when I'm gone.

—So I laughed at him, making light of his gloomy face, trying to jolly him up, you know. I said: Where, now, would you be thinking of going?

—Where all men go sooner or later, he said.

—That was the end of my laughing. That's no way for a man to talk, even if he has a premonition.

—Keep the book as a token, Paul said to me. You were never much for the poetry, I know. But your wife when you find her might be, or, perhaps, some of your children. You've a long road ahead of you yet, Pascal, all the way to ninety, and poetry can lighten the burden. That book was given to me long ago by the dearest friend I ever had. Until

I met yourself, he said. Long ago in a distant country and the wench is dead.

—Those were the last words I ever heard Paul speak, excepting the Latin of the mass next morning, for my bus passed the church gate before the mass was rightly over, and I had to run for it. But bloody odd words they were to come from Paul.

—Common enough words, I said. Anybody could have said them.

—But you didn't see the book, Pascal said. I'll show it to you.

He did, too, a week later. It was an exquisite little edition, lost on Pascal, I thought with some jealousy, both as to the perfection of the bookmaker's art and as to the text, which was William Morris telling us, there in a public house in Lislap, how Queen Guinevere had defended herself against the lies of Sir Gauwaine, and a charge of unchastity. Fondling the book, I was not above thinking how much more suitable than Pascal I would have been as a companion for old Paul. So that I felt more than a little ashamed when Pascal displayed to me with what care he had read the poem, underlining here and there in red ink to match the rubric of the capitals and the running titles on the tops of the pages. It was, almost certainly, the only poem to which he had ever paid any particular attention, with the possible exception of that bouncing parody on Shelley's skylark.

—It's like a miniature mass book, he said. Red and black. Only it was by no means intended for using at the mass. See here.

He read and pointed with his finger as he read: She threw her wet hair backward from her brow, her hand close to her mouth touching her cheek.

—Coming from the swimming-pool, Pascal said, when the dog-woods were in blossom. You never knew that Paul was a champion swimmer in his youth. Swimming's like tennis. Brings out the woman in a woman. Arms wide, flung-out, breasts up. Oh, there were a lot of aspects to Paul. And listen to this: Yet felt her cheek burned so, she must a little touch it. Like one lame she walked away from Gauwaine.

—Time and again, Pascal said, he had heard it said that lame women had the name for being hot. Once he had seen on the quays of Dublin a one-legged prostitute. The thought had ever afterwards filled him with curiosity, although at the time he wouldn't have risked touching her for all the diamonds in Kimberley.

—And her great eyes began again to fill, he read, though still she stood right up.

That red nurse, he remembered, had had great blue eyes, looking up at him like headlamps seen through mist.

—But the queen in this poem, he said, was a queen and no mistake.

And in the summer it says that she grew white with flame, white like the dogwood blossoms and all for this Launcelot fellow, lucky Launcelot, and such a pansy name. One day, she says, she was half-mad with beauty and went without her ladies all alone in a quiet garden walled round every way, just like the looney bin where I met that nurse. And both their mouths, it says, went wandering in one way and, aching sorely, met among the leaves. Warm, boy, warm. Then there's odd stuff here about a great God's angel standing at the foot of the bed, his wings dyed with colours not known on earth, and asking the guy or girl in the bed, the angel has two cloths, you see, one blue, one red, asking them, or him or her, to guess which cloth is heaven and which is hell. The blue one turns out to be hell. That puzzles me.

It puzzled both of us.

—But you must admit, said Pascal, that it was a rare book for a young one to be giving a young priest, and writing on it, look here, for Paul with a heart's love, by the Peaks of Otter in Virginia, on a day of sunshine never to be forgotten, from Elsie Cameron. Usually the women give breviaries to the priests, or chalices, or amices, or albs, or black pullovers. She must have been a rare one, Elsie Cameron. Would you say now that she might have had a slight limp? It's a Scottish name. Paul was forever talking about what he called the Scots Irish in Virginia and the fine people they were. All I know is that Scottish women are reputed to be very hot. They're all Protestants and don't have to go to confession.

Pascal had known a man who worked in Edinburgh who said that all you had to do to set a Scotswoman off was to show her the Forth Bridge, the wide open legs of it. That man had said that the Forth Bridge had never failed him.

When I said to Pascal that all this about Paul could have been as innocent as a rose, he said he was well aware of that: he wasn't claiming that Paul had done the dirty on the girl and left her to mourn out her life by the banks of the James River. But that it may all have been innocent for Paul and Elsie only made it the more mournful for Pascal. Fond memories and memories, and all about something that never happened.

—Any day henceforth, Pascal said, I'll go on a journey just to see for myself those Blue Ridge Mountains. Were they ever as blue as Paul thought they were? Cider's the same lousy drink the world over. What better could the orchards or women have been in Virginia than in Armagh? You see he was an imaginative man was old Paul, a touch of the poet, and soft as putty and sentimental away behind that granite mountainy face. Things hurt him, too. He told me once that one day walking he met that mad Maguire one from Cranny, the one with the seven children and no husband, and tried to talk reason to her, and she used language to him the like of which he had never heard, and he turned away with tears in his eyes. He said he saw all women degraded and the Mother of God sorrowful in Nancy Maguire who was as bad as she was mad. An odd thought. He should have taken the stick to her the way I once heard he did to a loving couple he found under the hedge.

But pleasures are like poppies spread, as Paul would say, walking the roads with Pascal *ad quietam conscientiam*, looking at mad Nancy and listening to her oaths, seeing Elsie Cameron under the apple tree under the Blue Mountains in faraway Virginia. Once I wrote a story about him and it was printed in a small little-known and now defunct magazine. That story was all about the nobility of him and the way he used to chant the words of Burns; and then about how he died.

He came home to his parochial house that morning after reading the mass and sat down, one of the cousins said, at the breakfast table, and sat there for a long time silent, looking straight ahead. That wasn't like him. She asked him was he well. He didn't answer. She left the room to consult her sister, who was fussing about in the kitchen. When she came back he had rested his head down on the table and was dead.

Looking straight ahead to Fincastle, Virginia, and seeing a woman white with flame when the dogwood blossomed, seeing the tall angel whose wings were the rainbow and who held heaven, a red cloth, in one hand, and hell, a blue cloth, in the other.

There was no place in that story of mine for Pascal Stakelum, the rural rake.

A Room in Linden

One day in the dark maze of the yew-hedges Sister Lua, who has arthritis, looks up at him from her wheelchair which he's pushing, and says: Tell me the truth. Don't be modest about it. Are you Nanki-Poo?

Since he is a bookish young man, it is an exciting thing for him to have history living along the corridor. The poet he's reading just before he leaves his room writes that there's a wind blowing, cold through the corridor, a death-wind, the flapping of defeated wings from meadows damned to eternal April. The poet has never seen it, but he could have been writing about this corridor. On its dull green walls, a mockery of the grass and green leaves of life, the sun never shines. All day and all night the big windows at the ends of the corridor, one at the east wing of the house and one at the west, are wide open, and from whichever airt the wind does blow it always blows cold. The rooms on the north side of the corridor are, as one might expect, colder and darker than the rooms on the south side, or would be if their light and heat depended totally on the sun.

Before the nuns got here and turned the place into a convalescent home it was lived in by a family famous for generations for a special brand of pipe tobacco. The old soldier, who is reluctantly, vociferously fading away in a room on the north side of the corridor, says: This house was built on smoke. Just think of that. Smoke.

The old soldier himself belongs to some branch of the family that emigrated to South Africa and made even more money out of burgundy than the people who stayed at home made out of smoke, and there was always as much soldiering as smoke in the family; and big-game hunting, too, to judge by the fearful snarling mounted heads left behind and surviving, undisturbed by nuns or convalescents, in the entrance hall.

—You'll be nice to the old man, won't you? Mother Polycarp had said to him. He'll bore you to death. But he needs somebody to listen to him. He hasn't much longer to talk, in this world at any rate.

So he talks to the old soldier in the evenings and, in the afternoons, to the old priest and historian, dying as methodically and academically as he has lived, checking references, adding footnotes, in a room on the south side of the corridor. At other times he reads in his own room, or has visitors, or wheels Sister Lua's wheelchair in the ample bosky grounds, or leaves the grounds on his own and goes through quiet suburban roads to walk slowly, tapping his stick, in the public park that overlooks, across two walls and a railway, the flat sand and the bay. It is not an exciting life, but it's not meant to be.

He wheels Sister Lua round and round the dark cloisters of the yew-hedge maze from the corner where Jesus is condemned to death to the central circle where he is laid in the tomb. He tells her that he is not Nanki-Poo.

—Well, I heard you had poems in that magazine. And I didn't see your name. And there is this poet called Nanki-Poo. And he's very good. About the missions.

—Not me, alas, sister. I was never on the missions.

—Know you weren't. A university student.

Although she is always sitting down and being wheeled she is also always breathless and never quite begins or finishes a sentence, and it is necessary to fill in her words and meanings as she goes along. Bird-like, he knows, isn't much of a description, but she is bird-like, little hands like claws because of the arthritis, of course, a little nose like a beak peeking out from under the nun's pucog. To the left corner of her pale unvarnished little mouth, so often twisted with patience in pain, there's a mole with two hairs. She loves the dark green maze that grew up, like the house, out of smoke and was used by the nuns as a setting for a via dolorosa with life-size figures; and backgrounds of good stone columns and arches robbed from the wreckage of some eighteenth-century mansion. His first faux pas with the old historian had to do with those stations of the cross. One dull evening when the talk wasn't going so well he had, just to make chat, said: Don't they have a big day here once a year? People coming in hundreds to do the stations of the cross. What day does that happen on?

The old man pulls the rug more tightly around his long legs. His feet are always cold. In large bodies, Edmund Burke held, circulation is slower at the extremities, but the coldness of the old man's feet is just the beginning of death. He snuffs black snuff expertly from the hollow between thumb and forefinger, he sneezes, he says with crushing deliberation: Good Friday, my good young man. Even the younger generation should be aware that the Lord was crucified on Good Friday.

He's a carnaptious old bastard and even for the sake of Mother Polycarp, the kindly reverend mother, who is always thanking God for everything, it's sort of hard to suffer him at times. But he has both made and written history, and poems, too, of a learned sort, and collected folksong, and the best people have written about him and discovered an old-world courtesy and all the rest of that rot behind his rude exterior: the old-world courtesy of a Scandinavian sea-rover putting the full of a monastery of shaven-pated monks to the gory hatchet. By comparison, the old soldier who has actually killed his man in faraway wars, is a gentleman. But then the old soldier is simply fading away, all battles fought and won, all comrades gone before him, all trumpets sounding from the other side. The old priest, still trying to work, has his last days aggravated by a mind that remembers everything and by the pain of a stomach cancer.

He leaves Sister Lua in the charge of a big red-headed nurse and walks down the main avenue towards suburbia and the park by the sea. The old white-haired vaudeville entertainer who has some sort of shaking paralysis, which he says is an occupational disease, waves to him from his seat by the grotto under the obelisk and gives him three letters to post at the postbox outside the gate. They are, he notices, all addressed to well-known celebrities of screen, stage and television: one in Dublin, one in London, one in New York. Out there is the world of healthy living people.

Life and playing children are, of course, all around him in the park by the sea but it isn't quite the same thing. There isn't enough of life there to help him to stop thinking of old men dying. He is very much on his own either because of his sullenness, or because he thinks that while he may be of interest to himself, he couldn't possibly be of interest to anybody else. Nothing humble about that, though. In that park he's really a visitor from a special sort of world, from a cold green corridor damned to eternal December: sort of exclusive, though, a rich old soldier, a famous old historian, the artist who is still in touch with the best people; and only the best die in that corridor.

One old man who sits on a green wooden seat, close to the playhall where the children run when it rains, talks to him as if he would gladly talk longer. He discourages that old man with abrupt sentences for he has, at the moment, enough of old men. He walks on beyond him and along by the tennis courts. A stout bespectacled girl with strong tanned legs plays awkwardly with a tall blond handsome fellow who wins every set and enjoys his superiority, while she seems to enjoy being beaten. A stranger from a strange land, he enjoys, as he passes or rests for a while on a seat and watches, the leaping of her legs. So everybody is happy and the park is beautiful. The blond boy isn't even good at the game and he, the stranger, knows that if it wasn't for the stiff hip, still slowly recovering, he could challenge him and beat him easily. But then the stout girl, legs excepted, isn't really interesting.

He himself is blond and doesn't take too well to the sun. So his favourite seat is in a shady corner under dark horse-chestnuts whose white candles are fading. He likes the place also because nobody else sits there. Strollers seem to accelerate as they walk past. Once in a while children run shouting, hooting through the dark tunnel, from one shire of sunshine into another. Through a fence of mournful laurels and copper beeches he sees the glitter of the sun on the lake. Out of the corner of his left eye he sees a well-built girl in white shorts flat on her back on the sunny grass. Sometimes she reads. Sometimes she raises her legs and, furiously with flashing thighs, pedals an invisible bicycle, faster and faster until it seems as if she has seven or seventeen legs, until the flash of her thighs takes the shape of a white circle. Her belly muscles must be jingling like springs. The joints in her hips, unlike his own, must be in perfect lubricated condition. She is at the moment one of the five women in his life: Polycarp thanking God for the rain and the sunshine, for the hail and the snow; Lua, twisted in her chair; she who, nameless, cycles on her back on the grass; the strong-legged tennis player whose name, he has heard the blond fellow shout, is Phyllis; and A. N. Other.

To the rear of his shady corner there is a privet hedge and a high wooden fence and a gate with a notice that says no admission except on business. That's exactly the way he feels. Adam in Eden must have had just such a corner where he kept his tools and experimented with slips and seeds. But then before Adam and Eve made a pig's ass out of a good arrangement the garden must have looked after itself and needed none of that sweat-of-the-brow stuff. What would old Thor the thunderer, brooding in his room, biting on his cancer, think of that?

Belloc, says the old priest, was a big man who looked as if all his life he had eaten too much and drunk too much. The best way to learn French is to read cowboy and injun stories. They hold the interest better than Racine.

Aware of his own inanity, he says: translations.

Before that face, oblong, seemingly about twelve feet long, like a head cut out of the side of some crazy American mountain, he is perpetually nonplussed into saying stupidities.

—Cowboys and injuns, my good young man, are not indigenous to the soil of France.

—There's a city called Macon in Georgia, USA.

—There's a city called everything somewhere in the States. Naturally they mispronounce the names.

So it goes on. You can't win with the old bastard.

—Darlington, he says, used to call on Hopkins to take him out for walks. Hopkins was for ever and always complaining of headaches. What else can you expect, Darlington would say to him, immured up there in your room writing rubbish. I'm not so sure that Darlington wasn't right.

He is at that time just entering his Hopkins phase and if he wasn't afraid of that granite face, eyes sunken and black and burning, jawbones out rigid like a forked bush struck by lightning, he would defend the poet, quoting his sonnet about the windhover which, with some difficulty, he has just memorised. Yet it still is something to hear those names tossed about by a man who knew the men, and was a name himself. He feels grateful to Mother Polycarp who, as a friend of his family, has invited him to this place for a while, after his year in orthopaedic, so that he can read his books and learn to walk at his ease. In all that green cold corridor, which is really a place for old men, he is the only person who is going to live. He searches for something neutral to say: Wasn't Hopkins always very scrupulous about marking students' papers?

—He was a neurotic Englishman, my good fellow. They never could make up their minds between imperialism and humanitarianism. That's what has them the way they are. Darlington was English, too, of course, the other sort, the complacent Englishman, thinking that only what is good can happen to him, and that all his works are good. Then a young upstart called Joyce put him in a book. That should have been a lesson to Darlington, if they have books in heaven or wherever he went to.

He should, as Mother Polycarp says, be taking notes, thank God, except he feels that if he did so, secretly even in his room, the old lion might read his mind and take offence. The old man laughs seldom but he's laughing now, perhaps at some memory of two English Jesuits marooned in Ireland, or at some other memory surfacing for a second in the dark crowded pool behind his square forehead. He has kept his hair, a dirty grey, standing up and out as if it had never encountered a comb. The long bony hands tighten the rug about his knees. The cold is creeping upwards.

In the green corridor he kneels for a while at the prie-dieu before the shrine, not praying, just thinking about age and death, and looking up at the bearded face of St. Joseph, pure and gentle, guardian of the savior child. With a lily in his hand. Another old man and, by all accounts, very patient about it. What in hell is St. Joseph, like Oscar Wilde or somebody, always doing with a lily in his hand? An awkward class of a thing for a carpenter to be carrying.

Before his hip betrayed him he has had a half-notion of being a priest, but a year in orthopaedic, bright nurses hopping all around him, has cured him by showing him that there are things that priests, in the ordinary course of duty, are not supposed to have.

—You're too young, the old soldier says, to be in this boneyard.

He's a small man with a red boozy face, a red dressing-gown, a whiskey bottle and a glass always to his right hand. The whiskey keeps him alive, thank God, Mother Polycarp says. He is, like St. Joseph, gentle but not so pure, rambling on about dirty doings in far-away places, Mombasa and Delhi are much mentioned, about Kaffir women, and about blokes who got knocked off in the most comical fashion. He laughs a lot. He doesn't need a considered answer or a balanced conversation, just a word now and then to show he's not alone. He shares the whiskey generously. He has bags of money and, when he dies, he'll leave the perishing lot to the nuns.

—They do good, you know. Keep perky about it, too. Who else would look after the likes of me? Ruddy boneyard, though. Elephants' graveyard. Get out of here and get a woman. Make sons. Before it's too late. Would get out myself only nobody would have me any more, and I couldn't have them. Only whiskey left. But I had my day. When I was your age I laid them as quick as my batman could pull them out from under me. Three women shot under me at the battle of Balaclava and all that. Fit only for the boneyard now and the nuns. They don't want it and I can't give it. But there's always whiskey, thank God, as the mother says. A field behind the barracks where old wind-broken cavalry mounts went on grass with the shoes off until they died. At least we didn't eat them like the bloody Belgians. Smell of slow death around this place.

He sniffs the whiskey and laughs and then coughs. By night the coughing is constant. Lying awake and listening, the young man has a nightmarish feeling that they are all in prison cells, all dying, which is true, all the living are dying, and after one night the sun will never rise again on the park, and every time the cycling girl spins her legs she's another circle nearer to the grave. His own healthy youth has already collapsed in illness. Life is one collapse after another. The coughing goes on and on. To be a brave soldier and to end up coughing in a lonely room. Let me outa here. No, Sister Lua, I am not Nanki-Poo.

—But every day that passes, Mother Polycarp tells him, brings you a day nearer to getting back to your studies, thank God. You made a great recovery in orthopaedic.

She is a tall woman with a long flat-footed step and more rattlings of keys and rosary beads than seem natural even in a nun. When he tells her that, she laughs and says, of course, that she has the keys of the kingdom, thank God. She has a good-humoured wrinkled mannish face, and she is famous everywhere for her kindness and her ability to gather money and build hospitals.

Does she say to the old men: Every day that passes brings you a day nearer heaven, thank God?

She naturally wouldn't mention death as the gate of heaven.

He has a feeling that none of them want to go any farther forward, they look backward to see heaven: on the day a new book was published or a new woman mounted or a new show went well. Heaven, like most things, doesn't last, or could only be an endless repetition of remembered happiness, and would in the end be, like dying, a bloody bore.

In her chair as he wheels her, Sister Lua, chirping like the little robin that she is, prays a bit and chats a bit and, because of her breathlessness and the way she beheads her sentences and docks the tails off them, he has to listen carefully to know whether she is chatting or praying. The life-size figures in the maze of dark yews – fourteen Christs in various postures, with attendant characters from jesting Pilate to the soldiers by the tomb – have acquired a sombre existence of their own. Do they relax at night, yawn, stretch stiff limbs, mutter a curse, light a cigarette, say to hell with show business? He must try that one out on the vaudeville man, shaking his way to the grave, on the seat by the grotto under the obelisk.

—Weep not for me, Sister Lua prays, but for yourselves and for your children.

The lord is talking to the weeping women of Jerusalem and not doing a lot to cheer them up. Some anti-semitical Irish parish priest must have written the prayers that Lua reels off. He didn't think much either of the kind of recruitment that got into the Roman army: These barbarians fastened him with nails and then, securing the cross, allowed him to die in anguish on this ignominious gibbet.

From the prayer book she has learned, by heart, not only the prayers but the instructions that go with them. She says, as the book instructs: Pause a while.

He pauses. The yew-hedges are a dark wall to either hand. Twenty paces ahead, the lord, in an arbour, is being lowered from the cross. The dying has been done.

—Nanki-Poo. Nanki-Poo.

—Sister, I am not Nanki-Poo.

—But I call you Nanki-Poo. Such a lovely name.

—So is Pooh-Bah.

—Pooh-Bah is horrible. Somebody making mean faces. Nanki-Poo, you must write a poem for Mother Polycarp's feast-day. So easy for you. Just a parody. Round Linden when the sun was low, Mother Polycarp the Good did go.

—There's a future in that style.

—You'll do it, Nanki-Poo?

—At my ease, sister. Whatever Nanki-Poo can do, I can do better.

By the laying of the lord in the tomb they encounter A. N. Other. She tries to escape by hiding behind the eighteenth-century cut-stone robbed from the old house, but Sister Lua's birds-eye is too quick and too sharp for her.

—Nurse Donovan, Nurse Donovan, the French texts have arrived.

—Yes, Sister Lua.

—When can you begin, Nanki-Poo?

—Any time, sister.

—So useful to you, Nurse Donovan, French, when you're a secretary.

She is a small well-rounded brunette who has nursed in the orthopaedic hospital until something happened to her health. He is in love with her, has been for some time. Nothing is to come of it. He is never to see her again after he leaves the convalescent home. The trouble is that Sister Lua has decided that the girl must be a secretary and that Nanki-Poo must teach her French, and it is quite clear from the subdued light in the girl's downcast dark eyes that she doesn't give a fiddler's fart about learning anything, even French, out of a book. Worse still: on the few occasions on which he has been able to corner the girl on her own, he hasn't been able to think of a damn thing to talk about except books. How can he ever get through to her that pedagogy is the last thing in his mind?

She wheels Sister Lua away from him to the part of the house where the nuns live. Between the girl and himself Sister Lua has thrown a barbed-wire entanglement of irregular verbs. No great love has ever been so ludicrously frustrated.

A white blossom that he cannot identify grows copiously in this suburb. Thanks be to God for the thunder and lightning, thanks be to God for all things that grow.

No, Sister Lua, I am not Nanki-Poo, am a disembodied spirit, homeless in suburbia, watching with envy a young couple coming, white and dancing, out of a house and driving away to play tennis, am a lost soul blown on the blast between a green cold corridor of age and death, and the children running and squealing by the lake in the park.

Beyond the two walls and the railway line the sea is flat and purple all the way to Liverpool. He envies the young footballers in the playing fields close to where the cycling girl lies flat on her back and rides to the moon on her imaginary bicycle. He envies particularly a red-headed boy with a superb left foot, who centres the ball, repeating the movement again and again, a conscious artist, as careless as God of what happens to the ball next, just so that he drops it in the goalmouth where he feels it should go. The footballer is on talking terms with the cycling girl. He jokes and laughs with her when the ball bounces that way. She stops her cycling to answer him. From his shadowy corner under the chestnuts Nanki-Poo watches and thinks about his latest talk with the vaudeville man on his seat by the grotto under the obelisk.

The obelisk has also been built on smoke to celebrate the twenty-first birthday of a son of the house who would have been the great-grand-uncle of the old soldier.

—Vanished somewhere in India, the poor fellow. There was a rumour to the effect that he was eaten by wild beasts. A damn hard thing to prove unless you see it happen. Anyway he did for a good few of them before they got him. Half of the heads in the hallway below are his.

The obelisk stands up on a base of a flowering rockery, and into the cave or grotto underneath the rockery the nuns have, naturally, inserted a miniature Lourdes: the virgin with arms extended and enhaloed by burning candles, Bernadette kneeling by a fountain of holy water that is blessed by the chaplain at its source in a copper tank.

—The candles, says the vaudeville man, keep my back warm.

He wears a faded brown overcoat with a velvet collar. His white hair is high and bushy and possibly not as well trimmed as it used to be. The skin of his shrunken face and bony Roman nose has little purple blotches and, to conceal the shake in his hands, he grips the knob of his bamboo walking-cane very tightly. When he walks his feet rise jerkily from the ground as if they did so of their own accord and might easily decide never to settle down again. The handwriting on the envelopes is thin and wavery as if the pen now and again took off on its own.

—You know all the best people.

—I used to.

He is never gloomy, yet never hilarious. Somewhere in between he has settled for an irony that is never quite bitter.

—You still write to them.

—Begging letters, you know. Reminders of the good old days. They almost always work with show people. I never quite made it, you know, not even when I had the health. But I was popular with my own kind. This one now.

He points to a notable name on one envelope.

—We met one night in a boozer in London when I wasn't working. He stood me a large Jameson straight away, then another, then another. He asked me to dine with him. We talked about this and that. When we parted I found a tenner in the inside breast pocket of my overcoat. While we were dining he had slipped into the cloakroom. No note, no message, just a simple tenner to speak for itself. He wasn't rich then, mark you, although as the world knows he did well afterwards. But he remembers me. He promises to come to see me. Do you know, now that I think of it, this was the very overcoat.

The cycling girl has stopped cycling and is talking to the red-headed footballer. He stands above her, casually bouncing the ball on that accurate left foot. Whatever he's saying the girl laughs so loudly that Nanki-Poo can hear her where he sits in gloom and broods on beggary. She has a good human throaty sort of a laugh.

The night there is no coughing, but only one loud single cry, from the next room, he knows that the old soldier has awakened for a moment to die. He rises, puts on slippers and dressing-gown, and heads down the corridor to find the night nurse. But Mother Polycarp is there already, coming stoop-shouldered, beads and keys rattling, out of the old man's room.

—Thank God, she says, he died peacefully and he had the blessed sacrament yesterday morning. He wandered a lot in his time but he came home in the end.

He walks down the stairway to the shadowy main hall. Do the animals in the half-darkness grin with satisfaction at the death of a man whose relative was eaten by one or more of their relatives? The front door is open for the coming of the doctor and the priest. Above the dark maze of yew-hedge the obelisk is silhouetted against the lights of the suburb. The place is so quiet that he can hear even the slight noise of the sea over the flat sand. This is the first time he has been out of doors at night since he went to orthopaedic. Enjoying the freedom, the quiet, the coolness, he walks round and round in the maze until his eyes grow used to the blackness and he is able to pick out the men and women who stand along the via dolorosa. They are just as motionless as they are during the day. When he comes back Mother Polycarp is waiting for him in the hallway.

—Now you're bold, she says. You could catch a chill. But every day that passes brings you nearer to freedom, thank God, and you can walk very well now.

She crosses herself as she passes the shrine in the corridor. She says: One thing that you could do now that you are up, is talk to himself. Or listen to him. He's awake and out of bed and lonely for somebody to talk to.

He is out of bed but not fully dressed; and, in a red dressing-gown that must have been presented to him by Mother Polycarp, he doesn't seem half as formidable as in his black religious habit. There is an open book on the rug that, as usual, covers and beats down the creeping cold from his thighs and knees. He is not reading. His spectacles are in their case on the table to his right hand. Above the light from the shaded reading-lamp his head and shoulders are in shadow. For once, since he is red and not black and half invisible, Nanki-Poo feels almost at ease with him.

From the shadows his voice says: Credit where credit is due, young man. The first Chichester to come to Ireland was certainly one of the most capable and successful robbers who ever lived. He stole most of the north of Ireland not only from its owners but even from the robbers who stole it from its owners. Twice he robbed his royal master, James Stuart, the fourth of Scotland and the first of England. The man who did that had to rise early in the morning. For although King James was a fool about most things he was no fool about robbery: it was he who got the Scots the name for parsimony. Chichester stole the entire fisheries of Lough Neagh, the largest lake in the British Isles, and nobody found out about it until after he died. *Age quod agis*, as the maxim says. Do what you do. At his own craft he was a master. I dealt with him in a book.

—I read it.

—Did you indeed? A mark in your favour, young man.

—As a matter of fact, sir, the copy of it I read had your name on the flyleaf. Father Charles from your monastery loaned it to me when I was in orthopaedic.

As soon as the words are out, he knows he has dropped the biggest brick of his career, and prays to Jesus that he may live long and die happy and never drop a bigger one. He has never known silence to last so long and be so deafening. Even the bulb in the reading-lamp makes a sound like a big wind far away. Blood in the ears?

—They're not expecting me back, so.

—What do you mean, sir?

—You know damned well what I mean. In a monastery when they know you're dead and not coming back they empty your room. There's another man in it now. They were kind and never told me. That room was all I had, and my books. They have sent me to the death-house as they so elegantly say in the United States. This here is the death-house. What do you do here, young man?

He is asking himself that question. So far no easy answer has offered itself.

—Books you build around you, more than a house and wife and family for a layman, part of yourself, flesh of your flesh, more than furniture for a monk's cell, a shell for his soul, the only thing in spite of the rule of poverty I couldn't strip myself of, and my talents allowed me a way around the rule, but man goeth forth naked as he came, stripped of everything, death bursts among them like a shell and strews them over half the town, and yet there are men who can leave their books as memorials to great libraries . . .

Sacred Heart of Jesus, he thinks, up there in the shadows there may be tears on that granite face.

—I'm sorry, sir.

—You didn't know, young man. How could you know?

—You will be remembered, sir.

—Thank you. The old must be grateful. Go to bed now. You have reason to rest. You have a life to live.

In his room he reads for what's left of the night. He has a life to live.

Through a drowsy weary morning he feels he wants to leave the place right away. Never again will he see the old soldier. Never again can he face the old scholar.

—Nanki-Poo, Nanki-Poo, you won't see your old friend again.

—No, sister. He died last night.

—Not him. Your old friend on the seat by the grotto.

Flying from French, A. N. Other cuts across their path through the maze. But she's moving so fast that not even Lua can hail her. Somewhere in the maze and as quietly as a cat she is stealing away from him for ever. Dulled with lack of sleep his brain is less than usually able to keep up with the chirpings of Lua.

—Is he dead too?

Let them all die. Let me outa here. I am not Nanki-Poo.

—A stroke, not fatal yet, but, alas, the final one.

—I'll go to see him.

But Mother Polycarp tells him there's no point in that: all connection between brain and tongue and eyes is gone.

—He wouldn't know whether you were there or not.

—Couldn't he see me?

—We don't know. The doctor says, God bless us, that he's a vegetable.

—I wondered had he any letters to send out. I used to post them for him.

—He can't write any more.

A silence. So he can't even beg.

—It's a blow to you, she says. You were his friend. He used to enjoy his talks with you. But it'll soon be over, thank God. Pray for him that he may pray for us. For some of us death isn't the worst thing and, as far as we can tell, he's content.

A vegetable has little choice. Refusing to lie down and rest in that green place of death, he walks dumbly through the suburb. The white blossoms blind him. When he leaves this place he will do so with the sense of escape he might have if he was running on a smooth hillside on a sunny windy day. But later he knows that the place will be with him for ever: the cry in the night, the begging letters sent to the stars, the pitiful anger of an old man finding another man living in his room. Crucified god, there's life for you, and there's a lot more of it that he hasn't yet encountered. He expects little, but he will sit no longer expecting it alone in any dark corner.

He would like to be able to tell the cycling girl a really good lie about how he injured his hip. The scrum fell on me on the line in a rather dirty game, just as I was sneaking away and over: that's how it happens, you know.

Or: An accident on a rockface in Snowdonia, a bit of bad judgment, my own fault actually.

Or: You've heard of the parachute club that ex-air force chap has started out near Celbridge.

He would prefer if he had crutches, or even one crutch, instead of a stick which he doesn't even need. A crutch could win a girl's confidence for no harm could come to her from a fellow hopping on a crutch unless he could move as fast as, and throw the crutch with the accuracy of, Long John Silver.

There he goes, thinking about books again. He'd better watch that.

The red-headed footballer is far-away and absorbed in the virtues of his own left foot. For the first time Nanki-Poo notices the colour of her hair, mousy, and the colour of her sweater, which today is mauve, because when she lay flat on the grass and he watched from a distance, she was mostly white shorts and bare circling thighs.

He sits down, stiffly, on the grass beside her. She seems not in the least surprised. She has a freckled face and spectacles. That surprises him.

He says: I envy the way your hips work.

If he doesn't say something wild like that he'll begin talking about books and his cause is lost.

—Why so?

—I was laid up for a year with a tubercular hip. I'm in the convalescent over there.

—Oh I know who you are. Sister Lua told me. You're Nanki-Poo. You write poetry.

He is cold all over.

You know Sister Lua?

—She's my aunt. I write poetry too. Nobody has ever printed it though. Yet. Sister Lua said that some day she'd ask you to read some of it.

—I'd be delighted to.

—I watched you sitting over there for a long time. But I didn't like to approach you. Sister Lua said you were standoffish and intellectual.

She walks back with him as far as the obelisk and the grotto. They will meet again on the following day and take a bus into a teashop in the city. They may even go to a show if Mother Polycarp allows him – as she will – to stay out late.

He suspects that all this will come to nothing except to the reading of her poetry which as likely as not will be diabolical. He wonders if some day she will, like her aunt, be arthritic, for arthritis, they say, like a stick leg, runs in the blood. But with one of his three friends dead, one estranged and one a vegetable, it is something to have somebody to talk to as you stumble through suburbia. He has a life to live. Every day that passes brings him a day nearer to somewhere else.

So thanks be to God for the rain and the sunshine, thanks be to God for the hail and the snow, thanks be to God for the thunder and lightning, thanks be to God that all things are so.

Maiden's Leap

The civic guard, or policeman, on the doorstep was big, middle-aged, awkward, affable. Behind him was green sunlit lawn sloping down to a white horse-fence and a line of low shrubs. Beyond that the highway, not much travelled. Beyond the highway, the jetty, the moored boats, the restless lake-water reflecting the sunshine.

The civic guard was so affable that he took off his cap. He was bald, completely bald. Robert St. Blaise Macmahon thought that by taking off his cap the civic guard had made himself a walking, or standing, comic comment on the comic rural constable, in the Thomas Hardy story, who wouldn't leave his house without his truncheon: because without his truncheon his going forth would not be official.

Robert St. Blaise Macmahon felt like telling all that to the civic guard and imploring him, for the sake of the dignity of his office, to restore his cap to its legal place and so to protect his bald head from the sunshine which, for Ireland, was quite bright and direct. Almost like the sun of that autumn he had spent in the Grand Atlas, far from the tourists. Or the sun of that spring when he had submitted to the natural curiosity of a novelist, who was also a wealthy man and could afford such silly journeys, and gone all the way to the United States, not to see those sprawling vulgar cities, Good God sir no, nor all those chromium-plated barbarians who had made an industry out of writing boring books about those colossal bores Yeats and Joyce, but to go to Georgia to see the Okefenokee Swamp which interested him because of those sacred drooping melancholy birds, the white ibises, and because of the alligators. Any day in the year give him, in preference to Americans, alligators. It could be that he made the journey so as to be able at intervals to say that.

But if he talked like this to the bald guard on the ancestral doorstep the poor devil would simply gawk or smirk or both and say: Yes, Mr Macmahon. Of course, Mr Macmahon.

Very respectful, he would seem to be. For the Macmahons counted for something in the town. His father's father had as good as owned it.

The fellow's bald head was nastily, ridiculously perspiring. Robert St. Blaise Macmahon marked down that detail for his notebook. Henry James had so wisely said: Try to be one of those on whom nothing is lost.

Henry James had known it all. What a pity that he had to be born in the United States. But then, like the gentleman he was, he had had the good wit to run away from it all.

The bald perspiring cap-in-hand guard said: Excuse me, Mr Macmahon. Sorry to disturb you on such a heavenly morning and all. But I've come about the body, sir.

Robert St. Blaise Macmahon was fond of saying in certain circles in Dublin that he liked civic guards if they were young, fresh from the country, and pink-cheeked; and that he liked Christian Brothers in a comparable state of development. In fact, he would argue, you came to a time of life when civic guards and Christian Brothers were, apart from the uniforms, indistinguishable. This he said merely to hear himself say it. He was much too fastidious for any fleshly contact with anybody, male or female. So, lightly, briefly, flittingly, trippingly, he now amused himself with looking ahead to what he would say on his next visit to town: Well if they had to send a guard they could have sent a young handsome one to enquire about the . . .

What the guard had just said now registered and with a considerable shock. The guard repeated: About the body, sir. I'm sorry, Mr Macmahon, to disturb you.

—What body? Whose body? What in heaven's name can you mean?

—I know it's a fright, sir. Not what you would expect at all. The body in the bed, sir. Dead in the bed.

—There is no body in my bed. Dead or alive. At least not while I'm up and about. I live here alone, with my housekeeper, Miss Hynes.

—Yes, Mr Macmahon, sir. We know Miss Hynes well. Very highly respected lady, sir. She's below in the barracks at the moment in a terrible state of nervous prostration. The doctor's giving her a pill or an injection or something to soothe her. Then he'll be here directly.

—Below in the barracks? But she went out to do the shopping.

—Indeed yes, sir. But she slipped in to tell us, in passing, like, sir. Oh it's not serious or anything. Foul play is not suspected.

—Foul what? Tell you what?

—Well, sir.

—Tell me, my good man.

—She says, sir, there's a man dead in her bed.

—A dead man?

—The very thing, Mr Macmahon.

—In the bed of Miss Hynes, my housekeeper.

—So she says, sir. Her very words.

—What in the name of God is he doing there?

—Hard to say, Mr Macmahon, what a dead man would be doing in a bed. I mean like in somebody else's bed.

With a huge white linen handkerchief that he dragged, elongated, out of a pants pocket, and then spread before him like an enveloping cloud, the guard patiently mopped his perspiration: Damned hot today, sir. The hottest summer, the paper says, in forty years.

The high Georgian-Floridian sun shone straight down on wine-coloured swamp-water laving (it was archaic but yet the only word) the grotesque knobbly knees of giant cypress trees. The white sacred crook-billed birds perched gravely, high on grey curved branches above trailing Spanish moss, oh far away, so far away from this mean sniggering town and its rattling tongues. It was obvious, it was regrettably obvious, that the guard was close to laughter.

—A dead man, guard, in the bed of Miss Hynes, my housekeeper, and housekeeper to my father and mother before me, and a distant relative of my own.

—So she tells us, sir.

—Scarcely a laughing matter, guard.

—No, sir. Everything but, sir. It's just the heat, sir. Overcome by the heat. Hottest summer, the forecast says, in forty years.

That hottest summer in forty years followed them, panting, across the black and red flagstones of the wide hallway. A fine mahogany staircase went up in easy spirals. Robert St. Blaise Macmahon led the way around it, keeping to the ground floor. The guard placed his cap, open end up, on the hall stand, as reverently as if he were laying cruets on an altar, excusing himself, as he did so, as if the ample mahogany hall stand, mirrored and antlered, were also a Macmahon watching, or reflecting, him with disapproval. It was the first time he or his like ever had had opportunity or occasion to enter this house.

In the big kitchen, old-fashioned as to size, modern as to fittings, the hottest summer was a little assuaged. The flagstones were replaced by light tiles, green and white, cool to the sight and the touch. She had always held on to that bedroom on the ground floor, beyond the kitchen, although upstairs the large house was more than half-empty. She said she loved it because it had French windows that opened out to the garden. They did, too. They would also give easy access for visitors to the bedroom: a thought that had never occurred to him, not once over all these years.

Earlier that morning she had called to him from the kitchen to say that she was going shopping, and had made her discreet escape by way of those windows. They still lay wide open to the garden. She was a good gardener as she was a good housekeeper. She had, of course, help with the heavy work in both cases: girls from the town for the kitchen, a healthy young man for the garden. All three, or any, of them were due to arrive, embarrassingly, within the next hour. Could it be the young man for the garden, there, dead in the bed? No, at least, thank God, it wasn't her assistant gardener, a scape-grace of a fellow that might readily tempt a middle-aged woman. She hadn't stooped to the servants. She had that much Macmahon blood in her veins. This man was, or had been, a stranger, an older man by far than the young gardener. He was now as old as he would ever be. The hottest summer was heavy and odorous in the garden, and flower odours and insect sounds came to them in the room. The birds were silent. There was also the other odour: stale sweat, or dead passion, or just death? The guard sniffed. He said: He died sweating. He's well tucked in.

Only the head was visible: sparse grey hair, a few sad pimples on the scalp, a long purple nose, a comic Cyrano nose. Mouth and eyes were open. He had good teeth and brown eyes. He looked, simply, surprised, not yet accustomed to wherever he happened to find himself.

—Feel his heart, guard.

—Oh dead as mutton, Mr Macmahon. Miss Hynes told no lie. Still, he couldn't die in a better place. In a bed, I mean.

—Unhousuelled, unappointed, unannealed.

—Yes, sir, the guard said, every bit of it.

—I mean he died without the priest.

With something amounting almost to wit – you encountered it in the most unexpected places – the guard said that taking into account the circumstances in which the deceased, God be merciful to him, had passed over, he could hardly have counted on the company of a resident chaplain. That remark could be adopted as one's own, improved upon, and employed on suitable occasions and in the right places, far from this town and its petty people.

—Death, said the guard, is an odd fellow. There's no being up to him, Mr Macmahon. He can catch you unawares in the oddest places.

This fellow, by heaven, was a philosopher. He was, for sure, one for the notebook.

—Quite true, guard. There was a very embarrassing case involving a president of the great French Republic. Found dead in his office. He had his hands in the young lady's hair. They had to cut the hair to set her free.

—Do you tell me so, sir? A French president? 'Twouldn't be the present fellow, DeGaulle, with the long nose would be caught at capers like that.

—There was a Hemingway story on a somewhat similar theme.

—Of course, sir. You'd know about that, Mr Macmahon. I don't read much myself. But my eldest daughter that works for the public libraries tells me about your books.

—And Dutch Schultz, the renowned American gangster, you know that he was shot dead while he was sitting, well in fact while he was sitting on the toilet.

—A painful experience, Mr Macmahon. He must have been surprised beyond measure.

Far away, from the highway, came the sound of an automobile.

—That, said the guard, could be the doctor or the ambulance.

They waited in silence in the warm odorous room. The sound passed on and away: neither the doctor nor the ambulance.

—But that fellow in the bed, Mr Macmahon, I could tell you things about him, God rest him.

—Do you mean to say you know him.

—Of course, sir. It's my business to know people.

—Try to be one of those on whom nothing is lost.

—Quite so, sir, and odd that you should mention it. For that fellow in the bed, sir, do you know that once upon a time he lost two hundred hens?

—Two hundred hens?

—Chickens.

—Well, even chickens. That was a lot of birds. Even sparrows. Or skylarks. He must have been the only man in Europe who ever did that.

—In the world, I'd say, sir. And it happened so simple.

—It's stuffy in here, Robert said.

He led the way out to the garden. The sound of another automobile on the highway was not yet the doctor nor the ambulance. They walked along a red-sanded walk. She had had that mulch red sand brought all the way from Mullachdearg Strand in County Donegal. She loved the varied strands of Donegal: red, golden or snow-white. To right and left her roses flourished. She had a good way with roses, and with sweetpea, and even with sunflowers, those lusty brazen-faced giants.

—He was up in Dublin one day in a pub, and beside him at the counter the mournfullest man you ever saw. So the man that's gone, he was always a cheery type, said to the mournful fellow: Brighten up, the sun's shining, life's not all that bad. The mournful one says: If you were a poultry farmer with two hundred hens that wouldn't lay an egg, you'd hardly be singing songs.

The plot, said Robert St. Blaise Macmahon, thickens.

—So, says your man that's inside there, and at peace we may charitably hope, how much would you take for those hens? A shilling a hen. Done, says he, and out with two hundred shillings and buys the hens. Then he hires a van and a boy to drive it, and off with him to transport the hens. You see, he knows a man here in this very town that will give him half-a-crown a hen, a profit of fifteen pounds sterling less the hire of the van. But the journey is long and the stops plentiful at the wayside pubs, he always had a notorious drouth, and whatever happened nobody ever found out, but when he got to this town at two in the morning, the back doors of the van were swinging open.

—The birds had flown.

—Only an odd feather to be seen. And he had to pay the boy fifteen shillings to clean out the back of the van. They were never heard of again, the hens I mean. He will long be remembered for that.

—If not for anything else.

—His poor brother, too, sir. That was a sad case. Some families are, you might say, addicted to sudden death.

—Did he die in a bed?

—Worse, far worse, sir. He died on a lawnmower.

—Guard, said Robert, would you have a cup of tea? You should be writing books, instead of me.

—I was never much given to tea, sir.

—But in all the best detective stories the man from Scotland Yard always drinks a cup o' tea.

—As I told you, sir, I don't read much. But if you had the tiniest drop of whiskey to spare, I'd be grateful. It's a hot day and this uniform is a crucifixion.

They left the garden by a wicket-gate that opened through a beech-hedge on to the front lawn. The sun's reflections shot up like lightning from the lake-water around the dancing boats. Three automobiles passed, but no doctor, no ambulance, appeared. Avoiding the silent odorous room they re-entered the house by the front door. In the dining-room Robert St. Blaise Macmahon poured the whiskey for the guard, and for himself: he needed it.

—Ice, guard?

—No thank you sir. Although they say the Americans are hell for it. In everything, in tea, whiskey, and so on.

Two more automobiles passed. They listened and waited.

—You'd feel, sir, he was listening to us, like for a laugh, long nose and all. His brother was the champion gardener of all time. Better even than Miss Hynes herself, although her garden's a sight to see and a scent to smell.

—He died on a lawnmower?

—On his own lawn, sir. On one of those motor mowers. It blew up under him. He was burned to death. And you could easily say, sir, he couldn't have been at a more harmless occupation, or in a safer place.

—You could indeed, guard. Why haven't I met you before this?

—That's life, sir. Our paths never crossed. Only now for that poor fellow inside I wouldn't be here today at all.

This time it had to be the doctor and the ambulance. The wheels came scattering gravel, up the driveway.

—He was luckier than his brother, sir. He died in more comfort, in a bed. And in action, it seems.

—That's more than will be said for most of us.

The doorbell chimed: three slow cathedral tones. That chime had been bought in Bruges where they knew about bells. The guard threw back what was left of his whiskey. He said: You'll excuse me, Mr Macmahon. I'll go and put on my cap. We have work to do.

When the guard, the doctor, the ambulance, the ambulance attendants, and the corpse had, all together, taken their departure, he sprayed the bedroom with Flit, sworn foe to the housefly. It was all he could think of. It certainly changed the odour. It drifted out even into the garden, and lingered there among the roses. The assistant gardener and the kitchen girls had not yet arrived. That meant that the news was out, and that they were delaying in the town to talk about it. What sort of insufferable idiot was that woman to put him in this way into the position of being talked about, even, in the local papers, written about, and then laughed at, by clods he had always regarded with a detached and humorous, yet godlike, eye?

He sat, for the sake of the experience, on the edge of the rumpled bed from which the long-nosed corpse had just been removed. But he felt nothing of any importance. He remembered that another of those American dons had written a book, which he had slashingly reviewed, about love and death in the American novel: To his right, beyond the open windows, was her bureau desk and bookcase: old black oak, as if in stubborn isolated contradiction to the prevalent mahogany. She had never lost the stiff pride that a poor relation wears as a mask when he or she can ride high above the more common servility. She was a high-rider. It was simply incomprehensible that she, who had always so rigidly kept herself to herself, should have had a weakness for a long-nosed man who seemed to have been little better than a figure of fun. Two hundred hens, indeed!

The drawers of the bureau-bookcase were sagging open, and in disorder, as if in panic she had been rooting through them for something that nobody could find. He had seldom seen the inside of her room but, from the little he had seen and from everything he knew of her, she was no woman for untidiness or unlocked drawers. Yet in spite of her panic she had not called for aid to him, her cousin-once-removed, her employer, her benefactor. She had always stiffly, and for twenty-five years, kept him at a distance. Twenty-five years ago, in this room. She would have been eighteen, not six months escaped from the mountain valley she had been reared in, from which his parents had rescued her. He closes his eyes and, as best he can, his nose. He remembers. It is a Sunday afternoon and the house is empty except for the two of them.

He is alone in his room reading. He is reading about how Lucius Apuleius watches the servant-maid, Fotis, bending over the fire: mincing of meats and making pottage for her master and mistress, the cupboard was all set with wines and I thought I smelled the savour of some dainty meats. She had about her middle a white and clean apron, and she was girdled about her body under the paps with a swathell of red silk, and she stirred the pot and turned the meat with her fair and white hands, in such sort that with stirring and turning the same, her loins and hips did likewise move and shake, which was in my mind a comely sight to see.

Robert St. Blaise Macmahon who, at sixteen, had never tasted wine except to nibble secretively at the altar-wine when he was an acolyte in the parish church, repeats over and over again the lovely luscious Elizabethan words of Adlington's translation from the silver Latin: We did renew our venery by drinking of wine.

For at sixteen he is wax, and crazy with curiosity.

Then he looks down into the garden and there she is bending down over a bed of flowers. She is tall, rather sallow-faced, a Spanish face in an oval of close, crisp, curling dark hair. He has already noticed the determination of her long lithe stride, the sway of her hips, the pendulum swish and swing of her bright tartan pleated skirt. For a girl from the back of the mountains she has a sense of style.

She has come to this house from the Gothic grandeur of a remote valley called Glenade. Flat-topped mountains, so steep that the highest few hundred feet are sheer rock-cliffs corrugated by torrents, surround it. One such cliff, fissured in some primeval cataclysm, falls away into a curved chasm, rises again into one cold pinnacle of rock. The place is known as the Maiden's Leap, and the story is that some woman out of myth – Goddess, female devil, what's the difference? – pursued by a savage and unwanted lover, ran along the ridge of the mountain, and when faced by the chasm leaped madly to save her virtue, and did. But she didn't leap far enough to save her beautiful frail body which was shattered on the rocks below. From which her pursuer may have derived a certain perverse satisfaction.

All through her girlhood her bedroom window has made a frame for that extraordinary view. Now, her parents dead, herself adopted into the house of rich relatives as a sort of servant-maid, assistant to the aged housekeeper and in due course to succeed her, she bends over a flowerbed as Fotis had bent over the fire: O Fotis how trimely you can stir the pot, and how finely, with shaking your buttocks, you can make pottage.

Now she is standing tall and straight snipping blossoms from a fence of sweetpea. Her body is clearly outlined against the multi-coloured fence. He watches. He thinks of Fotis. He says again: We did renew our venery by drinking of wine.

When he confronts her in this very room, and makes an awkward grab at her, her arms are laden with sweetpea. So he is able to plant one kiss on cold unresponding lips. The coldness, the lack of response in a bondswoman, surprises him. She bears not the slightest resemblance to Fotis. It was the done thing, wasn't it: the young master and the servant-maid? In the decent old days in Czarist Russia the great ladies in the landed houses used to give the maids to their sons to practise on.

The sweetpea blossoms, purple, red, pink, blue, flow rather than fall to the floor. Then she hits him with her open hand, one calm, deliberate, country clout that staggers him and leaves his ear red, swollen and singing for hours. She clearly does not understand the special duties of a young female servant. In wild Glenade they didn't read Turgenev or Saltykov-Schedrin. He is humiliatingly reminded that he is an unathletic young man, a pampered only child, and that she is a strong girl from a wild mountain valley. She says: Mind your manners, wee boy. Pick up those sweetpea or I'll tell your father and mother how they came to be on the floor.

He picks up the flowers. She is older than he is. She is also taller, and she has a hand like rock. He knows that she has already noticed that he is afraid of his father.

This room was not then a bedroom. It was a pantry with one whole wall of it shelved for storing apples. He could still smell those apples, and the sweetpea. The conjoined smell of flower and fruit was stronger even than the smell of the insect-killing spray with which he had tried to banish the odour of death.

That stinging clout was her great leap, her defiance, her declaration of independence but, as in the case of the Maiden of Glenade, it had only carried her halfways. To a cousin once-removed, who never anyway had cared enough to make a second attempt, she had demonstrated that she was no chattel. But she remained a dependant, a poor relation, a housekeeper doing the bidding of his parents until they died and, after their death, continuing to mind the house, grow the roses, the sweetpea and the sunflowers. The sense of style, the long lithe swinging stride, went for nothing, just because she hadn't jumped far enough to o'erleap the meandering withering enduring ways of a small provincial town. No man in the place could publicly be her equal. She was part

Macmahon. So she had no man of her own, no place of her own. She had become part of the furniture of this house. She had no life of her own. Or so he had lightly thought.

He came and went and wrote his books, and heard her and spoke to her, but seldom really saw her except to notice that wrinkles, very faint and fine, had appeared on that Spanish face, on the strong-boned, glossy forehead, around the corners of the eyes. The crisp dark hair had touches of grey that she had simply not bothered to do anything about. She was a cypher, and a symbol in a frustrating land that had more than its share of ageing hopeless virgins. He closed his eyes and saw her as such when, in his writing, he touched satirically on that aspect of life in his pathetic country. Not that he did so any more often than he could help. For a London illustrated magazine he had once written about the country's low and late marriage rate, an article that had astounded all by its hard practicality. But as a general rule he preferred to think and to write about Stockholm or Paris or Naples or Athens, or African mountains, remote from everything. His travel books were more than travel books, and his novels really did show that travel broadened the mind. Or to think and write about the brightest gem in an America that man was doing so much to lay waste: the swamp that was no swamp but a wonderland out of a fantasy by George MacDonald, a Scottish writer whom nobody read any more, a fantasy about awaking some morning in your own bedroom, which is no longer a bedroom but the heart of the forest where every tree has its living spirit, genial or evil, evil or genial.

At that moment in his reverie the telephone rang. To the devil with it, he thought, let it ring. The enchanted swamp was all around him, the wine-coloured water just perceptibly moving, the rugged knees of the cypress trees, the white priestly birds curved brooding on high bare branches, the silence. Let it ring. It did, too. It rang and rang and refused to stop. So he walked ill-tempered to the table in the hallway where the telephone was, picked it up, silenced the ringing, heard the voice of the civic guard, and then noticed for the first conscious time the black book that he carried in his right hand.

The guard said: She's resting now. The sergeant's wife is looking after her.

—Good. That's very good.

It was a ledger-type book, eight inches by four, the pages ruled in blue, the margins in red. He must, unthinkingly, have picked it up out of the disorder in which her morning panic had left the bureau-bookcase. For the first time that panic seemed to him as comic: it wasn't every morning a maiden lady found a long-nosed lover, or something, cold between the covers. It was matter for a short story, or an episode in a novel: if it just hadn't damned well happened in his own house. What would Henry James have made of it? The art of fiction is in telling not what happened, but what should have happened. Or what should have happened somewhere else.

The guard was still talking into his left ear, telling him that the doctor said it was a clear case of heart failure. Oh, indeed it was: for the heart was a rare and undependable instrument. With his right hand he flicked at random through the black book, then, his eye caught by some words that seemed to mean something, he held the book flat, focused on those words until they were steady, and read. The handwriting was thick-rubbed, black as coal, dogged, almost printing, deliberate as if the nib had bitten into the paper. He read: Here he comes down the stairs in the morning, his double jowl red and purple from the razor, his selfish mouth pursed as tight as Mick Clinton, the miser of Glenade, used to keep the woollen sock he stored his money in when he went to the market and the horsefair of Manorhamilton. Here he comes, the heavy tread of him in his good, brown hand-made shoes, would shake the house if it wasn't as solid on its foundations as the Rock of Cashel. Old John Macmahon used to boast that his people built for eternity. Thud, thud, thud, the weight of his big flat feet. Here he comes, Gorgeous Gussie, with his white linen shirt, he should have frills on his underpants, and his blue eyeshade to show to the world, as if there was anybody to bother looking at him except myself and the domestic help, that he's a writer. A writer, God help us. About what? Who reads him? It's just as well he has old John's plunder to live on.

The black letters stood out like basalt from the white, blue-and-red lined paper. Just one paragraph she wrote to just one page and, if the paragraph didn't fully fill the page, she made, above and below the paragraph, whorls and doodles and curlicues in inks of various colours, blue, red, green, violet. She was a lonely self-delighting artist. She was, she had been, for how long, oh merciful heavens, an observer, a writer.

The guard was saying: She said to the sergeant's wife that she's too shy to face you for the present.

—Shy, he said.

He looked at the black words. They were as distinct as that long-ago clout on the side of the head: the calloused hard hand of the mountainy girl reducing the pretensions of a shy, sensitive, effeminate youth.

He said: She has good reason to be shy. It is, perhaps, a good thing that she should, at least, be shy before her employer and distant relation.

—It might be that, sir, she might mean not shy, but ashamed.

—She has also good reason for being ashamed.

—She says, Mr Macmahon, sir, that she might go away somewhere for a while.

—Shouldn't she wait for the inquest and the funeral? At any rate, she has her duties here in this house. She is, she must realise, paid in advance.

So she would run, would she, and leave him to be the single object of the laughter of the mean people of this town? In a sweating panic he gripped the telephone as if he would crush it. There was an empty hungry feeling, by turns hot, by turns cold, just above his navel. He was betraying himself to that garrulous guard who would report to the town every word he said. It was almost as if the guard could read, if he could read, those damnable black words. He gripped the phone, slippy and sweaty as it was, gulped and steadied himself, breathed carefully, in out, in out, and was once again Robert St. Blaise Macmahon, a cultivated man whose education had commenced at the famous Benedictine school at Glenstal. After all, the Jesuits no longer were what once they had been, and James Joyce had passed that way to the discredit both of himself and the Jesuits.

—Let her rest then, he said. I'll think over what she should do. I'll be busy all day, guard, so don't call me unless it's absolutely essential.

He put down the telephone, wiped his sweating hand with a white

linen handkerchief, monogrammed and ornamented with the form of
a feather embroidered in red silk. It was meant to represent a quill pen
and also to be a symbol of the soaring creative mind. That fancy handkerchief was, he considered, his one flamboyance. He wore, working,
a blue eyeshade because there were times when lamplight, and even
overbright daylight, strained his eyes. Any gentleman worthy of the
name did, didn't he, wear hand-made shoes?

On the first page of the book she had pasted a square of bright yellow paper and on it printed in red ink: Paragraphs.

In smaller letters, in Indian black ink, and in an elegant italic script,
she had written: Reflections on Robert the Riter.

Then finally, in green ink, she had printed: By his Kaptivated
Kuntry Kusin!!!

He was aghast at her frivolity. Nor did she need those three excla-
mation marks to underline her bitchiness, a withdrawn and secretive
bitchiness, malevolent among the roses and the pots and pans, over-
flowing like bile, in black venomous ink. She couldn't have been long
at this secret writing. The book was by no means full. She had skipped,
and left empty pages here and there, at random, as if she dipped her
pen and viciously wrote wherever the book happened to open. There
was no time sequence that he could discern. He read: He says he went
all the way to the States to see a swamp. Just like him. Would he go all
the way to Paris to see the sewers?

—But the base perfidy of that.

He spoke aloud, not to himself but to her.

—You always pretended to be interested when I talked about the
swamp. The shy wild deer that would come to the table to take the bit
out of your fingers when you breakfasted in the open air, the racoon
with the rings round its eyes, the alligators, the wine-coloured waters,
the white birds, the white sand on the bed of the Suwannee River. You
would sit, woman, wouldn't you, brown Spanish face inscrutable, listening, agreeing, with me, oh yes, agreeing with me in words, but,
meanly, all the time, thinking like this.

Those brief words about that small portion of his dreamworld had
wounded him. But bravely he read more. The malice of this woman of
the long-nosed chicken-losing lover must be fully explored. She was

also, by heaven, a literary critic. She wrote: Does any novelist, nowadays, top-dress his chapters with quotations from other authors? There is one, but he writes thrillers and that's different. Flat-footed Robert the Riter, with his good tweeds and his brass-buttoned yellow waistcoat, has a hopelessly old-fashioned mind. His novels, with all those sophisticated nonentities going nowhere, read as if he was twisting life to suit his reading. But then what does Robert know about life? Mamma's boy, Little Lord Fauntleroy, always dressed in the best. He doesn't know one rose from another. But a novelist should know everything. He doesn't know the town he lives in. Nor the people in it. Quotations. Balderdash.

He found to his extreme humiliation that he was flushed with fury. The simplest thing to do would be to let her go away and stay away, and then find himself a housekeeper who wasn't a literary critic, a secret carping critic, a secret lover too, a Psyche, by Hercules, welcoming by night an invisible lover to her bed. Then death stops him, and daylight reveals him, makes him visible as a comic character with a long nose, and with a comic reputation, only, for mislaying two hundred hens, and with a brother, a great gardener, who had the absurd misfortune to be burned alive on his own lawn. Could comic people belong to a family addicted to sudden death? Somewhere in all this, there might be some time the germ of a story.

But couldn't she realise what those skilfully chosen quotations meant?

—Look now, he said, what they did for George MacDonald. A procession of ideas, names, great presences, marching around the room you write in: Fletcher and Shelley, Novalis and Beddoes, Goethe and Coleridge, Sir John Suckling and Shakespeare, Lyly and Schiller, Heine and Schleiermacher and Cowley and Spenser and the Book of Judges and Jean Paul Richter and Cyril Tourneur and Sir Philip Sidney and Dekker and Chaucer and the Kabala.

But, oh Mother Lilith, what was the use of debating thus with the shadow of a secretive woman who was now resting in the tender care of the sergeant's wife who was, twenty to one, relaying the uproarious news to every other wife in the town: Glory be, did you hear the fantasticality that happened up in Mr Robert St. Blaise Macmahon's big house? Declare to God they'll never again be able to show their faces in public.

Even if she were with him, walking in this garden as he now was, and if he was foolish enough thus to argue with her, she would smile her sallow wrinkled smile, look sideways out of those dark-brown eyes and then go off alone to write in her black book: He forgot to mention the Twelve Apostles, the Clancy Brothers, and the Royal Inniskilling Fusiliers.

All her life she had resisted his efforts to make something out of her. Nor had she ever had the determination to rise and leap again, to leave him and the house and go away and make something out of herself.

He read: He's like the stuck-up high-falutin' women in that funny story by Somerville and Ross, he never leaves the house except to go to Paris. He doesn't see the life that's going on under his nose. He says there are no brothels in Dublin. But if Dublin had the best brothels in the long history of sin . . .

Do you know, now, that was not badly put. She has a certain felicity of phrase. But then she has some Macmahon blood in her, and the educational advantages that over the years this house has afforded her . . . long history of sin, he'd be afraid of his breeches to enter any of them.

He says there are no chic women in Dublin. What would he do with a chic woman if I gave him one, wrapped in cellophane, for Valentine's Day? He says he doesn't know if the people he sees are ugly because they don't make love, or that they don't make love because they're ugly. He's the world's greatest living authority, isn't he, either on love or good looks?

On another page: To think, dear God, of that flat-footed bachelor who doesn't know one end of a woman from the other, daring to write an article attacking the mountainy farmers on their twenty pitiful acres of rocks, rushes, bogpools and dunghills, for not marrying young and raising large families. Not only does he not see the people around him, he doesn't even see himself. Himself and a crazy priest in America lamenting about late marriages and the vanishing Irish. A fine pair to run in harness. The safe, sworn celibate and the fraidy-cat bachelor.

And on yet another page: That time long ago, I clouted him when

BENEDICT KIELY

he made the pass, the only time, to my knowledge, he ever tried to
prove himself a man. And he never came back for more. I couldn't very
well tell him that the clout was not for what he was trying to do but
for the stupid way he was trying to do it. A born bungler.

The doodles, whorls and curlicues wriggled like a snake-pit, black,
blue, green, red, violet, before his angry eyes. That was enough. He
would bring that black book down to the barracks, and throw it at her,
and tell her never to darken his door again. His ears boomed with
blood. He went into the dining-room, poured himself a double
whiskey, drank it slowly, breathing heavily, thinking. But no, there was
a better way. Go down to the barracks, bring her back, lavish kindness
on her, in silence suffer her to write in her book, then copy what she
writes, reshape it, reproduce it, so that some day she would see it in
print and be confounded for the jade and jezebel that she is.

With deliberate speed, majestic instancy, he walked from the
dining-room to her bedroom, tossed the book on to her bed where
she would see it on her return and know he had read it, and that her
nastiness was uncovered. He had read enough of it, too much of it:
because the diabolical effect of his reading was that he paused, with
tingling irritation, to examine his tendency to think in quotations.
Never again, thanks to her malice, would he do so, easily, automatical-
ly, and, so to speak, unthinkingly.

Coming back across the kitchen he found himself looking at his
own feet, in fine hand-made shoes, his feet rising, moving forwards,
settling again on the floor, fine flat feet. It was little benefit to see ourselves as others see us. That was, merciful God, another quotation.
That mean woman would drive him mad. He needed a change:
Dublin, Paris, Boppard on the Rhine – a little town that he loved in
the off-season when it wasn't ravished by boat-loads of American
women doing the Grand Tour. First, though, to get the Spanish maid-
en of wild Glenade back to her proper place among the roses and the
pots and pans.

The guard answered the telephone. He said: She's still resting,
Mr Macmahon, sir.

—It's imperative that I speak to her. She can't just take this lying
down.

That, he immediately knew, was a stupid thing to say. On the wall before him, strong black letters formed, commenting on his stupidity.

There was a long silence. Then she spoke, almost whispered: Yes, Robert.

—Hadn't you better get back to your place here?

—Yes, Robert. But what is my place there?

—You know what I mean. We must face this together. After all, you are half a Macmahon.

—Half a Macmahon, she said, is better than no bread.

He was shocked to fury: This is nothing to be flippant about.

—No, Robert.

—Who was this man?

—A friend of mine.

—Do you tell me so? Do you invite all your friends to my house?

—He was the only one.

—Why didn't you marry him?

—He had a wife and five children in Sudbury in England. Separated.

—That does, I believe, constitute an impediment. But who or what was he?

—It would be just like you, Robert, not even to know who he was. He lived in this town. It's a little town.

—Should I have known him?

—Shouldn't a novelist know everybody and everything?

—I'm not an authority on roses.

—You've been reading my book.

She was too sharp for him. He tried another tack: Why didn't you tell me you were having a love affair? After all, I am civilised.

—Of course you're civilised. The world knows that. But there didn't seem any necessity for telling you.

—There must be so many things that you don't feel it is necessary to tell me.

—You were never an easy person to talk to.

—All your secret thoughts. Who could understand a devious woman? Far and from the farthest coasts . . .

—There you go again. Quotations. The two-footed gramophone.

What good would it do you if you did understand?

—Two-footed, he said. Flat-footed.

He was very angry: You could have written it all out for me if you couldn't say it. All the thoughts hidden behind your brooding face. All the things you thought when you said nothing, or said something else.

—You really have been reading my book. Prying.

The silence could have lasted all of three minutes. He searched around for something that would hurt.

—Isn't it odd that a comic figure should belong to a family addicted to sudden death?

—What on earth do you mean?

Her voice was higher. Anger? Indignation?

—That nose, he said. Cyrano. Toto the Clown. And I heard about the flight of the two hundred hens.

Silence.

—And about the brother who was burned.

—They were kindly men, she said. And good to talk to. They had green fingers.

It would have gratified him if he could have heard a sob.

—I'll drive down to collect you in an hour's time.

—He loved me, she said. I suppose I loved him. He was something, in a place like this.

Silence.

—You're a cruel little boy, she said. But just to amuse you, I'll give you another comic story. Once he worked in a dog kennels in Kent in England. The people who owned the kennels had an advertisement in the local paper. One sentence read like this: Bitches in heat will be personally conducted from the railway station by Mr Dominic Byrne.

—Dominic Byrne, she said. That was his name. He treasured that clipping. He loved to laugh at himself. He died for love. That's more than most will ever do. There you are. Make what you can out of that story, you flat-footed bore.

She replaced the telephone so quietly that for a few moments he listened, waiting for more, thinking of something suitable to say.

On good days, light, reflected from the lake, seemed to brighten every nook and corner of the little town. At the end of some old narrow winding cobbled laneway there would be a vision of lake-water bright as a polished mirror. It was a graceful greystone town, elegantly laid out by some Frenchman hired by an eighteenth-century earl. The crystal river that fed the lake flowed through the town and gave space and scope for a tree-lined mall. But grace and dancing light could do little to mollify his irritation. This time, by the heavenly father, he would have it out with her, he would put her in her place, revenge himself for a long-ago affront and humiliation. Body in the bed, indeed. Two hundred hens, indeed. Swamps and sewers, indeed. Bitches in heat, indeed. She did not have a leg to stand on. Rutting, and on his time, with a long-nosed yahoo.

The Byzantine church, with which the parish priest had recently done his damnedest to disfigure the town, struck his eyes with concentrated insult. Ignorant bloody peasants. The slick architects could sell them anything: Gothic, Byzantine, Romanesque, Igloo, Kraal, Modern Cubist. The faithful paid, and the pastor made the choice.

Who would ever have thought that a lawnmower could be a Viking funeral pyre?

The barracks, a square, grey house, made ugly by barred windows and notice-boards, was beside the church. The guard, capless, the neck of his uniform jacket open, his hands in his trouser pockets, stood in the doorway. He was still perspiring. The man would melt. There was a drop to his nose: snot or sweat or a subtle blend of both. Robert St. Blaise Macmahon would never again make jokes about civic guards. He said: I've come for Miss Hynes.

—Too late, Mr Macmahon, sir. The bird has flown.

—She has what?

—Gone, sir. Eloped. Stampeded. On the Dublin train. Ten minutes ago. I heard her whistle.

—Whistle?

—The train, sir.

—But the funeral? The inquest?

—Oh, his wife and children will bury him. We phoned them.

—But the inquest?

—Her affidavit will do the job. We'll just say he dropped while visiting your house to look at the roses.

—That's almost the truth.

—The whole truth and nothing but the truth is often a bitter dose, sir.

—As I said, guard, you are a philosopher.

He remembered too late that he hadn't said that, he had just thought it.

—Thank you kindly, sir. Would you chance a cup of tea, sir? Nothing better to cool one on a hot day. Not that I like tea myself. But in this weather, you know. The hottest day, the forecast says.

Well, why not? He needed cooling. The bird had flown, sailing away from him, over the chasm, laughing triumphant eldritch laughter.

In the austere dayroom they sat on hard chairs and sipped tea.

—Nothing decent or drinkable here, sir, except a half-bottle of Sandeman's port.

—No thank you, guard. No port. The tea will suffice.

—Those are gallant shoes, sir, if you'll excuse me being so pass-remarkable. Hand-made jobs.

—Yes, hand-made.

—Costly, I'd say. But then they'd last for ever.

—Quite true, guard.

—He's coffined by now. The heat, you know.

—Don't remind me.

—Sorry, sir. But the facts of life are the facts of life. Making love one minute. In a coffin the next.

—The facts of death, guard. Alone withouten any company.

—True as you say, sir. He was a droll divil, poor Byrne, and he died droll.

—Among the roses, guard.

—It could happen to anyone, God help us. Neither the day nor the hour do we know. The oddest thing, now, happened once to the sergeant's brother that's a journalist in Dublin. This particular day he's due to travel to Limerick City to report on a flower show. But he misses the train. So he sends a telegram to ask a reporter from another newspaper to keep him a carbon. Then he adjourns to pass the day in the upstairs lounge bar of the Ulster House. Along comes the Holy Hour as they call it for jokes, when the pubs of Dublin close for a while in the early afternoon. To break up the morning boozing parties, you understand. There's nobody in the lounge except the sergeant's brother and a strange man. So the manager locks them in there to drink in peace and goes off to his lunch. And exactly halfways through the Holy Hour the stranger drops down dead. Angina. And there's me man that should be at a flower show in Limerick locked in on a licensed prem- ises, the Ulster House, during an off or illegal hour, with a dead man that he doesn't know from Adam.

—An interesting legal situation, guard.

—Oh it was squared, of course. The full truth about that couldn't be allowed out. It would be a black mark on the licence. The manager might lose his job.

—People might even criticise the quality of the drink.

—They might, sir. Some people can't be satisfied. Not that there was ever a bad drop sold in the Ulster House. Another cup, Mr Macmahon, sir.

—Thank you, guard.

—She'll come back, Mr Macmahon. Blood they say is thicker than water.

—They do say that, do they? Yet somehow, in spite of what they say, I don't think she'll be back.

On she went, leaping, flying, describing jaunty parabolas. He would, of course, have to send her money. She was entitled to some- thing legally and he could well afford to be generous beyond what the law demanded.

—So the long-nosed lover died, guard, looking at the roses.

—In a manner of speaking, sir.

—Possibly the only man, guard, who ever had the privilege. Look thy last on all things lovely.

But the guard was not aware of de la Mare.

—That's what we'll say, sir. It would be best for all. His wife and all.

And no scandal.

—Days of wine and roses, guard.

—Yes, sir. Alas, that we have nothing here but that half-bottle of Sandeman's port. She was a great lady to grow roses, sir. That's how they met in the beginning, she told me. Over roses.

A Bottle of Brown Sherry

Mr Edward came home from hospital on the second day of the second summer holidays we spent at Delaps of Monellen.

That was the year old John Considine, the stone mason, laid the black basalt flagged floor in the hallway of the hotel. While the work was going on the guests used a side-door so that old John, the crafts-man, we, the four children, the only children allowed to holiday in that sedate house, and the stuffed brown bear, the ornamental organ that wasn't meant to play, and the framed photograph of the big bearded man leaning on a long rifle and with a dead antlered stag on his shoul-ders, had the hall all to ourselves. The big man in the picture had also, John told us, shot the bear. John, as he worked, told us an awful lot.

—There's nothing, he would say, like having a trade. Even if it's only cutting thistles.

He did not intend to belittle his own craft and, indeed, his old back arched with pride at his ability to lay the stones smoothly, gently as a mother would lay a child in a cot, on their bed of resilient red sand. Sand and stones came from the coast visible across parkland and over high trees from the top windows of Monellen, and so close that the dazzle of surf and sunshine could brighten the shade of the surround-ing greenery, and on a morning after a night of gale, salt and sand blurred the window-panes.

John wore an old bowler hat that he doffed for nothing or nobody, not even for the queenly grandeur of Miss Grania Delap herself, and although his work had him bending and straightening, kneeling and rising again, the hat held its place like a confident cormorant riding one familiar wave. The local louts had nicknamed him Apey Appey for he was hairless from birth as a ha'penny apple, and he had turned his back on all organised religion because he felt embarrassed about taking his hat off in church.

But his round purple cheeks showed that he worshipped frequently and publicly in the seaside taverns. As he bent and worked he puffed the cheeks out comically and talked in spurts, not to himself, but to the stuffed bear, to the tall hunter in the picture, to the flagstones and – although they were outside the house and too far away to hear him – to the three aproned servant-maids who, in sunny moments of leisure, took their sport on a swing under an oak tree in the centre of the lawn.

Once when he knelt at work a robin hopped, picking, in from the lawn and perched on his left heel, and he chatted to the robin, apologising in the end for the cramp that compelled him to move and unsettle his guest.

Of my twin brother and myself and our two sisters, also twins, he never seemed much aware, yet he never made us feel unwelcome. So we stayed with him and carried tools for him and tried to make out who and what he was talking to.

—Aren't you smooth now as a bottle of the best, and shiny black like a well-fed crow in a good harvest? Won't the visitors be coming in droves to see you?

That was his praise for one of the flagstones.

—Don't I smell the sea when I touch you, and see the cliffs you were quarried from? If it wasn't for you and your likes the ocean would be flowing over us, and nothing but fish in Monellen, instead of priests and doctors eating lobsters. Master Gerald there, with the stag on his back like a sack of meal, was the man for the cliffs, hail or shine, gale or calm. Up there, he said, he could expand his lungs like the Lord God. There'll be rich feet and fancy shoes stepping now on you that kept the ocean from flowing over us for so long. And the silver woman looking down on the miracle.

The silver woman was a decorative bare-breasted Juno who stood

with her peacock on the top of the highest dead pipe of the mute ornamental organ.

—'Tis you has the youth in you. 'Tis you're soople.

Slowly, caressingly, he rubbed a stone with the palm of his hand,
and could have been talking to the stone or to the bouncing blonde
maid who led the others in her frolics on the swing.

The hind-legs of the dead stag were under the armpits of the hunter
and pointing up. The fore-legs were over his shoulders and pointing
down, and laced to the hind-legs. The antlered head leaned sadly backwards. In a strong thick-nibbed hand an inscription was written under
the photograph. It read like this: Carrying a deer a few miles on one's
back stimulates a glorious dinner appetite. Love from Brother Gerald
and the Maple Leaf.

—Any man, John said, who would walk with that burden to work
up an appetite would be liable to get married, no matter how much the
family was set against it. Master Gerald, my man, you took all the
strength with you the day Edward and yourself saw the light. 'Tisn't
you they'd have to send like poor Edward to the doctors of Dublin to
have things unknown injected into you.

Straightening up, stamping on a flag to test its steadiness, fixing
with both hands the bowler more firmly on his head, he looked out at
the bright lawn, the windy woods beyond, and said in a singsong to
suit the rhythm of his feet: Swing, Nora Crowley, swing, you that never
knew a father, with your hair as bright as the silver woman, and your
mother before you that could swing like a branch in the wind.

The Misses Delap tolerated my father and mother bringing four children with them into that haven for elderly ladies, golfing clergymen
and doctors, because the Misses Delap were also twins, and Mr
Edward and the absent hunter, Mr Gerald, as well. The coincidence
intrigued Miss Grania – as so well it might.

Miss Deirdre painted beautifully, we thought, and did an ivy spray
on the dining-room overmantel so real that you would have thought it
was growing there. She gave us large round sweets as big as billiard
balls – they were called, and were, gob-stoppers – and allowed us to
stand, as round-jawed as John Considine, but mute and sucking, in her

attic studio while she copied old masters out of an art book. She was a
gamey old dame in the attic and she taught my brother and myself
how to wink, but anywhere lower down in the house she was only a
silvery silent wraith. For while she might paint and wink it was Miss
Grania bought the lobsters and was boss over all and, although they
were twins, Grania seemed and behaved like the elder of the two.

Deirdre's hair was a pale natural silver but Grania, to emphasise her
empery, had tinted her hair an assertive colour you might call red, anywhere except in the presence of cooked lobsters. Those morose,
doomed-to-be-boiled-alive crustaceans weren't red, of course, when
Donnelly from the harbour would tumble five or six of them out of a
sack on to the floor of the big basement kitchen. They still wore the
secretive colours of the sea and the rock clefts that had sheltered them
in a former life, and no lost soul precipitated into eternity could have
been more bewildered than they looked as they clacked helplessly on
the floor and stared from outshot eyes at the advance of Grania. If they
saw little else in their hell or their heaven they certainly saw her. For
she brought with her the power of life and death, and she was, at any
time, and particularly before her morning toilet, a sight to catch the
eye – even of a lobster. She was a tall woman, taller than her twin or
than Mr Edward. Her tinted hair was stiff with metal curlers that, as
old John once muttered, were like hedgehogs roasted in a burning
bush.

Her face, black and yellow with wrinkles, was alarmingly different
from the creamy mask it presented later in the day.

Touching a lobster smartly with her right foot, she would say: How
now brown cow.

The high-heeled, golden-coloured shoes she wore for that ritual
were never seen at any other time of the day, and it did seem to us that
they were special shoes for touching and choosing lobsters.

—How now brown cow number two and three and four. Put the
others back in the tanks, Donnelly, and give them a chance to repent.

To find themselves keeping guests for money was a comedown in the
world for the Delaps. Miss Grania, not so much by direct words as by
continuous tyranny, never allowed the guests to forget it. She talked

often and with solemn authority about low prices for farm produce and the crushing burden of rates on the owners of landed property. The implication was that only for those two reasons no paying guest would ever have crossed the threshold of Monellen.

After high rates and low prices, the next worst thing in the degenerating world seemed to be afternoon tea.

—Quite the thing, she would say, for salesmen and their wives in commercial hotels, I'm told, but it was never the custom at Monellen.

So it was sherry or port and biscuits, or nothing at all, in the dreamy, tree-surrounded afternoons. My mother, though, seemed to be a privileged person, for when the maids were having their afternoon meal it was permitted for one of them to bring her tea in her bedroom. Perhaps that was because she was that year in an ailing and expectant condition, and Miss Grania may have hoped to coax by kindness another set of twins into the world. As it turned out, she didn't.

But old widowed Mrs Nulty, who was eighty-five if she was a day, and whose brother was a bishop, had no such expectations and no such privileges. When at one ill-guided, dyspeptic lunch-time, she turned up her nose at a bread pudding made, with currants, by Miss Deirdre, the retribution descended on her – soft-spoken but relentless.

—So they tell me, Mrs Nulty, you didn't like Miss Deirdre's bread pudding. Perhaps it would suit us mutually if next year we severed connections. There are, I'm told, many more up-to-date establishments in the village and on the sea-front.

The brother, the bishop himself, had to exert his ghostly influence to save Mrs Nulty from banishment to Sea View or Ocean Lodge. His Christian name was Alexander and, if he ever had occasion to warm his hands at the drawing-room fire, he did so, standing at the side of the fireplace, and reaching out his fingertips, to the point almost of over-balancing, towards the flames. He wouldn't stand on the hearth-rug because he thought it was made of cat-skin and, like Lord Roberts of Pretoria and many a lesser man, he couldn't stand cats.

—But how little he knew, John Considine said, and all his learning. I snared the rabbits myself. As you may see, Monellen was a place with its own character, and Grania Delap an undoubted unchallenged queen. Deirdre, in her arty attic, dabbled in oils and water-colours, but the image of Grania could only have been cast in bronze, one conquering foot on a lobster large as a turtle. One of my sisters – greatly daring – once put her foot on the pet tortoise in the garden and hoarsened her voice to say: How now brown cow. But the effect wasn't even funny, and the four of us afterwards glanced around nervously in fear of detection and banishment.

For Monellen was a happy enough place for a holiday – with good food, freedom, open parkland, a toy lake, miles of magic wood, and the stream beyond; and one of the most exciting things about it was that other dominant image, not bronze, but muscled, living oak and iron, that the mediumistic mutterings of John Considine brought forth from the picture of the hunter in the hallway. Here was a giant of a man who shot bears and stags and who once from his foreign travels had brought back with him a dangerous stockwhip with which he demonstrated, beheading daisies on the lawn at thirty paces, and making cracks that set the grazing horses on the far side of the lake galloping wild in terror.

When a boy he had, for a dare and by moonlight, gone climbing for rooks' eggs up one of the highest trees in the woods, only to find when he got to the top that the birds, more matured than he had imagined, began to caw, and some of them even flew away.

—He was so vexed, John said, it was a God's wonder he didn't sprout wings and take after them.

For another dare he went when he was fourteen through the night woods to a pub at the harbour where the trawlers tied up, and drank whiskey, John said, until it came out of his ears; and walked home sober. It seemed likely, indeed, that from an early age he had carried, if not stags, horned goats, at least, on his shoulders.

Insignificant in the shadow of that great image, Mr Edward, back from hospital, shuffled about the house. John Considine told our father about the day in the winter when the two doctors, grey grave men, had stood over Edward and decided he needed hospital treatment.

—There they stood like two curers over a side of bacon. Smoke a bit here. Slice a bit there. Streaky in one place. Fat in another. They say in the Harbour Bar that Miss Crania sent him off to fit him for marrying to continue the line of the Delaps here in Monellen. Not that she was so pleased when the man in the picture there dirtied his bib out and out by marrying a foreign woman, as dark as these flagstones, and rearing the family in the heat of Africa; and he left the place to her and never faced home again. The Delaps when they kept at home were never much the marrying kind.

Our father's comment was: That reminds me of the woman who said that to have no children was hereditary in her family.

—But not all the doses or doctors in Dublin, John said.

He addressed himself again to his auditors, the stones, who never answered back or interpolated.

—Not all the doses or doctors in Dublin could make the poor sprissawn the man his brother was. A hunched little mouse of a man, creeping about in carpet slippers and apologising to the fresh air for taking liberties with it when he breathes. There does be an unholy difference in the natures of twins.

As if he was reading the future, he looked at the two of us morosely. Our sisters were upstairs having tea with our mother.

Then we all looked far away across the lawn where poor Edward, walking on a stick, mufflered and overcoated even in the sunshine, was going timid as a mole across the grass; and Nora Crowley, propelled by the pushes of the other laughing maids relaxing after their midday meal, was swinging, skirts fluttering, in a flying curve between grass and sky, her blonde hair bright against the dark green of the woods.

The day our sisters gave us the dare and we took it, the four of us were sitting concealed on the carpet of brown needles under a big Lebanon cedar on the fringe of the woods just beyond the swing. The tree made a tent around us. It was a windy sunny day. The maids had gone back to work. From our shelter we had peeped out at Edward on a garden seat, watching them at play, an open book fallen unheeded to the ground before him. Even when they had gone running and laughing away, he didn't bother to pick up the book. Then our father joined him and they talked. While our father had a sonorous rumble of a voice that, behind his red whiskers, rolled all words into one pleasant but meaningless sound, Mr Edward had a cutting whining beep-beep that would carry each word distinctly to the moon. We only half-listened to him because in taunting whispers under the cedar, the sisters were giving us the dare that implied that, even if we were in lands where they were to be found, we would never carry stags or kill brown bears.

Mr Edward said: Our lamented father often took the two of us, Gerald and myself, with him when he went to thin young plantations. It was an exhausting and exacting task under his leadership and surveillance. He expected us to be as good almost as he was himself. Gerald often was.

—Not even whiskey then, said Nora. Just a weeshy bottle of mangy abominable sherry.

She had tasted sherry once and simultaneously discovered the word abominable.

James had reasonably pointed out that we were too young, in these puny times, to be served with whiskey in the Harbour Bar. Things had been different in Mr Gerald's days – or nights.

—Pale or brown, I said, just to be difficult.

—Mr Gerald was different, said Nora, just to be nasty.

—Wet or dry, mocked Kathleen. The two of you would be feared to go through the woods by night.

—We never used big axes, Mr Edward said, only light hand implements made by Douglas McDonnell, the land steward.

—Why don't ye go yourselves?

—We're ladies.

—We know. Young ladies don't go out at night. They might wet their bloomers in the dew. But when we had to descend to offensiveness we knew they had us beaten.

—Douglas McDonnell's wife did housekeeper and baked yeast bread, getting the yeast from a friend of hers who had a small brewery in Altnamona. When she heard her friend was dead her only comment was that now she would be ill-fixed for barm.

—We'll make it easy for ye, Nora said. You don't have to drink the sherry in the Harbour Bar. Bring the bottle back with ye to show ye were there.

—We'll help to drink it, Kathleen said.

But Nora said not her, because sherry was abominable.

Except in their differing about the desirability of sherry our two red-headed sisters were enzygotics or identical twins. We never tested their fingerprints, as we did our own, to find – insofar as, not being Scotland Yard men, we could read them – that the books could be right in saying that the coincident sequence of papillary ridge characteristics had never been found to agree even in uniovular twins.

They both married. They were certainly identical in their love of hellery. They worked as one woman in taunting us and egging us on.

We pretended to be boys from Ocean View sent down for the bottle of brown sherry for our father who was sick in bed with a cramp.

—A sufferer, said one man at the counter of the Harbour Bar, from the Ocean View six-day joint, old cow to cottage pie in six painful moves.

My brother was quick-tongued. He said: No. It was last Friday's caviar gave him the heartburn.

Thanks to his wit, our exit from the pub, clutching the bottle, was on a flowing tide of appreciative kindly laughter, and not as shame-faced as it might have been. Yet it was not the exit of a young hero who had drunk whiskey until it came out of his ears and was still sailing on a steady keel.

In that windy August of sudden squalls the dinghies moored in the harbour jumped and tossed their heels on the full turbulent tide, like hairy Connemara ponies restless at a fair. The moon leaped to drown into racing clouds, then surfaced again with a bound and a brightness that made us feel the whole world was watching ourselves and our sinful bottle. So, to hide from its silver revelations, and for the general mystery of the thing, we made the first stages of the return journey by what we called the Secret Passage. There was nothing very secret about it. It was merely a narrow sunken roadway that went inland from east to west across Monellen land to the village of Altnamona, following a right of way that the village people had used, since God knew when, as a short-cut to the shore for shellfish or seaweed for manure, or to dig the succulent sand-eels from the wide white strand when the spring tides had ebbed and the moon was full. Three stone bridges carried over it the private roads generations of Delaps had driven on. We walked steadily in silence and shadow, and were, to be honest, more than a little out of breath with fear. I carried the bottle. Like a stick in the fist it was comfort and company.

—I don't mind the nights, said James, if it's windy.

For he felt, and I with him, that no evil thing could be abroad on a night when the wind bellowed so heartily and the moon and clouds played chasing games, and the sound of the orchestra of wind and swaying branches blotted out those subtle, unnerving, unidentifiable sounds that woods and the creatures in them make on calm nights. When we climbed up by the winding steps of an old belvedere to the main avenue, and saw the house, white in moonlight and distance, a curious exhilaration had conquered our fear. Afterwards, on long talk and reflection, we realised we had been possessed. Tall pines and cypresses lined the avenue, gracefully holding back two hunch-backed hordes of red oaks. One of the pines, leaning and sailing with the wind, must have been the highest tree in the world. We looked up, and the tip of it touched and pierced the moon, and at the moment of contact James said: To hell with those girls. We'll kill the sherry.

We were thirteen years apiece and not exactly novices. We had sampled on the sly everything we found at home in sideboard or undrained glass. As altar boys in the parish church we had nipped at the altar wine. Once, too, after a hasty gulp of whiskey James claimed that he had had in the bathroom the most comical double vision.

At my second gulp of the grocer's sherry I made a measured statement about the superiority of altar wine.

James was barking like a dog at the still impaled moon.

—Sure as God, he said, that was the tree he went up for the rooks' eggs.

—It tastes bloody, I said, but at least it's warm, and what better could you hope for from the Harbour Bar?

—Show me a bear and I'll shoot it and stuff it, he shouted. Show me a stag and I'll carry it to Miss Grania. How now brown cow?

He stamped his feet like a dancing Indian and howled into the blustery warm wind. We wrestled for the last drop of the brown sherry, and he had it and drank it, and tossed the bottle off spinning to some place where it fell in silence. We ran round and round in circles shouting about bears and lobsters, brown cows and stags. Then, James leading, we climbed the tree.

We went up easily into the light, regularly spaced branches as convenient as the rungs of a ladder. It was a comfortable tree to climb and for a while the swaying motion had a most comfortable effect on bellies warm with the cheap rough wine. Patterns of light and shadow, of pasture, tilled fields, woods, laid themselves out below us; and the lake was a glittering circle. Heads in the wild clouds, we turned dazzled eyes from the moon, and rested at the top of the tree, looked down at the lake and saw the moon again, and saw the sight, and thought at first that we were mad in the head with drink.

In days before the Delaps had made money in milling and bought the land, some eighteenth-century lord had brought from London a wandering Italian to plan that lake and the gazebo beside it. In classical afternoons, the lord and his ladies and friends would have been at their ease on the flat, tiled, octagonal roof. There now, in their space, on a stone seat was Mr Edward, as many overcoats on him as an onion, his head bent, his mouth to the nipple of a living enlarged Juno who had stepped down, leaving her peacock behind her, from the organ in the hallway: of Nora Crowley, before God, that never knew a father, and her mother before her that could swing like a branch in the wind and not a coat in the world on her, or a rag at all higher than her belly button.

She was laughing and tossing her blonde hair back, and pretending to push him away.

Hunched with the weight of his coats he was trotting after her round and round the octagon. They were back again at the stone seat. He was kneeling before her and cutting all sorts of capers. They were circling the roof again. We could hear nothing except the wind but we could see that she was still laughing. We laughed a little ourselves, but in sadness and mystery, because we felt sorry for Edward who had never frightened horses with a stockwhip. Yet we would have gone on watching, held by the night of wind and moon and by those antics that seemed to be part of it, if our father's voice hadn't bellowed up at us from the avenue: Come down, you misbegotten monkeys. Come down, you niggering night-owls. What games are you playing up there?

Juno, startled by mistake, vanished with a whisk, like a fish frightened from a clear pool into the shelter of reeds and rocks. Poor many-coated slow-moving Edward was left alone on the eighteenth-century octagon. We looked down into gloom and shadow, and the sherry settled, and our stomachs turned over at the prospect of descending, feet feeling for dark branches, to explain to our father where we had been and what we had been doing on the top of the tree.

—Bird-nesting, said James. Remember we were bird-nesting. For owls' eggs.

I repeated queasily: Bird-nesting.

The thought of soft eggs made me feel ill.

—Go carefully, my father bawled. Don't break your necks.

No cautionary words were needed. We were sick and shivering, and most anxious about our necks. The tree below us was the pit of darkness. When we stepped painfully from the lowest branches, and I opened my mouth to talk about bird-nesting for owl's eggs, release of tension struck me like a kick in the ribs and out came the sherry, not, alas, through my ears and a little the worse for wear. It spattered the grass and pine needles at my father's feet.

—Arboreal activities by moonlight, he was beginning to say. The woods stank of sour wine.

—Lord God what a reek, he said. Come home quick and wash your teeth before you put me off the drink for life.

The idea seemed to amuse him. So James, always an opportunist, snatched the chance of the moment to rattle out a doctored description of the sight we had seen while bird-nesting.

—He was sitting with Nora Crowley on the bench on the gazebo.

—By God and was he? By the bright silvery light of the moon. And what would he be at there?

—He had his arm round her and he was kissing her.

—Oh, sound man. Begod modern medicine can work the wonders.

He laughed a little, just as we had, and then stopped laughing. He said, half to himself: Get married or something quickly the four of you, and don't end up lost like poor Edward.

Absent-mindedly, and with a friendly thump apiece on the shoulder blades he left us at the foot of the back-stairs and we knew that he had, in private, to tell our mother all about it, and that there wouldn't be much more said about where the sherry that had bespattered the pine needles had come from.

Our sisters thought it the joke of the world when we told them precisely what Mr Edward had been kissing.

—Like a baby, they said.

And there were no secrets, not even the moon's secrets, to be kept from bald John Considine. On his knees, smoothing the listening flag-stones, he would go off into fits of shrill giggles and mutters which we, most efficient receiving sets, caught and elucidated: A bottle of brown sherry for two bad boys and a doll to play with for the third. They'll have to send him to the Dublin doctors again to have something else done to him to keep him in the house at night. Anyway, 'twas like the casting of a spell, 'twas the magic of having too many twins about the one house. 'Twas enough to bring Mr Gerald back over the seas to take possession of the place he owned. Wasn't there a man in Altnamona who talked like a Russian although he was never outside the parish?

So the hunter, we heard, had come back from Africa, or wherever he was, or stepped, stag on shoulders, out of the picture in the hallway, to walk in the stormy moonlit woods. We had more fellow feeling than ever for Edward because we knew that he wasn't the only man, on that night of gale and running moon, to be possessed by his brother's spirit. It was more than sherry had sent us climbing, and it was something more than our own efforts that had brought us safely down into dark-ness from the remote top of that tree.

When, at art in the attic, we asked Miss Deirdre about Mr Gerald, she wept a little tear and told us she often tried to get in touch with him by clairvoyance or telekinesis. She explained to us about clairvoy-ance and telekinesis. She said: You may think it impossible with your harsh practical young minds. But I assure you children that I have in my time seen some very remarkable things. When we were at Dover once there was a lady who had a crystal. This colonel asked her about his son who was somewhere at sea, out China way. The lady described him as having or not having a moustache, whichever was wrong, and said he was cleaning a bicycle. They thought this was a poor show. But shortly afterwards the colonel got a letter with a photograph showing his son either with or without a moustache, whichever the lady had said, and saying that as they were near port, and as he had heard the roads were good in China, he hoped to get a run on his bicycle. Then another lady whose husband was in South Africa was told by the lady with the crystal that her husband was on a pile of boxes in a lake. This, of course, sounded most unlikely, but the lady heard by the next post that there had been a cloudburst, and the only dry place he could get to sit on was a pile of empty ammunition cases . . .

She talked on for a long time.

Grania of the Lobsters, though, was a sceptic, and next year, summarily dismissed, swinging Nora Crowley was gone forever from Monellen.

A Ball of Malt and Madame Butterfly

On a warm but not sunny June afternoon on a crowded Dublin street, by no means one of the city's most elegant streets, a small hotel, a sort of bed-and-breakfast place, went on fire. There was pandemonium at first, more panic than curiosity in the crowd. It was a street of decayed Georgian houses, high and narrow, with steep wooden staircases, and cluttered small shops on the ground floors: all great nourishment for flames. The fire, though, didn't turn out to be serious. The brigade easily contained and controlled it. The panic passed, gave way to curiosity, then to indignation and finally, alas, to laughter about the odd thing that had happened when the alarm was at its worst.

This was it.

From a window on the top-most floor a woman, scantily-clad, puts her head out and waves a patchwork bed coverlet, and screams for help. The stairway, she cries, is thick with smoke, herself and her husband are afraid to face it. On what would seem to be prompting from inside the room, she calls down that they are a honeymoon couple up from the country. That would account fairly enough for their still being in bed on a warm June afternoon.

The customary ullagone and ullalu goes up from the crowd. The fire-engine ladder is aimed up to the window. A fireman begins to run up the ladder. Then suddenly the groom appears in shirt and trousers, and barefooted. For, to the horror of the beholders, he makes his bare feet visible by pushing the bride back into the room, clambering first out of the window, down the ladder like a monkey, although he is a fairly corpulent man; with monkey-like agility dodging round the ascending fireman, then disappearing through the crowd. The people, indignant enough to trounce him, are still too concerned with the plight of the bride, and too astounded to seize him. The fireman ascends to the nuptial casement, helps the lady through the window and down the ladder, gallantly offering his jacket which covers some of her. Then when they are halfways down, the fireman, to the amazement of all, is seen to be laughing right merrily, the bride vituperating. But before they reach the ground she also is laughing. She is brunette, tall, but almost Japanese in appearance, and very handsome. A voice says: If she's a bride, I can see no confetti in her hair.

She has fine legs which the fireman's jacket does nothing to conceal and which she takes pride, clearly, in displaying. She is a young woman of questionable virginity and well known to the firemen. She is the toast of a certain section of the town to whom she is affectionately known as Madame Butterfly, although unlike her more famous namesake she has never been married, nor cursed by an uncle bonze for violating the laws of the gods of her ancestors. She has another registered, name: her mother's name. What she is her mother was before her, and proud of it.

The bare-footed fugitive was not, of course, a bridegroom, but a long-established married man with his wife and family and a prosperous business in Longford, the meanest town in Ireland. For the fun of it the firemen made certain that the news of his escapade in the June afternoon got back to Longford. They were fond of, even proud of, Butterfly, as were many other men who had nothing at all to do with the quenching of fire.

But one man loved the pilgrim soul in her and his name was Pike Hunter.

Like Borgnefesse, the buccaneer of St. Malo on the Rance, who had a buttock shot or sliced off in action on the Spanish Main, Pike Hunter had a lopsided appearance when sitting down. Standing up he was as straight and well-balanced as a man could be: a higher civil servant approaching the age of forty, a shy bachelor, reared, nourished and guarded all his life by a trinity of upper-middle-class aunts. He was pink-faced, with a little fair hair left to emphasise early baldness, mild in his ways, with a slight stutter, somewhat afraid of women. He wore always dark-brown suits with a faint red stripe, dark-brown hats, rimless spectacles, shiny square-toed brown hand-made shoes with a wide welt. In summer, even on the hottest day, he carried a raincoat folded over his arm, and a rolled umbrella. When it rained he unfolded and wore the raincoat and opened and raised the umbrella. He suffered mildly from hay fever. In winter he belted himself into a heavy brown overcoat and wore galoshes. Nobody ever had such stiff white shirts. He favoured brown neckties distinguished with a pearl-headed pin. Why he sagged to one side, just a little to the left, when he sat down, I never knew. He had never been sliced or shot on the Spanish Main.

But the chance of a sunny still Sunday afternoon in Stephen's Green and Grafton Street, the select heart or soul of the city's south side, made a changed man out of him.

He had walked at his ease through the Green, taking the sun gratefully, blushing when he walked between the rows of young ladies lying back in deck-chairs. He blushed for two reasons: they were reclining, he was walking; they were as gracefully at rest as the swans on the lake, he was awkwardly in motion, conscious that his knees rose too high, that his sparse hair – because of the warmth he had his hat in his hand – danced long and ludicrously in the little wind, that his shoes squeaked. He was fearful that his right toe might kick his left heel, or vice versa, and that he would fall down and be laughed at in laughter like the sound of silver bells. He was also alarmingly aware of the bronze knees, and more than knees, that the young ladies exposed as they leaned back and relaxed in their light summer frocks. He would honestly have liked to stop and enumerate those knees, make an inventory – he was in the Department of Statistics; perhaps pat a few here and there. But the fearful regimen of that trinity of aunts forbade him even to glance sideways, and he stumbled on like a winkered horse, demented by the flashing to right and to left of bursting globes of bronze light.

Then on the park pathway before him, walking towards the main gate and the top of Grafton Street, he saw the poet. He had seen him before, but only in the Abbey Theatre and never on the street. Indeed it seemed hardly credible to Pike Hunter that such a man would walk on the common street where all ordinary or lesser men were free to place their feet. In the Abbey Theatre the poet had all the strut and style of a man who could walk with the gods, the Greek gods that is, not the gods in the theatre's cheapest seats. His custom was to enter by a small stairway, at the front of the house and in full view of the audience, a few moments before the lights dimmed and the famous gong sounded and the curtain rose. He walked slowly, hands clasped behind his back, definitely balancing the prone brow oppressive with its mind, the eagle head aloft and crested with foaming white hair. He would stand, his back to the curtain and facing the house. The chatter would cease, the fiddlers in the orchestra would saw with diminished fury. Some of the city wits said that what the poet really did at those times was to count the empty seats in the house and make a rapid reckoning of the night's takings. But their gibe could not diminish the majesty of those entrances, the majesty of the stance of the man. And there he was now, hands behind back, noble head high, pacing slowly, beginning the course of Grafton Street. Pike Hunter walked behind him, suiting his pace to the poet's, to the easy deliberate rhythms of the early love poetry: I would that we were, my beloved, white birds on the foam of the sea. There is a queen in China or, maybe, it's in Spain.

They walked between the opulent windows of elegant glittering shops, doors closed for Sunday. The sunshine had drawn the people from the streets: to the park, to the lush green country, to the seaside. Of the few people they did meet, not all of them seemed to know who the poet was, but those who did know saluted quietly, with a modest and unaffected reverence, and one young man with a pretty girl on his arm stepped off the pavement, looked after the poet and clearly whispered to the maiden who it was that had just passed by the way. Stepping behind him at a respectful distance Pike felt like an acolyte behind a celebrant and regretted that there was no cope or cloak of cloth of gold of which he could humbly carry the train.

So they sailed north towards the Liffey, leaving Trinity College, with Burke standing haughty-headed and Goldsmith sipping at his honeypot of a book, to the right, and the Bank and Grattan orating

Esto Perpetua, to the left, and Thomas Moore of the Melodies, brown, stooped and shabby, to the right; and came into Westmoreland Street where the wonder happened. For there approaching them came the woman Homer sung: old and grey and, perhaps, full of sleep, a face much and deeply lined and haggard, eyes sunken, yet still the face of the queen she had been when she and the poet were young and they had stood on the cliffs on Howth Head, high above the promontory that bears the Baily Lighthouse as a warning torch and looks like the end of the world; and they had watched the soaring of the gulls and he wished that he and she were only white birds, my beloved, buoyed out on the foam of the sea. She was very tall. She was not white, but all black in widow's weeds for the man she had married when she wouldn't marry the poet. Her black hat had a wide brim and, from the brim, an old-fashioned veil hung down before her face. The pilgrim soul in you, and loved the sorrows of your changing face.

Pike stood still, fearing that in a dream he had intruded on some holy place. The poet and the woman moved dreamlike towards each other then stood still, not speaking, not saluting, at opposite street corners where Fleet Street comes narrowly from the east to join Westmoreland Street. Then still not speaking, not saluting, they turned into Fleet Street. When Pike tiptoed to the corner and peered around he saw that they had walked on opposite sides of the street for, perhaps, thirty paces, then turned at right angles, moved towards each other, stopped to talk in the middle of the street where a shaft of sunlight had defied the tall overshadowing buildings. Apart from themselves and Pike that portion of the town seemed to be awesomely empty; and there Pike left them and walked in a daze by the side of the Liffey to a pub called The Dark Cow. Something odd had happened to him: poetry, a vision of love?

It so happened that on that day Butterfly was in the Dark Cow, as, indeed, she often was: just Butterfly and Pike, and Jody with the red carbuncled face who owned the place and was genuinely kind to the girls of the town, and a few honest dockers who didn't count because they had money only for their own porter and were moral men, loyal to wives or sweethearts. It wasn't the sort of place Pike frequented. He had never seen Butterfly before: those odd slanting eyes, the glistening highpiled black hair, the well-defined bud of a mouth, the crossed legs, the knees that outclassed to the point of mockery all the bronze globes in Stephen's Green. Coming on top of his vision of the poet and the woman, all this was too much for him, driving him to a reckless courage that would have flabbergasted the three aunts. He leaned on the counter. She sat in an alcove that was a sort of throne for her, where on busier days she sat surrounded by her sorority. So he says to Jody whom he did not yet know as Jody: May I have the favour of buying the lady in the corner a drink?

—That you may, and more besides.

—Please ask her permission. We must do these things properly.

—Oh there's a proper way of doing everything, even screwing a goose.

But Jody, messenger of love, walks to the alcove and formally asks the lady would she drink if the gentleman at the counter sends it over. She will. She will also allow him to join her. She whispers: Has he any money?

—Loaded, says Jody.

—Send him over so. Sunday's a dull day.

Pike sits down stiffly, leaning a little away from her, which seems to her quite right for him as she has already decided that he's a shy sort of man, upper class, but shy, not like some. He excuses himself from intruding. She says: You're not inthrudin'.

He says he hasn't the privilege of knowing her name.

Talks like a book, she decides, or a play in the Gaiety.

—Buttherfly, she says.

—Butterfly, he says, is a lovely name.

—Me mother's name was Trixie, she volunteers.

—Was she dark like you?

—Oh, a natural blonde and very busty, well developed, you know. She danced in the old Tivoli where the newspaper office is now. I'm neat, not busty.

To his confusion she indicates, with hands moving in small curves, the parts of her that she considers are neat. But he notices that she has shapely long-fingered hands and he remembers that the poet had admitted that the small hands of his beloved were not, in fact, beautiful. He is very perturbed.

—Neat, she says, and well-made. Austin McDonnell, the fire-brigade chief, says that he read in a book that the best sizes and shapes would fit into champagne glasses.

He did wonder a little that a fire-brigade chief should be a quotable authority on female sizes and shapes, and on champagne glasses. But then and there he decided to buy her champagne, the only drink fit for such a queen who seemed as if she came, if not from China, at any rate from Japan.

—Champagne, he said.

—Bubbly, she said. I love bubbly.

Jody dusted the shoulders of the bottle that on his shelves had waited a long time for a customer. He unwired the cork. The cork and the fizz shot up to the ceiling.

—This, she said, is my lucky day.

—The divine Bernhardt, said Pike, had a bath in champagne presented to her by a group of gentlemen who admired her.

—Water, she said, is better for washing.

But she told him that her mother who knew everything about actresses had told her that story, and told her that when, afterwards, the gentlemen bottled the contents of the bath and drank it, they had one bottleful too many. He was too far gone in fizz and love's frenzy to feel embarrassed. She was his discovery, his oriental queen.

He said: You're very oriental in appearance. You could be from Japan.

She said: My father was, they say. A sailor. Sailors come and go.

She giggled. She said: That's a joke. Come and go. Do you see it?

Pike saw it. He giggled with her. He was a doomed man.

She said: Austin McDonnell says that if I was in Japan I could be a geisha girl if I wasn't so tall. That's why they call me Butterfly. It's the saddest story. Poor Madame Buttherfly died that her child could be happy across the sea. She married a sailor, too, an American lieutenant. They come and go. The priest, her uncle, cursed her for marrying a Yank.

—The priests are good at that, said Pike who, because of his reading allowed himself, outside office hours, a soupçon of anticlericalism.

Touched by Puccini they were silent for a while, sipping champagne. With every sip Pike realised more clearly that he had found
what the poet, another poet, an English one, had called the long-await-
ed long-expected spring, he knew his heart had found a time to sing,
the strength to soar was in his spirit's wing, that life was full of a triumphant sound and death could only be a little thing. She was good
on the nose, too. She was wise in the ways of perfume. The skin of her
neck had a pearly glow. The three guardian aunts were as far away as
the moon. Then one of the pub's two doors – it was a corner house –
opened with a crash and a big man came in, well drunk, very jovial.
He wore a wide-brimmed grey hat. He walked to the counter. He said:
Jody, old bootlegger, old friend of mine, old friend of Al Capone, serve
me a drink to sober me up.

—Austin, said Jody, what will it be?

—A ball of malt, the big man said, and Madame Butterfly.

—That's my friend, Austin, she said, he always says that for a joke.

Pike whose face, with love or champagne or indignation, was taut
and hot all over, said that he didn't think it was much of a joke.

—Oh, for janey's sake, Pike, be your age.

She used his first name for the first time. His eyes were moist.

—For Janey's sake, it's a joke. He's a father to me. He knew my
mother.

—He's not Japanese.

—Mind your manners. He's a fireman.

—Austin, she called. Champagne. Pike Hunter's buying champagne.

Pike bought another bottle, while Austin towered above them,
swept the wide-brimmed hat from his head in a cavalier half-circle,
dropped it on the head of Jody, whose red carbuncled face was thus
half-extinguished. Butterfly giggled. She said: Austin, you're a scream.
He knew Trixie, Pike. He knew Trixie when she was the queen of the
boards in the old Tivoli.

Sitting down, the big man sang in a ringing tenor: For I knew Trixie
when Trixie was a child.

He sipped at his ball of malt. He sipped at a glass of Pike's champagne. He said: It's a great day for the Irish. It's a great day to break a

fiver. Butterfly, dear girl, we fixed the Longford lout. He'll never leave Longford again. The wife has him tethered and spancelled in the haggard. We wrote poison-pen letters to half the town, including the parish priest.

—I never doubted ye, she said. Leave it to the firemen, I said.

—The Dublin Fire Brigade, Austin said, has as long an arm as the Irish Republican Army.

—Austin, she told Pike, died for Ireland.

He sipped champagne. He sipped whiskey. He said: Not once, but several times. When it was neither popular nor profitable. By the living God we was there when we was wanted. Volunteer McDonnell, at your service.

His bald head shone and showed freckles. His startlingly blue eyes were brightened and dilated by booze. He said: Did I know Trixie, light on her feet as the foam on the fountain? Come in and see the horses. That's what we used to say to the girls when I was a young fireman. Genuine horsepower the fire-engines ran on then, and the harness hung on hooks ready to drop on the horses as the firemen descended the greasy pole. And where the horses were, the hay and the straw were plentiful enough to make couches for Cleopatra. That was why we asked the girls in to see the horses. The sailors from the ships, homeless men all, had no such comforts and conveniences. They used to envy us. Butterfly, my geisha girl, you should have been alive then. We'd have shown you the jumps.

Pike was affronted. He was almost prepared to say so and take the consequences. But Butterfly stole his thunder. She stood up, kissed the jovial big man smack on the bald head and then, as light on her feet as her mother ever could have been, danced up and down the floor, tight hips bouncing, fingers clicking, singing: I'm the smartest little geisha in Japan, in Japan. And the people call me Rolee Polee Nan, Polee Nan.

Drowning in desire, Pike forgot his indignation and found that he was liking the man who could provoke such an exhibition. Breathless, she sat down again, suddenly kissed Pike on the cheek, said: I love you too. I love champagne. Let's have another bottle.

They had.

—Rolee Polee Nan, she sang as the cork and the fizz ascended.

—A great writer, a Russian, Pike said, wrote that his ideal was to be idle and to make love to a plump girl.

—The cheek of him. I'm not plump. Turkeys are plump. I love being tall, with long legs.

Displaying the agility of a trained high-kicker with hinges in her hips she, still sitting, raised her shapely right leg, up and up as if her toes would touch the ceiling, up and up until stocking-top, suspender, bare thigh and a frill of pink panties, showed. Something happened to Pike that had nothing at all to do with poetry or Jody's champagne. He held Butterfly's hand. She made a cat's cradle with their fingers and swung the locked hands pendulum-wise. She sang: Janey Mac, the child's a black, what will we do on Sunday? Put him to bed and cover his head and don't let him up until Monday.

Austin had momentarily absented himself for gentlemanly reasons. From the basement jakes his voice singing rose above the soft inland murmur of falling water: Oh my boat can lightly float in the heel of wind and weather, and outrace the smartest hooker between Galway and Kinsale.

The dockers methodically drank their pints of black porter and paid no attention. Jody said: Time's money. Why don't the two of you slip upstairs. Your heads would make a lovely pair on a pillow.

Austin was singing: Oh she's neat, oh she's sweet, she's a beauty every line, the Queen of Connemara is that bounding barque of mine.

He was so shy, Butterfly said afterwards, that he might have been a Christian Brother and a young one at that, although where or how she ever got the experience to enable her to make the comparison, or why she should think an old Christian Brother less cuthallacht than a young one, she didn't say. He told her all about the aunts and the odd way he had been reared and she, naturally, told Austin and Jody and all her sorority. But they were a kind people and no mockers, and Pike never knew, Austin told me, that Jody's clientele listened with such absorbed interest to the story of his life, and of his heart and his love-making. He was something new in their experience, and Jody's stable of girls had experienced a lot, and Austin a lot more, and Jody more than the whole shebang, and all the fire-brigade, put together.

For Jody, Austin told me, had made the price of the Dark Cow in a basement in Chicago. During the prohibition, as they called it, although what they prohibited it would be hard to say. He was one of five brothers from the bogs of Manulla in the middle of nowhere in the County of Mayo. The five of them emigrated to Chicago. When Al Capone and his merry men discovered that Jody and his brothers had the real true secret about how to make booze, and to make it good, down they went into the cellar and didn't see daylight or breathe fresh air, except to surface to go to Mass on Sundays, until they left the USA. They made a fair fortune. At least four of them did. The fifth was murdered.

Jody was a bachelor man and he was good to the girls. He took his pleasures with them as a gentleman might, with the natural result that he was poxed to the eyebrows. But he was worth more to them than the money he quite generously paid after every turn or trick on the rumpled, always unmade bed in the two-storeyed apartment above the pub. He was a kind uncle to them. He gave them a friendly welcome, a place to sit down, free drink and smokes and loans, or advances for services yet to be rendered, when they were down on their luck. He had the ear of the civic guards and could help a girl when she was in trouble. He paid fines when they were unavoidable, and bills when they could no longer be postponed, and had an aunt who was reverend mother in a home for unmarried mothers and who was, like her nephew, a kindly person. Now and again, like the Madame made immortal by Maupassant, he took a bevy or flock of the girls for a day at the seaside or in the country. A friend of mine and myself, travelling into the granite mountains south of the city, to the old stone-cutters' villages of Lackan and Ballyknockan where there were aged people who had never seen Dublin, thirty miles away, and never wanted to, came upon a most delightful scene in the old country pub in Lackan. All around the bench around the walls sat the mountainy men, the stone-cutters, drinking their pints. But the floor was in the possession of a score of wild girls, all dancing together, resting off and on for more drink, laughing, happy, their gaiety inspired and directed by one man in the middle of the floor: red-faced, carbuncled, oily black hair sleeked down and parted up the middle in the style of Dixie Dean, the famous soccer centre-forward whom Jody so much admired. All the drinks were on generous Jody.

So in Jody's friendly house Pike had, as he came close to forty years, what he never had in the cold abode of the three aunts: a home with a father, Austin, and a brother, Jody, and any God's amount of sisters; and Butterfly who, to judge by the tales she told afterwards, was a motherly sort of lover to him and, for a while, a sympathetic listener. For a while, only: because nothing in her birth, background, rearing or education, had equipped her to listen to so much poetry and talk about poetry.

—Poor Pike, she'd say, he'd puke you with poethry. Poethry's all very well, but.

She had never worked out what came after that qualifying: But.

—Give us a bar of a song, Austin. There's some sense to singing. But poethry. My heart leaps up when I behold a rainbow in the sky. On Linden when the sun was low. The lady of Shalott left the room to go to the pot. Janey preserve us from poethry.

He has eyes, Jody told Austin and myself, for no girl except Butterfly. Reckon, in one way, we can't blame him for that. She sure is the smartest filly showing in this paddock. But there must be moderation in all things. Big Anne, now, isn't bad, nor her sister, both well-built Sligo girls and very co-operative, nor Joany Maher from Waterford, nor Patty Daley from Castleisland in the County Kerry who married the Limey in Brum but left him when she found he was as queer as a three-dollar bill. And what about little Red Annie Byrne from Kilkenny City, very attractive if it just wasn't for the teeth she lost when the cattleman that claimed he caught gonorrhoea from her gave her an unmerciful hammering in Cumberland Street. We got him before he left town. We cured more than his gonorrhoea.

—But, Austin said, when following your advice, Jody, and against my own better judgment, I tried to explain all that to Pike, what does he do but quote to me what the playboy of the Abbey Theatre, John M. Synge, wrote in a love poem about counting queens in Glenmacnass in the Wicklow mountains.

—In the Wicklow mountains, said Jody. Queens! With the smell of the bog and the peat smoke off them.

Austin, a great man, ever, to sing at the top of his tenor voice about Dark Rosaleen and the Queen of Connemara and the County of Mayo, was a literary class of a fireman. That was one reason why Pike and himself got on so well together, in spite of that initial momentary misunderstanding about the ball of malt and Madame Butterfly.

—Seven dog days, Austin said, the playboy said he let pass, he and his girl, counting queens in Glenmacnass. The queens he mentions, Jody, you never saw, even in Chicago.

—Never saw daylight in Chicago.

—The Queen of Sheba, Austin said, and Helen, and Maeve the warrior queen of Connacht, and Deirdre of the Sorrows and Gloriana that was the great Elizabeth of England and Judith out of the Bible that chopped the block of Holofernes.

—All, said Jody, in a wet glen in Wicklow. A likely bloody story.

—There was one queen in the poem that had an amber belly.

—Jaundice, said Jody. Or Butterfly herself that's as sallow as any Jap. Austin, you're a worse lunatic than Pike.

—But in the end, Jody, his own girl was the queen of all queens. They were dead and rotten. She was alive.

—Not much of a compliment to her, Jody said, to prefer her to a cartload of corpses.

—Love's love, Jody. Even the girls admit that. They've no grudge against him for seeing nobody but Butterfly.

—They give him a fool's pardon. But no doll in the hustling game, Austin, can afford to spend all her time listening to poetry. Besides, girls like a variety of pricks. Butterfly's no better or worse than the next. When Pike finds that out he'll go crazy. If he isn't crazy already.

That was the day, as I recall, that Butterfly came in wearing the fancy fur coat – just a little out of season. Jody had, for some reason or other, given her a five-pound note. Pike knew nothing about that. And Jody told her to venture the five pounds on a horse that was running at the Curragh of Kildare, that a man in Kilcullen on the edge of the Curragh had told him that the jockey's wife had already bought her ball dress for the victory celebration. The Kilcullen man knew his onions, and his jockeys, and shared his wisdom only with a select few so as to keep the odds at a good twenty to one.

—She's gone out to the bookie's, said Jody, to pick up her winnings. We'll have a party tonight.

Jody had a tenner on the beast.

—She could invest it, said Austin, if she was wise. The day will come when her looks will go.

—Pike might propose to her, said Jody. He's mad enough for anything.

—The aunts would devour him. And her.

—Here she comes, Jody said. She invested her winnings on her fancy back.

She had too, and well she carried them in the shape of pale or silver musquash, and three of her sorority walked behind her like ladies-in-waiting behind the Queen of England. There was a party in which even the dockers joined, but not Pike, for that evening and night one of his aunts was at death's door in a nursing home, and Pike and the other two aunts were by her side. He wasn't to see the musquash until he took Butterfly on an outing to the romantic hill of Howth where the poet and the woman had seen the white birds. That was the last day Pike ever took Butterfly anywhere. The aunt recovered. They were a thrawn hardy trio.

Pike had become a devotee. Every day except Sunday he lunched in Jody's, on a sandwich of stale bread and leathery ham and a glass of beer, just on the off-chance that Butterfly might be out of the doss and abroad, and in Jody's, at that, to her, unseasonable hour of the day. She seldom was, except when she was deplorably short of money. In the better eating places on Grafton Street and Stephen's Green, his colleagues absorbed the meals that enabled higher civil servants to face up to the afternoon and the responsibilities of State: statistics, land commission, local government, posts and telegraphs, internal revenue. He had never, among his own kind, been much of a mixer: so that few of his peers even noticed the speed with which, when at five in the evening the official day was done, he took himself, and his hat and coat and umbrella, and legged it off to Jody's: in the hope that Butterfly might be there, bathed and perfumed and ready for wine and love.

Sometimes she was. Sometimes she wasn't. She liked Pike. She didn't deny it. She was always an honest girl, as her mother, Trixie, had been before her – so Austin said when he remembered Trixie who had died in a hurry, of peritonitis. But, Janey Mac, Butterfly couldn't have Pike Hunter for breakfast, dinner, tea and supper, and nibblers as well, all the livelong day and night. She still, as Jody said, had her first million to make, and Pike's inordinate attachment was coming between her and the real big business, as when, say, the country cattle men were in town for the market. They were the men who knew how to get rid of the money.

—There is this big cattle man, she tells Austin once, big he is in every way, who never knows or cares what he's spending. He's a gift and a godsend to the girls. He gets so drunk that all you have to do to humour him is play with him a little in the taxi going from pub to pub and see that he gets safely to his hotel. The taximen are on to the game and get their divy out of the loot.

One wet and windy night, it seems, Butterfly and this philanthropist are flying high together, he on brandy, she on champagne, for which that first encounter with Pike has given her a ferocious drouth. In the back of the taxi touring from pub to pub, the five pound notes are flowing out of your man like water out of a pressed sponge. Butterfly is picking them up and stuffing them into her handbag, but not all of them. For this is too good and too big for any taximan on a fair percentage basis. So for every one note she puts into her handbag she stuffs two or three down into the calf-length boots she is wearing against the wet weather. She knows, you see, that she is too far gone in bubbly to walk up the stairs to her own room, that the taximan, decent fellow, will help her up and then, fair enough, go through her bag and take his cut. Which, indeed, in due time he does. When she wakes up, fully clothed, in the morning on her own bed, and pulls off her boots, her ankles, what with the rain that had dribbled down into her boots, are poulticed and plastered with notes of the banks of Ireland and of England, and one moreover of the Bank of Bonnie Scotland.

—Rings on my fingers, she says, and bells on my toes.

That was the gallant life that Pike's constant attendance was cutting her off from. She also hated being owned. She hated other people thinking that she was owned. She hated like hell when Pike would enter the Dark Cow and one of the other girls or, worse still, another man, a bit of variety, would move away from her side to let Pike take the throne. They weren't married, for Janey's sake. She could have hated Pike, except that she was as tender-hearted as Trixie had been, and she liked champagne. She certainly felt at liberty to hate the three aunts who made a mollycoddle out of him. She also hated, with a hatred that grew and grew, the way that Pike puked her with poethry. And all this time poor Pike walked in a dream that he never defined for us, perhaps not even for himself, but that certainly must have looked higher than the occasional trick on Jody's rumpled bed. So dreaming, sleep-walking, he persuaded Butterfly to go to Howth Head with him one dull hot day when the town was empty and she had nothing better to do. No place could have been more fatally poetic than Howth. She wore her musquash. Not even the heat could part her from it.

—He never let up, she said, not once from the moment we boarded the bus on the quays. Poethry. I had my bellyful.

—Sure thing, said Jody.

—Any man, she said, that won't pay every time he performs is a man to keep a cautious eye on. Not that he's not generous. But at the wrong times. Money down or no play's my motto.

—Well I know that, Jody said.

—But Pike Hunter says that would make our love mercenary, whatever that is.

—You're a great girl, said Austin, to be able to pronounce it.

—Your middle name, said Jody, is mercenary.

—My middle name, thank you, is Imelda. And the cheek of Pike Hunter suggesting to me to go to a doctor because he noticed something wrong with himself, a kidney disorder, he said. He must wet the bed.

—Butterfly, said Austin, he might have been giving you good advice.

—Nevertheless. It's not for him to say.

When they saw from the bus the Bull Wall holding the northern sand back from clogging up the harbour, and the Bull Island, three miles long, with dunes, bent grass, golfers, bathers and skylarks, Pike told her about some fellow called Joyce – there was a Joyce in the Civic Guards, a Galwayman who played county football, but no relation – who had gone walking on the Island one fine day and laid eyes on a young one, wading in a pool, with her skirts well pulled up; and let a roar out of him. By all accounts this Joyce was no addition to the family for, as Pike told the story, Butterfly worked out that the young one was well under age.

Pike and Butterfly had lunch by the edge of the sea, in the Claremont Hotel, and that was all right. Then they walked in the grounds of Howth Castle, Pike had a special pass and the flowers and shrubs were a sight to see if only Pike had kept his mouth shut about some limey by the name of Spenser who landed there in the year of God, and wrote a poem as long as from here to Killarney about a fairy queen and a gentle knight who was pricking on the plain like the members of the Harp Cycling Club, Junior Branch, up above there in the Phoenix Park. He didn't get time to finish the poem, the poet that is, not Pike, for the Cork people burned him out of house and home and, as far as Butterfly was concerned, that was the only good deed she ever heard attributed to the Cork people.

The Phoenix Park and the Harp Club reminded her that one day Jody had said, meaning no harm, about the way Pike moped around the Dark Cow when Butterfly wasn't there, that Pike was the victim of a semi-horn and should go up to the Fifteen Acres and put it in the grass for a while and run around it. But when, for fun, she told this to Pike he got so huffed he didn't speak for half an hour, and they walked Howth Head until her feet were blistered and the heel of her right shoe broke, and the sweat, with the weight of the musquash and the heat of the day, was running between her shoulder-blades like a cloudburst down the gutter. Then the row and the ructions, as the song says, soon began. He said she should have worn flat-heeled shoes. She said that if she had known that he was conscripting her for a forced march over a mountain she'd have borrowed a pair of boots from the last soldier she gave it to at cut-price, for the soldiers, God help them, didn't have much money but they were more open-handed with what they had than some people who had plenty, and soldiers didn't waste time and breath on poetry: Be you fat or be you lean there is no soap like Preservene.

So she sat on the summit of Howth and looked at the lighthouse and the seagulls, while Pike walked back to the village to have the broken heel mended, and the sweat dried cold on her, and she was perished. Then when he came back, off he was again about how that white-headed old character that you'd see across the river there at the Abbey Theatre, and Madame Gone Mad MacBride that was the age of ninety and looked it, and known to all as a roaring rebel, worse than Austin, had stood there on that very spot, and how the poet wrote a poem wishing for himself and herself to be turned into seagulls, the big dirty brutes that you'd see along the docks robbing the pigeons of their food. Butterfly would have laughed at him, except that her teeth by this time were tap-dancing with the cold like the twinkling feet of Fred Astaire. So she pulled her coat around her and said: Pike, I'm no seagull. For Janey's sake take me back to civilisation and Jody's where I know someone.

But, God sees, you never knew nobody, for at that moment the caveman came out in Pike Hunter, he that was always so backward on Jody's bed and, there and then, he tried to flatten her in the heather in full view of all Dublin and the coast of Ireland as far south as Wicklow Head and as far north as where the Mountains of Mourne sweep down to the sea.

—Oh none of that, Pike Hunter, she says, my good musquash will be crucified. There's a time and a place and a price for everything.

You and your musquash, he tells her.

They were wrestling like Man Mountain Dean and Jack Doyle, the Gorgeous Gael.

—You've neither sense nor taste, says he, to be wearing a fur coat on a day like this.

—Bloody well for you to talk, says she, with your rolled umbrella and your woollen combinations and your wobbly ass that won't keep you straight in the chair, and your three witches of maiden aunts never touched, tasted or handled by mortal man, and plenty of money and everything your own way. This is my only coat that's decent, in case you haven't noticed, and I earned it hard and honest with Jody, a generous man but a monster on the bed, I bled after him.

That put a stop to the wrestling. He brought her back to the Dark Cow and left her at the door and went his way.

He never came back to the Dark Cow but once, and Butterfly wasn't on her throne that night. It was the night before the cattle-market. He was so lugubrious and woebegone that Jody and Austin and a few merry newspaper men, including myself, tried to jolly him up, take him out of himself, by making jokes at his expense that would force him to come alive and answer back. Our efforts failed. He looked at us sadly and said: Boys, Beethoven, when he was dying, said: Clap now, good friends, the comedy is done.

He was more than a little drunk and, for the first time, seemed lopsided when standing up; and untidy.

—Clap now indeed, said Jody.

Pike departed and never returned. He took to steady drinking in places like the Shelbourne Hotel or the Buttery in the Hibernian where it was most unlikely, even with Dublin being the democratic sort of town that it is, that he would ever encounter Madame Butterfly. He became a great problem for his colleagues and his superior officers in the civil service, and for his three aunts. After careful consultation they, all together, persuaded him to rest up in Saint Patrick's Hospital where, as you all may remember, Dean Swift died roaring. Which was, I feel sure, why Pike wasn't there to pay the last respects to the dead when Jody dropped from a heart attack and was waked in the bedroom above the Dark Cow. The girls were there in force to say an eternal farewell to a good friend. Since the drink was plentiful and the fun and the mourning intense, somebody, not even Austin knew who, suggested that the part of the corpse that the girls knew best should be tastefully decorated with black crepe ribbon. The honour of tying on the ribbon naturally went to Madame Butterfly but it was Big Anne who burst into tears and cried out: Jody's dead and gone forever.

Austin met her, Butterfly not Big Anne, a few days afterwards at the foot of the Nelson Pillar. Jody's successor had routed the girls from the Dark Cow. Austin told her about Pike and where he was. She brooded a bit. She said it was a pity, but nobody could do nothing for him, that

those three aunts had spoiled him for ever and, anyway, didn't Austin
think that he was a bit astray in the head.

—Who knows, Butterfly? Who's sound or who's silly? Consider
yourself for a moment.

—What about me, Austin?

—A lovely girl like you, a vision from the romantic east, and think
of the life you lead. It can have no good ending. Let me tell you a story,
Butterfly. There was a girl once in London, a slavey, a poor domestic servant. I knew a redcoat here in the old British days who said he preferred
slaveys to anything else because they were clean, free and flattering.

—Austin, I was never a slavey.

—No, Butterfly, you have your proper pride. But listen: this slavey
is out one morning scrubbing the stone steps in front of the big house
she works in, bucket and brush, carbolic soap and all that, in one of
the great squares in one of the more classy parts of London Town.
There she is on her bended knees when a gentleman walks past, a
British army major in the Coldstream Guards or the Black Watch or
something.

—I've heard of them, Austin.

—So this British major looks at her, and he sees the naked backs of
her legs, thighs you know, and taps her on the shoulder or somewhere
and he says: Oh, rise up, lovely maiden and come along with me,
there's a better life in store for you somewhere else. She left the bucket
and the brush, and the stone steps half-scrubbed, and walked off with
him and became his girl. But there were even greater things in store for
her. For, Butterfly, that slavey became Lady Emma Hamilton, the
beloved of Lord Nelson the greatest British sailor that ever sailed, and
the victor of the renowned battle of Trafalgar. There he is up on the top
of the Pillar.

—You wouldn't think to look at him, Austin, that he had much
love in him.

—But, Butterfly, meditate on that story, and rise up and get yourself out of the gutter. You're handsome enough to be the second Lady
Hamilton.

After that remark, Austin brought her into Lloyd's, a famous house
of worship in North Earl Street under the shadow of Lord Nelson and

his pillar. In Lloyd's he bought her a drink and out of the kindness of his great singing heart, gave her some money. She shook his hand and said: Austin, you're the nicest man I ever met.

Austin had, we may suppose, given her an image, an ideal. She may have been wearied by Pike and his sad attachment to poetry, but she rose to the glimmering vision of herself as a great lady beloved by a great and valiant lord. A year later she married a docker, a decent quiet hard-working fellow who had slowly sipped his pints of black porter and watched and waited all the time.

Oddly enough, Austin told me when the dignity of old age had gathered around him like the glow of corn-stubble in the afterwards of harvest.

He could still sing. His voice never grew old.

—Oddly enough, I never had anything to do with her. That way, I mean. Well you know me. Fine wife, splendid sons, nobody like them in the world. Fine daughters, too. But a cousin of mine, a ship's wireless operator who had been all round the world from Yokohama to the Belgian Congo and back again, and had had a ship burned under him in Bermuda and, for good value, another ship burned under him in Belfast, said she was the meanest whore he ever met. When he had paid her the stated price, there were some coppers left in his hand and she grabbed them and said: give us these for the gas-meter.

But he said, also, that at the high moments she had a curious and diverting way of raising and bending and extending her left leg – not her right leg, which she kept as flat as a plumb-level. He had never encountered the like before, in any colour or in any country.

The Weavers at the Mill

Baxbakualanuxsiwae, she said to herself as she walked by the sea, was one of the odd gods of the Kwakiutl Indians, and had the privilege of eating human flesh. That pale-faced woman with the strained polite accent would devour me if her teeth were sharp enough. She even calls me, intending it as an insult, Miss Vancouver, although she knows damned well in her heart and mind, if she has a heart, that I don't come from Vancouver.

She loved the vast flat strand, the distant sea, the wraithlike outline of rocky islands that looked as if they were sailing in the sky, the abruptness with which a brook cradled by flat green fields became a wide glassy sheet of water spreading out over the sand.

A thatched cottage, gable end to the inshore gales, was palisaded against the sea by trunks of trees driven deep into the sand. On the sea-front road that curved around the shanty village, wind and water had tossed seaweed over the wall so regularly that it looked like nets spread out to dry. All the young men she met on the road wore beards they had grown for the night's pageant: not the melancholy, wishy-washy, desiccated-coconut pennants of artistic integrity but solid square-cut beards or shaggy beards that birds could nest in. To walk among them was a bit like stepping back into some old picture of the time of Charles Stewart Parnell: stern men marching home to beleaguered cabins from a meeting of the Land League.

That woman would say: They are all so handsome.

She was long-faced, pale and languid, the sort of woman who would swoon with craven delight at the rub of a beard. Yet she could never persuade the old man to abandon his daily careful ritual with cut-throat razor, wooden soap bowl, the strop worn to a waist in the middle, the fragments of newspaper splattered with blobs of spent lather and grey stubble.

—Eamonn, she would say to her husband, if you'd only grow a beard, you'd look like Garibaldi with his goats on the island of Caprera.

—I have no knowledge of goats. I'm not on my own island any more.

To the girl she would say: If your bags are packed I'll run you at any time to the station.

—My bags are always packed. There's only one of them. A duffle-bag, she'd answer. But if it doesn't inconvenience you too much I'd like to stay another day. There are a few details I want to fill in.

It needed nerve to talk to a woman like that in her own house. But what could the girl do when the old man was plaintively urging her not to go, not to go, pay no heed to her, stay another day.

They had breakfast in bed every day and lunch in their own rooms, and all the time until four in the afternoon free. It was in some ways the most relaxed life the girl had ever known. She had been there for a week since she had come from London across England, Wales, the Irish Sea and a part of Ireland, to write one more article in the magazine series that kept her eating. It was a series about little-known heroes of our time.

The woman had met her at the train. She drove a station-wagon piled high in the back with hanks of coloured wool. They drove round the village, foam glimmering in the dusk to their right hand, then across a humped five-arched stone bridge and up a narrow, sunken, winding roadway to the old Mill House in the middle of gaunt, grey, eyeless ruins where – above the river foaming down a narrow valley – two hundred men had worked in days of a simple local economy. Four grass-grown waterwheels rusted and rested for ever.

—Only my weavers work here now, she said. That's what the wool's for. Aran sweaters and belts – criosanna, they call them here – and scarves and cardigans. We sell them in the States where you come from.

She sounded as friendly as her over-refined, Henley-on-Thames voice could allow her to sound.

—Canada, the girl said. British Columbia. My father worked among the Kwakiutl Indians.

—Can't say I ever heard of them. What do they do?

—They were cannibals once. For religious reasons. But not any longer. They catch salmon. They sing songs. They carve totem poles. They weave good woollens, too. With simplified totem designs.

—How interesting.

The car went under a stone archway topped by a shapeless mass that she was to discover had once represented a re-arising phoenix – until rain and salt gales had disfigured it to a death deeper than ashes. They were in a cobbled courtyard and then in a garage that had once been part of a stables.

—You want to write about my husband's lifeboat exploits when he was an islandman.

—The famous one. I was asked to write about it. Or ordered. I read it up in the newspaper files. It was heroic.

She slung the duffle-bag over her shoulder and they walked towards the seven-windowed face of the old stone house. From the loft above the garage the clacking of looms kept mocking time to their steps. The woman said: Do you always dress so informally?

—I travel a lot and light. Leather jacket and corduroy slacks. You need them in my business. A protection against pinchers and pawsey men.

—You're safe here, said the woman. The men are quiet. All the young ones have just grown lovely beards for a parish masque or a pageant or something. You mustn't tire him too much. Sometimes he can get unbearably excited when he remembers his youth.

His youth, the girl reckoned, was a long time ago.

She spread out her few belongings between the old creaking mahogany wardrobe and the marble-topped dressing-table, and tidied herself for dinner, and remembered that she had left her typewriter, smothered in wool, in the station-wagon. The newspaper that had told her about the rescue had been fifty years old; and Eamonn, the brave coxswain and the leader of the heroic crew, had been then a well-developed man of thirty. The newsprint picture had faded, but not so badly that she couldn't see the big man, a head taller than any of his companions, laughing under his sou'wester with all the easy mirth of a man who had never yet been afraid.

From her bedroom window she could look down into the courtyard and see girls in blue overalls carrying armfuls of wool from the wagon up an outside wooden stairway to the weaving shed. The thatched roofs of the village were, from her height, like a flock of yellow birds nestling by the edge of the sea and, far across the water, the outlines of the islands of Eamonn's origin faded into the darkness, as distant and lost for ever as his daring youth and manhood. Yet she knew so little, or had reflected so little, on the transfiguring power of time that she was ill-prepared for the gaunt, impressive wreck of a man who came slowly into a dining-room that was elaborately made up to look like a Glocamorra farmhouse kitchen. He sat down on a low chair by the open hearth and silently accepted a bowl of lentil soup with fragments of bread softening in it. He didn't even glance at the low unstained oak table where the girl sat most painfully, on a traditional three-legged wooden chair. Dressed in black, her black hair piled on her head, her oblong face, by lamplight, longer and whiter than ever, the woman sat aloof at the head of the table. Two girls, daytime weavers magically transformed by the touch of the creeping dusk into night-time waitresses, blue overalls exchanged for dark dresses, white aprons, white collars, served the table; and a third stood like a nurse behind the old man's chair. He slopped with a spoon, irritably rejecting the handmaiden's effort to aid him. He recited to himself what was to the girl an unintelligible sing-song.

—Merely counting, the woman said. In Gaelic. One, two, three, and so on. He says it soothes him and helps his memory. I told him what you want. He'll talk when he's ready.

Suddenly he said: She cracked right across the middle, that merchant vessel, and she stuffed as full as a fat pig with the costliest bales of goods and furniture and God knows what. I can tell you there are houses on this coast but not out on the islands where the people are honest and no wreckers, and those houses are furnished well to this day on account of what the waves brought in that night.

The voice came out like a bell, defying and belying time, loud and melodious as when he must have roared over the billows to his comrades the time the ship cracked. Then he handed the empty soup bowl to the nervous weaver-handmaiden, sat up high in his chair, bade the girl welcome in Gaelic, and said to the woman: She's not one of the French people from the hotel.

—From London, said the woman.

—There's a fear on the people in the village below that there won't be a duck or a hen or any class of a domestic fowl left alive to them with the shooting of these French people. The very sparrows in the hedges and God's red robins have no guarantee of life while they're about. They came over in the beginning for the sea-angling and, when they saw all the birds we have, nothing would satisfy them but to go home to France for their guns. They say they have all the birds in France shot. And the women with them are worse than the men.

—Les femmes de la chasse, said the woman.

—Patsy Glynn the postman tells me there's one six feet high with hair like brass and legs on her like Diana and wading boots up to her crotch. God, Pats said to me, and I agreed, the pity Eamonn, you're not seventy again, or that the Capall himself is dead and in the grave. He'd manipulate her, long legs and boots and all.

—Our visitor, said the woman, is not here to write about the Capall.

—Then, girl from London, 'tis little knowledge you have of writing. For there have been books written about men that weren't a patch on the Capall's breeches. A horse of a man and a stallion outright for the women. That was why we called him the Capall.

With a raised right hand and cracking fingers the woman had dismissed the three girls. This was no talk for servants to hear.

—That John's Eve on the island, the night of the bonfires and midsummer, and every man's blood warm with poteen and porter in Dinny O'Brien's pub. Dinny, the old miser that he was, serving short measure and gloating over the ha'pennies. But, by God, the joke was on him and didn't we know it. For wasn't the Capall in the barn-loft at the back of the house with Dinny's young wife that married him for money, for that was all Dinny had to offer. She had to lie down for two days in bed, drinking nothing but milk, after the capers of the Capall and herself in the loft. He walked in the back door of the bar, his shirt open to the navel, no coat on him and the sweat on him like oil. Two pints he drank and saw for the first time the new barmaid, a niece of Dinny, that had come all the way from Cork City, and the fat dancing on her and her dress thin. So he lifted the third pint and said: *Dhia! Is trua nach bhfuil dara bud ag duine.*

Feeling that she did understand, and close to coarse laughter, the girl said that she didn't understand. Coldly and precisely the woman said: To put it politely he regretted that he was merely one man, not two.

—But he saved my life did the Capall. For the gale swept us, and the eight men we took off the broken vessel, eastwards before it to a port in Wales. There was no turning back in the teeth of it. There we were trying to moor the boat by the mole in another country when, with weariness and the tossing of the water, didn't I slip and go down between the wall and the boat, to be crushed, sure as God, if the Capall hadn't hooked his elbow in mine and thrown me back into the boat the way a prize wrestler would. Remember that bit, girl, when you write the story, and thank God you never met the Capall on a lonely road. He came from a place called the Field of the Strangers that was the wildest place on the whole island. From the hill above it you could see the wide ocean all the way to Africa, and the spray came spitting in over the roofs of the little houses, and the salt burned the grass in the fields. There was no strand in it, no breakwater, no harbour or slip for boats. Nothing man ever built could stand against that ocean. You held the currach steady and leaped into it from a flat rock as you shot out to sea. But there were men of strength and valour reared there who could conquer valleys before them and throw sledge-hammers over high houses. Dried sea bream we ate, boiled or roasted over hot sods, the strongest sweetest food in the world. And rock birds taken in nets where they'd nest in the clefts of the cliffs. Bread and tea for a treat, and potatoes boiled or brusselled in the *gríosach*.

The woman explained: Roasted in the hot peat ashes.

—Then a cow might break a leg in a split in the rocks and have to be destroyed. A black disaster in one way. But in another way a feast of fresh meat and liver with the blood running out of it, food for men. All out of tins nowadays, and nobody has his own teeth.

The woman said: You were, Eamonn, talking about the lifeboat.

—Good for its own purpose the lifeboat, he said. But you couldn't feel the heart of the sea beating in it as you could in the canvas currach. We had one fellow with us that night who always had ill luck with currachs. Three of them he lost, and once he nearly lost his life. So we put him in the crew of the lifeboat to break his ill-fortune, and the trick worked. It could be that the sea didn't recognise him in his new yellow oilskins. Three days in that Welsh town we sweated in knee-boots and oilskins, having nothing else to wear, and the gales blowing in against us all the time. But the welcome we got. Didn't a deputation of ladies come to us with a white sheet of cloth to draw our names on, so that they could embroider our names for ever on the flag of the town's football team. Didn't the Capall write himself down as Martin McIntyre the Horse. There was the laughing, I can tell you, when the ladies wanted us to tell them why we put the title of the horse on Martin. They made heroes out of us. It was a sea-going town and there wasn't a woman in it hadn't a son or a husband or a lover on the salt water.

The attendant girls had come back silently. His great head, shaggy with uncombed white hair, sank down. With a napkin one of the girls mopped a splatter of soup from the green leather zipper jacket and, startlingly, with the yeeow of a shout a young fellow would give at a country dance, he came awake and slapped her buttocks before she could leap, laughing and blushing, and seemingly well used to the horseplay, out of his reach. The woman looked at the servant and then at her food. She said: Don't tire yourself.

—Never saw the tired day, he said, that the smell of a young girl wouldn't put life into me.

—Tell me more, said the girl, about the sea.

—What would you want to know about the sea and you from the smoky heart of London?

—I'm not from London.

—From Canada, said the woman. Her girlhood companions were cannibalistic Indians.

—On an island, the girl said.

He was wide awake, and interested, and upright. How tall he was when he sat up straight.

—Tell me, he said, about your wild Indians and your island.

Because he had hard blue eyes with a compelling icy light in them, and because for her benefit he had so carefully dredged his memory, she wanted to tell him. She wanted to tell him even more because as soon as he showed interest she had sensed the first stirrings of antagonism in the woman.

—Eamonn, the woman said, our guest may be tired.

—Tell me a little, he said. It's lucky to begin a story by lamplight.

—Nothing much to tell, she said. Don't think of me as sitting in the middle of a pack of noble savages, chewing on a hunk of Tyee salmon while they ate long pig. I didn't grow up with drums and war chants throbbing around me. I was some miles distant, on the other side of the hill. Of course I had plenty of contact with the confused no-man's-land Indian that the white man has made. Studied their history and sociology at college. But when I was a little girl the closest I got to them was to run to the top of the hill and peep down through cedar branches at the noble Indians pulling the guts out of salmon. Sounds bitter I know. But beauty and nobility had left them for a long while. And in our village the groups were so divided that not even the minds of the children could meet. When I was a girl I remember trying to get a little Indian girl to tell me some of her words. She stayed sullen and very silent. Then finally she and her little friend giggled and spat out one word. Matsooie – that was what it sounded like. I found out later that she had simply been saying: what's the matter with you? It was a rebuff.

—It's sad, he said, when people don't understand you, no matter what you do or try to do. We'll talk more tomorrow, girl, when you've rested after your journey.

—I've talked too much, she said. I came to listen to you.

He rose alertly when she passed him and shook her hand in a solemn old-fashioned way. He belonged to a time when men shook hands elaborately at every meeting and parting.

Later – very much later – she thought drowsily that she heard his slow tread on the old creaking stairs, his coughing in the next room as he lay down on his bed, and far away the faint sound of the sea along the shore and around the islands.

She carried two notebooks always in the right-hand pocket of her leather jacket.

All women, said the hopeful man she had met on the Irish Mail, are lascivious.

One of the notebooks was paper-backed, spined with spiral wire, and with tear-out leaves. It was for ephemera and temporalities – in other words, her work. The other book was stiff-backed, with stable, ruled leaves for the recording of the experiences she would use when the day would come and she'd sit down really to write. The stiff-backed book had another quality: it kept the weaker member straight in her jacket pocket, for she found nothing more maddening than note-taking on a page that was bent like a crescent.

The people she met she divided into two classes: tear-outs or stiff-backs.

This wonderful old man, an aged hero recalling islands, immured here by a female dragon, was as notable a stiff-back as she had ever encountered.

When the clacking of looms awoke her in the morning, she sat up in bed and reached for ball-point and stiff-back where she had left them in readiness on the bedside table. Or was it the looms had awakened her or the purring of the motor-car engine in the cobbled yard or the morning coughing of the old giant in the next room? For an ancient stone house, she thought, the walls were thin. But then she studied the slant of the ceiling, and realised that her room was only half a room and that the sound of coughing came to her, not through old stone, but through a wooden partition. She went to the window and looked out at three of the blue weaving girls walking in single file from the station-wagon to the weaving-shed and carrying hanks of coloured wool: obedient African kraal girls with burdens on their heads and disciplined by some wrinkled Zulu queen. Then the woman drove away under the faceless phoenix. When the girl was settled back in bed again, he spoke to her through the wall: I can hear you're awake. Has she driven off to do the shopping?

—Good morning, she said. She's driven off somewhere.

—Good morning to you, girl. Did you sleep well?

Her answer was lost in a fit of his coughing, and when his throat had cleared again, he said: No more rising with the lark for me. Nor the seagull itself. I'm old and lazy now. But I mind my father the oldest day he was, walking barefoot in the dawn, the old greasy sailor's cap on his head, to the flagstone at the corner of the house, to look at the sea and the surf on the white strand, to sniff the wind and to tell the weather for the day to come. He had his own teeth to the age of ninety. If he was inland and far from the sea, he could tell by the smell of the wind whether the tide was ebbing or flowing. But it wasn't often he went inland, and he was never happy in an offshore wind.

This was the most wonderful way in the world to conduct an interview. The metallic voice came muted, but clear, through the timber. The looms, the sea, and the river made their noises. The wind muttered around grey stone. She could sit snug in bed, both notebooks open, and make notes at her ease without embarrassing her subject.

—Tell me more, she said.

He said: Tell me about your wild Indians.

So to entice him to talk, she talked about Quathiaski Cove at the mouth of the river, and about the wits among the Scots and Irish settlers who nicknamed it Quart of Whiskey Cove, about the great argonauts of salmon homing up the Campbell River, about people of many nations, Scots, Swedes, Irish, Indians, Chinese, Japanese, living in one way or another on the rich red body of the salmon.

—The very air in that place smells of salmon. When my mother first took me to visit Vancouver I thought there was something wrong with the place, something missing. Finally she told me I felt that way because I could no longer smell the salmon.

—Like myself, he said, when I came here with her. This far inland you can't sniff the salt properly.

—And tell me about their songs, he said. In my days on the island

197

there were sweet singers and old men who could tell stories to last the night.

So, for his sake, she remembered that when she had been a little girl she had sneaked out one night to listen to the singing of the Indians. One song particularly stayed in her memory. Years afterwards when she and her people had long left the place, she went north by boat with her father to revisit the haunts of her childhood. To one old noble chieftain she spoke of the songs – and of that special song. He answered her about all the forms of songs: morning songs, harvest songs, giving songs to be chanted at the potlatch when a man gave all he had to his neighbours, gambling songs, lullabies. And song after song he sang until she stopped him and said: That's it. That's the song I loved when I was a little girl.

Then, with tears in his eyes, the old chieftain said: That's my gambling song, written for me by my own songwriter.

Her story faded into coughing that rattled the partition between them. Later he said in a hoarse carrying whisper: Don't go away soon, girl. Stay as long as you can whether she wants you to or not.

It wasn't easy to think of any response.

—She doesn't like strangers about the place. She's cold, God help her, and has no *fáilte* in her. Even when I was married to my first wife, and herself only a stranger visiting the islands, she was always jealous to find me in the middle of a crowd.

—You were married before?

—To a woman of my own people. And year after year herself came as a tourist until my wife died. Then I went away with her and we were married in London. A watery class of a wedding they give you in cities. It wasn't love, as they call it. She was too grand for that. But she was there always – and willing. The islands do something to visiting women. And with creams and perfumes and the best clothes out of the London shops she was different from any woman I'd ever smelled or seen. You know how it is with a strong imaginative young fellow, and he only a few months married.

—I can guess, she said. Some minor poet said something about white arms beckoning all around him.

—Minor or major he was poet enough to know what he was

talking about. We haven't slept heads on one pillow for twenty years now, but in secret corners in those old days we'd play hide and seek in our pelt on the bare rocks – when it was a sin moreover. And look at me now here wrapped in coloured wool, and broken in health, and surrounded by stupid women, weaving.

Propped by pillows, and taking notes, she squatted like a tailor, and made up her mind. She would stay a week if she could, just to please the old man and – her blood warming to the conflict – to spite that cold dried fish of a woman. In his youth, to judge by his talk, the old man had eaten better.

When he heard the station-wagon returning he said: I'll doze for a while now. She wouldn't like to hear us talking through the wall. She was hinting last night she'd run you to the station for the late train. But don't go, don't go, stay as long as you can.

They had a week of mornings together talking through the wall. Reading her notes afterwards she found that morning mingled with morning. One morning, though, was distinct because it had been a morning of gale and rain. The coy red-and-purple blossoms were being whipped off the tormented fuchsia bushes, and when she stepped out for her daily walk – the sea was too tossed for a swim – the sand and salt were in her eyebrows and gritting between her teeth. Bloated by a night of rain the brown mad river bellowed around the dead mill-wheels and for once, the clack, the mocking one-two-three of the looms couldn't be heard.

Through the wall and the frequent fits of coughing he had said to her: I've grown younger since you came. A gift to me from the god of the sea himself, a beautiful young girl from a far island.

As a clergyman's daughter, the object of as many jokes as an Aberdonian, she was calmly aware of her looks: neither better nor worse than they were. She laughed. She said: I've a nose like a pack saddle, and a square face and freckles, although they tell me I've honest eyes.

—But you're young, he said.

After a silence she heard his dry choking laughter: There's a lump on my own nose still where I had it broken and I no more than a boy. The way it happened is a story will tickle you. There was this free and easy girl, a rare thing on the islands I can tell you – with the close way we lived. She wasn't an island girl, whatever. She came from the main-land in the tourist season and, as the song says, her stockings were white and you'd love to be tickling her garter, even if she was no better than a servant-maid in a lodging-house. This evening weren't we lined up to see her, like penitents going to confession, at the bottom of the orchard behind the house she worked in, and when Pat's Jameseen stepped out of his fair place in the line to go ahead of me, I fought him and, although he cracked my nose, hammered him back.

The dry laughter went on, choking now not with phlegm but with remembered devilment.

—That was the way with me when I was young. A chieftain among my own people, like your fine Indian, and respected by all. Then when my first woman died I never wanted to see the islands again. The English woman had it easy to carry me to the smoke of London, where, as God is my judge, I came near to choking. The islands pulled at me again, even though I got only this far and no farther. Old as I am, I think at times I'll take a boat and return. But they don't want me any more since I married a stranger, and grew grand, and left.

—It would be fun, said the girl, if we could go to an island I know in Spain. Life is simple and gentle there, and the food good, cooked over an open fire. Some rough wine, wild and coarse, but with a kind flavour. A little music and reading and story-telling by lamplight, and water all around.

—That would be a holiday to remember, he said.

With the gale that morning they didn't hear the station-wagon returning, and it was the woman opening the door of the old man's room that interrupted them. Afterwards, while the old man slept, she said, over black coffee, to the girl: Any time you're ready I'll run you to the station.

A conflict like this was, in some ways, worse than blows or eye-scratching. As steadily as she could the girl said: If it doesn't upset your arrangements too much I'd love to see the pageant. It would add colour to the story.

—Colour, the woman said. Well, the beards, yes. Please yourself. But don't talk to the girls so much. It holds them up at their work.

They lose. I lose. They're paid by piece-work.

Walking out into the gale the girl, for the sake of peace and the old man, avoided the weaving-shed where, she had been glad to think, the sullen faces of the underpaid weavers brightened when she entered. She loved the soft coloured wool, the intricacies of warping mills and heddles, the careful spacing of the threads. When you looked at the process, you were as much part of it as the woolwinder and the sound of the looms was comforting, not mocking.

In the hotel bar the French hunters, driven in by the tempest that had also driven the birds to shelter, clustered around Diana who wore tight red pants and sneakers. Through a red beard like a burning bush the barman told her how five years ago the old man had run amok: Terrified the bloody country for a week. Wandering around with a loaded shotgun. Shooting and spearing salmon in the pool below the old mill. Then pleurisy laid him low and he was never the same again. Out on the islands they're savages. Half-crazy with inbreeding.

The raised wind-driven sea was sucking around the tree trunks that palisaded the white cottage. She walked, fighting the gale, along the thin line of sand the water had not devoured.

Baxbakualanuxsiwae, she recalled, shared his house with his wife, Qominoqa, a frightful female who cooked his ghoulish meals. A female slave, Kinqalalala, rounded up victims and collected corpses, well-hung meat in the house of the gods.

The thunder of the waves made her want to run and shout. One Sunday morning the small, deep-toned drums of the potlatch had set the whole village vibrating, until her father was forced to abandon his pulpit and say with a good humour more than Christian: Let us marvel at the force of tradition which is also one of the works of the Lord.

Once, in one of the books in her father's library, she had read that the Dinka people of the southern Sudan had a special sort of priest known as Masters of the Fishing Spear. These men, if they had great names as heroes, could be honourably killed when old and failing, by being buried alive at their own request and before all their assembled kin.

The islands, lost in spume and low-running clouds, were not to be seen.

In the dusk the bearded young men came in twos and threes under the featureless phoenix, across the courtyard, out by another gateway at the back of the weaving-shed, and up the hill to the mounded rath that was to be the open-air, torch-lit stage for their pageant. They wore white shirts and saffron kilts, cowskin pampooties made on the islands and dyed all colours, and thick woollen stockings cross-gartered to the knees. Most of them carried long wooden spears with silvered cardboard heads, and cardboard shields bright with brassy tacks. Some of them carried and some of them even played the bagpipes.

The blue weaving girls gathered on the landing outside the door of the shed, and cat-called, and addressed the bearded heroes by their ordinary everyday names and nicknames. They asked with irony if the men were going to the wars or to stick flounder on the flat sands with the flowing tide. When one bandy-legged, hairy-kneed veteran tottered past carrying a huge harp, and preceded by the curate who was directing the pageant, the blue girls held each other up, embracing in paroxysms and pantomimes of suppressed mirth.

—Never yet, the old man said, did I hear tell of one of these pageants that wasn't a holy laugh in the end. The Orangemen in the North, they say, had a pageant about the landing of King Billy in Carrickfergus harbour. But the sea was choppy that day and the boat tilted and didn't his majesty land on his arse in the water. And in Straide in Mayo they had a pageant about the eviction of the family of Michael Davitt who founded the Land League. But they built the mock cabin so strong that all the guns of Germany, let alone the battering rams of the boys who were pretending to be the bailiff's men, couldn't knock it down. Still and all, for the laugh, we'll go up to the rath and drink porter and eat pork sausages with the rest. It'll be a fine night with a full moon.

—At your age, Eamonn, that's the worst thing you could do.

—At my age?

He tossed aside the blackthorn he leaned on and, on the flat flag at the door of the house, hopped, but stiffly, from one foot to the other.

—These days I'm a two-year-old. The Indian maiden here will lead me up the slope. Minnehaha.

The woman's eyelids came down – it seemed one after the other, and very deliberately – to hide her eyes.

—Please yourself, then. Those girls have wasted enough time. I'll go up later with coffee and sandwiches.

His arm was around the girl's shoulders as they walked up a twisting boreen towards bonfires reddening in the dusk.

—Kings lived on this high hill, he said. All gone now, and dead and buried, generations of ancient kings, but the mounds and the ramparts are as solid as the day they were raised.

For one night, she thought, the kings had returned. She sat beside him on a rug on the mound. They were sheltered by a blossoming whitethorn from the light seawind. She held his hand. A huge round moon was motionless in a cloudless sky. Under its influence, and in the glow of a dozen bonfires, the bearded, cross-gartered country boys, the one decrepit harper, were no longer comic.

It was a masque, not a pageant. In a hut in a forest a dozen old broken men, remnants of a beaten clan, waited sadly and with little hope for the fulfilment of a prophecy that told of the coming of a young hero to lead them back to victory.

—This, said the oldest of them, is the last day of the year of our foretold salvation, and the last hour of the last day, yet the prophecy still stands even if it was made by one of the faery women who make game of men.

Her own old man moved closer to her on the rug.

The blue girls were just ending the long day's weaving. The coffee and sandwiches, and the woman with them, were still a good hour away; and also the thought that her duffle-bag and typewriter had been stored, for simpler departure, in the hotel with the red-bearded barman. She felt a brute, but she had a job to do – such as it was – and an old man's dream couldn't go on for ever, nor could she any longer defy a woman who didn't want her about the place.

When he pressed her hand she returned the pressure. She felt the great bones from which the flesh had melted away. She could have wept.

—The pity, he said, I didn't meet you when I was a young blade.

—I wasn't born then.

—We'd have found our own island and lived on it.

—There was a Japanese poet, she said, who was born in 1911, the year after Halley's Comet. He reckoned with a sad heart that he'd never see the comet since it wouldn't come again until 1986. That it was the same case with human encounters. His true friend would appear after his death. His sweetheart had died before he was born.

—A fine young man there, he said.

For who should arrive at that moment but the red barman himself striding from darkness into the glare of the fires. Spear on shoulder. With the firelight glinting in his bush of a beard he could only be the hero who was promised. The crowds, seated on the slopes of the rath, cheered him. He was a popular man. For the broken old men he brought venison from the forest, cakes impaled on spears, and rolling barrels of ale from an enemy fortress he had that day captured single-handed. Also a sackful of golden goblets, made out of cardboard and all the tokens, including a severed head in a sack, to prove he was the man of destiny. The exigencies of the drama did not, mercifully, call for the production of the severed head.

Then the harper harped on his harp and, far away in the shadows, the pipers played, slowly advancing towards the circle of fires to show that they were an army of young men following their unique leader. The watching crowds broke up into groups to eat sausages and pigs' feet and to drink porter. The dancing began on the rough dry grass. Led by two of the pipers, the dancers moved to find a better surface between the weaving-shed and the millhouse. Then the woman was there, and the curate with her helping her to carry cups and sandwiches and the coffee pot.

—Not pigs' feet, Eamonn. Not all that greasy fat.

—Tisn't often now I have a night out under the moon.

—A midsummer night, she said. Madness.

—I could leap through bonfires, woman. I feel like twenty. Pour milk on the ground for the good people who lived here before kings were heard tell of. It's not lucky to let them go hungry.

—What silly waste, the woman said.

Slowly the girl tilted her cup and let the coffee drain down to the grass. She said: They might fancy coffee.

His great hand was in the bowl of brown sugar and the fistful he took he tossed into the air, scattering it over the crowd. Faces, some laughing, some curious, turned towards them in the firelight.

—The world knows, he said, that the good people have a sweet tooth. Halley's Comet, Minnehaha, will come again.

They laughed loudly together. She noticed that they were again hand in hand. The curate, pretending to answer a call from one of the bearded men, moved away. The woman poured more coffee. By the farthest fire the girl saw the red man standing and beckoning. He probably had notions above his state in life, but he could give her a lift to the nearest town, and her leather jacket was stout enough to resist even the paws and the pinches of a man mentioned in prophecy. When the barman moved off down the slope towards the millhouse, she excused herself.

—Come back soon, Minnehaha, the old man called after her. Don't delay. It's a fine night for seeing comets.

—Eamonn, isn't it time you went in out of the night air?

Like in movies about Italy, the girl thought, everything ends with a carnival. She walked down the slope, taking his second youth with her, towing the sailing islands behind her. She was the sea receding for ever from a stranded master of the sea.

By torchlight in the cobbled courtyard blue weaving girls danced with bearded warriors who had cast aside their spears.

She walked on under the stone phoenix that could never arise again because it had merely decayed, never been purified by fire and burned to ashes.

With car, duffle-bag and typewriter, the red barman was waiting. She sat beside him and was driven off to find her next little-known hero.

Down Then by Derry

The first time Tom Cunningham ever saw Sadie Law's brother, Francie, that brother was airborne between the saddle of a racing bicycle and a stockade filled with female lunatics. Francie is not the chief part of this story, nor is his sister, but since he has been mentioned, it might be fair to his fame and memory to say who he was and what he was doing in the air in that odd place.

A resident medical officer in the district's mental hospital had, years before, been a believer in athletics as curative therapy for the crazy: running and jumping and the lord knows what. So he set those who were out of cells and strait-jackets, and otherwise capable, at the running and jumping, barring, for good reasons the throwing of the hammer or the discus, or the tossing of the caber – which can be dangerous occupations even for the sane. Then the medical officer, to introduce a sanative, competitive spirit, organised an annual sports meeting, with cups, shields and lesser prizes. The thing grew and grew. That medical officer died and went to Valhalla. The annual meeting continued to grow until it was one of the most notable sporting events in that part of the country. Professionals competed. The crazy men and women, those of them who could be out and about, were now only two small corralled sections among the spectators. They had been pushed back into the shouting or gibbering shadows where everybody, except the man in Valhalla, thought they belonged.

Francie Law was a famous track cyclist. That was how he came to be there in the air. There was one bad corner on the packed cinder track. This day there was a pile-up and Francie was catapulted clean, to land among the lunatic ladies. He survived. It was as a hero-worshipper bearing grapes to Francie's hospital bedside – Francie, wherever he was, always smelled of embrocation – that Tom Cunningham first met Francie's sister, Sadie, who was almost as famous as her brother, but not for track-cycling.

—She's Number One, according to all the talk, Tom said to his favourite friend who was five years younger than him.

Tom was nineteen.

—And she liked me, Tom said. We have a date. She wore a black leather coat with a belt. There was a good warm smell off it. Like the smell of the plush seats at the back of the cinema where all the feeling goes on. Hot stuff, boy. Also the smell of embrocation. Rub it up good. Frank Mullan told me she was okay and easy to get, if you once got to know her. And the May devotions are on the way. Long evenings. Warm grass. And Frank Mullan should know. He knows them all.

Of course it goes without saying that the devotions on May evenings in the parish church, with the high, limping, Gothic spires, went away back to something far before the worship of holy purity and the blessed virgin, to some pagan festival of the rites of spring. This he found out afterwards by reading, and by much dull talk, in more sophisticated places, heaven help us, than his own native town. But in the spring of that year he neither knew nor worried about such things, as he knelt beside Tom Cunningham in the side aisle to the left hand of the high altar.

Oh, those brown angels cut in wood of a slightly lighter colour than the wood of the beams to which they provided a figurehead finish. They swooped out towards each other over the nave and eyed the pray-ing people. Once he had tried to write a poem about them:

> In church the angels cut in wood,
> In row on row arranged,
> Stand always as before they stood,
> And only I am changed.

But it wouldn't work. The angels weren't standing, for God's sake, they had no legs or feet to stand on, or, if they had, those legs were buried in the wood of the beams from which winged torsos and long-haired oaken heads seemed to have instantaneously, ecstatically, emerged. Times, he still saw those angels in his dreams, soaring, in a sort of a way, over altar, incense, monstrance, praying priest, responding mumbling people, over Tom Cunningham in the side aisle making cute sideways eyes and secret signs at Sadie Law who knelt with her favourite friend directly under the angels in the nave. Whatever about bullshit talk and the rites of spring, the devotions on May evenings was where you met people for good or evil; and all around the church, high on a hill with its hopalong spires, the rolling country was rich in deep grass and the birds were making mocking calls along hidden lovers' lanes. The high grassy embankments along the railways that went out of the town to the Donegal sea at Bundoran, or to Dublin or Belfast or down then by Derry to the northern sea, were a sort of secret world where only lovers went in the long evenings. No respectable girl would be seen walking along the railway. The art was in not being seen.

His daughter, who was eighteen years of age, said to his mother who admitted to being eighty-five: Dad must have been happy here in this town in his schooldays. He's always singing a song. Well, not singing exactly. It has no particular tune. No beat. Dad's a bit of a square. It goes more like an African chant.

—Wallawalla boom boom, said his son who was fourteen.

—John, said the daughter, mind your manners. Granny doesn't dig Swahili. No granny. The song begins like this. Thrice happy and blessed were the days of my childhood and happy the hours I wandered from school, by green Mountjoy's forest, our dear native wildwood, and the green flowery banks of the serpentine Strule.

—Mountjoy forest, he said, was part of the estate of Lord and Lady Blessington. Back in the days of the great Napoleon. That was an old song.

—He was a good scholar, his mother said. He was very fond of reading poetry out loud. In the mornings after breakfast. Before he went to school.

As if he wasn't there at all. His daughter giggled.

He was accustomed to his mother rhapsodising in this way, talking about him to other people in his presence. Once she had said to a friend of his: He would be the best man in Ireland if it wasn't for the little weakness.

Afterwards his friend had said with great good humour: with you standing there I couldn't very well ask her which weakness she meant.

Another time and under similar circumstances she had said to the same friend: His father, God rest him, put on some weight when he passed forty, but he never swelled like that.

Pointing to him. As if, by God, the son, had had a dropsical condition.

To her grand-daughter and grandson she said: He read Shelley. If Winter comes can Spring be far behind. I liked that. Shelley was a good poet. Although my own mother could never understand about Tennyson and the brook. She used to say: Poor fellow, could nobody stop him. I think she thought it was about some unfortunate man that had something astray with his bowels. Then there was one poet that droned on and on about Adam and Eve and the fall of Satan.

She spat mildly and politely towards the fireplace where, winter or summer, there was always a fire. She preserved many old country customs. One was to spit when, by inadvertence or necessity, one mentioned a name of the devil – and his names were legion.

Twenty-eight years later he was still a little ashamed that he had inflicted on his mother's patient ears the monotony of Milton, even to the utter extremity of the Latin verses.

—Milton, he said, a bit of a bore.

But nobody paid the least attention to him. So he closed his eyes and his mind to the lot of them: the mother, old, wrinkled, wearing a battered old felt hat that looked like a German helmet, but with an eye as bright and inquisitive as it must have been when she was a lively singing country girl, and the man she was to marry was walking round and round the South African veldt; and he himself wasn't even a fragment of an imagination, or a gleam or a glint in his father's eye; the daughter, pert, small, lively, endlessly talkative; the son, tall, easygoing, slouching when he walked – as his grandfather had done. It was uncanny to observe such resemblances.

Since not one of the three of them paid any attention to him he shut his eyes and his mind to them and went on his own through the town, and back to the past that had made the town and him.

The two tall limping Gothic spires rose high above the hilly narrow streets. Those two spires and the simple plain spire of the Protestant church – that would be Church of Ireland, for the Methodists and Presbyterians did not rise to spires – could be seen for a distance of ten miles. They soared, they were prayers of a sort, over the riverine countryside.

The taller spire was all of two hundred and thirty feet high, thirty of that being for the surmounting cross. To climb up the inside of that spire you went first by a winding stone stairway to the organ loft, then by a steep straight wooden stairway to the shaky creaky platform where the sexton stood when he pulled the bell-rope, then up a series of perpendicular ladders to the place where the two bells were hung, sullen and heavy, but ready at the twitch of a rope to do their duty. From that eminence, one hundred and fifty feet up, you could look down on everything. The town was almost flat, no longer all humps and hills and high-ridged roofs and steep narrow streets. Down there was the meeting place of two rivers, the Camowen and the Drumragh: a sparkling trout-water, a sullen pike-water. Who could comprehend the differences there were between rivers, not to speak now of the Amazon and the Seine and the Volga and the Whang-ho and the Ohio, but even between neighbouring rivers destined to marry and to melt into one? United, the waters of Drumragh and Camowen went on under the name of the Strule, sweeping in a great horseshoe around the wide holm below the military barracks, tramping and tossing northwards to meet yet another river, the Fairywater, then to vanish glistening into a green-and-blue infinity.

Except you were the sexton, or some lesser person authorised by him, you were not, by no means, supposed to be up there at all. Dusty boards, with crazy, dizzy gaps between them, swayed and bent under your feet. Vicious jackdaws screeched. The blue-and-green infinity into which the sparkling water vanished was the place where Blessington's Rangers had once walked, speaking Gaelic, great axes on shoulders. They cut down the trees to make timber for war against Bonaparte, and money to keep Lord and Lady Blessington, their daughter, and the ineffable Count D'Orsay gallivanting.

One day coming home from school alone – that was a time of the day when it wasn't easy to be alone but, with cunning, it could be managed – he had found the door at the foot of the stone stairway open and had taken the chance that it was open by accident. It was. He made the climb. He saw the world. He was alone with the jackdaws and the moan of the wind. Then on the way down the perpendicular ladders he had missed a rung, slipped, screamed with the jackdaws, grabbed desperately and held on. Just about where the sexton would stand to pull the bell-rope, he had vomited a sort of striped vomit that he had never seen before. Even in boyhood there was the fear of death.

Nobody, thank God, had ever found out who had thus paid tribute, made offertory, in the holy place. For weeks afterwards he had felt dizzy even when climbing the stairs to his bedroom.

When the war was over and Boney beaten, the gallivanting lords and ladies had no more use for the woodsmen of Mountjoy. For the last time they walked down there below in the old Flax Market that hadn't changed much since 1820: in their rough boots and frieze coats, axes on shoulders, speaking a guttural language that was doomed almost to die, singing, drinking, fighting among each other, but standing shoulder to shoulder or axe to axe against the world. The paltry townsmen and shopkeepers must have breathed easily when the woodsmen went north to Derry to board the American boat.

As a boy he had known of them and walked among their shadows in the Old Market: No more will we see the gay silver trouts playing, or the herd of wild deer through its forest be straying, or the nymph and gay swain on its flowery bank straying, or hear the loud guns of the sportsmen of Strule.

On those May evenings the steeplejacks were swinging on the spires, tiny black dwarfs sitting in wooden chairs at the ends of ropes. They were pointing the stones, which meant that they smeared in fresh cement, netted the soaring prayers in nets of new white. Snug and secure in deep warm grass on a railway embankment from which there was a view both of the tips of the roofs of the town and of one deep curve of the slow pike-infested Drumragh River, Tom and Sadie, Tom's friend and Sadie's friend, lay on their backs and watched the dwarfs on the steeples.

—Why, Angela said, did they not build one steeple as long as the other?

—As high, he said, you mean.

—High or long, she said, what's the difference?

She had a wide humorous mouth that, some evening, with the help of God he would get around to kissing.

—It all depends, Tom said, on which way you're going. Like up or down or sideways.

—Why? she repeated.

She was a stubborn girl. He held her hand.

—In this life, Tom said, there is nothing perfect.

—No, he said.

Because he knew.

—Two men were killed on the smaller steeple. So they stopped.

—Brian, said Tom, always has a better story. Say us a poem, Brian.

—That's no story. It's gospel truth.

Tom and Sadie were kissing, gurgling. Angela tickled his palm.

—That's a job, he said, I wouldn't have for all the tea in China. He meant being a steeplejack.

Tom surfaced. He said: I'm not so sure. I wouldn't mind being able to get up as high as that.

Sadie said: You could always try.

With her left hand she gently massaged Tom's grey-flannelled crotch. He watched Sadie's small moving hand. He wondered how many people within a ten-mile radius, in the town, in villages, from farmhouse doorways, walking along laneways, or fishing, or lying on grass, were watching the steeplejacks on the spires.

For no reason that he could explain he thought it would be exciting to see that face again, the wide humorous mouth, the brown hair that curled like two little brown horns over her temples, the plump fresh cheeks. The hair, though, wouldn't be brown any more. Don't forget that. Look for something older. Three years older than yourself: a reasonable gap of years, once upon a time, for a girl who could teach and a boy who was willing, even afraid, to learn.

—That woman, his daughter said, who writes you those letters from Indiana. What part of this town did she live in? When she was a girl, I mean.

The three of them were walking down the steep High Street. Behind and above them, where two narrower streets met to form the High Street, was the eighteenth-century courthouse, high steps before it and Doric columns, dominating the long undulations of High Street and Campsie Avenue until the houses ended and the point of vision was buried in deep trees.

He told them that there had once been in the town a policeman so lazy that he hated to walk. So he sat all day, when the day was sunny, on the courthouse steps. When his superior officers asked him what he thought he was at, he defended himself by saying that he had the whole town under observation.

This grey day, the last sad day but one of the old year, would have been no day for sitting on the steps.

They laughed at the memory of the lazy policeman, and descended the steep street. The daughter said: You never met her, all the times you were in the States?

—I never even met her, I only saw her, when we were young together here in this town. She's a shadow, a memory.

—Shadows, she said precisely, don't write letters. Memories might.

—One time last year, he said, I had hoped to meet her. I was, so to speak, passing that way. That is, within a few hundred miles or so of where she lives. That's not far, out there.

—Just next door, his son said.

—It was in March, he said, and I was on the way north to give a lecture in Minnesota. I crossed Indiana.

—See any Injuns dad? said the son.

—No, what I mostly remember about Indiana is big barns and ducks, the big ducks that we call Muscovy ducks. Never saw so many Muscovy ducks, anywhere else in the world.

—But then dad, his daughter said, you never were in Muscovy.

—Or if he was, said the son, he never told us.

In March in Indiana the endless flat brown land still shivered. The harness-racing tracks by the roadside were soggy and empty. The last of the snow lay here and there in sordid mounds. Cattle, with a certain guilty look about them, foraged among the tall battered corn-stalks of last year's harvest. There was ice at the fringes of creeks and rivers that looked far too small to negotiate such interminable expanses of flat land. Great round-roofed barns stood aloof from, yet still dwarfed, the neat houses. Flat and sombre the land went every way to a far horizon . . .

—A small American penny, his daughter said, for your wandering thoughts.

He told her that in one small field near the city of Lafayette he had seen a flock of more than two hundred Muscovy ducks. The field had been between a railway and a line of power pylons.

—Nothing, he explained, more emphasises distance in flat land than a line of pylons striding on and on for ever, giants marching, carrying cables on their shoulders, until they vanish east or west.

—Or north or south, his son said.

—Now, she said sweetly, we know all about electricity. Dad, you're such a dear old bore. We couldn't care less about ducks or pylons. We want to know about the woman who writes you those marvellous letters from Indiana.

—She was an orphan, he said. In an orphanage. In Derry City.

—So far so good, his son said.

—She was taken out of the orphanage by this woman and reared in this town. She suffered a lot from illness. She wore a leg-splint when she was a child. She grew up. She read books. My father used to talk a lot about her. He used to say: You should meet that young woman. She's a wonder.

—But I was in college in Dublin, by that time, coming and going and somehow or other I never did get the opportunity of speaking to her. My memory is of a rather long beautiful face, sort of madonna, and fair hair. Framed like an old picture in glass and wood, against a background of coloured magazines and paperbacked books. Because my last recollection of her is that she was working in the bookstall in the railway station. During the war she went off to London, married an American. Then seven or eight years ago she read something I'd written and wrote to me. That's the whole story.

She had written: You may have a vague recollection of who I am when you read my name. Then again you may not. It's been a long time. About thirty years. But I remember you very well, indeed: on your way to school, to church, walking the roads around our town, always, it seemed to me, alone.

That would be a romantic young girl confusing an average sullen lout of a fellow with her private image of Lord Byron.

—We rarely said more than hello. We lived in the same town all our growing years. We walked the same roads, knew the same people, and didn't meet at all. We might have shared a common interest. I loved books, poetry, music, but had little opportunity to enjoy any of them. I did manage to read quite a lot, and to remember poetry, and get a little music on an old radio. I walked, and thought of the books I'd read, and repeated the poetry to myself, and could hear the music again along the quiet roads. Thus I survived the town I was born in. Though mostly I remember it with love, because of Margaret, the woman who reared me. She was gentle, poor, uneducated, but with a lively mind and kind to all things living – especially to me when she took me from the nightmare of the orphanage in Derry, haunting me even now with its coldness, the crooked hilly streets of Derry, the jail, the Diamond, the wide Foyle which is really our own Strule, and the ships.

—Another penny for your thoughts, his daughter said. Or a measly nickel.

They turned right from the Market Street along the Dublin Road, past a filling station and a Presbyterian church, a toy-like gasworks, the old white houses of Irishtown. Beyond Irishtown, he told them, was the Drumragh River and the old humped King's Bridge where James Stuart, falling back from the walls of Derry, had watched the town burn behind him.

Then they were ascending through a pleasant affluent suburb.

—No, he said, this wasn't the part of the town she lived in. We're not going that way just at the moment.

They were, in fact, walking to say a prayer at his father's grave. Everywhere he went he carried with him for luck a white stone from the grave. A white stone from the grave of a kind man would have to be lucky, wouldn't it, if there was the least pick of reason in the universe? But in a drunken moment in Dubin City he had loaned the stone to a man who ran greyhounds, and this particular greyhound had won, and the man begged to be allowed to keep the stone. Today he would say his prayer and take away with him another white stone.

The Protestants lay to the left of the cemetery's main avenue, the Catholics to the right, and between them, on a slight rise, the stone oratory, cold and draughty, where on harsh days the last prayers were said over the coffins. He never remembered the wind around the corners of that oratory as being, even in summer, anything but bitterly cold. This last dead day, but one, of the year it was unbearable. Bravely the boy and girl knelt on the damp earth and prayed. He knelt with them, not praying, talking without words to the man under the clay, or somewhere in the air around him, and around him wherever in the world he went: the dead hover for ever over the living.

Low dark clouds travelling, or being forced to travel, fast, bulged with rain. To the lee of the empty oratory the three of them stood and looked over the forest of obelisks and Celtic crosses, Sacred Hearts and sorrowing mothers, at the distant sweep of the flooded Drumragh, at where the railway line used to cross it by a red metal bridge. The bridge was gone and the railway too – sold for scrap. But three hundred yards to the east of the river, there was still the stone bridge under the embankment – it looked like a gateway into an old walled city – and the lovers' lane that led into the fields, and across the fields to the wooded brambly slope above one of the deepest, most brooding of the river's pike-pools.

Would it be sin or the beginning of living to touch the hidden flesh of Angela? His dream of fair women was all about the creeping hand, the hair, the warmth. That was all that Tom and the other boys talked about.

She lay on her back in the brambly wood – the pike hovering in the pool below them – and he fumbled fearfully, and tickled her, his hand timidly outside her dress. But when she reached for him he rolled away. She laughed for a longer time than seemed necessary. From the far side of a clump of bushes he heard Tom say to Sadie: There must be nothing in Brown's house that doesn't smell of embrocation.

—The grave was very weedy, the daughter said.

—So I noticed. Your grandmother pays good money to have it kept clean and covered with white stones. On the way out I'll call to the caretaker's house and talk to him.

The clay in the centre of the grave had sunk. He was glad that neither son nor daughter had noticed that. It would be so painful to have to explain to young people, or even to oneself, that clay sank so when the coffin underneath had collapsed.

The hotel they stopped in was a mile outside the town, a domed mid-nineteenth-century house, miscalled a castle, on a hill top with a view of the heathery uplands the Camowen came from, and quite close to a park called the Lovers' Retreat, but known to the soldiers in the barracks as Buggers' Den.

The aged mother was safely at home in bed, in her small house across the narrow street from those gigantic limping spires. She liked to be close to the quietness of the church, the glowing red circle around the sanctuary lamp where she remembered and prayed for and to the dead man.

Leaving her in peace they had walked through the lighted crowded town, along a quiet dim suburban road, over a bridge that crossed the invisible talkative Camowen – there was a good gravelly trout pool just below that bridge. They dined late in a deserted dining-room. Along a corridor there was the noise of merriment from the bar. His son asked him which room had been the haunted room in the days when the hotel had been a castle.

—For the sake of the ghost, the daughter said, let's hope it wasn't where the bar is now.

—Ghosts, he told her, might like company.

—Not mine I pray, she said.

—Fraidy cat, the son said. A ghost couldn't hurt you.

—That ghost, he told them, couldn't hurt anyone. The story was that the people who lived here called in the priest and he blessed the room and put the ghost in a bottle.

—Poor ghost, she said.

—But where, she wondered, did the priest put the bottle?

—On the river, the son said. And it floated over the sea, to England, and somebody found and opened it, and got a ghost instead of a message.

He saw them to their rooms. No ghost could survive in such up-to-date comfort. No ghost could rest in peace in any of the coloured bottles in the bar. The noisy local drinkers had gone home, taking their din with them. A few commercial men, talking of odds and ends, drinking slowly but with style, sat in an alcove. He joined them.

—Did you like it out there? they asked him.

—You were a friend of Tom Cunningham, they said.

—It's good out there. Fine people. Hospitable. The sort of people I meet.

—Tom went into the Palestine police after the war, they said. Then he went farther east. Never heard of since.

—Chasing the women in China, they said.

—But the crime in America, they said. Did you ever come up against that?

—It's there. But I never came up against it. Except in the newspapers.

—By God, they said, they have picturesque murders out there. We never have anything here except an odd friendly class of a murder. But out there. That fellow in Chicago and the nurses. And the young fellow that made the women in the beauty parlour lie down like the spokes of a wheel and then shot the living daylights out of them.

—The one that sticks most in my mind . . .

They were all attention.

. . . was the girl in the sump. This sump is an overflow pond at the back of a dry-cleaning plant. One morning a man walking by sees a girl's leg standing up out of the water.

—Clothed in white samite, they said. Mystic, wonderful.

—Seems she had been by day a teller in a bank and by night a go-go dancer in a discotheque. One day she walks out of the bank with a bagful of thousands of dollars. She is next encountered in the sump, one leg surfacing, her hands tied behind her back, her throat cut, the bag and the dollars gone. A barman from the discotheque is also missing.

—All for love, they said.

The long cold day, the search for the past, the drink, the warm company, had made him maudlin.

—When I read the newspapers today there are times I think I was reared in the Garden of Eden.

—Weren't we all, they said.

But it hadn't been the Garden of Eden for one waif of a girl, now a woman in far-away Indiana. From Atlanta, Georgia, where he had been for two years he had remailed to her the local newspapers that had come to him from this town.

She had written: That photograph of the demolition of the old stone railway bridge at Brook Corner saddened me. I recall that bridge with affection. When I'd spent about fourteen months flat on my back in the County Hospital, and was at last permitted up on crutches, I headed, somewhat shakily, under that bridge to begin the first of many walks. I still remember the bridge framing the road beyond like a picture, and the incredible green of the fields, the flowering hedges, the smell of hawthorn. The bridge became for me a gateway: to happy solitude. When I had trachoma and thought I might go blind my bitterest thought was that I might never again see the world through that bridge. Margaret's brother, Fred, was my companion and consolation in those dark days. He had been hired out at the age of six to work with a farmer and Margaret remembered seeing the golden-curly-haired child going off in the farmer's trap.

—Perhaps that was why Fred never cared to work. He hadn't, for about twenty-five years before he died, not because he couldn't but simply because he didn't want to. Oh, on a number of occasions he worked, briefly, for farmers at harvest time, was rarely paid in cash but in kind; and only on condition that his dog, Major, could accompany him. Major barked all day, every day, as though indignant at his master's labours, and much to the chagrin of the other workers and the farmer. But since, when he wanted to, Fred could work as well as the others, his services were always desired and he was permitted to stay, dog and all.

—He was a strange silent man who sat by the fire all day with a far-off look in his eyes. He had very blue eyes. He rarely spoke to anybody outside the house. He was my sole companion during many long hours when I was confined to bed. I would read to him and ask him to spell and he would deliberately mis-spell and would be delighted when I would sharply correct him. I never knew how much I loved him until he died.

—Margaret house-kept for Morris, the lawyer, who lived in the Georgian house beside the church with the high spires, and that left Fred and me a lot alone, and Fred would cook for me. Once, after I had been with Margaret several months, some sadistic neighbour woman told me that I was being sent back to the orphanage. So terri-fied was I that I hobbled up to the church and stood for hours across the street from the lawyer's house, waiting, the wind moaning away up in the spires in the darkness, until Margaret came and comforted me, led me home by the hand to Fred and Major and numerous cats, and a one-legged hen who had a nest in the corner and who was infuriated if another hen ever came to the back door in search of scraps.

His room was haunted, sure enough. He had sat too late, drunk too much, perhaps released the ghosts from the bottles. Oaken angels sang from the ceiling. A tearful crippled girl waited in the darkness at the foot of spires lost also in the windy darkness, no longer magic towers from which one could see the world. The leg of a girl who had stolen for love stood up like a stump of wood out of stagnant water.

Very cautiously he had asked his mother: Do you remember a family called Law? Are they still in the town? One of them, I think, was a famous racing cyclist.

Cautiously: because in her eyes there were times when he was still fourteen or less and there were people that he wasn't supposed to know.

—Oh, I remember the Laws. They were famous, indeed.

Around the house she had a fancy for dressing as if she were a pirate chief. Or perhaps it was a gipsy queen. Sometimes instead of the hel-met-shaped hat she wore a white gipsy head-handkerchief; and a long red dressing-gown and a Galway shawl with the corners tucked back under her oxters and pinned behind.

—One of them called in to see me one morning after Sunday mass. A Law or a half-Law or a quarter-Law or a by-Law. You wouldn't have much time for the like of them. Not condemning anyone for the weakness, but there were more distant cousins in that clan than was natural. Or godly.

That seemed to be that.

—You wouldn't have expected much of the Laws, she said. But it's heartrending to see the fate of some families that had every chance that God and man could give them.

—Like who, for instance?

—Like many I've seen. Like the Glenshrule family, for one.

The red bull of Glenshrule roared through his haunted dreams.

—Glenshrule's sold, she said, and in the hands of strangers. The bull, he supposed, had been sold to make bovril.

Two private roadways led into the old house at Glenshrule, one from the steep by-road along which the crippled girl had hobbled to find peace, one from the road that led west to the Donegal sea. To either hand on either road it was all Glenshrule land, green, bountiful, a little unkempt, cattle country, little tillage. The three bachelor brothers of Glenshrule were gentlemen farmers: which meant whipcord breeches and booze and hunting horses. But they were frank, reckless, generous, easy in their money and good breeding, and made no objection to the townspeople using their private roads for circular walks on Sunday afternoons. Roving boys used those roads all the time, and the fields around them, and the only prohibiting notice to be seen told you to beware of the red bull.

—Christ, look at the size of him, Tom cried with an artist's enthusiasm. Boy, if you were built like that, you'd be welcome anywhere.

They sat on a five-barred iron gate. Between them and the bull's private meadow was the additional fortification of a strong wooden gate. He was an unruly bull. His red coat shone. He had a head near as big as the head of the mouldy bison they had seen in the Old Market in Bostock and Wombell's travelling menagerie. He rooted at the ground with one fore-foot. The great head rose and fell. He didn't roar.

He rumbled all the time like a train, far away, going into a tunnel.

—There's a lot to be said, Tom said, for being a bull.

—Everybody puts up with your tantrums.

—There's more to it than that.

Then the lady of Glenshrule, the one single sister of the three bachelor brothers, rode by on a bay mare. To acknowledge that they existed she raised her riding-crop, she smiled and said: Don't tempt him. Don't enter the meadow. Bulls eat boys.

—Boys, Tom muttered.

He was very bitter.

—There's also a lot to be said, he said, for being a bay mare.

She was bareheaded. She was blonde. She was twenty-five. She was blonde, she was blonde, she was blonde and calm-faced, and all the officers in the barracks pursued her. Years afterwards – altering the truth, as memory always does – he thought that he had then thought about queen and huntress, chaste and fair. But he hadn't. He had been too breathless to think of anything except, perhaps, that Sadie and Angela, lively and provoking as they could be, were still only in the servant-maid class.

She rode on towards the Donegal road. The sound of the hooves died away. The red bull, calmed, had lain down on the grass.

—One Sunday evening I sat beside her in the church, Tom said. My right leg against her left. It burned me. I can feel it still.

He rubbed his right thigh slowly, then sniffed his hand.

—I swear to God, he said, she pressed her thigh against mine. It made short work of the holy hour.

That was the year Tom and himself had been barred from the town's one cinema because Tom, ever an eager and enquiring mind, had discovered the anti-social use of hydrogen sulphide. A few sizzling test tubes planted here and there in the darkness could have tumultuous effects on the audience. Old Mr Pritchard – he was so old that it was suspected he had fought in the Zulu war – was heard to say in a barracks-square voice that some bloke here needed a purge of broken bottles. But three burly ushers simply purged Tom and his companion from the audience, two of them to hold Tom, the other to herd the companion before him.

Such a splendid deed and its consequences gave the two of them the glory of outlaws among their contemporaries. And to be barred from the delights of Eddy Cantor's Rome, or of Broadway with its gold-diggers, or of Wallace Beery's Big House, meant more nights in the Old Flax Market. That was fair enough, because the Old Flax Market was the place for outlaws. Black-uniformed constables patrolled the streets but, unless there was very audible drunken disorder, they left the Old Flax Market alone. No flax was ever sold there any more.

—The ghosts of the woodsmen are still here, he told Tom. This was their place when they came to town.

—You and those bloody woodsmen. You're a haunted man.

The unpaved three acres of the Old Market were sodden and puddled. A sharply defined half-moon cut like a cleaver through wispy running clouds. He shouted at the moon: No more will the fair one of each shady bower hail her dear boy of that once happy hour, or present him again with a garland of flowers that they oft times selected and wove by the Strule.

—And poetry, boy, will be your ruination. Poetry will get you nowhere with Angela. Move in, man. Angela demands action.

The moon, even if it was only half a moon, was useful to outlaws in a land of outlaws. For there were only three gas-lamps in the whole of the Old Flax Market and gas-lamps were little use on windy nights or when somebody, for fun or hellery, wished to quench them. One lamp was on a wall-bracket at the corner of a rowdy dance hall. It lighted, when it was allowed to, the wooden stairway to the door of the dance hall, and the people ascending or descending or standing in groups making noise. One lamp lighted the covered cobbled entry-way from the High Street. The third lighted the muddy uncovered exit to a dark riverside walk from which an irate lover had, about that time, heaved his fancy into the river.

—Let's have a look, Tom said, at the Jennet's corner. You'd see things there you never saw at the pictures.

—But look, he said, there goes the Bluebottle, her legs like eleven-pence marked on a new bucket.

The drum boomed, the horn blared from the dance hall. The

half-moon coldly shone on the Strule waters that flowed by one side of
the Old Market.

—If your woodsmen ever walked here, you can bloody well guess
what they were after.

A tall thin girl in a blue coat was being eased into the shadows by
a drunken man.

—Would you believe it, Tom said, she fought like a cat here one
night with one of the Fighting McDermotts. The one with the dinge
in his temple where some decent man brained him with a bottle of
port-wine. When she wouldn't go with him, he shouted he'd tell her
father that sent her out for money, and her uncle that broke her in. She
tore the red face off him.

—He rings the bell, her uncle.

—They say he rang the bell for her when she was thirteen.

There then was the terror of the dark walk by the river. The uncle
who rang the bell as one of the last town-criers was a figure out of a
German fairy-tale, a pied piper, tall hard hat, tailed coat, long grey
moustache, a small man with a voice of thunder, swinging his hand-
bell, shouting out fragments of news: that a group of strolling players
would perform in the town hall, that the water supply would be turned
off – for repairs to pipes in this or that part of the town, that such and
such a house property would be auctioned. Was it credible that a comic
fairytale figure should also be a part of some sniggering story? The
Bluebottle vanished ahead of them into some riverside bushes. Where
the river made an elbow bend, a group of smoking muttering men
waited at the Jennet's corner. Her shady bower was a wooden shelter
put there by the town council to protect Sunday walkers from sudden
showers. The council had not intended to cater for the comfort of the
Jennet and her customers. She was a raw-boned red-headed country
girl whose husband was in the mental hospital.

—Good-natured and charges very little, Tom said.

Some of the shadowy courtiers called after them.

—But, boy, a little bit too open to the general public for men of
taste like ourselves. Take me back to sweet sinful Sadie. Or the lady of
Glenshrule on her bay mare.

She rode on to the Donegal road, the hooves dancing clippety-clop, and the bull lay down in the meadow.

—What went wrong there? he said to his mother. They had everything.

—What would go wrong but debt and drink and the want of wit. The three brothers fled to Canada.

—They followed the woodsmen.

His mother didn't hear him.

—And my, she said, she looked lovely when she rode out astraddle on that bay mare.

—Tom Cunningham would have agreed with you.

—Oh, Tom Cunningham was a rare one. Very freckled when he was a little boy. And curly-haired. I'm amazed you remember him. He went to the war and never came back when it was over. But then you always had a good memory.

—I always had.

—She lived alone after the brothers left, and she never married, and went on drinking. There was a bit of scandal, too. But I never paid much attention to that sort of talk. She died in the ambulance on the way to hospital. But not, thank God, without the priest. For one of the curates was driving past just at that moment.

On the road she had ridden over on the bay mare.

—The Lord, his mother said, has everything mixed with mercy.

—He must have a lot of mercy for orphans, he said.

—Tell granny that story, dad, about the girl in the rain. The woman who writes to you. When she was a child, I mean.

She could still be outside there, the ghost of a frightened child, standing in the darkness at the foot of the spires. But one day in the orphanage playground she had broken out in rebellion.

—A sudden storm came up. The nuns called us in. We were to shelter, cold and miserable, in a sort of arcade or cloister. I started in with the rest, but suddenly I stopped and ran back to the playground. It was pouring. I was alone. The nuns called me. I wouldn't come. I danced around that playground in my bare feet, hair and dress soaking wet. Repeated calls failed to move me. Two nuns came after me. I ran and danced from one side to the other, dodging the hands that tried to clutch me. I laughed and danced in the wind and rain. I'd wait until they got close and then I'd run like the wind. Their long robes were heavy with water. They were exhausted. But I was exhilarated. Until suddenly I collapsed and was dragged inside. Mute and terrified and expecting to be lashed. I don't know why, but my defiance was forgiven.

—It was a ballet, his daughter said. The truant in the rain.

—Nuns on the run, said the son.

The German poet, long ago, went walking in the botanical gardens, saw plants, that elsewhere he had seen only in pots or under glass, growing cheerfully under the open sky. Might he not discover among them, the original plant from which all others are derived? After all, the poet thought, it must exist, the innermost nucleus.

A crazy idea. A wise old woman dressed like a gipsy or a pirate chief. A pert young girl curious about the American woman who had once been an orphan child in this town. Sadie Law with her leather coat and the smell of embrocation. A blonde horse-riding queen and huntress dying of drink in the back of an ambulance. Two sad creatures, nicknamed, one for the colour of her only coat and the hard meagre shape of her body, the other because it was said, with sniggers, that she was hopeless of progeny and disreputable in her ancestry. Angela running hand in hand with him on a wet Saturday afternoon through the Old Flax Market.

The place was empty that day. Not even the ghosts of the woodsmen walked in the grey light and the rain. He couldn't remember where Sadie and Tom had been at that time. The Jennet's corner was also empty. In the wooden shelter, hacked with names and odd obscenities and coy references to local love affairs, they sat on a creaky seat and kissed and fumbled. Then around a corner of the shelter came the Jennet herself, leading a staggering cattle-drover, his ash-plant in his hand.

—Wee fellow, he said with great camaraderie, I suppose you're at the same game as myself.

—He's too bashful, Angela said.

—He'll live to learn, the Jennet said. They all do.

The rain ran down her bony face. Wet yellow hair stuck out from under a red tam o'shanter. Her eyes were of such a bright blue as to make her seem blind.

—The good book, the drover said, says that the wise man falls seven times. And, as sure as my name is Solomon, I'm going to fall now.

So the wee fellow retreated from the shelter, dragging Angela with him for a little way until she dug her heels into the muddy ground. The river was a brown fresh, taking with it broken branches and hay from flooded meadows, sweeping on, down then by Derry our dear boys are sailing. Now he remembered that that day Angela had been wearing a sou'wester and Sadie's black coat, a little big for her but a stronghold against the rain.

—What do we need to run for? You might learn something. He said nothing.

—Wee boy, she said. I'm going back for a peep.

He stood alone looking at the turbulent river, looking across the river at the limping spires, one proud and complete, one for ever unfinished, a memory of defeat and death. What would a wild woodsman have done? Down along the river valley it was said that there were trees on which the woodsmen, just before they left, had carved their names so strongly that the letters could still be read. But that must be a fable, a memory out of the old song: Their names on the trees of the rising plantation, their memories we'll cherish, and affection ne'er cool. For where are the heroes of high or low station that could be compared with the brave boys of Strule?

—That was as good as a circus, Angela said. You've no idea in the world what you missed.

At breakfast in the hotel in the morning the chatty little waitress shook his belief in himself by saying to him and his children that she had never heard of anybody of his name coming from this town.

—The great unknown, his daughter said.

—Fooling us all the time, the son said. He came from Atlanta, Georgia.

But then it turned out that the waitress came from a smaller town twenty miles away and was only eighteen years of age.

—Off we go now, said the daughter, to see where granny came from.

—Bring no whiskey to Claramore, his mother said. There was always too much whiskey in Claramore. Returned Americans coming and going.

The son and the daughter wished her a happy new year.

—Drive down the town first, she said. I owe a bill I must pay.

—Won't it wait?

She was dressed in high style: widow's black coat, high hat and veil, high buttoned boots for walking in country places.

—Never begin the new year in debt was a good maxim. I'll stick to it while I have breath.

Her grand-daughter, sitting beside her in the back of the hired car, giggled. Sourly he accepted the comments, one unconscious, one conscious, of two other generations on his own finances.

He drove down the High Street. They waited for her outside a hardware shop. The sky was pale blue, cloudless, and last night's unexpected white frost lay on the roofs and spotted the pavements. His daughter said: Granny never heard of a credit card.

More sordidly the son said: Nor hire purchase. Nor a post-dated cheque.

—It was a different world, mes enfants. They paid their way or went without.

But he knew that he had never worked out where – in the world that he had grown into – that terrifying old-fashioned honesty had gone: no debt, no theft, no waste. Beggars were accepted, because Joseph and Mary and the Child Jesus had gone homeless into Egypt. But debt was a sort of sin.

—Eat black bread first, she would say. But let no man say you're in his debt.

He had never taken to black bread. He hadn't told her that in a briefcase in the boot he had two bottles of Jack Daniels as a gift for his cousin – and for himself. A decent man could not with empty hands enter a decent house, and two bottles of American whiskey would be a fit offering to a house that had sent so many sons and daughters to the States.

She was back in the car again, settling herself like a duchess, her small red-headed grand-daughter helping her to tuck a rug around her knees. She refused to believe that a moving vehicle could be heated like a house.

It was a twelve-mile drive, first down the Derry road, over the steep hill that, in spite of all the miracles of macadam, was called, as it had been called in the eighteenth century, Clabber Brae. Then west, over the Drumquin railway crossing. There was no longer any railway to cross. Once upon a time the crossing-keeper's daughter had been as famous as Sadie Law. Then by Gillygooley crossroads where, one June day, Tom and himself, coming tired from fishing perch in the Fairywater, had seen Angela climbing a gate into a ripe meadow just opened for the mower. Her companion was a stocky-shouldered black-avised soldier. That much they could see. A hundred yards ahead, Tom rested from his cycling and was silent for a long time. Then he said: Boy, I'd leave that one alone for the future.

—She's leaving me alone. Who's she with?

—The worst in the barracks. Fusilier Nixon. And he'll never rank higher.

—Why so?

—Four years ago when he came back from India he was all but drummed out for raping a slavey in the soldiers' holm.

—There's a great view of the holm from the tall spire.

—If you had been up there you could have seen the fun. His bacon was saved by a major whose life he saved, or something, in India. And God help the slaveys. The offspring of that bit of love at first sight is now toddling around Fountain Lane. I'll point him out to you some day. You'd have something in common.

They cycled on.

—I'll tell Sadie, Tom said, what we saw. Sadie has some sense. She wouldn't want to be seen in the company of Fusilier Nixon.

Their bicycles bumped over the railway crossing. The keeper's daughter waved, and called: Hello, Tom Cunningham.

—Cheer up, boy. You'll get another girl.

—I suppose I will.

—From here to China the world's full of them.

—I liked Angela.

He found it hard not to sob. Angela peeping around a corner at the animals in the circus. Angela in the clutches of a black-chinned brute. He had, too, really liked her. More than thirty years later he foolishly looked for her face on the streets of the old town and the face he looked for could not, in reason, ever be there. He would see, instead, a Madonna – whom, also, he had never known – against a background of the coloured covers of magazines.

Now as he drove on, he looked at the gate that Angela had climbed into the meadow. But one gate was very like another and, under white frost, all meadows were the same. Although this valley to him would always be summer holiday country. Every mile of it he had walked or cycled. A hay-shed by a prosperous farmhouse meant for him mostly the sultry July hush before the rain came, the smell of sheds and barns, heavy rain on tin roofs, or soda bread and strong tea by peat fires on open hospitable hearths.

There now across the stilled, white fields was the glint of water at the pool where Tom and himself would first strike the Fairywater. The road climbed here, up over the stony place of Clohogue, then switch-backed for miles in and out of hazel glens, over loud rough brooks, then on to a plateau, high, very high; and visible in such clear frosty air, and a good seventy miles away by the edge of the Atlantic, the pig-back of Muckish Mountain, the white cone of Mount Errigal, the Cock of the North. Claramore was just below the plateau. It was a place of its own, in a new valley.

From the Barley Hill beyond the old long white farmhouse you could also see those two far-away mountains and, in the other direction and looking down the valley of the Fairywater, the tips and crosses of the two limping Gothic spires, but not the smaller plain spire of the Protestant church.

—On a calm evening, his cousin said, they seem so close that you'd imagine you could hear the bell ringing for the May devotions.

He asked his cousin: Do the young people still climb Drumard in autumn to pluck the blayberries?

—We've heard a lot about those same blayberries, his daughter said.

To pluck and eat them, dad says, was a memory of some ancient pagan feast.

—The young people, his cousin said, have their own pagan feasts.

The four of them walked on the boreen that crossed the Barley Hill to the place where the men were building a house for his cousin's son and the bride he would bring home with him in three months' time. Hard frost had slowed up the building work. Among the men, half-loitering, working just enough to keep warm, keeping as close as possible to an open brazier, his cousin passed round one of the bottles of bourbon. They drank from cracked cups and tin mugs, toasted the health of the visitors, of the bride-to-be, wished luck for ever on the house they were building. High above a jet plane, westward-bound out of Prestwick, made its mark on the cold pale blue.

—They'll be in New York before you, his son said.

The drinking men, circling the brazier, saluted the travellers in the sky and raised a cheer. It was only a few hours to New York from the Barley Hill or the pagan blayberries of Drumard. Breath ascended in puffs as white as the jet's signature. On the far side of the hill from the long farmhouse the Fairywater, glittering black, looped through frosted bottom-land.

—Phil Loughran, that used to work for you, he said. He was about my age. Where did he go?

The Black Stepping Stones were at that bend of the Fairywater, the seventh bend visible from where they stood; and above the Black Stones the pool where the country boys went swimming. Willows drooped over it. The bottom was good yellow sand. The water had the brown of the peat and was nowhere more than four feet deep. It was an idyllic place, had been an idyllic place until the day he had that crazy fight with Phil Loughran.

—He went to Australia, his cousin said. We hear he's doing well. The family, what's left of them, are still living here on my land.

Even to this day, and in the frosty air, he blushed to think of the lies he had told to Phil Longhram down there by the Black Stones – blushed all the more because, country boys being so much more cunning than towny boys, Phil almost certainly hadn't believed a word he said. Phil as he listened would have secretly laughed.

—So her name is Angela, he said.

Phil was a squat sallow-faced young fellow, dressed in rough corduroys and heavy nailed boots, his brown hair short-cropped, his eyes dark brown and close together. There was always a vague smell of peat smoke, or stables or something, from those corduroys.

—Angela the walking angel, he said.

They were dressing after a swim. Three other boys splashed and shouted in the pool. A fourth hung naked from a trailing willow, swinging like a pendulum, striking the water with his feet.

—So you tell us, Phil, you had the little man out of sight.

He made a sideways grab, as Angela had done on the wooden brambly slope above the pike-pool on the Drumragh. He was laughing. He said: Little man, you've had a busy day.

Then the two of them were rolling on the grass, swiping at each other, Phil still laughing, he sobbing, with temper, with the humiliation of having his tall tales of conquest made mockery of. Four naked dripping boys danced and laughed and shouted around them. It was the last day but one that he had been at the Black Stones. He had come second best out of that fight but he had a mean miserable sort of vengeance on his very last visit to the place.

Phil in his best corduroys – since it was Sunday – is crossing the water, stepping carefully from stone to stone, in his right hand the halter with which he is leading a love-stricken Claramore cow to keep her date with a bull on the farm on the far side of the river. So he calls to Phil to mind his Sunday-go-to-meeting suit and Phil, turning round to answer, is off his guard when the restive beast bolts. It is, fair enough, his turn to laugh, sharp, clear and cruel, as Phil, bravely holding on to the halter is dragged through the shallow muddy water below the stones. There are seventeen in Phil's family, and he is the eldest, and those corduroys will not be easily replaced.

Over the hard frosted fields his own laughter came back to him.

—I'm glad to hear he did well in Australia.

—They were a thrifty family, his cousin said. A sister of his might visit us this evening, the youngest of the breed, a god-daughter of mine.

The trail of the jet was curdling in the cold sky. The men had gone back to work. For penance he told his cousin and son and daughter how he had laughed on the day the cow dragged Phil through the muddy water. They stood by a huge sycamore a little down the slopes from the unfinished house. Icicles hung from bare branches. He said nothing about how Phil had mocked his boasting.

—Weren't you the beast, dad, his daughter said.

—But it was funny, the son said.

—The young, his cousin said, can be thoughtless. Present company excepted.

For the daughter, the face of a good mimic distorted with mock fury, was dancing towards the cousin to stab him with an icicle broken from the sycamore.

—No, but seriously, he said when they had played out their pantomime of fury and terror: a grey man over sixty with a restful singing sort of voice and a pert little girl of sixteen.

—Seriously. Look at the sycamore. It was planted here more than a hundred years ago by an uncle of mine who was a priest. He died young, not long after ordination. He planted this tree on the day he was ordained, and blessed the earth and the sapling. You may recall, when you were young yourselves, some of his books were still about the house. Mostly Latin. Theology. Some novels. I told you about one of them and you rushed to get it. *The Lass of the Barns*, you thought I said. But, man alive, were you down in the mouth when you discovered it was the *Last of the Barons*.

—Oh dad, his daughter said.

—But I know the age of this tree by checking on the date on the priest's tombstone in Langfield churchyard. And my son says to me: We'll cut it down. It'll spoil the view from the new house. So I said: The house may fall, but this tree will stand while I do. The old have a feeling for each other.

—Lucky tree, the daughter said, that has somebody to stand up for it.

They went, laughing, back down the Barley Hill towards the warmth of the great kitchen of the farmhouse. Under the pall of the white frost it seemed as if nothing here would ever change: not the sycamore, not his cousin, nor the ancient sleeping land. Nothing would change, no matter how many airliners swept westwards up there, leaving nothing behind them but a curdling dissolving mark on the sky. All the ships that had carried all those people westwards, even so many sons and daughters of this house, and the ocean was still unmarked and the land here as it had been. It was elsewhere in the world the changes happened.

—But this fatal ship to her cold bosom folds them. Wherever she goes our fond hearts shall adore them. Our prayers and good wishes will still be before them, that their names be remembered and sung by the Strule. The pond at the corner of the avenue was frozen over. He had fallen into it once, climbing the fence above and beyond it to chase a wandering bullock out of a field of young oats. The fence-post he had been holding on to had broken. The water, he had always imagined, had tasted of duck-dirt. But then how in hell would one be expected to know what duck-dirt tasted like? The fence-post, he noticed, was now made of iron, and that might be some indication, even here, of change. But not much.

The ash-grove to the left before you came to the stables – in that grove he had once criminally broken a young sapling to make a fishing rod – was now a solid wall of grown strong trees, a windbreak on days of south-westerly gales.

Would the horses in the stables be the same, with the same names, as they had been thirty years ago? He was afraid to ask, to be laughed at, to be told what he knew: that even here, even loved familiar farmhorses didn't live for ever. The dogs seemed the same – collies, with more sprawling pups underfoot than had ever seemed natural. The pattern of farming though, had changed somewhat, he had been told: more barley, more pigs fed on the barley, less oats, less root crops, more sucking calves bred in season on the open pasture, taken early from their mothers and sold to be fattened somewhere in confinement, and slaughtered.

In the house ahead of them somebody was playing a melodeon, softly, slowly, and that was something that hadn't changed, because in the past in that house there had been great country dances to pipe, fiddle and melodeon. That was before so many of his cousins, all much older than himself, had gone to the States.

His mother had enjoyed herself. She was red in the face and moist-eyed from sitting by the open hearth with its high golden pyramid of blazing peat; from remembering, for the instruction of a younger generation, the comic figaries of her dear departed dowager of a sister, Kate, who, as a widow in her thirties, had ruled not only Claramore but half the countryside: and from, let it be admitted, sipping at the bourbon. For while she was a great one to lecture about the dangers of drink, she was liable the next minute to take from her sideboard a bottle of brandy and a bottle of whiskey, to ask what you were having, and to join you herself, and she instinctively thought the worst of a man who neither smoked, drank, swore, nor rode horses.

—The young people, she said, are growing up well, God bless them. They haven't forgotten the old ways. That house was never without music and dancing.

The Claramore people had stood around the car, under a frosty moon, and sang Auld Lang Syne as their guests departed.

—That Loughran girl was a good hand at the melodeon. Did you all see her making up to the widow man, the returned American?

She poked him between the shoulder-blades as he drove slowly over the icy plateau.

—She sat on your knee, dad, the daughter said.

He could still feel the pressure of the underparts of the girl's thighs. She was conventionally slim and dark and handsome, with wide brown eyes; in appearance most unlike her eldest brother. She had sat on his knee in the dancing kitchen to tell him that Phil, in every letter he wrote from Australia, enquired about him. She stayed sitting there while his cousin sang: There was once a maid in a lonely garden when a well-dressed gentleman came passing by.

—Was that story true granny? the son asked. The one about the lone bush.

—Would I tell it if it wasn't.

They descended into the first hazel glen. Over the rushing of its brook they could hear the roaring of another jet, out of Prestwick, bound for New York.

—They're lining up to get into America, the son said.

—To get out of it too, son.

Six hours or so to the bedlam of Kennedy airport: But now our bold heroes are past all their dangers. On America's shores they won't be long strangers. They'll send back their love from famed Blessington's Rangers to comrades and friends and the fair maids of Strule.

People who travelled by jet left no shadows in old market-places. Generations would be born to whom the ache and loneliness in the old songs of exile would mean nothing.

—Jordan Taggart the cobbler, as I said, had his house on the road from Claramore to Carrickaness, and a small farm to boot. Against the advice of all, even against Father Gormley the priest that cured people, he cut down a whitethorn that grew alone in the middle of his meadow and, at nightfall, he dragged it home behind him for kindling. In the orchard before his house he saw two small children, dressed in white, and he spoke to them but they made no answer. So he told his wife and his three sons, who were also cobblers, that there were two shy children waiting, maybe for mended shoes in the orchard. But when two of the sons went out and searched they saw nothing. Then Jordan ate the supper of a healthy man and went to bed and died in his sleep.

—But he wasn't really dead, the son said.

—No, the white children took him. God between us and all harm.

In the darkness in the car she spat, but slightly and politely, and into her handkerchief.

The daughter said nothing.

They were back again in the meadow country where Angela had climbed the gate and, except for one last meeting, had climbed out of his life for ever. They bumped over the Drumquin crossing where there was no longer any railway to cross, no easy girl to call longingly after Tom Cunningham, who was chasing girls in China and never wrote to enquire about anybody.

The daughter was alert again. She was giggling. She said: Dad, Granny wants to do something about the way you dress.

—I was only thinking about his own good, his mother said.

Although he was carefully driving the car over Clabber Brae, he knew by the way she talked that he was no longer there.

—But when I was by the seaside at Bundoran I saw these young fellows wearing loose coloured patterned shirts outside their trousers. I was told it was an American fashion, and I was sure that he would be wearing one of them when he came home.

He said: I'm no young fellow.

—What I thought was that it would cover his middle-aged spread.

As they descended by the military barracks into the town the daughter's giggles rocked the car.

—A maternity shirt, she said.

—For how could he expect anyone to look at him at his age and with a stomach like that.

Castle Street went up so steeply that it seemed as if it was trying to climb those dark grotesque spires.

—A young one, for instance, like that Loughran girl who sat on his knee because the chairs were scarce.

—That one, he said. All that I remember about the Loughrans is that her bare-footed elder brothers were always raiding Aunt Kate's cherry trees and blaming the depredation on the birds.

In the hotel bar only two of the commercial men were left. They said: What do you think now of your happy home town?

—How do you mean?

—Last night's tragic event, they said. Didn't you hear? Didn't you read the paper?

—I was in the country all day.

Back in the past where one didn't read the newspapers.

—A poor man murdered, they said. What your American friends would call a filling-station attendant.

—Robbed and shot, they said. Just when we were sitting here talking about murder.

The grandfather clock in the hallway chimed midnight.

—The New Year, he said. May it be quiet and happy.

In the ballroom in the far wing of the hotel the revellers were clasping hands and singing about old acquaintance.

—We should be there singing, he said.

—The second murder here this year, they said. The other was a queer case, two young men, a bit odd. Things like that usen't to happen. This town is getting to be as bad as Chicago.

—It isn't as big or as varied.

They laughed. They agreed that the town was still only in a small way of business. He asked them was the park called the Lovers' Retreat still where it had been.

—If that's the way you feel, it is.

More laughter.

—But it's gone to hell, they told him. It's not kept as it used to be. The young compulsory soldiers in national service wreck everything. They haven't the style of the old Indian army, when the empire was in its glory. Children's swings uprooted now. Benches broken. One of the two bridges over the millrace gone completely. The grass three feet long.

—Nothing improves, they said.

When they left him he sat on for a long time, drinking alone. Was it imagination, or could he really hear the sound of the Camowen waters falling over the salmon leap at the Lovers' Retreat? That place was one of the sights of the town when the salmon were running: the shining curving bodies rising from the water as if sprung from catapults – leaping and struggling upwards in white foam and froth. But one year the water was abnormally low, the salmon a sullen black mass in the pool below the falls – a temptation to a man with Tom Cunningham's enterprise. The water-bailiff and his two assistants and his three dogs came by night and caught Tom and his faithful companion with torch and gaff and one slaughtered salmon. But since the bailiff, a bandy-legged amiable man, was also the park-keeper he said not a word to the police on condition that the two criminals kept the grass in the park mowed for a period of six months.

—Hard labour, by God, boy. He has us by the hasp. The Big House with Wallace Beery. You be Mickey Rooney.

The bad news travelled and was comic to all except the two mowers. Then one day from the far side of the millrace that made one boundary to the park they heard the laughter of women, and saw Sadie and Angela, bending and pointing.

—Two men went to mow, they sang, went to mow the meadow.

—Grilled salmon for all, they called.

Tom crossed the millrace by leaping on to the trunk of a leaning tree that was rooted on the far bank. Sadie, laughing, screaming in mock terror, and Tom in pursuit, vanished into the bluebell woods. Tom's companion crossed the millrace prosaically by one of the wooden footbridges. Was it the one that the wild young resentful compulsory soldiers had destroyed? She didn't run. She wasn't laughing any more. Her brown hair no longer curled in little horns on her temples but was combed straight back. But the wide mouth, in spite of the black fusilier, was to him as inviting as ever. She said: You're a dab hand at mowing. You've a future in cutting grass.

He said: I never see you any more.

—Little boys should take what's offered to them, when it's offered. Go back to your scythe.

—Go back to the fusilier, he said.

He went back to his scythe by climbing along the trunk of the leaning tree and leaping the millrace. The grass that fell before his scythe was crimson in colour and swathed in a sort of mist. The swing of the scythe moved with the rhythm of the falling water sweeping on to meet the Drumragh, to become the Strule, to absorb the Fairywater and the Derg and the Owenkillew, to become the Mourne, to absorb the Finn, to become the Foyle, to go down then by Derry to the ocean, taking with it the shadows of the woodsmen, the echoes of the brass and pipes and tramping feet of the army of a vanished empire, the stories of all who had ever lived in this valley.

He knew he was drunk when he heard the woman's voice speak respectfully to him and saw her through the crimson mist through which long ago he had seen the falling grass. She said: You wouldn't remember me, sir.

He didn't. She wore the black dress, white collar and cuffs of the hotel staff. She would be sixtyish. She said: We saw you on the teevee one night and I said to Francie who you were. But he said he didn't know you. He knew your elder brother better.

—My brother was well known.

—Francie's my brother. You might remember he used to ride racing bicycles. I saw you in the dining-room. I work in the kitchen. I knew it was you when I saw your son, and from the teevee.

—You're Sadie Law.

—I didn't like to intrude on you and the children.

He said there was no intrusion. They shook hands. He asked her how her brother was.

—He's in a chair all the time. He broke his back at the tom-fool cycling. But he does woodcarving, and I work here. We manage. I never married.

Her face did not remind him of Sadie Law, but then he found that he could not remember what Sadie Law's face had looked like.

—Nobody, he said, could replace Tom Cunningham.

She neither smiled nor looked sorrowful. Her face remained the same. She said: Oh, Tom was a card. He went away.

Some revellers from the ballroom came in, drunk, singing, wearing paper hats. She said: I must be off.

—I'll see you in the morning.

—I'm off duty then. Because of the late dance tonight. But we hope you'll come back often to see the old places.

—Do you ever remember, he asked, a Fusilier Nixon, a wild fellow?

She thought: No. But there were so many fusiliers. A lot of them we'll never see again.

—We'll look out for you on the teevee, she said.

They shook hands again.

They said goodbye to his mother and drove away. His daughter said: Dad, this isn't the Dublin road.

—There's a place I want to see before we leave.

It was the place that Tom and himself used to go to when they considered that the mental strain of school was too much for them. For it was an odd thing that in all the comings and goings of that railway station nobody ever thought of asking a pair of truants what they were doing there. Everybody thought that everybody else was waiting for somebody else, and there were always porters and postmen who knew what you were at, but who kept the knowledge to themselves, and would share talk and cigarettes with runaway convicts, let alone reluctant schoolboys. No police hunted for drifters or loiterers, as in

American bus stations: and the sights were superb and you met the best people. They had spent several hours one day with Chief Abidu from southern Nigeria and his Irish wife and honey-coloured brood. He danced on broken glass and swallowed fire in a wooden booth in the Old Market, and, beating on his breast, made the most wonderful throaty noises; and came, most likely, from Liverpool.

—I understand, she had written, that the railway station is closed now. Only the ghosts of those who passed through it abide there. Some were gentle, some were violent men, morose or gay, ordinary or extraordinary. I had time to watch them passing by. It is pain that they died so young, so long ago.

The tracks were gone, the grass and weeds had grown high through the ballast. The old stone buildings had been turned into warehouses. Two men in dusty dungarees kept coming and going, carrying sacks of meal, at the far end of the platform. But if they spoke to each other they were too far away for their voices to be heard, and the cold wind moved as stealthily in grass and weeds as if it were blowing over some forlorn midland hillside. Where the bookstall had been there was just a scar on the granite wall, where she had stood, framed against coloured books and magazines, and watched the soldiers coming and going.

—The young English poet you mention, I knew briefly. He came to buy books. At first he had little to say, simply polite, that's all. Then one day he and another young man began to talk. They included me. But mostly I listened. It was fascinating. After that, when he came he talked about books. He asked questions about Ireland. He was uneasy there, considered it beautiful but alien, felt, I think, that the very earth of Ireland was hostile to him, the landscape had a brooding quality as though it waited.

—He was five or six months garrisoned in our town. They told me he could be very much one of the boys, but he could also be remote. He treated me kindly, teased me gently. But he and a brilliant bitter Welshman gave me books and talked to me. Sometimes they talked about the war.

—It was only after he was reported missing in Africa that I learned he was a poet. But I think I knew anyway.

—I never heard if the Welshman survived. I had several long letters from him and that was all.

Ghosts everywhere in this old town.

—Now I have a son who may pass through a railway station or an airport on his way to war.

He said to his daughter: That's where the bookstall was.

—Will you go to see her, dad? In the States, I mean.

—In a way I've seen her.

He was grateful that she didn't ask him what on earth he was talking about.

—As the song says, I'll look for her if I'm ever back that way.

The ghost of his father stood just here, waving farewell to him every time he went back after holidays to college in Dublin.

They walked through the cold deserted hall, where the ticket offices had been, and down the steps, grass-grown, cracked, to the Station Square, once lined with taxis, now empty except for some playing children and the truck into which the dusty men were loading the sacks. From the high steeple the noonday angelus rang.

—How high up is the bell? his son asked.

He told him, and also told him the height of the spire and of the surmounting cross, and why one spire was higher than the other, and how he had once climbed up there, and of the view over the valley, and of how he had almost fallen to doom on the way down, and of the vertigo, the fear of death, that followed.

—And a curious thing. Once, on top of the Eiffel Tower, that vertigo returned. And once over the Mojave desert when I thought the plane was going to crash. But I didn't see Paris or the Mojave desert. I saw that long straight ladder.

The bell ceased. The spires were outlined very clearly in the cold air, looked as formidable as precipices. Around them floated black specks, the unbanishable jackdaws.

—Once I got a job from the parish priest because I was a dab hand with a twenty-two. The job was to shoot the jackdaws, they were pests, off the spires. It was going fine until the police stopped me for using a firearm too close to a public highway. The sexton at the time was a tall man in a black robe down to his feet, more stately than a bishop. One day, when he was watching me at work, a bird I shot struck one of those protruding corner-stones and came soaring, dead, in a wide parabola, straight for the sexton. He backed away, looking in horror at the falling bird. But he tripped on his robe, and the bird, blood, feathers, beak and all got him fair in the face. At that time I thought it was the funniest thing I had ever seen.

—Grisly, his daughter said.

—But once upon a time I laughed easily. It was easy to laugh here then.

High Street, Market Street, the Dublin Road. A stop at the grave where the caretaker's men had already done their job. The weeds were gone, the sad hollow filled, new white stones laid.

Then on to Dublin, crossing the Drumragh at Lissan Bridge where, it was said, Red Hugh O'Donnell had passed on his way back from prison in Dublin Castle to princedom in Donegal and war with Elizabeth of England. The wintry land brooded waiting, as it had always done, and would do for ever.

He sang at the wheel: There was once a maid in a lovely garden.

—Oh dad, his daughter said.

So he thought the rest of it: Oh, do you see yon high high building? And do you see yon castle fine? And do you see yon ship on the ocean? They'll all be thine if thou wilt be mine.

There are Meadows in Lanark

The schoolmaster in Bomacatall or McKattle's Hut was gloved and masked and at his beehives when his diminutive brother, the schoolmaster from Knockatatawn, came down the dusty road on his high bicycle. It was an Irish-made bicycle. The schoolmaster from Knockatatawn was a patriot. He could have bought the best English-made Raleigh for half the price, but instead he imported this edifice from the Twenty-six into the Six Counties and paid a mountain of duty on it. The bike, and more of its kind, was made in Wexford by a firm that made the sort of mowing-machine that it took two horses to pull. They built the bikes on the same solid principle. Willian Bulfin from the Argentine who long ago wrote a book about rambling in Erin had cycled round the island on one of them and died not long afterwards, almost certainly from over-exertion. There was a great view from the saddle. Hugh, who was the son of the schoolmaster from Bomacatall, once on the quiet borrowed the bike and rode into the side of a motorcar that was coming slowly out of a hedgy hidden boreen. He was tossed sideways into the hedgerow and had a lacework of scratches on his face. The enamel on the car was chipped and the driver's window broken. The bike was unperturbed.

The little man mounted the monster by holding the grips on the handlebars, placing his left foot on the extended spud or hub of the back heel and then giving an electrified leap. This sunny evening he dismounted by stepping on to the top rail of the garden fence at

Bomacatall. He sat there like a gigantic rook, the King Rook that you hear chanting bass barreltone in the rookery chorus. He wore a pin-striped dark suit and a black wide-brimmed hat. He paid no attention to the buzzing and swarming of the bees. The herbaceous borders, the diamond-shaped beds at Bomacatall would blind you. There was a twisting trout stream a field away from the far end of the garden. To his brother who was six feet and more the little man said: I have a scheme in mind.

From behind the mask the big man said: Was there ever a day that God sent that you didn't have a scheme in mind?

—It would benefit the boy Hugh. *Cé an aois é anois?*

That meant: What age is he now?

—Nine, God bless him.

—Time he saw a bit of the world. Bracing breezes, silvery sands, booming breakers, lovely lands: Come to Bundoran.

That was an advertisement in the local newspaper.

—You could sing that if you had a tune to it, said the man behind the mask.

—The holiday would do him good, the King Rook said, and for three weeks there'd be one mouth less to feed.

That was a forceful argument. The master from Knockatatawn, or the Hill of the Conflagrations, was a bachelor. Hugh was midways in a household of seven, not counting the father and mother.

The bees settled. The bee-keeper doffed the mask and wiped the sweat off a broad humorous face. He said: James, like St Paul you're getting on. You want another to guide you and lead you where thou would'st not.

—John, said the man on the fence, in defiance of Shakespeare, I maintain that there are only three stages in a man's life: young, getting-on, and not so bad-considering. I've a sad feeling that I've got to the third.

The nine-year-old, as he told me a long time afterwards, was all for the idea of Bundoran except that, young as he was, he knew there was a hook attached. This was it. At home on the Hill of the Conflagrations there wasn't a soberer man than the wee schoolmaster, none more precise in his way of life and his teaching methods, more just and exact in the administering of punishments or rewards. But Bundoran was for him another world and he, when he was there, was another man. He met a lot of all sorts of people. He talked his head off, behaved as if he had never heard of algebra or a headline copybook, and drank whiskey as if he liked it and as if the world's stock of whiskey was going to run dry on the following morning. Yet, always an exact man, he knew that his powers of navigation, when he was in the whiskey, were failing, that – as Myles na Gopaleen said about a man coming home from a night at a boat-club dance in Islandbridge – he knew where he was coming from and going to, but he had no control over his lesser movements. He needed a pilot, he needed a tug, or both combined in one: his nephew. There was, also, this to be said for the wee man: he was never irascible or difficult in drink, he went where the pilot guided him and the tug tugged him. He was inclined to sing, but then he was musical and in the school in Knockatatawn he had a choir that was the terror of Féis Doire Cholmcille, the great musical festival held in Derry in memory of St Colmcille. He even won prizes in Derry against the competition of the Derry choirs – and that was a real achievement.

So for one, two, three, four years the nephew-and-uncle navigational co-operation worked well. The nephew had his days on the sand and in the sea. He even faced up to it with the expert swimmers at Roguey Rocks and the Horse Pool. By night while he waited until his uncle was ready to be steered back to the doss he drank gallons of lemonade and the like, and saw a lot of life. With the natural result that by the time the fifth summer came around, that summer when the winds were so contrary and the sea so treacherous that the priest was drowned in the Horse Pool, the nephew was developing new interests: he was looking around for the girls. At any rate, Bundoran or no Bundoran, he was growing up. Now this was a special problem because the schoolmaster from Knockatatawn had little time for girls, for himself or anybody else and, least of all, for his nephew who, in the fifth summer, had just passed thirteen.

One of the wonders of the day on which they helped the schoolmaster from Knockatatawn to the hotel and happed him safely into bed by four o'clock in the afternoon was that Hugh saw a woman, one of the Scotchies, swimming at her ease in the pool where the priest had been drowned. She was a white and crimson tropical fish, more blinding than the handsomest perch in the lake at Corcreevy or the Branchy Wood: white for arms, shoulders, midriff and legs, crimson for cap and scanty costume. Women were not supposed to be in the Horse Pool on any account but so soon after the drowning, the usual people were shunning it, and that woman either didn't know or didn't care. The Scotchies who came to the seaside to Bundoran in the summer had a great name for being wild.

In the hotel bedroom the sun came in as muted slanted shafts through the cane blinds. The shafts were all dancing dust. Carpet-sweepers weren't much in use in that hotel. They helped the wee man out of his grey sober clothes and into a brutal pair of blue-and-white striped pyjamas. He was a fierce hairy wee fellow. Arms long like an ape and a famous fiddler when he was sober. The big purple-faced schoolmaster from Lurganboy said: Begod, you're like a striped earthenware jar of something good.

The little man waved his arms and tried to sing and once slipped off the edge of the bed and sat on the floor and recited word-perfect:

A Chieftain to the Highlands bound
Cries: Boatman, do not tarry,
And I'll give thee a silver crown
To row me o'er the ferry.

The lot of it, every verse, all about how the waters wild swept o'er his child and how Lord Ullin's daughter and her lover were drowned. The drowning of the priest must have put it into his mind. The purple-faced man from Lurganboy, rocking a little, listened with great gravity, his head to one side, his black bushy eyes glistening, his thick smiling lips bedewed with malt. He said: In the training college he was renowned for his photographic memory. And for the fiddle.

Hugh said nothing. He was sick with delight. His uncle was a blue-and-white earthenware jar of Scotch whisky, as full as it could hold. He always drank Scotch in Bundoran, out of courtesy, he said, to the

hundreds of Scotchies who came there every year on their holidays and
spent good money in the country. The music of hurdy-gurdies and
hobby-horses and the like came drifting to them from the strand, over
the houses on the far side of the town's long street. This blessed day the
blue-and-white jar could hold no more. He would sleep until tomorrow's dawn and Hugh was a free man, almost fourteen, and the world
before him.

—He'll rest now, said the red-faced master from Lurganboy.

They tiptoed out of the room and down the stairs.

—What'll you do now, boy?

—Go for a walk.

—Do that. It's healthy for the young.

He gave Hugh a pound, taken all crumpled out of a trouser pocket.

Then nimbly, for such a heavy man, he sidestepped into a raucous
bar and the swinging doors, glass, brass and mahogany, closed behind
him. It was an abrupt farewell, yet Hugh was all for him, and not only
because of the crumpled pound, but because in him, man to man and
glass for glass, the schoolmaster from the Hill of the Conflagrations
had for once taken on more than his match. Several times as they
helped the little man towards his bed the unshakeable savant from
Lurganboy had said to Hugh: Young man, you are looking at one who
in his cups and in his declining years can keep his steps, sir, like a
grenadier guard.

He had the map of his day already worked out in his head. The Scotchy
girl wouldn't be sitting on the high windowsill until seven o'clock. She
was there most evenings about that time. She and God knew how
many other Scotchies, male and female, lived in a three-storeyed yellow boarding-house at the east end of the town. There was a garden in
front of it, a sloping lawn but no fence or hedge, and the two oval
flower-beds were rimmed with great stones, smoothed and shaped by
the sea, tossed up on the beach at Tullaghan to the west, gathered and
painted and used as ornaments by the local people. This Scotchy girl
was one that liked attention. The way she went after it was to clamber
out of a bedroom window on the third floor and to sit there for an
hour or more in the evening kicking her heels, singing, laughing,

pretending to fall, blowing kisses, and shouting things in unintelligible Scottish at the people in the street below, throwing or dropping things, flowers, chocolates, little fluttering handkerchiefs and once, he had heard, a pair of knickers. He had only seen her once at those capers when one evening he navigated past, tug before steamship, with his uncle in tow. But a fella he knew slightly told him she was to be seen there at that time most evenings. She sure as God was there to be seen. It wouldn't have been half the fun if she'd worn a bathing-suit, but a skirt with nothing underneath was something to tell the fellas about when he got back to Bomacatall. Not that they'd believe him, but still.

Behind her in the room there must have been thirty girls. They squealed like a piggery. That was a hell of a house. A randyboo, the wee master called it. Bomacatall, Knockatatawn and Corcreevy all combined never heard the equal of the noise that came out of that house. On the ground floor the piano always going, and a gramophone often at the same time, and a melodeon and pipes, and boozy male voices singing Bonny Doon and Bonny Charlie's noo awa' and Over the Sea to Skye and Loch Lomond and The Blue Bells of Scotland and Bonny Strathyre and Bonny Mary of Argyle and, all the time and in and out between everything else:

> For I'm no awa tae bide awa,
> For I'm no awa tae leave ye,
> For I'm no awa tae bide awa,
> I'll come back an' see ye.

—They work hard all year, the wee master said. In the big factories and shipyards of Glasgow. Then they play hard. They're entitled to it. The Scots are a sensitive generous people and very musical.

This was the map that was in Hugh's mind when the red- or purple-faced master from Lurganboy left him outside the swinging doors of the saloon bar. That Lurganboy man was a wonder to see at the drink. When he moved, Hugh thought, he should make a sound like the ocean surf itself with the weight of liquid inside him. He had also said something remarkable and given Hugh a phrase to remember. For as they'd steered the Knockatatawn man round a windy corner from the promenade to the main street, a crowd, ten or eleven, of Scotchy girls had overtaken them, singing and shouting, waving towels and skimpy bathing-suits, wearing slacks and sandals, bright blouses, short skirts, sweaters with sleeves knotted round their waists and hanging over rumps like britchens on horses.

—This town, said the master from Lurganboy, is hoaching with women.

That was the northern word you'd use to describe the way finger-lings wriggle over and around each other at the shallow fringes of pools on blinding June days.

—Hoaching. Hoaching with women, Hugh said to himself as he set out to follow the map he had drawn in his mind that would bring him back at seven o'clock to the place where the daft girl kicked her heels and more besides on the windowsill.

From the house of glass to the Nuns' Pool by way of the harbour where the fishing boats are. It isn't really a house of glass. This shopkeeper has a fanciful sort of mind and has pebbledashed the front wall of his place with fragments of broken glass. The shop faces east, catching the morning sun; the whole wall then lives and dances like little coloured tropical fish frisking, hoaching, in a giant aquarium. Hugh can look down on it from his window which is right on top of the hotel across the street. Some people say the wall is beautiful. Some people say the man is crazy. The seer from Knockatatawn says that's the way with people.

Westward the course towards the Nuns' Pool. Passing the place where the sea crashes right into the side of the street, no houses here, and only a high strong wall keeps it from splattering the traffic. Here in the mornings when the tide is ebbed and the water quiet, a daft old lady in a long dress walks out along rocks and sand, out and out until she's up to her neck in the water, dress and all, and only her head and wide-brimmed straw hat to be seen. Then she comes calmly out again and walks home dripping. Nobody worries or bothers about her. The bay is her bath tub. She lives here winter and summer.

This day the harbour is empty, a few white sails far out on the bay, pleasure boats. He sits on the tip of the mole for a while and looks down into the deep translucent water. On the gravelly bottom there are a few dead discarded fish, a sodden cardboard box, and fragments of lobster claws turned white. If he could clamber around that sharp rock headland and around two or three more of the same he could peep into the Nuns' Pool and see what they're up to. Do they plunge in, clothes and all, like the mad woman in the morning? It's hard to imagine nuns stripping like the Scotchy in the pool where the priest was drowned. Surely the priests and the nuns should share the one pool and leave Roguey Rocks and the Horse Pool to the men and the wild Scotchies. The strand and the surf are for children and after five summers he knows he's no longer a child.

But he's also alone and he knows it. Tugging and steering his mighty atom of an uncle has taken up all his time and cut him off from his kind. On the cliff top path by the Nuns' Pool there are laughing girls by the dozen, and couples walking, his arm as tightly around her as if she had just fainted and he is holding her up. In corners behind sod fences there are couples asprawl on rugs or on the naked grass, grappled like wrestlers but motionless and in deep silence. Nobody pays the least attention to him. Fair enough, he seems to be the youngest person present. Anyone younger is on the sand or in the surf. Or going for rides on donkeys. He is discovering that, unless you're the tiniest bit kinky, love is not a satisfactory spectator sport.

Steep steps cut in rock go down to the Nuns' Pool. Was it called after one nun or gaggles of nuns, season after season? It must have been one horse. But what was a horse ever doing out there on rocks and sea-weed and salt water? He sees as he walks a giant nun, a giant horse. The steep steps turn a corner and vanish behind a wall of rock as big as Ben Bulben mountain. Only God or a man in a helicopter could see what goes on in there. Do they swim in holy silence, praying perhaps, making aspirations to Mary the Star of the Sea? He listens for the sort of shouts and music and screaming laughs that come from the house where the girl sits on the windowsill. He hears nothing but the wash of the sea, the wind in the cliffside grass, the crying of the gulls. What would you expect? It is ten minutes to five o'clock.

He has time to walk on to the place where the Drowes river splits into two and goes to the sea over the ranked, sea-shaped stones of Tullaghan, to walk back to the hotel by the main road, feast on the customary cold ham and tomatoes and tea, bread and butter, wash his hands and face and sleek his hair with Brylcreem and part it up the middle, and still be on good time and in a good place for the seven o'clock show. He does all this. He is flat-footed from walking and a little dispirited. On the stony strand of Tullaghan there isn't even a girl to be seen. If there was he could draw her attention to the wonderful way the sea forms and places the stones, rank on rank, the biggest ones by the water line and matted with seaweed, the smallest and daintiest right up by the sand and the whistling bent-grass. They are variously coloured. The tide has ebbed. Far out the water growls over immovable stones.

He rests for a while by the two bridges over the Drowes river. If there was a girl there he could tell her how the river flows down from Lough Melvin, and how the trout in the lake and the trout in the river have the gizzards of chickens and how, to account for that oddity, there's a miracle story about an ancient Irish saint. There is no girl there. A passing car blinds him with dust. Has the evening become more chilly or is that just the effect of hunger? He accelerates. He knows that while a Scotchy girl might show some interest in stones shaped and coloured into mantelpiece or dressing-room ornaments, she would be unlikely to care much about trout or ancient miracles. In the hotel the master is sound asleep in blue-and-white bars, the bedclothes on the floor. He doesn't snore. Hugh eats four helpings of ham and tomatoes, two for himself, two for the recumbent fiddler from the Hill of the Conflagrations.

The evening is still ahead of him and the fleshpots delectably steaming. There is no glitter from the house of glass. The hot tea and ham, the thought of the kicking girl on the high windowsill have done him a lot of good. In the evening most of the children will be gone from the strand, the Palais de Danse warming up, the hoaching at its best.

He wasn't the only one watching for the vision to appear, and right in the middle, like a gigantic rugby-football forward holding together a monumental serum, was the purple-faced man from Lurganboy. The Assyrian, Hugh thought, came down like a wolf on the fold and his cohorts were gleaming in purple and gold. He wasn't his uncle's nephew for nothing, even if he wasn't quite sure what a cohort meant. As he told me long afterwards in the Branchy Wood, or Corcreevy, if his literary education had then advanced as far as Romeo and Juliet he would have been able, inevitably, to say: But soft what light through yonder window etc. The man with the face as purple as cohorts saw it differently. To the men that ringed him round he said: Lads, I declare to me Jasus, 'tis like Lourdes or Fatima waiting for the lady to appear. All we lack is hymns and candles.

—We have the hymns, one voice said, she has the candles.

—*Ave ave*, said another voice.

The laughter wasn't all that pleasant to listen to. They were a scruffy enough crowd, Hugh thought, to be in the company of a schoolmaster that had the benefit of education and the best of training; the master from Bomacatall, kind as he was, would have crossed the street if he'd seen them coming. Shiny pointy toes, wide grey flannels, tight jackets, oiled hair; the man from Lurganboy must, at last, like the stag at eve, have drunk his fill or he wouldn't, surely to God, be in the middle of them. Hugh dodged. There was a fine fat flowering bush, white blossoms, bursting with sparrows when the place was quiet, right in the middle of the sloping lawn. He put it between himself and the waiting watching crowd. His back was to the bush. He was very close to the high yellow house. The din was delightful, voices male and female, a gramophone playing a military march, somebody singing that there are meadows in Lanark and mountains in Skye – and he was thinking what a wonderful people the Scots were and what a hell and all of a house that must be to live in, when the high window went up with a bang and there she was, quick as a sparrow on a branch, but brighter, much brighter.

He had heard of a bird of paradise but never had he, nor has he up to the present moment, seen one. But if such a bird exists then its plumage would really have to be something to surpass in splendour what Hugh, in the dying western evening, saw roosting and swinging on the windowsill. Far and beyond Roguey Rocks the sun would be sinking in crimson. The light came over the roofs of the houses across the street, dazzled the windows, set the girl on fire. Long red hair, red dress, pink stockings, red shoes with wooden soles. She was so high up, the angle was so awkward, the late sunlight so dazzling, that he could find out little about her face except that it was laughing. The scrum around the Lurganboy man cheered and whistled. He knew she was laughing, too, because he could hear her. She was shouting down to the Lurganboy contingent, the *caballeros*, but because of the noise from the house and the street he couldn't pick out any words and, anyway, she would be talking Scottish. Nor could he be certain that he had been correctly informed as to what, if anything, she wore underneath the red dress although when he got home to his peers in McKattle's Hut or Bomacatall he sure as God wouldn't spoil a good story by unreasonable doubts.

All told it was an imperfect experience. She twisted and tacked so rapidly, agile as a monkey, that a man could see nothing except crimson. He couldn't even have known that her red shoes had wooden soles if it hadn't been that, with the dink of kicking, one of them came unstuck, and landed as surely as a cricket-ball in his cupped palms where he stood in hiding behind the bush. It was in the pocket of his jacket before he knew what he was doing. Cinderella lost her slipper. He was off through the crowd in a second and nobody but the girl saw him go. The eyes of Lurganboy and his men were on the vision. She screamed high and long. From the far end of the crowd he glanced back and saw her pointing towards him. But nobody bothered to look the way she was pointing. The map of his evening was as clear in his mind as the strand before him, as sure as the shoe in his pocket, and hunt-the-slipper was a game at which anything might happen.

The people in this place have, like the tides, their own peculiar movement. Evening, as he expected, draws most of the children away from the strand to a thousand boarding-house bedrooms. The promise of the moon draws the loving couples, the laughing and shouting groups away from the westward walk by the Nuns' Pool to dry sheltered nooks between strand and dunes, to the hollows in the grassy tops of the high cliffs above Roguey, to the place where later the drums will begin to feel their way in the Palais de Danse. Every night, including Sunday, in the palais there is not only a dance but a few brawls and a talent competition.

No moon yet. No drums yet. The last red rays are drowned in the ocean. The light is grey. The strand is pretty empty and a little chilly, the sea is far out. But as he runs, ankle deep in churned sand, down the slope from the now silent motionless hobby-horses and hurdy-gurdies, he sees a slow, silent procession of people coming towards him around the jagged black corner of Roguey Rocks. The sea washes up almost around their feet. They step cautiously across a shelf of rock, then more rapidly and boldly along the slapping wet sand by the water's edge. Four men in the lead are carrying something. He runs towards them, all girls forgotten. Whatever chance, anyway, he had of meeting a girl during the day he can only have less now in this half-desolate place. The red shoe will be his only souvenir, yet still something to show to the heathens in Bomacatall. Halfways across the strand a distraught woman in shirt and cardigan, hair blowing wild, stops him. She says: Wee boy, see if it's a wee boy with fair hair. He's missing for an hour and I'm distracted. Jesus, Mary and Joseph protect him. I'm afraid to look myself.

But it isn't a wee boy with fair hair. It isn't even the crimson-and-white Scotchy girl who had been swimming in the Horse Pool and whom the sea might have punished for sacrilege, for surely a dead drowned priest must make some difference to the nature of the water.

What he sees is nothing that you could exactly put a name to. The four men carry it on a door taken off its hinges. It's very large and sodden. There's nothing in particular where the face should be – except that it's very black. A woman looks at it and gasps. Somebody says: Cover that up, for God's sake.

A tall red-headed man throws a plastic raincoat over the black nothing in particular. Hugh walks back to the woman in the skirt and cardigan. He tells her that it isn't a wee boy with fair hair. She thanks God.

—It's a big person that must have been a long time in the water.

But she has moved away and isn't listening. He falls in at the tail of the procession. People leave it and join it, join it and leave it. It's a class of a funeral. An ambulance comes screaming down the slope from the long town and parks beside the stabled silent hobby-horses. Two civic guards come running, a third on a bicycle. Behind on the strand one single man in a long black coat walks, fearing no ghosts, towards Roguey Rocks. No couples or laughing groups are to be seen, even on the grassy clifftops. He fingers the shoe in his pocket to remind him of girls. A drum booms, a horn blares from the Palais de Danse which is halfways up the slope towards the town. He gets in, and for free, simply by saying that he's singing in Irish in the talent competition.

The hall was already crowded because the evening had turned chilly and the threat of rain was in the air. He found a seat in a corner near the ladies where he could watch the procession coming and going. They came and went in scores and for all the attention any of them paid to him he might have been invisible. He was grateful for the anonymity. He was too weary to carry on with the hopeless chase and that grim vision on the beach had given him other things to think about. It was still fun to sit and watch the women, all shapes and sizes and colours, and moods. They went in demure and came out giggling. That was because most of them, he had heard, kept noggins of gin and vodka concealed in the cloakroom. It was a great world and all before him. The band was thunderous, the floor more and more crowded until somebody thumped a gong and everybody who could find a chair sat down: girls who couldn't sitting recklessly on the knees of strangers, nobody on his. So he stood up and gave his chair to a girl who didn't even say thanks. The band vanished. A woman sat at the piano, a man with a fiddle and a young fellow with a guitar stood beside her. This was the talent competition.

A grown man long afterwards in the Branchy Wood, or Corcreevy, he couldn't remember much of it. The time was after eleven, he had been on foot all day, his eyes were closing with sleep. A man with long brown hair and long – the longest – legs and big feet came out, sang in a high nervous tenor about the bard of Armagh, then tripped over the music stand and fell flat on his face. That act was much appreciated. A little girl in a white frock and with spangles or something shining in her hair, tiptoed out, curtsied, holding the hem of her skirt out wide in her hands, danced a jig to the fiddle, then sang a song in Irish that meant: There are two little yellow goats at me, courage of the milk, courage of the milk. This is the tune that is at the piper, Hielan laddy, Hielan laddy. And more of the same. A fat bald man sang: While I'm jog jog jogging along the highway, a vagabond like me. Then there were tin whistles and concertinas, six sets of Scottish and two of Irish or Uillean pipes, piano accordions, melodeons, combs in tissue paper and clicking spoons, cornet, fiddle, big bass drum, something, something and euphonium. As the song says.

He lost interest. His insteps ached. He would unnoticed have slipped away only a crowd and girls hoaching was always better than a lonely room. Surveying the crowd from China to Peru he saw in the far corner the man from Lurganboy, like the old priest Peter Gilligan, asleep within a chair, his legs out like logs, hands locked over splendid stomach and watch-chain and velvet waistcoat, chin on chest, black hat at a wild angle but bravely holding on to his head. No angels, as in the case of Peter Gilligan, hovered over him, none that Hugh could see. Five other adults sat in a row beside him, all awake except Lurganboy. Angels that around us hover, guard us till the close of day. Singing that, the Knockatatawn choir had once won a first prize in Derry city.

As Hugh watched, Lurganboy awoke, pulled in his legs, raised his head, gripped the arms of his chair and hoisted himself to sit erect. The ballroom was silent. Was it the oddness of the silence made the sleeper awake? No, not that, but something, Hugh felt, was going to happen. The drummer was back on the stage. He struck the drum a boom that went round the room, echoing, shivering slowly away. Then the compère said: Ladies and gentlemen.

He said it twice. He held up his right hand. He said again: Ladies and gentlemen, while the judges, including our old, true, tried and stalwart friend from Lurganboy are making up their minds, adding up points, assessing the vast array of talent, not to mention grace and beauty, we will meet again an old friend, a man who needs no introduction, a man who many a time and oft has starred on this stage and who, in days gone by but well remembered has worn more laurels for music than—

The cheers hit the roof, and out on the stage like a released jack-in-the-box stepped the wee master from Knockatatawn, sober as a judge, lively as a cricket, dapper as a prize greyhound, fiddle in one fist, bow in the other. When the cheering stopped he played for fifteen minutes and even the gigglers, resurfacing after gin and vodka, kept a respectful silence. Lord God Almighty, he could play the fiddle.

It could be that the way to get the women is to be a bachelor and play the fiddle, and drink all day and pay no attention to them. For I declare to God, the schoolmaster from Corcreevy said long afterwards, I never saw anything like it before or since, flies round the honey-pot, rats round a carcase, never did I see hoaching like that hoaching, and in the middle of it and hopping about on the stage like a wound-up toy, a monkey on a stick, the red Scots girl from the windowsill, and her shoe in my pocket. Radar or something must have told her where it was. She saw me, isolated as I was, standing like a pillar-box in the middle of the floor, for the crowd was on the stage or fighting to get on the stage, and the drum was booming and the compère shouting and nobody listening. She came towards me slowly and I backed away and then ran for the beach, and then stopped. The moon was out between clouds. There was a mizzle of rain.

He stopped running and looked at the moon and the moonlight on the water. This was destiny and he had no real wish to run from it. The moon shines bright, on such a night as this. As he is now, a moonlit beach always reminds him of loneliness, a crowded beach of faceless death. She was a little monkey of a girl and she crouched her shoulders and stooped when she talked. Her red hair was down to her hips. She said: Wee laddie, will ye no gie me back ma shoe?

He was learning the language.

—I'm as big as ye are, yersel.

—Will ye no gie me back ma shoe?

She wasn't pleading. She wasn't angry. He knew by her big eyes that it was all fun to her, all part of the holiday. She really wasn't any taller than himself and her foot fitted into his pocket.

—It's no here. It's in ma room.

—You'll bring it tae me.

—For sure. It's no awa tae bide away.

—Guid laddie. Do ye dance?

—Thon's my uncle wi' the fiddle.

—Ye're like him. Ye were quick away wi' ma shoe. I'll no tell him ye're here.

The red shoe was his ticket of admission to the wild happy house. Nothing much, naturally, came of that except a lot of singing and some kisses in the mornings from a sort of elder sister. He learned to talk and understood Scots and to this day, and in his cups, can sing that he's no awa tae bide awa with the best Glaswegian that e'er cam doon frae Gilmour hill. Like his uncle he enjoyed his double life. Not for years, though, not until he had been through college and had his own school in Corcreevy or the Branchy Wood, did he tell the tale to the old man who by that time was retired and able to drink as he pleased. The old fellow, mellow at the time, laughed immoderately and said: Seemuldoon, I always hold, is a land of milk and honey if you keep your own bees and milk your own cow.

That was a favourite and frequently irrelevant saying of his. Seemuldoon, meaning the dwelling-place of the Muldoons, was, in all truth, the place he came from, and not Knockatatawn. Nor did the man from Lurganboy really come from Lurganboy: I used the name just because I like it, and when people ask me to go to Paris and places like that I say no, I'll go to Lurganboy. Because you don't *go* to Lurganboy, you find yourself there when you lose the road going somewhere else.

Bloodless Byrne of a Monday

Three tall men excuse themselves politely, close the door gently behind them, hope he doesn't mind. But they are exhausted putting fractious Connemara ponies on a boat for a show and sale in Britain. Odd caper to be at so early on a Monday morning, they admit. And, as well, they're all Dublin men by accent, and may never have seen the Twelve Bens or Clifden or the plains of Glenbricken.

—Fair enough, they admit. They are most courteous.

The tallest of the three says he knows the West of Ireland well, and knows the song about Derrylee and the greyhounds and the plains of Glenbricken and about the man who emigrated from Clifden to the other West, the Wild West, to hunt the red man, the panther and the beaver, and to gaze back with pride on the bogs of Shanaheever.

The tallest man also says that from an early age he has been into horses, the big ones, his father drove a four-wheeled dray. Then into hunters with a man on the Curragh of Kildare. Then, on his own and by a lucky break, into ponies. A bleeding goldmine. He is not boasting. The colour of his money is evident in three large whiskeys for himself and his colleagues, and a brandy and ginger for the stranger up from . . .

—Sligo, he says.

—On a bit of a blinder, he adds.

To be civil and companionable. They are three very civil, companionable men. And he craves company. The need of a world of men for me. And round the corner came the sun.

To the tallest man the fat redheaded man says: Bloodless Byrne was a friend of your father.

The smallest of the three, the man with the peaked cloth-cap, says: Bloodless Byrne of a Monday morning. The brooding terror of the Naas Road. Very vengeful. Bloodless drove a dray for the brewery.

—Bloodless Byrne of a Monday morning, the tallest man repeats. He wears strong nailed boots and black, well-polished leather leggings.

—It became a sort of a proverb, he explains. Like: Out of the question, as Ronnie Donnegan said. Bloodless. A face on him like Dracula without the teeth. They tried calling him Dracula Byrne. But it didn't stick. He didn't fancy it. He was vengeful. Vindictive. He'd wait a generation to get his own back. He didn't mind being called Bloodless. They say he wrote it when he filled in forms.

—Mad about pigeons, says the stout redheaded man.

—Bloodless Byrne of a Monday. My father told me how that came about.

Carefully the tallest man closes the other door that opens into the public bar, cuts off the morning voices of dockers on the way to work, printers on the way home.

—Bloodless, you see, is backing his horse and dray of a Monday into a gateway in a lane back of the fruit and fish markets in Moore Street. Backs and backs, again and again. Often as he tries, one or other of the back wheels catches on the brick wall. So finally he takes his cap off, throws it down, puts his foot on it, stares the unfortunate horse full in the face, and says: You're always the same of a fuckin' Monday.

—Deep voice he had too. Paul Robeson.

The shortest man removes his cloth cap to reveal utter baldness. A startling transformation, forcing the strange gentleman from Sligo to blink tired eyelids upon tired eyes. The shortest man says: Bloodless Byrne of a Monday.

—Pigeons, says the stout redheaded man.

Bangers, the barman, belying his nickname, steps in most politely, making no din, to gather up empties and hear requests: so the gentleman from Sligo places the relevant order. These men are true companions. And prepared to talk. And what he needs most at the moment is the vibration of the voices of men. And he wants to hear more about those pigeons. And Bloodless Byrne. And why Ronnie Donnegan said it was out of the question, and what it was that was.

Drinks paid for, he has five single pound notes to survive on until the banks open and he can acquire a new chequebook.

—Out of the question, he says tentatively.

But the emphasis is on pigeons and the tallest man is talking.

—Fellow in America, Bloodless says to me, wrote a play about a cat on a hot tin roof. Bloodless never saw it. The play. He saw the poster on a wall. Could you imagine Bloodless at a play? Up above in the Gaiety with all the grandees. A play. Bloodless tells me the neighbour has three cats on a black tin roof, hot or cold, and says he wouldn't like to tell me what they're at, night and day. Bloodless has no time for cats.

—Pigeons, says the stout redheaded man.

—No time for the neighbour either. No love lost. No compatibility. No good fences. So one day . . . .

—Cats and pigeons, says the stout redheaded man.

—One day the neighbour knocks on the door and says very sorry there's your pigeons, and throws in a potato sack, wet and heavy. Dead birds.

It is difficult not to join in the chant when the stout redheaded man says again: Cats and pigeons.

—What does the bold Bloodless do? Nothing. Simply nothing. He bides his time. He waits and watches. June goes by, July and August and the horse-show, and one day in September he throws a plastic sack, very sanitary, in at the neighbour's door and says sorry, mate, them's your cats. Just like that. Them's your cats. In a plastic sack.

There is nobody in the snug, nobody even in the packed and noisy public bar but Bloodless Byrne, nothing to be seriously considered but his vengeance: Sorry, mate, them's your cats.

Face like Dracula without the teeth, he broods over the place for the duration of several more drinks which must have been bought by the ponymen: for the five pound notes are still intact and the ponymen are gone, and never in this life may he know what it was that was out of the question. His clothes are creased and rumpled. He needs a bath and a shave and a long rest. The noise outside is of water relaxing from shelving shingle. The snug is silent. The old boozy Belfast lady fell asleep in the confessional and when the priest pulled across the slide, said: Another bottle, Peter, and turn on the light in the snug.

His eyes are moist at the memory of that schoolboy joke.

June, July, August, and then in September: Sorry, mate, them's your cats.

He should telephone his wife and say he is well and happy and sober. Anyway he wouldn't be here and like this if she hadn't been pregnant so that, to some extent, she is at fault: and he laughs aloud at the idea, and rests his head back on old smoke-browned panelling, and dozes for five minutes.

How many years now have we been meeting once a year: Niall and Robert, Eamonn and little Kevin, Anthony and John and Sean and big Kevin, and Arthur, that's me? Count us. Nine in all. Since two years after secondary school ended in good old St Kieran's where nobody, not even the clerical professors, ever talked about anything but hurling and Gaelic football, safe topics, no heresies possible although at times you'd wonder a bit about that, only a little blasphemy and/or obscenity might creep in when Kilkenny had lost a game: but no sex, right or wrong, sex did not enter in. No sex, either, on this meditative morning. As you were. That wash of waves retreating in the public bar is now as far away as the high cliffs of Moher on the far western shore of the county Clare.

Day of a big game in Dublin, Kilkenny versus Tipperary who have the hay saved and Cork bet, the nine of us come together by happy accident: a journalist and a banker, a student of law, a civil servant, a student of art and theatre, another journalist, a student of history, an auctioneer and valuer, that's me. There's one missing there somewhere. Count us, as they do with the elephants at bedtime in Duffy's circus. N'importe. Bangers looks in and pleasantly smiles, but the glass is still brimming and the five pound notes must be held in reserve until Blucher gets to the bank. Nine old school-friends meet by happy accident and vow to make the meeting annual. Tipperary lost. How many years ago? Ten? More than ten. Twenty? No, not twenty. Then wives crept in. Crept in? Came in battalions, all in one year, mass madness,

Gadarene swine, lemmings swarming to the sea: and college reunions and laughter and the love of friends became cocktails and wives who don't much like each other: and dinner dances. So nothing to worry about when this year Marie is expecting, and all I have to do is meet the men and make excuses and slip away, odd man out: which seemed a good idea at the time, late in the afternoon yesterday, or early in the evening, for in this untidy town afternoon melts un-noted into evening and, regrettably and returning as the wheel returns, it is now in a day as we say in the Irish when we say it in the Irish: and here I am, here I am, here I'm alone and the ponymen are gone, and five pound notes is all between now and the opening of the banks . . . .

Outside, the translucent stream, as he once heard some wit call it, slithers, green and spitting with pollution, eastwards to the sea. The sun is bright without mercy. His eyes water. His knees wobble. Where had he got to after he left the lads to get with their good, unco guid, wives to the dinner dance? The sequence of events, after their last brandy and backslapping, is a bit befogged.

This town is changing. For the worse. Nothing to lean on any more. Where, said Ulysses, where in hell are the pillars of Hercules. The Scotch House is gone. Called that, I suppose, when a boat went all the way from the North Wall to Glasgow, and came back again, carrying Scotsmen who would look across the river and see the sign and feel they were at home. Scotsmen were great men for feeling at home anywhere, westering home with a song in the air, at home with my ain folk in Islay, home no more home to me whither must I wander, and the Red Bank Restaurant gone, it's a church now, and the brewery barges that used to bring the booze downstairs to the cross-channel cargo boats gone forever and for a long time. He's just old enough to remember when he first made a trip to Dublin and saw the frantic puffs of the barges when they broke funnels to clear the low arch, and the children leaning over the parapet, just here, and yelling: Hey mister, bring us back a parrot. A monkey for me, mister. A monkey for me.

And slowly answered Arthur from the barge the old order changeth yielding place to new. That went with a drawing in a comic magazine at the time: a man in hock-coat and top-hat standing among the beer barrels on a barge, Arthur Guinness of course, immortal father of the brewery bring me back a monkey, bring me back a parrot. And God fulfils himself in many ways, over from barges to motor-trucks.

Sorry, mate, them's your cats.

There in that small hotel the nine of us met the day Tipperary lost the match, and met there every year until the hotel wasn't grand enough for the assembled ladies. Then it descended lower still to include a discotheque: and that was that. Nine of us? Dear God, that was why this morning I counted only eight the second time round, for Eamonn, who discovered that little hotel and liked it, even to the ulti-mate of the discotheque, Eamonn up and died on us and that's the worst change of all.

Somewhere last night I was talking mournfully to somebody about Eamonn, mournfully remembering him: and God fulfils himself in many ways.

Out all night, and cannot exactly remember where I was, and did not get home to my own hotel which, and this is another sign of the times, is away out somewhere in the suburbs. Once upon a time the best hotels were always in the centre. Like America now, the automo-bile rules okay, the centre of the city dies, and far away in ideal homes all are happy, and witness a drive-in movie from the comfort and secu-rity of your own automobile: and the gossip and the fevers of the mid-dle-ages, middle between which and what, fore and aft, I never knew, are no more: and I am dirty and tired now, and want a bath and a shave and sleep. Samuel Taylor Coleridge emptied the po out of a first-floor window. While admiring the lakeland scenery.

But this other hotel outside which he now stands is still, and in spite of the changing times and the shifting pattern of urban concen-trations, one of the best hotels in town. At this moment he loves it because he knows it will be clean, as he certainly is not. In the pubs of Dublin the loos can often be an upset to the delicate in health.

So up the steps here and in through the porch. There is a long porch. Jack Doyle, the boxer, used to sit here with an Alsatian dog, and read the papers and be photographed. That was away back in Jack's good days. As a boy he used to study those newspaper photos of hand-some Jack and the big dog, and envy Jack because it was said that all the girls in Dublin and elsewhere were mad about him.

He has heard that a new proprietor of this hotel has Napoleonic delusions: and, to prove the point, *l'empereur* in a detail reproduced from David and blown up to monstrosity, is there on the wall on a horse rearing on the hindlegs, pawing with the forelegs. The French must fancy that pose or position: Louis the Sun King on a charger similarly performing is frozen forever in the Place des Victoires.

Tread carefully now, long steps, across the foyer for if that horse should forget himself, I founder.

A porter salutes him, a thin sandy man, going bald. He nods in return.

Were we here last night? Could have been, for the nine of us used to meet here: and the eighteen of us, until that changing city pattern swept the dinner dance away somewhere to the south.

This morning anything is possible. He raises his left hand to reinforce his nod, and passes on. Upstairs or downstairs or to my lady's chamber? Destiny guides him. So he walks upstairs, soft carpets, long corridors, perhaps an open, detached bathroom even if he has no razor to shave with. Afterwards, a barber's shave, oh bliss, oh bliss. He finds the bathroom and washes his face and those tired eyelids and tired eyes, and combs his hair and shakes himself a bit and shakes his crumpled suit, and polishes his shoes with a dampish handtowel. A bit too risky to chance a bath and total exposure, although he has heard and read the oddest stories about deeds performed in hotel bathrooms by people who had no right in the world to be there. Bravely he steps out again. A brandy in the bar, and the road to the bank and his own hotel and sobriety, and home: Bright sun before whose glorious rays.

Sorry, mate, them's your pigeons.

Before him the corridor a door opens and a man steps out.

This man who steps out is in one hell of a hurry. He swings left so fast that his face has been nothing more than a blur. A black back to be seen as he hares off down the corridor to the stairhead. Hat in one hand, briefcase in the other. Off with quick short steps and down the stairs and away, leaving the door of the room open behind him. His haste rattles me with guilt. That man has somewhere to go and something to do.

To sleep, to die, to sleep, to sleep perchance to dream, and his eyes are half-closed and a mist rolling at him, tumbling tumbleweed, up the corridor from the spot where the man has vanished: and the door is open and the devil dancing ahead of him. There is no luggage in the room, not in wardrobe nor on tables, racks nor floors, no papers except yesterday's evening papers discarded in the waste-basket, no shaving-kit in the bathroom: and the towels, all except one handtowel, all folded as if they have not been used. No empty cups nor glasses nor anything to prove that the robin good fellows or good girls of room service have ever passed this way. That's odd. The black-backed hurrying man must carry all his luggage in that briefcase: but, now that he remembers, it was a big bulging briefcase, brown leather to clash badly with the black suit, big enough to hold pyjamas but scarcely big enough to accommodate anything more bulky than a light silk dressing-gown. Woollen would not fit. N'importe. There are two single beds, one pillowless and unused, all the pillows on the other, which is tossed and tumbled. That man must have had a restless night. But who in hell am I supposed to be or what am I playing at? Sherlock Holmes?

The phone on the table on the far side of the rumpled bed would do very well for his expiatory call to Sligo. He reaches across first for it and then, the most natural thing in the world it seems for him to subside, not just to subside but to allow himself to subside, gravity and all that: and to close his eyes. The bed is quite cold even to a man with his clothes on, and that's also odd because the man with the brown briefcase had moved so fast that his couch should not yet have had time to cool. Perhaps he had genuinely passed such a restless night that he had tumbled on the bed for a while, then sat up or walked the floor until dawn. To hell with Holmes and Dr Watson or Nigel Bruce and Basil, Basil, the second name eludes me. Pigeons fly high over a black roof that is crawling with spitting cats.

Opening his eyes again he reads seventeen in the centre of the dial and, with the phone in his hand, says not Sligo but: Room seventeen speaking, room service could I have, please, a glass of brandy and a baby ginger, not too well this morning, a slight dyspepsia, nervous dyspepsia, something I'm liable to.

The explanation perhaps was an error, too long, too apologetic,

BENEDICT KIELY

never apologise, like Sergius in the Shaw play, just barge ahead and hope for the best. Not too late yet to cut and run but, to hell with poverty we'll kill a duck, here's a pound note for a tip on the table between the beds, charge the brandy to the black-backed man's bill, any man who moves so fast would need a brandy: now down, well down under the bedclothes, nothing to be seen but the crown of my head: and your brandy, sir, the ginger sir, will I pour it sir, do please, mumble but be firm, and thank you, that's for yourself and have one on me, and thank you, sir. It was a man's voice. A porter, not a chambermaid. You can't have everything. And where is the chambermaid? as the commercial traveller said in the Metropole in Cork when his tea was carried to him in the randy morning by, alas, the nightporter. Can't say, sir, about the chamber but the cup and saucer are the best Arklow pottery. Oh God, hoary old jokes: but then my mind is weakening or I wouldn't be here.

The door closes. This is the sweetest brandy he has ever tasted and cheap at a pound. Four notes left. Let me outa here. But gravity strikes again and, eyes closing, he is drifting into dreams when the phone rings and, before he can stop himself, he picks it up and the voice of the female switch says: Call for you, sir.

—Thanking you.

—That you, Mulqueen? Where the hell are you?

A rough, a very rough, male voice.

—Room seventeen.

—Balls. What I mean is what the hell are you up to?

That would by no means be easy to explain to a man I've never seen and on behalf of a man I've never really met.

Mumble: Up to nothing.

—Can't hear you too well. You sound odd. Are you drinking? A bloody pussyfoot like you might get drunk in a crisis.

That's the first time, the reely-reely first time, I was ever called a pussyfoot. Say something. Mumble something. What to say? What to mumble? Have another slow meditative sip. Never gulp brandy, my uncle always told me, it's bad for your brain and an insult to a great nation.

—Mulqueen, are you there? Are you bloody well listening?

—Everything's fine. Not to worry.

—Never heard you say that before, Mulqueen. You that worried the life out of yourself and everybody else. But I should bloodywell hope everything is fine. Although I may as well tell you that's not what the bossman thinks out here in the bloody suburbs. He's called a meeting. You'd better be here. And have the old alibis in order.

—I'll be there. When the roll is called up yonder I'll be there. I'll be . . .

Perhaps he shouldn't have said that, but the brandy, brandy for heroes, is making a new man out of Pussyfoot Mulqueen or whoever he is. Anyway, and God be praised, it put an end to that conversation for the phone at the far end goes down with a dangerous crash that echoes in his ears, if not even in the bedroom. He finishes the brandy, beats time with his left hand and chants: I'll be there, I'll be there, when the roll is called up yonder I'll be there, oh I wonder, yes I wonder do the angels fart like thunder, when the roll is called up yonder I'll be there!

Sips at the empty glass and draws his breath and continues: At the cross, at the cross, where the jockey lost 'is 'oss: send down sal, send down sal, send down salvation from the lord catch my flea, catch my flea, catch my fleeting soul.

And orders another brandy and ginger, and plants another pound, and submerges, and all goes well, and surfaces and drinks the brandy, and realises that he must not fall asleep, must out and away while the going is good and the great winds westward blow, and is about to get on his feet when the phone is at it again. Here now is a dilemma, emma, emma, emma, to answer or not to answer, dangerous to answer, more dangerous not to answer, the ringing may attract attention, the not answering may bring searchers up. It is a woman's voice.

—Is that you, Arthur? Arthur is my name.

—Who else?

—You sound odd.

—The line is bad.

—Your hives are flourishing.

My hives? I don't have hives. Good God, the man's a beekeeper, an apywhatisit.

—But Arthur, I'm worried sick about you. What is it? What is wrong? She is crying.

—O'Leary rang looking for you. I told him where you might be.

—That was unwise.

—I had to. He said things were in a bad way.

—He would.

—Arthur. You sound very peculiar.

—I feel very peculiar.

—What were you up to?

He still doesn't know what he was up to. He says: these things happen. So does Hiroshima. So does the end of the world.

—Arthur, how can you talk like that? You don't sound in the least like yourself. And there is something wrong with your voice.

Best put the phone down gently and run. But she will only ring again before he can get out the door and away.

—Laryngitis. Hoarse as a drake.

He coughs.

—Don't do anything desperate. Promise me.

—Promise.

—In the long run it will be better to face the music. Think of the children.

—I always do.

—You have been a good father. You were never unkind.

She is crying again and he feels like the ruffian he is for bursting in on the sorrows of a woman he has never seen, may never see, pray God. Then his self-respect is restored and his finer feelings dissipated by a male voice, sharp and clear and oh so nasty: You blackguard. Mary is much too soft with you. She always has been.

Nothing better to say than: Who's speaking?

—Very well you know who is speaking, you dishonest automaton, this is your brother-in-law speaking, and a sorry day it was that you ever saw Mary or she ever saw you, or that you brought a black stain, the only one ever, on the name of this family, get over to your office this minute and face the music, it will make a man of you, a term in jail . . . .

Christ save the hastening man who has this faceless monster for a brother-in-law. I am shent, or somebody is, Pussyfoot the automaton is shent as in Shakespeare. But what to say? So unable to think of anything better he says: Bugger off.

Somebody must stand up for Mulqueen who is not here to stand up for himself.

—Filthy language now to make a bad job worse, your father and mother were decent people who never used words like that . . . .

—They never had to listen to the like of you.

—I'll offer up my mass for you, as a Catholic priest I can think of nothing else.

And slam goes the phone and the gates of hell shall not prevail, and the Lord hath but spoken and chariots and horsemen are sunk in the wave: sound the loud timbrel o'er Egypt's dark sea: and he is halfway to the door when the loud timbrel sounds again. Let it sound. Divide the dark waves and let me outa here. And the bedroom door opens and in steps the thin sandy porter, going bald, with a third brandy and ginger on a tray, and puts the tray down carefully, and picks up the phone and says hello and listens, and cups his hand carefully over the mouthpiece and says: It's for Mr Mulqueen, sir. It might be as well to answer it. Just for the sake of appearances at the switch below.

Sounds, he means. Appearances do not enter into this caper. It's a wonderful world. As the song assures us.

A woman's voice, husky, says: Arthur, this is Emma.

Emma, dilemma, dilemma, dilemma.

He says: Emma.

—Arthur love, don't bother about what they say. Come over here to me.

Which at the moment he feels he might almost do, if he knew where she was. Or who. That voice.

—Arthur, do you read me?

—Loud and clear.

—Are you coming?

—Pronto.

And puts down the phone, and turns to face the porter and the music.

So the porter pours the ginger into the brandy and hands it to him and says: You sat here for a while last night, sir. After the others had gone.

Remembering Eamonn. Now he begins to remember something of the night.

—Nine of you used to meet here.

—Eamonn Murray and the rest of us.

—Poor Mr Murray, God be good to him. One decent man. He thought the world and all of you.

A silence. The phone also is mercifully silent.

—About Mr Mulqueen, sir.

—Who?

—Mulqueen, sir. His room, you know.

—Of course. Face the music, Mulqueen.

—You know him, sir?

—Not too well. A sort of passing acquaintance.

—You'll be glad to hear he's well, sir. They fished him safely out of the river. Nobody here knows a thing about it yet. An errand boy came in the back and told me. I sent him about his business. No harm done.

Another silence. He puts the last three notes on the table between the beds, flattens them down under an ashtray: That's for your trouble, Peter Callanan.

Memory, fond memory brings the light.

—How much do I owe you for the brandy?

—It came out of the dispense, sir.

—The name's Arthur.

—They won't miss it for a while.

—But we can't have that. I'll be back as soon as the banks open.

—No panic. No panic at all. You're old stock. Nine of you. And Mr Murray. The flower of the flock.

—What did he do that for? Jump?

—God knows, sir. He seemed such a quiet orderly man. Never touched a drop. And in broad daylight. Stood up on the wall and jumped with the city watching. He couldn't have meant it. Missed a moored dinghy by inches. But he did miss it.

—He had luck, the dog, 'twas a merry chance.

—What's that, sir?

—Oh, nothing. A bit of an old poem. How they kept the bridge of Athlone.

—Athlone. It's a fine town. I worked there for a summer in the Duke of York. Mr Murray was a great man for the poetry. He could recite all night. Under yonder beechtree. And to sing the parting glass.

He leads the way along the corridor and down the backstairs to the basement, then along a tunnel with store-rooms like treasure-caves to right and left. They shake hands.

—Many thanks, Peter.

—Good luck, sir.

—Them's your cats.

Two cats are wooing in the carpark across the laneway.

—What's that, sir?

—Oh, nothing. Just a sort of a proverb where I come from.

—Like out of the question as Ronnie Donnegan said.

—Something like that.

Bloodless Byrne to the right, Ronnie Donnegan to the left, he walks away along the laneway. He hasn't had the heart to ask Peter Callanan what it was that was out of the question. Ahead of him Eamonn walks, forever reciting: Under yonder beechtree, single on the greensward, couched with her arms beneath her golden head, blank a blank a blanky, blank a blank a blanky, lies my young love sleeping in the shade.

He must ring Sligo and tell her that all is well. All is well. Somewhere poor Pussyfoot Mulqueen is being dried out through the mangle. All may not be well. The music is waiting.

There is a group of seven or eight people by the river-wall. One young fellow points. As if Mulqueen had made a permanent mark on the dark water. He has never seen the man's face. Shared his life for a bit. Shared it? Lived it.

And he goes on over the bridge to the bank.

A Letter to Peachtree

Always I prefer not to begin a sentence with an I, so I'm beginning this sentence and letter with the word always. Which can be a beautiful or a terrible word, all depending on where you are, how you feel, who you are with, what you are doing, or what is being done to you. Days may not be bright always and I'll be loving you always. That last bit I really do mean, you, over there, soaking in the Atlantan sun on Peachtree.

Do you know that there was an Irish poet and novelist, a decent man who, as they would say over here, never laid his hand on a woman, and who tore up his mss. and died a Christian Brother, and who wrote a love song to say that he loved his love in the morning, he loved his love at noon, he loved his love in the morning for she like the morn was fair. He loved his love in the morning, he loved his love at noon, for she was bright as the Lord of Light yet mild as Autumn's moon. He loved his love in the morning, he loved his love at Even. Her smile's soft play was like the ray that lights the western heaven. He loved her when the Sun was high. He loved her when he rose. But best of all when evening's sigh was murmuring at its close.

Clear, godamned clear that he knew nothing about it. How could he keep it up, always?

Howandever, as Patrick Lagan says, here we are on this crowded train, the cameraman called Conall, and Patrick and Brendan and Niall and myself, and this plump girl in jodhpurs, well, and a red sweater as well, and good horsey boots to walk about in. And a mob of people, a jampacked train, dozens standing in the corridors, and going towards the wide open spaces of the Curragh of Kildare where the great horses run. There's a man with a melodeon sitting on the seat in the john, merely because he has nowhere else to sit, his big, square-toed boots nonchalantly over the threshold, the melodeon tacit, the man sucking an orange. Jodhpurs leans her right shoulder, her round cheeks flushed, against my necktie spreading like the Shannon between Limerick and the sea, the tie you gave me when I took off for Ireland, a tie wide, I say, as the Shannon, a basic blue and green and, floating on that, slices of orange, a bloodred cherry and a branch of blossoming dogwood. Some tie. The tie that binds us.

This all about Jodhpurs I tell you not to make you jealous but to explain to you how crowded the train is and to give you a general idea of the style and spirit of the journey. Conall the cameraman has asked Jodhpurs to pose against my tie, your tie. She has been on the train with some friends on the way to the races. But when she sees Conall she drops out and joins us. She has the hots for Conall. He is quite a guy. Italianate handsome, dark wavy hair, quick gestures, good tweeds, and style, and as tough as a hawser and, to add the little dusting of pimento, a slight stutter, only noticeable when he's sober. But good-humoured and talking all the time.

Now let me tell you something.

My grandmother came from Ballintubber in the county of Mayo. She had the old belief about how it was ill-luck to meet a redheaded woman on the way to market. Jodhpurs is sure as hell redheaded. But how about, for added value, a redheaded man, big as Carnera, dressed in rust-coloured chainmail tweed, whose too-tight trousers betray him and burst wide-open between the legs when he is strap-hanging in this crowded train? What would you do on an occasion like that? Walk the other way? Look the other way? As any lady would or should.

One little railway-station, two, three, four little railway-stations whip by, then wide-rolling, green spaces with racing-stables, a silhouetted water-tower, a line of exercising horses. Conall says that over there in the national stud by Kildare town he once did a set of pictures of a famous stallion, and he, the stallion, was the smallest thing you ever saw, everywhere and every way no bigger than a pony, Conall says, and says that he, Conall, was himself better hung and I'm prepared to take his word for it. But he is clearly meditating on the goodness of God to the big man who burst. Who has had to borrow a mac from somebody to cover his glory, or his shame. Which it just about does. He is a very big man. Seems to me that that earthquake or revelation, or whatever, just about sets the tone for all that is to follow. Conall puts his curse on crowded trains and on the sharp corners of the leather case he carries his camera in, and says that if there isn't a fight at the play tonight his time will have gone astray. Because of the crowd on the train he missed a proper, or improper, shot of the red man who burst: at the actual instant of bursting, that is. But he knows the red man and the red man's two comrades. Three army officers, out of uniform for a day at the races. The big red man has not, say the other two, been out of uniform, except when in bed, for years. So they have almost forcibly fitted him, or stuffed him into that tweed which, under strain, has not proved a perfect fit from Brooks Brothers.

Then the crowd leaves us at the railway halt, one platform and a tin hut, out on the great plain of Kildare: and off with them all to the races. Conall, who already has had some drink taken, must have sucked it out of the air, no jug visible at any time since Dublin, sings after the racegoers that the cheeks of his Nelly are jolting like jelly as she joggles along up to Bellewstown hill. Which Lagan assures me is a bit of a ballad about another race-meeting somewhere to the north. He promises Jodhpurs, whose cheeks, fore and aft, are firm and by no means jolting like jelly, that he will sing it for her later on. He's a good man to sing a ballad or quote a poem. She latches on to us, and to hell with the races, and we are elsewhere bound, and not to any market.

But how did we all come to be on that there train when the red man was unseamed from the nave to chaps? Listen!

The previous evening, a lovely May evening, Dublin looking almost like one of those elegant eighteenth-century prints, I walked over the Liffey at O'Connell Bridge, then along Eden Quay and for once, the name seemed apt: and into the Abbey bar to meet Patrick Lagan, a man I've mentioned in previous letters. Like, when I went to Brinsley MacNamara to talk to him about his novels and my dissertation, he passed me on to Patrick Lagan. He said that Lagan had more of his books than he had himself, all autographed by me, I mean all autographed by Brinsley. He said that Lagan knew more about his books than he himself did. Curious thing, he said. Brinsley begins many statements with those two words: Curious thing.

Life seems to him almost always absurd and he may well be right about that. He even made a collection of some of his short stories and called it: *Some Curious People*.

Along Eden Quay, then, and left round the corner at the Sailors' Home, and past the burned-out shell of the old Abbey Theatre. Which has recently gone up in smoke, taking all sorts of legends and memories with it. With Brinsley I walked through the rubble, a big man, Brinsley, once a great walker by the river Boyne, but now moving slowly, arthritic feet, and leaning on a stick, and remembering and remembering many curious people.

But the Abbey Bar, round yet another corner, still survives, and Lagan was there in all his glory and a few of his friends with him. There was a lawyer and a professor of history, and a bank-manager, who is also a music critic and who plays the organ in a church, and two actors from the Abbey Theatre, and two reporters from the paper Lagan works on, and one cameraman from same: a mixed and merry throng. And Brinsley, dominating all in physical size and mental dignity, and being treated by all with the respect which is only his due.

Curious thing, he says, how landscape, buildings, environment, physical surroundings can affect the character of people. Take, for instance, your average Dublin workingman. A rough type. A man with a young family, he goes out to the pub in the evening. He drinks a pint, two pints, three, four, five, six, perhaps ten pints. He's a noisy fellow. He sings. He talks loud. He argues. He may even quarrel. He staggers, singing, home to the bosom of his family, in tenement apartment or corporation house, goes to bed quietly and, soundly, sleeps it off. But down in the so soft midlands of Meath and Westmeath, where I come from, things are different. The heavy heifers graze quietly, and the bullocks, all beef to the ankles. The deep rivers flow quietly. Your average workingman there is a bachelor. Living most likely with his maiden aunt, and in a labourer's cottage. In the quiet, green evening he cycles six or so miles into the village of Delvin for a drink. He drinks quietly. One pint, two, three, anything up to ten or more. In the dusk he cycles quietly home and murders his maiden aunt with a hatchet.

Curious thing, environment. Curious thing.

The name of Conall, the cameraman, is also Lagan, but no relation to Patrick. Patrick says that Patrick was a saint but that Conall Cearnach was a murderous bloody buff out of the mythologies before Christ. There's a poem about the fellow, Lagan says, you'll hear it from me sometime, as I feel we will, he's a helluva man to quote poetry. In a booming bass barreltone that would put Ariel to sleep.

Then, when I tell Conall that I am over here from Harvard to write about Brinsley's novel, *The Valley of the Squinting Windows* about village and small town hatreds, and in relation to Sinclair Lewis and the main street of Gopher Prairie . . . .

How are you over there on Peachtree Street in sunny Atlanta? Think of me in the Margaret Mitchell museum.

And in relation to Edgar Lee Masters and all the tombstones on the Spoon River, and Sherwood Anderson away out there in Winesburg, Ohio, and a Scotsman called George Douglas Brown and his House with the Green Shutters, about whom and which Brinsley has put me wise, and about all the dead life of small places . . . .

Well, then, Conall Cearnach he says to me, but man you have to come with us to where we are going. You'll be missing copy if you don't. This is going to be it.

At this stage Brinsley leaves us but only briefly and only to travel as far as the john and back again. We are sitting in a nook or corner of the bar. The door of the john is right in there. For the reason that his feet give him some discomfort, Brinsley doesn't stand up rightaway but slithers, sitting, right up to the door of the locus. Niall of the Nine Hostages, ancient Irish King, and Brendan the Navigator, ancient Irish saint, who sailed an open boat all the way almost to Peachtree, who are sitting between Brinsley and the holy door, stand respectfully out of his way. Then he stands up finally to his most majestic height.

Curious thing, he says. This reminds me of the only good parody I ever heard on the style of John Millington Synge. It was the work of that great player, J. M. Kerrigan, and it began like this. Was it on your feet you came this way, man of the roads? No, 'twas not, but on my arse surely, woman of the house. As in the *Shadow of the Glen*.

Then with an amazing agility for a man so big, he dives into the john and we laugh at the joke and respectfully hold our conversation until he returns. When Conall tells me that there is this company of travelling players and that, in this country town, they are planning to put on in the parochial hall this play, says Conall, by a French jailbird about a Roman Catholic cardinal taking off his clothes in a kip. Or worse still, says Conall, about two women, a madame and a hoor (anglice: whore), disrobing or disvesting or devestmentising a peacock of a cardinal, and think of that, for fun, in an Irish country town. So the parish priest naturally, or supernaturally, prohibits the use of the parochial hall and, having done so, takes off for the Eucharistic Congress in Antananarivo, or somewheres east of Suez. He didn't have to read that play to know it was no go, and the players have booked another, non-sectarian hall and are going ahead and, Conall says, the man who owns that hall must fear not God nor regard the parish priest, and must be so rich and powerful that he needn't give a fuck about King, Kaiser or cardinal.

But there is this organisation called Maria Duce, like the Mother of God up there with Mussolini, which will picket the hall to keep the clothes on the cardinal, and a riot is confidently expected, says Conall, and if you want to see what life is like in an Irish country-town, man, you gotta be there.

Conall lowers his voice.

Even Brinsley himself at his worst and wildest, he says, never thought of that one. A cardinal in a kip. In the buff.

For kip, here read brothel. Not kip as in England where it may mean merely a place to sleep in.

So here we are on the train, Patrick and Conall and his camera, and myself, and Brendan and Niall and Jodhpurs: and the world and his mother are off to the races: and, somewhere ahead, a red cardinal is roosting and waiting to be depilated: and the priest of the parish is awa, like the deil with the tailor in Robert Burns, to Antananarivo: and Patrick is singing that on the broad road we dash on, rank, beauty and fashion, it Banagher bangs by the table of war. From the couch of the quality down to the jollity, bouncing along on an old lowbacked car. Though straw cushions are placed, two foot thick at the laste, its concussive motion to mollify, still, the cheeks of my Nelly are jolting like jelly as she joggles along up to Bellewstown hill.

Onwards and upwards. The play's the thing.

Eighty miles from Dublin town.

The poet Cowper points out, as I would have you know, that not rural sights alone but rural sounds exhilarate the spirit and restore the tone of languid nature, that ten thousand warblers cheer the day and one the livelong night.

He means the nightingale. I reckon.

What lies ahead of us is not going to be exactly like that.

The gallant lady who leads the strolling players holds back the raising of the curtain for our arrival. But with the best or the worst intentions in the world, or with no godamned niggering intentions whatsoever, we succeed in being late and the play is well advanced when we get there. We have been delayed in the bar in one of the town's two hotels. Not drinking has detained us but a sudden attack of love, or something, not on me, already, as you know, wounded and possessed, but on Conall the fickle, the flaky, the volatile, the two-timer of all time, who wouldn't even curb his bronc until Jodhpurs had gone for a moment and what else to the powder-room. No, just one look over the bar-rail at the barmaid and he was hogtied, and said so out loud, very very loud. Like I love my love in the ginmill, I love her in the lounge. A mighty handsome brunette she is.

Jodhpurs, though, takes it all mighty cool. She is by no means in love with Conall, just lust, and she tells me that he does this everywhere and all the time, and Lagan intones like a monk of Solesmes: O'er Slieve Few with noiseless trampling through the heavy, drifted snow, Bealcú, Connachia's champion, in his chariot tracks the foe: and, anon, far-off discerneth in the mountain hollow white, Slinger Keth and Conall Cearnach mingling hand-to-hand in fight.

Prophetic?

Wait and see.

That's the beginning of the poem about the ancient hero or whatever.

Lagan explains in considerable detail that Slieve Few is a mountain in the heroic north, and in the mythologies. A few notes I make. Research? You can never tell.

For Connachia read Connacht.

Conall is now behind the bar. He went over it, not through it. He's a pretty agile guy. His arm is around the barmaid's waist. She is laughing most merrily. Nobody by now in the place except the four of us. For Brendan and Niall have really gone ahead to the theatre. But when Conall had first attempted to go over the top, Lagan and myself decided it might be wiser to stick around and keep a snaffle, Lagan said spancell, on him. That may be not all that easy.

Jodhpurs, I may tell you, has the same surname as myself. Except that she spells it differently. Carney, not Karney. So much I found out by standing beside her when she was filling in the hotel register. Waiting my turn I was. With the register.

We are now at last in the theatre. Or in the substitute hall. Which is by no means in the most elegant part of the town. There are no praying pickets. Conall is outraged. No pickets, no picture.

Perhaps they have prayed and picketed and departed before we got here. But no. Later we are to hear that they were never there. Also flown to Antananarivo?

To get to the hall we go through a dark entryway. Seventeenth century at the least. Footpads? Stilettos? Christopher Marlowe? No. Bludgeons? Newgate calendar? No. Nothing but bad lighting and pot-holed ground underfoot. Easy here to sprain an ankle. We are in an ancient market-place, long ago forsaken by markets and by everything and everybody else. A hideyhole for Art? A last refuge for strolling players? Then up a covered and creaking wooden stairway that climbs the wall, then down four shaky wooden steps and here we are, and where is the kip and where is the cardinal?

But there is no kip. There is no cardinal at the moment to be seen.

Conall, as is his custom, has got it wrong. Or so Lagan later booms.

What we are looking at is a weeping broad in a long, black dress, kneeling down before a roaring Franciscan friar. Or a fellow roaring, and wearing what might be a Franciscan habit except that it's so badly battered from strolling with the players that it's hard to tell. He could be Guy Fawkes or Johnny Appleseed or Planters' Peanuts or the man who broke the bank at Monte Carlo. But whoever or whatever he is, he sure as hell is giving that broad hell. Boy, is he giving her hell. What I mean is, he is telling her in considerable detail where she will find herself she doesn't mend her ways and get smart, and get real smart and give up that old wop trick of screwing her brother. If you can tell by a slight protuberance, she seems to be in the family way by her brother.

Curious thing, Brinsley is later to say, but there was always a soupçon of that in the midlands where I come from. John Ford, not the man who makes the cowboys, seems to have been much possessed by the idea. As T. S. Eliot said Webster was by death. Curious fellow, Ford. And Webster. And Eliot.

Brinsley met Eliot when Eliot was round the corner from the Abbey Bar to give a lecture in the Abbey Theatre that was. My research proceeds. Curious thing.

But listen to the friar as the broad is listening or pretending to listen.

He is telling her about a black and hollow vault where day is never seen, where shines no sun but flaming horror of consuming fires, a lightless sulphur choked with smoky fogs in an infected darkness: and in that place dwell many thousand thousand sundry sorts of never dying deaths, and damned souls roar without pity, gluttons are fed with toads and adders, and burning oil poured down the drunkard's throat, and the usurer is forced to sip whole draughts of molten gold, and the murderer is forever stabbed yet never can he die, and the wanton lies on racks of burning steel.

—Watch it, chick, watch it.

The friar also wises her up about lawless sheets and secret incests. About which, we may reckon, she knows more than he does. And tells her that when she parks her ass in that black and gloomy vault she will wish that each kiss her brother gave her had been a dagger's point.

Jasus Christ, says Conall, this is worse than any sermon I ever heard at any mission. What was the parish priest beefing about? He couldn't do better himself.

He says all that out quite aloud and several people hush him up, and the friar thinks they mean him and gets rattled, and, to my high delight, the incestuous broad giggles. For her it is mighty obvious that hell hath no furies.

To you, down there on Peachtree, a mission would be a sort of a tent-meeting, hellfire a-plenty, the Baptist tabernacle in Marietta, yeah Lord Amen, and washed, when the time is ripe, in the blood of the Lamb or the Chatahoochie river. What has the Good Lawd done for you, as the preacher roared and pointed by mistake at the harelipped, hunchbacked cripple, and the harelipped, hunchbacked cripple, in so far as his cleft palate would allow him to articulate, whistled back that the Good Lawd damn near roont me.

Then when the curtain creaks down to separate the scenes, something has to separate them, and the lights come up in the body of the house, Conall stands up to take pictures and to make a speech.

Jesus and Amen!

We are *in tempore opportune*, to find out that the valiant woman, far and from the farthest coasts, who leads the strolling players was so annoyed with the parish-priest that she cancelled the kip and the cardinal for something in which, when most of the cast has been massacred, another cardinal and the Pope get any loot that's left.

For we're off to Antananarivo in the morning.

Then and thereafter Conall has bad luck with his photographs. For why? He keeps dropping the camera. The audience love it. Light relief. Charlie Chaplin. The audience need it. Some of them know Conall very well. He has been around. They cheer when he drops the camera. But in a mild, friendly, appreciative sort of way and not so as to disturb the players. Overmuch.

Conall's speech begins by thanking the audience on behalf of the valiant woman and the strolling players. Then he thanks the players and the woman on behalf of the audience. Then he sits down where his seat is not, or a place to put it. He has a standing ovation for that one. Then Brendan and Niall and Jodhpurs persuade him: into a corner at the back of the hall and hold him there, good old Jodhpurs, and the curtain creaks up again, it sure as God creaks, and here we are back in Renaissance Parma and nothing worse going on than incest and multiple murder.

Not one picture all night long did Conall capture.

Up on the stage, Grimaldi, a Roman gentleman, has just knocked somebody off, the wrong person, as it so happens, or, at any rate, not the person he means to knock off. The cardinal, when the matter is drawn to his attention by the citizens of Parma, is inclined to take a lenient view. For why? See text. The cardinal, in brief, argues that Grimaldi is no common man even if he is somewhat inclined to first-degree homicide. Grimaldi is nobly born and of the blood of princes and he, the cardinal, has received Grimaldi into the protection of the Holy Father.

Hip, hip hurrah, cries Conall, for the Holy Father. Send Grimaldi to the Eucharistic Congress.

There are some murmurs but more laughs among the audience. Stands to reason they're the laughing rather than the murmuring sort of audience. Otherwise they wouldn't be here.

Then Soranzo, who is a nobleman, who wishes to marry Annabella and who thinks he has all the boys in line, is raising his glass which he has filled from the weighty bowl (see text), to Giovanni who is screwing Annabella, but not just then and there, who is, as I may have already explained, Giovanni's sister, and Soranzo, in all innocence or something, is saying: Here, Brother Grimaldi, here's to you, your turn comes next though now a bachelor.

Then to Annabella Soranzo says: Cheer up, my love.

Conall repeats that, and shouts something that sounds like: Tighten up there, M'Chesney.

Lagan basebarrelltones: Gag him, for God's sake.

And the house is hilarious.

Then enter Hippolita, masked, followed by several ladies in white robes, also masked and bearing garlands of willow. Music offstage. They do a dance. Not the Charleston, you may safely speculate. Soranzo says: Thanks, lovely virgins.

Conall says: How do you know?

The house rocks.

You see the joke, such as it may be, is that Soranzo has been having it off with Hippolita and now wishes to jettison cargo, and she, knowing this, is out to waste him but before she can do so, Vasquez, a low type and no nobleman, slips her the old trick of the poisoned cup, and the friar, wise guy, says, fairly enough, that he fears the event, that a marriage is seldom good when the bride banquet so begins in blood. He sure is the greatest living authority on hell and matrimony.

Curious thing.

Read the rest of it for yourself.

Enter Soranzo, unbraced and dragging in Annabella, and calling out: Come strumpet, famous Whore.

Conall: Give the girl a break. She'll come on her own.

Soranzo: Wilt thou confess and I will spare thy life?

Annabella: My life. I will not buy my life so dear.

Soranzo: I will not slack my vengeance.

Conall: They're not getting on. There's a rift in the flute.

Soranzo: Had'st thou been virtuous, fair, wicked woman.

Conall: Thou can'st not have everything.

Soranzo: My reason tells me now that 'tis as common to err in frailty as to be a woman. Go to your chamber.

Conall: Politeness is all. Carry the chamber to her, sir.

Conall seems to know his Shakespeare.

Curious thing.

Three pictures are taken.

Not by Conall Cearnach of whom, the original warrior I mean, more hereafter. But by Brendan the Navigator, who proves to be a good man in a crisis. He is a blond block of a man in a brown, serge suit. He is a Fingallian. That means that he comes from the north of the County Dublin, or Fingal, the land of the fairhaired foreigners where, Lagan assures me, some of the old farmhouses still preserve the high, pointed, Scandinavian gables, a style brought in there a thousand or so years ago by sea-rovers who settled.

One picture Brendan takes of Giovanni entering from left with his sister's heart impaled on a dagger, and dripping. A red sponge, I'd say, soaked, for additional effect, in some reasonably inexpensive red wine.

All hearts that love should be like that. Mayhap, they are.

One picture he takes when the banditti rush in and the stage is strewn with corpses, and Vasquez, I told you he was a low type, tells the banditti that the way to deal with an old dame called Putana, whose name's a clue to character, is to carry her closely into the coal-house and, instantly, put out her eyes and, if she should be so unappreciative as to scream, to slit her nose for laughs.

Exeunt banditti with Putana.

And that's about the next best thing to the riot that didn't arise.

The survivors are the cardinal, and Richardetto, a supposed physician, and Donado, a citizen of Parma, and Vasquez, the villain, who rejoices that a Spaniard can, in vengeance, outgo an Italian. Giovanni has just cashed in his chips. So the cardinal wisely advises those who are still able to stand up, that they should take up those slaughtered bodies and see them buried: and as for the gold and jewels, or whatsoever, since they are confiscate to the canons of the church, he, the cardinal, or we, as he calls himself, will seize them all for the Pope's proper use.

Conall: To pay for the . . .

But Jodhpurs has put her strong hand over his mouth. Hautboys.

Sennet sounded.

Curtain.

The third picture Brendan takes is of the valiant lady making her curtain speech, and all the players, to the relief and felicity of all of us, resurrected and reunited. She thanks the audience. She thanks the gentlemen of the press. She thanks Conall personally and as Conall Lagan and not, as Patrick says she should have done, as Conall Carnage. To loud applause. Even I am astounded. Ireland is a more wonderful place than I ever thought it could be. Later I find out that Conall and the valiant woman are firm friends, that she even loves Conall as a mother might love a wayward son. Also find out that to make absolutely certain of a good house, she took no money at the door: and that the picketers did not bother their ass picketing because the priest was far awa, far awa, and the weather was raining.

Up to that moment none of us have noticed or mentioned the weather.

And the next act opens back in the bar in the hotel.

The night is in full swing.

We return to our festivity and do our best to put the corpses of Parma out of our thoughts. We manage to do so.

To tell you the whole truth as I have promised always to do, well to tell as much of the whole truth as a lady should hear or wish to hear, we sit drinking, slowly, sipping, no gulping, spilling or slobbering, and the talk is good. We sit for several hours after official closing time and in the learned company of two uniformed police-officers and two detectives in plain clothes. One of the detectives has been among the audience and thinks the play the funniest thing he ever laid eyes or ears on since he saw Jimmy O'Dea, a famous comedian, in the Olympia theatre in Dublin when he, the detective, was in training in the Phoenix Park.

Jasus, the detective keeps saying, I tought dey'd never stop. And de coming in wit her heart on a breadknife. I could have taken me oat as a pig's kidney. And Himself dere was de best part of de play.

The detective comes from a fairly widespread part of Ireland where they have problems with a certain dipthong.

By Himself he means Conall whose constancy and endurance is astounding, for talking and dancing and singing and telling the women he loves them: Jodhpurs in one breath, the barmaid in the next, with a few words to spare for any woman in the place, under or over sixty. He sits with us for a space. Then he is up at the bar or behind the bar and occasionally kissing the barmaid who objects, but mildly. To much general laughter. He is, believe it or not, most courteous. He knows *tout le monde* and it knows and likes him and I do notice that he seldom renews his drink, and I wonder is it booze that sets him going or is he just that way by nature. Outgoing. Extrovert. You could say all that again. He can dance. He can sing. He does both at intervals. He even wears a wedding ring. He uses all his talents to the full.

We may be forced, Lagan says, to hogtie Conall as his namesake,

Conall Cearnach, was hogtied by Bealcú, or Houndmouth, from Ballina, the champion of Connacht before Christ was in it. Not that Christ ever had much influence in certain parts of Connacht.

Nothing I know can stop Lagan. He will boom and drone on now until the sergeant and the guard and the two men in plain clothes, and anybody else who cares to listen, will know all about the wounding and healing of the ancient hero. But, hell, what am I here for? Research is research. And where is my notebook?

Lagan explains to the plain-clothes men and the guard that when Bealcú urges his charger and, ergo, his chariot across the snow to the place where he has seen the two warriors in combat, Slinger Keth lies dead and Conall Cearnach, wounded, lies at point to die. The guard and the plain-clothes men show every evidence of interest. The sergeant is up to something else. He has the ear of Brendan, the Viking sea-rover or the sanctified navigator, what you will. He, the sergeant, is saying slowly, spacing out the words carefully: Soap . . . necktie . . . chocolates . . . cigarettes . . . pipe and tobacco-pouch . . . book or book token . . . shaving-cream or aftershave . . . socks . . . record or record-player . . . pen . . . handkerchiefs . . . .

Or rather he is reading those mystic words out of the newspaper that employs Lagan, Conall, Brendan and Niall. He asks Brendan what he thinks of all that. Brendan says: Aunt Miriam is a very good friend of mine. And a most considerate and efficient colleague.

This is extremely curious. Niall is, for the moment, at the far end of the bar, engaged at conversation with some friends he has encountered.

Lagan says: Put jockstrap on the list. For Conall over there.

Seems Lagan can narrate to four men and simultaneously listen to a fifth. There is much general laughter at mention of the jockstrap. Over at the bar, but on this side of it, Conall has one arm around the barmaid and the other around Jodhpurs. All seem happy. Am I losing contact? Events mingle and move too fast for me. It is a long way from here to Spoon River.

But aside from all that: When Houndmouth sees Cearnach flat on his ass on the snow he proceeds to badmouth him. Calling him a ravening wolf of Ulster which is where Conall, hereinafter to be known as Cearnach, comes from. Who answers: Taunts are for reviling women.

That's pretty good.

—Hush up, he says, to Bealcú, and finish me off.

But no, Bealcú will not have it noised abroad that it took two Connachtmen to knock off one Ulsterman. His game is to bring Cearnach home with him to Ballina or wherever, to have him patched up by the Connacht medicos and then, for the glory of Bealcú, and whatever gods may be in Connacht, to kill him in single combat. So Bealcú binds Cearnach in five-fold fetters, which is what Lagan thinks we should do with our Conall, then heaves him up or has him heaved up on the chariot, to be somewhat cheesed when he tries to lift the Ulsterman's war-mace.

What a weight it was to raise!

Brendan interrupts, reading out aloud from the newspaper. This is what he reads: The girl in the picture is playing with her white mice. Do you have a pet mouse? If so what colour is it? Do you like mice? If not, write and say why. Could you write a poem about a mouse? Try.

—Christ of Almighty, says Lagan. What are you all up to?

And the sergeant says that his sixteen-year-old daughter is a magician all-out at the painting and drawing, and can turn out a poem should be printed.

Brendan explains. Mostly or totally for my benefit. The others know all about Aunt Miriam. Which is the name of the mythical lady who edits the page from which the sergeant and Brendan have been reading: Aunt Miriam's Campfire Club.

The sergeant's daughter and a slew (sluagh, in the Irish) of her schoolfriends wish to join. Brendan says that he will look after all that. He reads further to explain to me about that odd list of objects: Choosing birthday presents for fathers, uncles or older brothers can sometimes be quite difficult. So what about carrying out a birthday survey? Ask your father, brother, uncle, teacher or any man over twenty-fiveish to put the birthday presents on this list in order of their choice. Bring your completed list into class next week. Check the answers and count up in class how many men put socks or soap . . .

Or de jockstraps, says one of de plain-clothes men.

Let joy be unconfined.

It is early in de morning. Am I losing my diptongs?

Brendan later admits, blushingly, that Aunt Miriam is his beloved wife. That is not true. Aunt Miriam, in fact, is a somewhat eccentric and retired clergyman. That is supposed to be a well-kept secret. But Brendan writes down the names and addresses of the sergeant's daughter and all her friends. He says that he will see to it that Aunt Miriam's secretary, who doesn't exist, will send to each and every one of those young enthusiasts the Campfire Crest, a sort of badge. He promises that the letters they write to Aunt Miriam will be printed in the paper. And the poetical works of the sergeant's daughter. All this, for sure, he looks after when back in Dublin. But the entente he sets up between us and the sergeant is to prove real precious some hours later when Brendan and Niall are on the road, by automobile, to Limerick city where they have something else to report. Or on which to report. Even in Ireland, English is English.

Action stations!

The clock strikes three.

Jodhpurs says she will hit the hay. A challenging thought. The barmaid has vanished. Brendan and Niall have taken the road for Limerick city. Conall and Lagan and myself would seem to be the only living people left. One of those corrugated things has been pulled down and the bar is closed. Lagan and myself set sail for the bottom of the main stairway. But is that good enough for Conall? No, no, by no means no. He says that he wants one more drink. But he is a lot more sober than he pretends to be and he has something else, as you may imagine, in his calculating mind. We try to reason with him. To talk him into calling it a night, or a day. No use, no use. Down a long corridor that leads towards the back of the building he sees, and so do we, a light burning. That, it may appear, is where the barmaid has found covert. So hitching his wagon to that star, Conall Carnage steams (block that metaphor), down the corridor and through the heavy-drifted snow, and thunders on the door of the room of the light as if he owned the world, and barges in, and finds . . . .

Two young clergymen drinking-up. The curates, or assistants, or lootenants of the parish. The mice relaxing while the tomcat is farawa, farawa in Antananarivo. One of them turns angry-nasty. Through embarrassment, it may be, at being found out. Tells Conall, and in a clear shrill voice, that this is a private room. The barmaid is nowhere to be seen. So Conall demands to know what in heaven, or hell, two clerics are doing drinking-up and being merry in a private room in a public house at three o'clock in the morning. And why are they not at home writing sermons and banning plays as any zealous sacerdotes should be. Cleric Number Two asks him, politely enough, to leave. Then Lagan grabs Conall and begins to urge him out and Lagan, although an anti-clerical of the old style, apologises to the polite priest, explaining that Conall has a drop too many taken. Out of nowhere the proprietress appears, a tough sort of a lady in late middle-age. She exhorts Conall to have some respect for the cloth. From halfways up the stairs Conall intones: Bless me, fathers, for I have sinned.

Lagan chants, but only so as to be heard by Conall and myself: *Dies irae, dies illa, solvet saeclum in favilla* . . .

We propel Conall as far as and into his room. That day, we reckon, has been called a day.

So Bealcú urges charger and chariot westward through the borders of Breffny. Bearing with him the corpse of Keth the Slinger and the wounded and captive Cearnach. They come to a place called Moy Slaught where the ancient Irish used to worship a pretty formidable idol called Crom Cruach. He was a hunk of stone or something and his twelve apostles, twelve lesser hunks, sat round him in a ring. Along came Jones, meaning St Patrick, and thumbs old Crom with his Bachall Iosa, or the staff of Christ, and Crom bears forever the mark of the bachall, and the earth swallows and the twelve lesser idols: and, just at that moment in Lagan's narration, all hell breaks loose in the street outside the hotel.

Lagan and myself are sharing a room. Where Jodhpurs has vanished to, we do not know. Jealousy, at last, may have driven that tolerant girl to roost in some faraway place. The hotel is a corner house. Our room is right on the corner and right above the main door. On which door Crom Cruach and his sub-gods twelve seem at this moment to be beating. Where, cries Lagan, is the staff of Jesus.

He looks out one of our two windows but the angle is awkward and he can see nothing. The beating at the door lessens. Then ceases. But there is a frenzy and a babel of voices. Then the door of our room opens and the sergeant steps in. And says most modestly: Mr Lagan, as the eldest member here present of the press-party, could you please come down and put a tether on this young fellow before he wrecks the town.

For Carnage is off on the warpath again, with or without benefit of chariot. Meantime, back at the ranch, Cearnach has been unceremoniously dumped on the fairgreen of Moy Slaught where he is getting a poor press from all the widows he, in happier times, has made in the West of Ireland.

And Bealcú says: Let Lee, the leech, be brought.

And Lee, the gentlefaced, is brought from his plot of healing herbs. Like Lagan walking down the stairs to see what healing he can bring to Conall Carnage in the hall below. Followed, at a safe distance, by myself and the sergeant who gives me a brief breakdown on what has caused the brouhaha. Seems Conall made down again to the door of the lighted room. To find it locked and bolted. To Carnage that presented no problem. He bangs on the door and roars out that he wants somebody to hear his confession. Lest he die in sin. Then comes a-running the lady of the house and with her a big guy she has somewhere drafted so as to throw Conall out. This big guy is a mighty-big big guy. So he pushes our Conall back as far as the main hall where Conall, who is nifty, steps backwards up two rungs of the stairs, so as to gain purchase, and throws a hard, roundhouse swing at the big guy, who is also nifty. And ducks. And Conall knocks down the lady, and the lady screams bloody murder, and the big guy and the clerics just about manage to heave Conall out the front door and lock it, and Conall goes to work with fists and feet, raising holy hell on the oak, three inches thick, and ringing the bell, and roaring Bless me, fathers, for I have sinned, and lights going on and children crying all over the town as if, says the sergeant, Jesus had come again, and the lady phones the fuzz, and here we are again, happy as can be, and Jodhpurs, neat girl, and one of the plain-clothes men are holding Conall, and Lagan is saying that Conall is a good kid, and the lady is shouting that he's a pup, a pup, a pup.

Lagan shows himself to be some diplomat. M. de Norpois. Hit the Guermantes trail. The matronly presence of Aunt Miriam is still there to aid him. He and the sergeant mutter together in one corner. Conall calms down. Jodhpurs is good for him. Like Hector in Homer she is well known as a tamer of horses. Then Lagan and the sergeant come to this arrangement. That Conall will go for the night to the calaboose with the lawmen. For no way in hell will the lady have him for the night in her hotel. What, she says, will my husband say when he comes home and hears that I was assaulted under my own roof. What, says Lagan, will the parish priest say when he comes home from wherever in heaven he is and I tell him that his two curates were drinking in your office at three o'clock in the morning?

Détente.

The lady screams that right away she wants to prefer charges. The Sergeant, gently but firmly, says that she must wait until the next day or, to be exact, daylight of the same day. She screams again that Conall's swipe has smashed her spectacles. For corroboration, the big guy has already gathered up the fragments, *colligite fragmenta ne pereant*, into a brown paper-bag. Evidence? Or second-class relics? Jodhpurs, gallant girl, offers to go with Conall. To burn on his pyre. But Conall, like a hero going into transportation, kisses her farewell, several times, advises her to catch a few hours' sleep, she may need them: that the night to come, and still so far ahead, is yet another night. The lady of the house is about to have a fit. So the big guy leads her away. The clerics have vanished. Up the chimney! Then Conall marches off, taking the lead with the sergeant, the plain-clothes man bringing up the rear. But halfways across the street, the plain-clothes man stops, shakes hands with Conall and goes off another way: Home to his bed and his wife, if he has one. Conall marches on, under escort, to his lonely prison cell. Or so I sadly and foolishly think.

Carnage now lies in the hoosegow. Cearnach lies under the care of Lee the Leech. Who, gentlefaced as he is, still strikes a hard bargain with the victorious and vengeful Bealcú. Has Lee, like the sergeant, a soft, melancholy voice and a moustache that droops as if the humid heat had gotten to it?

—Do you know what he said to me? Lagan says.

Not Lee the Leech, but the sergeant.

When the two of them, Lagan and the sergeant, were muttering in the corner.

—He said to me, Lagan says, that if the lad never did worse than knock that damsel down, he won't do much wrong in the world. She would skin a flea. (For the price of its hide: a native colloquialism.) 'Tis well known, says the sergeant, that she adulterates the whiskey. Anyway, the lad never hit her.

No direct hit. The wind of his passing, like that of a godamned archangel, simply flattened her.

—Anyway, the sergeant said. The lad struck out in self-defence. And missed. The only bruise would be on her backside where she sat down with a thump. He that cares to feel that way may find it.

—But keep an eye on things here, the sergeant said. You and the Yank. And I'll watch the young fellow. We want no trouble. Nor capers in the courtroom. We're overworked as it is. And that's the true.

Then Jodhpurs kisses us goodnight.

And that's the true, as the sergeant says.

And we rest our weary heads. And somewhere in gardens, and on the fringe of the town, and all over Ireland, the birds are beginning to sing.

—Curious thing, Brinsley says to me through my tumbling half-sleep.

—Curious thing. Georgia is famous for peaches. Or that's what the Irish Christian Brothers told me.

Once I had told him that there was a dame on Peachtree Street, Atlanta, Georgia. Meaning you. Well aware I am that there are many and various dames on Peachtree.

He capped my statement by telling me that there was once, he had heard or read, a dame in Belmont, richly left, and she was fair . . . .

Then he went on about the peaches.

Seems there is or was a geography compiled by an Irish Christian Brother for use in schools run by the Irish Christian Brothers. It lists or listed the chief products of various places. Inchicore, a portion of Dublin, has rolling-stock. Georgia has peaches.

It is the dawn. The summer dark, the poet said, is but the dawn of day. That's Lagan quoting. He is up and shaving at the handbasin. No rooms with bath here. Rise up, he says, and do begin the day's adorning. He is a healthy man. He needs no cure. He tells me that Lee the Leech says that healing is with God's permission, health for life's enjoyment made. My American head is a purple glow and my belly full of the linnet's wings: and Lee the Leech agrees to heal Cearnach but insists that when the healing is perfected there shall be a fair fight and no favour, and that if Conall is triumphant he is to have safe conduct back to the Fews, his native part of Ulster. Also: that while the healing is in process no man shall steal through fences to work the patient mischief or surprise. He demands an oath on the matter: to Crom the God, to the sun, to the wind.

Lagan pulls open the heavy window-curtains and the sun comes through with a scream.

All quiet on the street outside. The good folk here do not arise betimes.

What healing is there for my hapless head?

My eyes I close and see viscous, bubbling peaches.

What healing for Carnage in his dungeon drear?

Lee the Leech has unlocked Cearnach's fetters.

Valiantly I face the razor.

—Curious thing, Brinsley says, Plato never bothered his barney about anachronisms. Curious thing.

But I swear by God and Abraham Lincoln, and by the body of Pocahontas, lovely as a poppy, sweet as a pawpaw in May, he is there in the dining-room and leathering-in (as Jodhpurs says), to his breakfast when she, me and Lagan get downstairs to the dining-room. He? Who? Brinsley? Plato? Bealcú? Lee the Leech? Conall Cearnach? Crom the God? No, but our own dear Conall Carnage for it is he. Eating egg and bacon and sausage and black pudding and drinking black coffee by the bucket. And eating butter, putting it into his mouth in great globs. Lubrication, he tells me. Oil the wheels. And the big end. Never did I see the like. Almost threw up to watch him. The lady of the house hovers in the background. Out of arm's reach and the swing of the sea. Amazed me that they served him anything. But he's a hell of a hard man to resist. Jodhpurs is all joy. Growing boys need food, she says. She glows. She is, I blush to say it, looking ahead to the night ahead.

Then while Carnage roisters and we nibble he tells us about the night or the remnants of a night just passed. Seems he never had it so good. Here is what happened. Conall and the sergeant walked back to the barracks. Who should be there but the second plain-clothes man (as in Shakespeare), and the garda or guard who had been drinking with us earlier in the night. Conall asked if they were going to lock him up and they said no way. Then another garda appeared with a tray and teapot and bread and jam. Everybody was, as Conall put it, fierce polite. Then the lot went home except Conall and one man or guard or garda, or what-in-the-hell, who was on night-duty. Who placed six chairs in strategic positions. Then produced a spring and a mattress which he balanced on the chairs. Then the all-night man said hop in and the two of them, and the town and the cattle in the fields and the birds in the bushes, slept until the sergeant came in at dawn, and with a bottle of wine from faraway Oporto. There were drinks and hand-shaking all round and that was that. Curious country, Ireland.

The healing of Conall Cearnach is, by now, well under way. He is still on his bed or on the scratcher (a Dublin usage), and he heaves thereon, Lagan quotes, as on reef of rock the ocean wildly tosses. Don't quite get that. The bed, the ocean, should be tossing, not Cearnach, the Rock. And the sons of Bealcú are worried. What is Lee the Leech up to? How fares the Ulsterman, the man from the Fews? So from a distance the sons of Bealcú spy, as best as they can, on the medical treatment. The patient no longer tosses on the bed nor does the bed toss under him. Now he is up and about even if he is pallid as a winding-sheet. Swear I do to Edgar Allan Poe that I do not know, nor could wildly guess at the pallidity of a winding-sheet.

Now Cearnach is out of his chamber. This isle of is full of chambers.

Cearnach is walking on his feet. What else?

We have paid our bill to the barmaid who is doubling in reception and who has the giggles. She giggles beautifully. All over. She kisses Carnage a fond farewell. The lady of the house is not there to be seen. Nor to see. We walk on our feet, all four of us, on eight feet, through the town to the other of the two hotels. It is an ancient and historic town. And looks the part. But I have a hunch that we have become part of the history. For the people on the pleasant side-walks are peeping at us and trying to pretend that they are not peeping. As are the sons of Bealcú peeping away out west, not in Kansas, but on the fair green of Moy Slaught. To see Cearnach, a ghastly figure, on his javelin propped he goes. But day follows day and Cearnach convalesces and convalesces, and with herbs and healing balsams he burgeons like a sere oak under summer showers and dew, and the sons of Bealcú are fearful for the future of their father.

Or the Dazee, as Carnage puts it.

Another Dublin usage.

Carnage is beginning to show some interest in the story of the healing of his namesake.

We have reached the other hotel. A mighty handsome place. But it is now bright morning and, after last night and all that happened where we were, even a roominghouse on Ponce de Leon, which flows into and out of the street of the Peachtrees, as you know, could be a mighty handsome place.

The valiant woman is here, having her morning gin, and some of her players around her. She is a widow. Her husband, who was a playwright, had a long enmity with Brinsley who is, also, a playwright. But valiantly she did her best to keep the peace between them. She tells me a lot. Research, research, research. The hardships of strolling players in rural Ireland. The money she is losing. Sean O'Casey, she tells me, is a cantankerous bastard when it comes to giving permission to anyone to put on his plays in Ireland. He wants money, for God's sake, money. Ah well. To make him madder still the Maria Mussolini Duce people picketed a play of his in the Gaiety in Dublin, and the Sinn Féiners, long ago, nearly wrecked the old Abbey over *The Plough and the Stars*, and one old nut of a theatre-goer roared at O'Casey that there were no prostitutes in Dublin, and O'Casey said, mildly, in return, that he had been accosted three times on his way to the theatre and the old nut cracked back that if there were prostitutes in Dublin it was the British army put them there.

—Good on the army, Carnage says.

Lagan hushes him up.

But all that about O'Casey is history. Away back in the 1920s.

Return to the here and now.

We have one hell of a lunch. The valiant lady pays.

Then honking in the street and shouting at the door come Niall and Brendan, all bright and glittering in the lunchtime air, and all the way from Limerick city, and all ready to drive you all back to Dublin town.

They have had their own adventures.

For on the way to Limerick city they rested for a while in a roadside tavern. Not a roadhouse. Just an Irish pub, open day and night and to hell with the law. Niall had driven that far. And in the tavern they got to talking with this elderly farmer who lived back in the boondocks in mountains called the Silvermines. He sang songs. He hobbled on a stick. So kindhearted Brendan reckoned that the old-timer was too old and too hirpled (an Ulster usage) to walk home. Off with the three of them, and a bottle of whiskey, through a network of mountain roads to a shack where Senex lived alone. Brendan uncorked the whiskey. Senex produced three cracked and yellowing mugs. Out with Niall to the henhouse to rob the nests. Shall it be my lot, he thought, in the screeching and fluttering dark, to be beaten to death by the wings of hens in a cró, or hutment, on the slopes of the Silvermine mountains. Then out of all the eggs he could find he made he says, the world's biggest-ever bloody omelette, chopped it into three fair halves, and they ate the lot and drank the whiskey, and Senex staggered safely to bed and with Brendan the Navigator at the wheel, the pair of them set out to try to escape from the mountains. Which does not prove to be all that easy. For the dustroads go round and round about to find the town of Roundabout that makes the world go round. Nor is an over-dose of whiskey the best navigational aid. In the chill dawn, with

Brendan asleep and Niall at the wheel, they stumble on Limerick city which is beautiful, as everybody knows, the river Shannon, full of fish, beside that city flows: and Niall, shaking Brendan awake, says where is Hanratty's hotel, and Brendan sings out: You find Hanratty's. I discovered Limerick.

Then they find the hotel and are no sooner asleep than the phone rings from the Dublin office to say that it has heard that a pressman has assaulted a woman during or after the performance of the banned play, and would somebody please tell the other end of the phone what in hell is going on down there.

Enter now the garda of the previous night.

Not into Limerick city but into that handsome hotel in which we are washing down our lunch. Seems the lady of the other hotel has called the Dublin office to report the disorderly behaviour of two cameramen, Patrick Lagan and John Karney, meaning me. Now I have become a cameraman and a knockerdown of ladies. She has threatened legal action. The old blackmail – settle-out-of-court trick. The office disowns both of us. Lagan is on holidays and I was never there, and even Conall Carnage is under semi-suspension for some previous misdemeanour and, anyway, he hasn't been mentioned. So Lagan calls the lady and says that if she wants legal action or counteraction she is more than welcome any time, and that those two young clergymen would sure smile to be subpoenaed, and about the hell there would be to pay when the boss gets back from Antananarivo.

Enter the sergeant.

To approve of Lagan's diplomacy, or whatever. To bid us godspeed and a safe journey, and to say that things will surely settle if we see Carnage safely back to Dublin.

Exeunt omnes.

One little town. Two little towns. Three little towns.

No stops, Niall says, until we're safe in Dublin. Or, at any rate, as far as Roche's of Rathcoole.

Meaning a famous singing public-house about twenty-five miles from the city centre. The public-house does not sing. Only the people in it. Well, they try. A master of ceremonies at the piano. Ladies and gentlemen, one voice only, please. And the saddest man in the house stands up and wails: Caan, I forget you, when every night reminds me . . . .

Well you know that I cannot forget you. Accept this letter in lieu of vows.

Anyway, Lagan is quoting: Forbaid was a master-slinger. Maev, when in her bath she sank, felt the presence of his finger from the further Shannon bank . . . .

—That guy, says Carnage, had a mighty, long finger.

Jodhpurs smacks him. But gently. She is sitting on his knee. It is a small auto. We are six people. We are counted, Brendan says, like the elephants, after they are washed, at bedtime in Duffy's circus.

Lagan annotates his quotation. Research.

Conall Cearnach, do you follow me, had killed Aleel, the last husband of Maev, queen of Connacht. Aleel and Maev started a war when they quarrelled in their bed because he had a bull and she hadn't.

—So, Carnage says, that we don't have to be professors or literary editors to know what that was about.

Again Jodhpurs smacks him. Then they kiss. Niall who is at the wheel says that somebody or something is rocking the boat.

Then, after the killing of Aleel, Maev retires to an island on Lough Ree in the river Shannon. Once a day and at dawn she takes her bath in a springwell on that island. Vain woman, she thinks there isn't a peeper in Ireland dare peep on a queen. But Forbaid of Ulster has long sight as well as a long finger, and spots her from afar, and comes in the dusk secretly to the well and, with a linen thread, measures the distance back to the far shore. Then he stretches the thread on the ground, in a safe and secret place, plants a wooden fence-pole at each end of it, puts an apple atop of one pole, stands at the other, practises with his sling or handbow until he can take the apple ten times out of ten. Then one fine morning he stands where the river Shannon's flowing and the three-leaved shamrock grows and, across the wide water, where my heart is I am going to my native Irish rose, he clobbers the queen between the eyes with a two-pound rock, and she falls into the well, and that is the end of a queen who was longer in the bidnis than Queen Victoria: and the moment that I meet her with a hug an' kiss

I'll greet her, for there's not a colleen (cáilín), sweeter where the river Shannon flows.

—Smart guy, Carnage says. But he hadn't much to peep at. She must have been a hundred if she was a day.

More smacks and kisses. Niall heaves to. Threatens irons for mutiny. Jodhpurs kisses back of Niall's neck. On we go.

Then more kisses, did I stop them when a million seemed so few?

That was Lagan. Courtesy of Mr Browning.

Wait for it, Carnage says.

Then we get the entire spiel about Oh Galuppi, Baldassaro, this is very hard to find, I can scarcely misconceive you it would prove me deaf and blind, but although I take your meaning 'tis with such a heavy mind . . . .

And much more of the same.

That's Lagan's party piece. Or one of them.

We know now, Carnage says, who broke up the party in Fitzwilliam Square.

Much laughter. For the benefit of the visitor Lagan explains: It is, John, one of the many afflictions of my life to have the same surname as our dear friend, Carnage. Here and now happily restored to us, through my, shall we say, diplomacy, and the friendship of the sergeant. Although, if the case had gone to court, even the most humane District Justice would have felt compelled to give him six months without the option. For last night's performance and, furthermore, for his previous record. That gold ring he so proudly wears. Consider it.

Carnage raises and swivels an elegant right hand. The ring glows.

That ring is by no means his ring, Lagan informs me. He is not married. Do not think it. Not a woman in Ireland would have him. In wedded bliss, that is. No, that ring belongs to a lady with whom he is, shall we say, familiar. Who received it from her husband. From whom she is now sundered.

Life, life, says Carnage.

And twists the ring on his finger.

Who to support herself, Lagan says, ventures out occasionally on the scented and sacred sidewalks of Dublin.

We all, says Jodhpurs, have to do our best. Poor Maryanne.

Jodhpurs has a lot of heart.

So Carnage has a friend, Lagan explains. Odd as it may seem, he still has friends. This friend lives in an apartment in Fitzwilliam Square. A select area. And invites Carnage and Maryanne to a party. Invitation instantly accepted. Conall Carnage is hell for parties. And two or three or four, accounts and authorities differ as in Edward Scribble Gibbon, two or three or four cab loads arrive somewhat noisily in the elegant Square, Carnage and Maryanne, and some of Maryanne's business colleagues, and some of their friends, and create such immortal havoc that the gardaí or the guards or the police or the coppers or the bobbies or the peelers or the fuzz or the pigs or the gendarmes or the effing Royal Irish Constabulary or whatever in hell you visiting American scholar, or embryo scholar, may care so to describe them, are called by the startled and highly respectable neighbours, and the unfortunate man is evicted from his apartment in Fitzwilliam Square . . . .

With more kisses, who could stop them, Jodhpurs is keeping Carnage quiet.

Does that sentence, or does it not, need a question mark. This one does????

Niall is singing about the sash his father wore.

Brendan, his voyaging o'er, is asleep.

The green countryside flows past.

And the great and much-appreciated joke, Lagan says, was that the news went round the town that I was the Lagan responsible.

More green countryside. Beautifully sunlit. One more small town.

How lucky, Lagan says, was Conall Cearnach to live so long ago.

But the sons of Bealcú are on the warpath and one of them reminds the other of the method by which Forbaid, the master-slinger, had fingered Maev, the Queen. Every morning from afar they watch Cearnach grow stronger and they fear for their father, and watch Cearnach coming at dawn to the fountain or well-margin to drink: while Cearnach is thinking, in the words of the poet, how a noble virgin, by a like green fountain's brink, heard his own pure vows one morning, faraway and long ago, all his heart to home was turning and the tears began to flow . . .

Jodhpurs likes that bit.

Not many pure vows, she says, do I hear. Nor Maryanne, in the course of her career.

So Lagan explains that Cearnach is thinking, while he weeps, of the wife and the weans (children, to you), back home in Ulster in Dunseverick's windy tower. Then up he leaps in a fit, runs round like a whirlwind, swings the war-mace, hurls the spear, and Bealcú, also peeping, but from another point of vantage and unseen by his sons, has the crap frightened out of him.

Cearnach, Carnage opines, has had his morning gin-and-tonic. There must be good stuff in that there fountain. Mayo poteen? Mountain dew? Georgia Moon Cawn whiskey?

Which may be more-or-less what Bealcú thinks. Not in relation to booze but about a god who, Bealcú thinks, may be in the fountain and to whom Cearnach prays, and Bealcú reckons he might just sneak in and, himself, mention the matter to the god.

But what about his vow? cries Jodhpurs. His vow to Crom Cruach and the sun and the wind.

She seems to know more about the story than a man might imagine.

She and Carnage are cheek-to-cheek.

Even if not dancing.

Has she tamed him?

Briefly we pause at Roche's of Rathcoole. Just long enough to hear six times on the jukebox one of Niall's favourite songs. Idaho, Idaho, I lost her and I found her at the Idaho State Fair, he broke twenty broncos and one grizzly bear, but she broke one cowpoke at the Idaho State Fair, Idaho, Idaho . . . .

Once in my life I passed, by Greyhound, through Boise, Idaho.

No singing customers are present in Roche's of Rathcoole. It is too early in the evening.

Caan I forget you . . . .

No question mark here needed.

But this is not Dunseverick's windy tower. No, we are back somewhere in the environs of Dublin and we are in a tower, one of four, and one

of them at each corner of an ancient castle. For Lagan, Patrick, has
been invited to a party in this tower. A friend of his rents it. Just the
one tower. He is a prominent painter, this friend. We get there about
midnight. There is a tree in the courtyard that was planted there more
than five hundred years ago. At Lagan's suggestion Carnage tears off a
bit of the bark and some leaves to send to you. They are safely in a
small box and I will bear them with me across the broad Atlantic.
There is a tradition that Edmund Spenser ate his first meal in Ireland
in this castle. As for myself, I ate there what, but for the grace of God,
might have been my last meal on earth: the ghost of the poet, perhaps,
looking over my shoulder and babbling of a goodly bosom like a strawberry bed, a breast like lilies e'er their leaves be shed, and all her body
rising like a stayre, and you know the rest of it, and I love my love in
the morning, I love my love at noon . . . .

Poor fellow. No wonder he entered the Christian Brothers. Not
Spenser. But that other gentle poet.

But speaking of ghosts, this castle is haunted by a peculiar shade.
Or by peculiar footsteps that are heard going up the winding stairs.
But never coming down. Steps only. No person. No wraith.

Carnage says: Don't blame me.

The Castle has other associations which I will enumerate when I see
you. A pleasant seat which I was unable to see. For it is now past midnight. We enter the great hall. Not of the castle. But we enter a pretty
commodious room halfways up the tower. To see a fine throng, glasses
in hands. And to be welcomed. And to see a distinguished-looking,
elderly, mustachioed gentleman trying to climb the wall. Uttering foul
oaths the while. Seems that he has been attempting to climb the wall
for several hours. Nor is he alone at that caper. Several of the guests are
having a go. A hop, step and jump across the room. Then a roar and a
run and a leap at the wall. Does not make sense at first. Then it dawns
on me. The aim of the game is to leap higher than the door, turn round
in mid-air and end up seated on the wide lintel shelf. Solid oak. Only
one guest succeeds. A small man with a Chaplinesque moustache. A
painter. Or, also, a circus acrobat. He is rewarded by a bottle of champagne. Which he drinks while sitting on the shelf.

Lacking the long finger of Forbaid, the master-slinger I stay safely on the carpet. For the wear and tear of the journey to renaissance Parma and back is beginning to tell, and all I want to do is to lie down. So up with me, up the haunted, twisting stairway, up two more floors, the furore dying away below me. No rough men-at-arms do I meet, cross-gartered to the knees or shod in iron. No footfalls do I hear but mine own. A small room I find and, joy of joys, a bed. On which, fully clothed, I collapse with a crash. Then down below in the Hall of Pandemonium, Carnage becomes aware of my absence and is worried. Believe it or not, but Carnage is a real human being. He begins searching all over for me. He runs downstairs and looks all around. All around the grounds and in the pouring rain. Checking all the cars. Climbing the ancient tree. Then, systematically, he begins to search the tower from the ground up. Where, at the end of an hour, he, inevitably, finds me. Shakes me awake to find out if I am still alive. Puts a pillow under my head. Tucks blankets around me. All the while assuring me that I should come downstairs and have another drink to help me to sleep. He is very concerned about me. He says that he mainly worries because I seem so tall, blond, thin and innocent, and mild-mannered, that I can only come to harm among the rougher Irish. Even the women are hard, he assures me, and you have got to be tough to stand up to them. He is taking care of me all the time, talking to me like a worried father to a not-too-bright, not-too-strong son. He is twenty-one. As you know I am twenty-five and have survived even the army.

At four in the morning I arise to begin the day's adorning. Still slightly stupefied. Go down the haunted stairway. My host gives me coffee and sandwiches and tells me that I should write not about Brinsley but about Joyce. He is actually a relation. Not of Brinsley. But of Joyce.

So in honour of James Joyce we go for a morning swim off the Bull Wall where Stephen Dedalus walked and saw the wading girl and cried out heavenly god and all the rest of it. Research, research! Oh, the delights of a dawn plunge in the nude in the dirty water of Dublin Bay. Jodhpurs and all, or Jodhpurs without her jodhpurs. My eyes I modestly avert. Credit that if you can. She swims well. Not Dedalus himself, when he walked into that epiphany, ever saw the like. So strip I do and clamber down the rocks. Brendan, who has more sense, stays clothed and warm and holds my spectacles for me. The water is colder than ice and about as comfortable as broken glass. But it almost restores us to sobriety. We splash around there for thirty minutes or so and nobody, praise the Lord and hand me down my bible, is cramped or drowned. Then we sit on the rocks and watch the day coming up over Dublin city, and over the bay, and over Clontarf where Brian Boru bate the Danes, the dacent people, Lagan had said, without whom there never would have been a Dublin. For Brian, Lagan had argued, was a wild man from Limerick or thereabouts, as bad as or worse than Carnage or Bealcú . . . .

Now Lagan has gone. For unlike the rest of us he has a home and a family to attend to, and Jodhpurs tells to the end the tale of the killing of Bealcú, another sore case of mistaken identity. She has read the poem, or has had it read to her, at school. Seems hard to believe that a strong broad like Jodhpurs ever went to school or to anywhere except the racing-stables. But Carnage says she was very bright at school, prizes and scholarships, and still is, and in all sort of places and ways, and can hold her own in talk on such topics even with the learned Lagan himself who is, says Carnage, as you have noticed, a sound man, and he will have my suspension lifted, he has the decency, he has the influence and he doesn't really mind being mistaken for me, it gives him stories to tell, and you may have noticed that he has a weakness for telling stories.

It is now the intention of Carnage to finally (Lagan would violently object to the split infinitive but since he's not here to hear me I'll split it wider still), get in the sack with Jodhpurs, when she will be once again divested of her jodhpurs, and Jodhpurs is raising no objection. As for me, I walk alone because to tell you the truth I am lonely, I don't mind being lonely when my heart tells me you're lonely too . . . .

Then Karnage, who is kind, forgive that one, says come home with him to his apartment, he has a spare room and Maryanne is not, at the moment, in it, and he wants me to sleep for eight hours while he and

Jodhpurs do what they have to do, and he loves his love in the morning and all the way to noon. So he hits the gas and speeds back towards Dublin city. Only the three of us left. The roads are wet and slippery. They almost always are in Ireland. We turn a corner. We approach a bridge. We go into a spin, an all-out spin. To you I pray. We ram the brick wall of the bridge. It rams us. Karnage is thrown out of the Kar. The front windshield kisses me, my only kiss since I left Atlanta. But it holds up under the strain and Jodhpurs gets the reins, the wheel, and tames the horse and all is almost well. What I sustain, you may be glad to hear, is, merely a stunned elbow, a bruised black-and-white forearm and a cut finger. They will be perfect again when I get to Peachtree.

We are now somewhere on the outskirts of Dublin city. It is very early on a Sunday morning and nobody to be seen and, to top it all, it begins once again to pour rain. We try to push the car over off the road into a vacant lot. But the front right fender is crushed into the tyre and will not allow the wheel to move. We pull, we push, we grunt, we strain. No deal. Well, we make twenty-five yards but that gets us nowhere except into the middle of the road. But, God a mercy, along comes a big milk-truck, ties a rope to the battered bumper or fender, drags the wreck into the vacant lot. The rain continues. We start to walk downtown. The truck is going the other way. Another truck. Going my way. Offers us a ride. Do we accept? You're goddamn right we do. And gratefully settle back. To travel half a block when Truck Number Two cranks out. Oh Gawd! We walk on. The rain continues.

In the north of Dublin city there stands a small hotel. More than one, but one will do.It's not the Ritz or the Savoy but the door is open and the coffee hot and strong. Karnage has left his Kamera in the Kastle. Now we krack. Karnage and I. Not Jodhpurs. She pours the coffee. We sit in the lounge. Just the three of us. But when Karnage talks to me I hear instead the booming voice of Lagan. Not imagination. Really, the booming voice of Lagan. He sings about the sash my father wore. He sings in Irish about a maiden in Donegal whose cheeks were like the roses and her little mouth like brown sugar. Honey with the mouth like brown sugar. A good beat for a black combo. He recites about dear

Pádraig of the wise and seacold eyes, so loveable, so courteous and so noble, the very west was in his soft replies. But Lagan is nowhere to be seen. He says that free speech shivered on the pikes of Macedonia and later on the swords of Rome. He says Love that had robbed us of immortal things, and I rise to protest, but he is not there.

This is ghastly and I tell Karnage who says that, Good God, he hears him too.

We search the lounge. But he is nowhere to be found. Nobody anywhere to be seen except an unconcerned and bored female clerk. We pay for our coffee. We depart.

In the spare room of Karnage I lie down and try to sleep, remembering Thee, on Peachtree. But right away the room is full of voices and above them all the voice of Lagan intoning that by Douglas Bridge he met a man who lived adjacent to Strabane before the English hung him high for riding with O'Hanlon.

Then up I leap and dress, and tiptoe, almost running, out of the house to walk, in a daze, the awakening streets and find a restaurant, and eggs and coffee. Then I go to my lodgings.

I might not have bothered to tiptoe. Karnage later tells me that when he has done the gentlemen by Jodhpurs they sleep, off and on, for thirty-six hours. You may have noticed that I have just broken one of my rules.

Stretched out again on a bed and sleeping, I suppose, I have this strange dream. This poem I have written and I am reciting it to a group of Roman citizens. It ends like this: A wooden sagging is in my shoulders and wood is dogma to an infidel.

Those words I take from my dream exactly as dreamt. No meaning. No connection with anything. But in my dream they made sense. Housman said that each man travels with a skeleton. Lagan had been booming about Wenlock Edge and the wood in trouble and then 'twas the Roman now 'tis I. Perhaps I was trying to say that each man carries within himself a cross, the shoulders the crossbar, the spine the upright.

Damned if I know. Or care.

Time Passes.

We are back in the Abbey, the bar not the theatre. A lawyer, or professor of history, a bank-manager who is also a music-critic and who plays the organ in a church, two actors from the theatre, and Niall and Brendan and Karnage and Lagan. No Jodhpurs. No Maryanne. Maryanne I am never to meet. But Brinsley honours us by his entrance. Huge, stately, brown overcoat, wide-brimmed hat. Leaning on stick.

Karnage has confiscated your, or my, necktie of many colours which he is wearing with wild ostentation. Cleverly he conceals the coloured body or expanse of it under a modest pullover, then whips it out like a lightning flash to startle and dazzle each and every newcomer. Lagan says that he and Karnage will wear your necktie, week about, so that they will never forget me nor the voyage to Parma. I am touched. (For a second time I have broken one of my rules.) Leaving that resplendent necktie with them, I know that as long as it lasts, and the material is strong and well-chosen, I will be remembered and spoken of in the land of my forefathers.

And Lagan has used his influence and Karnage is no longer suspended.

They go off to work together.

Time passes.

Curious thing, Brinsley says to me, but there are young fellows who say about me that I belong to a past time. I don't mean a pastime. But a previous period in history. But there is no time that is absolutely past, and little time in the present, it passes so quickly and, for all you or I or anybody knows, there may be no time in the future. Only eternity, we have been told. A most dismal idea. Imagine listening to (he mentions a well-known name), and God help and preserve him and lead him to a better and happier way of life, but imagine listening to him forever. So here's to the young fellows who think they know more than their elders. The total sum or aggregate or whatever you call it of knowledge, or whatever, in the human brain is always about the same. You might as well listen to your elders. You'll end up like them and nothing much accomplished. Lagan, though, is different. He raises his cap, mentally, to men older than himself. He admits that we have been here first and he knows that he is on the way to join us. Curious thing.

Time passes.

But whatever exactly did happen to Bealcú who broke his vows to the god, to the sun, to the wind. The poem I will read to you when I meet you, as arranged, in Washington D.C. My vows I have kept and will keep. All of the forty-one verses of four lines each I will read to you when you have the leisure to listen.

Conall Cearnach is safely back in Ulster.

Time passes.

If anybody in time to come ever reads this letter, found in a tin box in a hole in the ground on Kennesaw mountain, it may be said that it is merely a zany folktale from an island that once was, way out in the eastern sea. All parish priests and all that. And drink. Well, there are a lot of parish priests in Ireland and there is an amount of drink consumed. Apart from a curious crowd called the Pioneers. Not a damn thing to do with Dan'l Boone and the New River that runs west where so many rivers run east.

Here I give you a genuine slice, or bottle, of old Ireland, as I ate, or drank, it.

There may yet be worse things than parish priests in store for the new Ireland.

Time passes.

My money from home has arrived.

To Lagan I owe ten pounds. Not that he would remind me. In an envelope I fold the notes, and leave them, no message enclosed, at the counter in the front-office of his office. Way back behind, the machines are rattling for the morning paper.

Farewells I abhor.

So from the far shore of the Liffey I salute his lighted window and walk home to pack. Peachtree, here I come.

By way of Cork city and Cobb and a liner over the wide Atlantic.

Look for my ghost on Eden Quay. Round the corner from the Sailors' Home ... ...

Afterword:
The Long Way Round
by Ben Forkner

I hope it seems fitting that I begin this talk, in homage to the master, with a digression. Of course no one can compete with Ben Kiely at full gallop. I can't remember the occasion, but he once told me that no story should ever interfere with a good digression. This was a variation on what his father had told him about never allowing mere truth to stand in the way of a good story. Ben Kiely's digressions, of course, were never gratuitous. They always turned out to be vital to the story's final purpose, and absolutely faithful to the strange revelations of the human voice, free to seek its way forward, and backward, hunting down every turn and twist of memory, inspiration, and whim, and rejoicing all the time in the promise of the search. As anyone who has read a Kiely story, or has heard him speak, can affirm, there is far more to the Kiely voice than its uncanny swerves and spins, as I hope to suggest later on. But at least I know I have his approval for trying a modest digression or diversion of my own before turning back to the highway home.

Home today will be his last published short story, or, as my old Southern Baptist preacher would announce, while the deacons roved the aisles with the large collection plates, my text today will be 'A Letter to Peachtree,' the title story of his final collection. The reference to the old preacher is deliberate. When I first met Benedict Kiely, in Angers,

France, where he had been invited to give a reading, I introduced him with a memory of one of my favourite relatives in the small southern town where I grew up. Uncle Dewey loved to talk, and loved to take advantage of one of the rituals of the church. After the sermon, the preacher would ask the congregation if there were questions or comments. The church was a sizeable one for the town, with around two hundred members in the congregation. There was no air-conditioning in those days, and each member, man, woman, and child, held a large stiff paper fan to wave back and forth during the sermon. When the preacher had finished, and asked if there were any questions, the fans that had slowed down as the preacher droned on suddenly revived. They knew that Uncle Dewey had been given his cue. One hundred and ninety-nine fans beat a little faster, brushing the air all at once, like a whispering chorus. The one that had stopped was always Uncle Dewey's. He had put down his fan when he stood up at the preacher's challenge, usually to disagree, with a word-perfect quotation from the Bible to make his point, and a flamboyant phrase or two completely out of the blue, just for the pure pleasure of the verbal effect. There was never anything aggressive or contentious in his rising up or in whatever he had to say. He was simply assuming his democratic right to speak his mind, and everyone, even the preacher, enjoyed listening. Uncle Dewey was a small town lawyer, and may have envied the preacher a captive audience. But he was a gifted actor, with a gentle wit and a flair for speaking on his feet, and he made Sunday mornings come alive with a spontaneous performance that was never dull.

When I had finished with my introduction, and handed the microphone over to Ben, I expected him to say a few polite words, and then proceed to the task at hand, which was the reading of one of his new stories. Little did I know Ben Kiely then, and how well he could 'out dewey' anyone's uncle. He reached for the microphone with a smile, and immediately picked up the thread with an impromptu recollection of his own. As I later discovered to my joy and amazement on many an occasion afterwards, like the legendary dairy farmer Joe Sutton, in one of Ben's stories, 'Soldier, Red Soldier,' Bendict Kiely had 'a verse to meet every need.' Fortunately there was a tape recorder on, and we were able to transcribe his improvisation. Here is what he said, word for word:

I want to tell Ben Forkner that in Omagh Town, County
Tyrone, where I was reared, we also had Baptists. And I
worked in the Post Office for seven months of my life with
a very charming young man called Elwood Grier. And there
was this Miss Annie Mullen who was Baptist, 'Dippers' we
used to call them. That's because of their being drenched in
the river and baptized. 'Leave well alone, I hate immersion,'
Dr Johnson said, I think, about baptism by immersion. But
Miss Annie Mullen liked me because I could quote the
Bible, the Authorized Version. And the simple reason was
that when I was a young fellow – I should have been in
Duffy's Circus – I had a freak memory. Anything I read, I
could quote it. I've lost the gift now, alas. Annie liked me
for that reason. But Elwood Grier was standing by Miss
Mullen. She was tall, she wore a long, sort of greyish, cardigan. And she had a waist as wide as a bookcase. And Elwood
was sorting letters you see, and he was sorting a letter for
some place that was on the far side of Miss Mullen. Being
such a perfect gentleman, he wouldn't reach across in front
of her to post the letter, so he reached around behind her,
and she struck him: 'How dare you, Mr Grier.' Annie
thought that Elwood was embracing her. He wasn't of
course. He married a very nice girl who worked in the Post
Office at the time and Miss Mullen was not his ambition.

The improvision did not stop with Annie Mullen and Elwood
Grier. It continued without a hesitation or a hitch, weaving in other
stories, and memories, snatches of song and quotation, even a complete theory on the art of the short story, before launching into his
reading. The story he read, by the way, was 'Bloodless Byrne of a
Monday,' later included in *A Letter to Peachtree*, and one of the great
short stories of our times. This was my first experience of Ben Kiely's
extraordinary gift for counter-telling, for matching one story with
another, for creating a seamless narrative of voices and stories reaching
on endlessly, as long as the occasion, or as life itself, permitted. After
his reading, once the drinking and dining had begun, I sat back and

waited for more, relishing the thought that all I had to do as host was to relax and listen. Lo and behold, howandever, as he might have said, he reversed the roles and began asking me questions about Uncle Dewey, Southern Baptists, and growing up in a small country town in the lower latitudes. For three days during his visit to Angers, we talked about the South.

He mentioned that he had lived there as a visiting professor, but did not elaborate. He asked questions, and listened. I began by telling him about my childhood in Florida, in a small coastal town settled mainly by self-exiled farmers from Georgia. At the beginning of the century, in fact, the whole impoverished South had been dazzled by dreams of better lives in the Florida sunshine. My mother's family had moved there from south Georgia, near a remote hamlet called Homerville (James Joyce knew there was a Dublin in Georgia, but I know he never heard of Homerville). It was near the Okefenokee Swamp, a lost wilderness that Benedict Kiely had actually visited. My father's people lived in Decatur, Georgia, near Atlanta. They had moved there from the mountains of east Tennessee, right after the Civil War. After my father's death in the Pacific, at the end of World War II, my mother returned to Florida to be with her parents.

When I was growing up, my town had two or three prosperous families, the owners of cattle ranches and orange groves, but the main population, black and white, consisted of hard-working farmers, shop-keepers, and one-boat commercial shrimpers and fishermen. Many black families had joined the migration from Georgia, leaving behind their grim working conditions as sharecroppers and the harsher racial segregation. In our town there were no chain stores, no shopping malls, and no suburbs. We lived on sun-baked streets within walking distance of the centre of the town on the Indian River. It was in many ways a typical southern town. The accents were all southern, from the precise Mississippi whistle to the high lonesome Kentucky drawl. But the town happened to be located in the middle of a semi-tropical par-adise. Along with the twisted live oaks hanging with Spanish moss, there were coconut trees, royal palms, hibiscus hedges, giant poinciana trees, oranges, grapefruit, lemons, kumquats, guavas, pineapples, and mangoes. The river, the mile-wide Indian River, was actually a salt

BEN FORKNER

water lagoon, filled with small islands and hidden coves where a boy
with a small boat and a fishing pole and a bucket of live shrimp for bait
could disappear for a summer day. We were in fact surrounded by
water. To the north was the Banana River, to the south the St Lucie
River, and to the west the great Lake Okeechobee. A few hundred feet
east of the Indian River was the Atlantic Ocean, and a beach that
stretched for miles north and south, without a single building or
tourist to spoil the view.

When I talked about this to Ben, he was fascinated by the idea of
the remnants of the old south, as it were, washed up on a tropical
beach. When I told him the size of the population, around fifteen
thousand, and the names of my friends, the Callahans, the Moodys,
the Moomeys, the Cadenheads, the Stokes, the O'Briens, he said it
sounded much like the Omagh of his youth, without the mangoes.

Omagh was on his mind too, I think, when he spurred me on with
more questions. My friends and I never had to look far afield, or to
strain our wits, in order to leapfrog boredom and lope through the
long afternoons. Our escapades reminded him of his own boyhood.
After all, we both had been given the wide world of nature and all the
open countryside at our doorsteps. As he said, 'it was great to be out
and be a boy.' Even violent weather did not often keep us indoors.
Nothing will ever quite match the thrill of sitting on a bamboo raft on
a dark inland river during a sudden downpour. Under a wild magnolia
tree that drummed with rain, three of us watched in wonder as the
storm threw pitchforks of lightning out of the blackness. I told Ben
how much time I had spent on horseback. Well-trained cowhorses
were easy to come by from the ranches west of town, and we all had
two or three. One favourite sport was to race them through abandoned
orange groves, throwing rotten oranges at each other while trying to
dodge the zebra-striped spiders hanging from their great webs between
the trees. I should have remembered, but did not, that Omagh had
horses too, along with the Baptists. Think of Tony in 'The Shortest
Way Home.' Tony is the old horse Ben and his school friends 'the four
horsemen' stop and admire as they take the long way round back to
Omagh. Tony may be the oldest horse in literature, with 'white spots
of age on his hide like stabs of lichen on old stone.' What I like best is

Ben's description of Tony's 'lovely smile.' It takes a fine eye to recognise that horses will always smile, when relaxed, and in good company.

As boys do, Ben and his friends in that same story trade legends of the strong men they admire, Big Mick O'Neill, the local railway porter, and Patrick Sheehan, the Dublin policeman. I remember Ben's knowing look when I told him about working with 'Foots,' the strongest man on the Indian River. Foots was the black foreman in the fertilizer yard. I had first heard his name one summer at the ice house, listening to the black workers talk about him while my friends and I sat on the bags of crushed ice waiting to be carried to the fishing boats. I learned he had the biggest feet in Florida, and had won a contest to prove it. As a young man, he had beaten every rival in the dance-hall fights on Saturday nights, but he hated fighting. I met him a few years after the ice house stories when I took a job at the fertilizer yard. He was everything I had heard, a giant of a man who could lift with each hand hundred pound sacks of sludge as if they were filled with foam. But he was a gentle giant, one of the kindest and most courteous men I have ever met. He would have made mincemeat of the heavyweights today. He would not have wanted me to say it, but mincemeat they would be.

During our three-day meeting in Angers, thanks to Ben's questions, and his manifestations of genuine interest, I rambled on a great deal about my early days in Florida. One effect of so much talking, of course, was the way one memory would call forth another. It took me some time to realise that these convivial attentions were at the heart of a long-proven Kiely method. His questions were aimed at drawing me out, and drawing me in. They urged me to let my own story, however ordinary in my eyes, and however locked up in the past, reveal itself as worthy of being remembered and told. The same method can be found in much of his fiction, especially in the short stories, in which the narrator, almost always Kiely himself, prompts and lures the main story out of whomever he is talking with, whether it be an old friend or a chance encounter on the road. There are stories everywhere, but it helps to have a Benedict Kiely close at hand to bring them back to life. In my case, I soon discovered, Ben had private, or at least personal reasons for sounding me out. As I have mentioned, there was a powerful

Georgia note in my memories. In the Florida town where I was born and raised I was surrounded by Georgians, including my mother, my grandmother and grandfather, and uncles and aunts and older cousins too numerous to count. Listening to their stories, as I told Ben and as I wrote down later, I was never allowed to completely shake the sensation of a having been displaced from a more authentic source. Georgia was north of Florida, but much deeper in the south. Especially in my grandparents' memories of rural Georgia, life was harder and heartier. There was more pain, but more resistance to pain. The threats of sudden violence were constant: disease, accidents, wild animals, treacherous strangers. Death came in the form of lockjaw, cottonmouth moccasins, rabid dogs, and midnight murder. But apparently these could be overcome: otherwise my grandmother and grandfather would not be there speaking to me on the front porch, and around the kitchen table.

My mother's stories of her childhood in Homerville, on the edge of the Okefenokee swamp, were the ones that left the deepest impression. As Ben knew, and as I found out, they were counter-stories of a past that was not mine, but that had as much a claim on my life as my own boyhood in Florida. The past is filled with counter-stories of the present, or it may be the other way around. And I cannot think of any writer who demonstrates this truth with more vividness, and with more conviction, than Benedict Kiely. Ben wanted to know more about my mother. I told him two or three stories. In one, she is a barefoot girl sitting on her front porch with her mother (my grandmother of course) when she saw a Model T Ford come by with two men in the front seat, and a woman in the back. Her mother told her: 'There goes Sheriff Lee taking Miss Cora Sweat to Milledgeville.' By Milledgeville she meant the home of the state insane asylum. An hour later the Model T came back again in the opposite direction, this time with the woman driving and the two men in the back.

Ben enjoyed my mother's obvious love of the Georgia she had left, despite the suffering and pain some of her stories described. She took me around with her on summer trips, stopping to tell me about places connected with the family, or with historical events, much as Benedict Kiely's father does in the story 'A Journey to the Seven Streams.' She knew the flaws and failures of the past, and had no illusions about the sad human history of her land, but it was hers, and through her it became mine. She amused me, and herself, by calling the Civil War the War of Northern Aggression. When I told Ben this, he answered that when he lived in Atlanta he had climbed to the top of Kennesaw Mountain to look the way the invasion came.

Looking back now, I think there were at least two reasons Ben pressed me on about my mother. One was Georgia, where Ben had lived for two years. He had just written his own Georgia story when we met in Angers, but it had not yet been published, and he did not mention it. This was his last story, 'A Letter to Peachtree,' which I will turn to eventually, I promise, after another digression, or two. The other reason was his faith in counter-telling. After his spontaneous response to my Uncle Dewey story, he was deliberately reserved in answering my stories with his own. These would come in later meetings, and in our correspondence over the years. For the moment, he was content to listen to my mother's stories counter and complete my own.

I realise now that long before he encouraged me to talk about Florida in Angers, the stories Ben Kiely had written demonstrate again and again the fundamental bond of memory and identity. Ben is one of the great memorial writers, not just in the sense of celebrating experience, which he always does, but in his insight into the way a man's mind holds on to certain stories as affirmation of his existence, and perhaps even of existence itself. Certainly it is only in countering the stories we hear with the stories we tell that we know we belong to the world, though the word world is far too grandiose and biblical a term to use here. I would not want Uncle Dewey springing from the grave to object. Let him rest in peace. Suffice to say that necessary cycles of stories cling to every man's life. From the first solitude of childhood, they move back and forth between family and friends, carrying us along into the future, and backward in time to fuse with the repeated memories of the older clan or community. That is probably enough. We can feel that the stories we remember lead us directly into the dark mystery of identity, whatever that may be. They are certainly dearer to our lonely bones than all the weary theories of nationality, and closer than any claim of nationality to the greater idea of the human family. I suspect Benedict Kiely would agree. In fact I know he would, given the power of the stories he has written, and the enduring life and appeal of the voices they contain.

Because of these voices, including his own, on the page and in the flesh, Ben Kiely has often been singled out as one of the last great Irish storytellers. No one could argue with that. But I would want to add that his skill at counter-telling makes him far more of a singularity, and more of a revolutionary, than is often recognised, especially in the rich tradition of the modern Irish short story. This is no small achievement. It may be almost as great a feat to renew a tradition as to create one.

Everyone knows that in Ireland the old high value placed on the spoken word reached well into the twentieth century. This may help explain Ben's lifelong interest in the South, where a similar value stubbornly persisted long after it had lost ground elsewhere. To a large degree, southern writing spilled straight from the overflow of talk in the country store, in the barber shop, on the church steps, right into the mainstream of literary modernism. Think of William Faulkner's short story 'Dry September' or Eudora Welty's 'Petrified Man' as proof of the point. The modern southern writer, like all moderns, is self-conscious, ironic, and sceptical, but he continues to believe that the human voice, inner and outer, is the one sure key to character. The radical southern voice is the origin of William Faulkner, just as the radical Irish voice is the origin of W. B. Yeats. Memory and identity, voice and character; these ideas are not easy to unravel one from the other, and probably do not need to be. Thankfully, as far as I am concerned, I can only touch on them here. Still, they do pull us back home, I hope, and back to Ben and the Irish short story.

One or two examples should be enough to find our way. It is an odd fact to contemplate, but the modern Irish short story began on a stage. The Abbey Theatre was founded by Yeats in 1904. During the summer of that year, young James Joyce watched as the old Mechanics Institute was being transformed into the new theatre. Joyce admired Yeats immensely. He tried at first to involve himself in the grand project, but he did so half-heartedly, with the growing conviction that he could never belong to a movement of any kind. But there was another reason for his frustration. Yeats planned the Abbey as the place where a new Irish community would be reborn. It would fulfil its purpose, and fill its halls, by searching backward toward the Irish Celts and outward toward the peasant hinterland and the old forgotten landed estates. It was there, he believed, that the folk and the gentry would reveal the voice of the future because they were the only ones left who spoke the living voice of the past. For Joyce, there were two problems with Yeats's vision of Ireland. Its heroic casting of the Irish character flew full in the face of Joyce's modern anti-heroism. And then too, there was the glaring absence of Joyce's Dublin in Yeats's new world. Here was a dramatic irony, so to speak, that struck Joyce with the shock of a divine mission. If Yeats's Irish theatre insisted on excluding the Dubliner from the resurrection taking place in the middle of his own city, there was one doubting Dubliner ready to take up the challenge.

It is imposssible to pinpoint the hour and the day when Joyce conceived of *Dubliners* as a complete cycle of stories. I like to think the inspiration came to him as he fell on his back in a drunken stupor after attending one of the pre-Abbey rehearsals that summer. From this perspective, so to speak, he could look at Ireland from the bottom up. A very colourful account of the incident is commemorated in *Ulysses*. Whatever the exact moment, the modern Irish short story was born, and with it a more doubtful and dismissive assessment of the human community (all too human, Joyce would have reminded us) and the true Irish voice. What is truth? we can hear Joyce echo.

Joyce's parade of lost souls and failed lives in his book of *Dubliners* is bleak, but the very title itself suggests, however faintly, the hope of community that *Ulysses* openly celebrates on a June day that same summer. And the language the reader hears in certain stories, 'Ivy Day in the Committee Room' for one, is as witty and unpredictable as anything in *Ulysses*. In fact, before the short stories of Ben Kiely appear on the scene, 'Ivy Day in the Committee Room' may be the most vocal story in modern fiction. The motley gathering of men in a theatrically unlit room on Wicklow Street, across the river from the Abbey, never cease talking. They talk to little purpose, like out-of-work actors remembering broken lines from all the roles they never performed. But the language itself is full of energy and life, just like the spirit of the dead Parnell who moves through the story with more life than the living. What is missing in all the talking, all the repetitions, hearsay, gossip, and mimicry, is the presence of an independent voice, and without that there can be no community, no communion, and no counter-telling. There is no contradiction in Joyce's attitude. Our minds are filled with all manner of voices we hear and repeat from the beginning to the end. It is easier to let these voices possess us, than to develop our own.

After Joyce, and after *Dubliners*, self-possessed voices enter the Irish short story with a vengeance. This is especially true of the second generation of writers, dominated by Frank O'Connor. Perhaps Joyce's negative example provoked them to opposition, just as Yeats had provoked Joyce. There are many strong individual voices in O'Connor's stories, but they are usually heard speaking outside and against the community, thus in a kind of denial of the concept itself. O'Connor's families and social clans are often grim and forbidding in their conformities. We usually see them through the eyes and words of a victim, or an outcast, voluntary or not, but always beyond the pale. O'Connor developed his own theory of the short story as the literary form best suited to the solitary vision, and wrote a critical study called *The Lonely Voice* to justify it. There is nothing wrong in saying that few stories better demonstrate his argument of lonely voices than his own. They are remarkable stories, and well deserve the honour of a theory custom-made to match.

Benedict Kiely knew and admired Frank O'Connor, but just as O'Connor absorbed Joyce and had the genius to move the Irish story into new directions, Kiely absorbed Joyce and O'Connor, and all the others, and had the genius to carry the tradition beyond and elsewhere, creating a form of short story that to my mind ranks in originality with the best stories of our time, bar none.

I will not surprise you, by now, in saying that one source of that originality is Ben's gift in counter-telling, in creating a narrative capable of shifting from one voice, one story, to another, from the present to the past, and back again, all meeting to flow toward a single revelation of the human condition. I like to think he was able to pull all these voices and stories together in one deep current for two reasons. First of all, he had a strong independent voice himself, strong enough to hold his own in any exchange, in any circumstance, high, low, and in-between. That voice, open, engaging, and liberated, and thus liberating in others, is present in every one of his stories. Unlike Joyce, who called on the artist to hide behind his handiwork, Kiely thrusts himself forward in his stories with absolute honesty. When you sense Benedict Kiely is speaking and searching for himself, you may be sure that is the case. Then, there is his memory of Omagh. All the force of his narrative art flows out of the Omagh of his youth.

Omagh is not, or was not, in Kiely's mind, the ideal community. As a committed realist, he did not expect, or even desire, perfection of life. There can be no ideal community, given the perversity of the human soul, and the accidents of fate. Still, unlike the exclusive clans of O'Connor, Omagh was good enough, even better than good enough. It provided Kiely with an image of human cohesiveness, a mid-sized town, like many others, striving for growth and completeness even if completeness could never be reached. Much of the striving came through speaking, and the speaking seldom stopped. It was a town and a time where voices bursting with life and love of company could be heard everywhere, in couples and in clusters, morning to night, and Benedict Kiely seems to have remembered every single one, his own among them.

This is one reason we should be wary of thinking of Ben Kiely in the guise of a traditional storyteller, as a town crier or a communal voice. His gift allows the community to speak for itself, in all its voices, the whole human comedy, living, dying and dead. As we all know, the human comedy is more tragic than comic, a warning that we should not insist too much on Benedict Kiely's far-famed wit and jocularity. They are there on every page, but so are the voices of loss and frustration and broken hearts. In a town like Ben's Omagh, these lonely voices wander through the side streets and on the river banks never too far not to be overheard, and young Ben did not miss a syllable.

Think of his masterpiece, 'Down Then by Derry,' one of many. There are lines in it that make me laugh out loud at every reading. But it is one of the saddest stories ever written. There is enough loneliness and longing in it to fill any number of empty wells. I mention it here not so much because of its layers of grief, but because it is a good example of Kiely's counter-telling weaving back and forth with the greatest of ease and effect between present and past.

As you know, 'Down Then by Derry' is the story of a family reunion in Omagh and a nearby village during the New Year holiday. Benedict Kiely is just back from his two-year stay in Atlanta (Georgia again!). He is called Brian in the story, but Ben he is. With his daughter and son, the sixty-year-old writer, now without a wife, is paying a visit to his mother. Once in Omagh, the memories leap back to when he was a fourteen-year-old troubled by the first stirrings of sexual desire. One memory generates another, and one story swirls around another. There are far too many to mention here, but it helps to think of the main story as a cycle of three, a mysterious trinity of stories that cannot be separated. One is the memory of his boyhood, one is the account of the family reunion, and the third the story of an orphan girl he remembers seeing but never met, and who now has moved to the United States. She has read his books, and writes him letters about her lonely life as a child in Omagh. How these three stories counter and circle round each other is a wonder to behold. And so are the individual human portraits each contains.

There is Tom Cunningham, the nineteen-year-old rake, and his free-spirited girlfriend, Sadie Law. Tom tries to enlighten young Ben in the ways of the world, even to the extent of showing him Bluebottle and the Jennet, two fallen women who ply their sad trade in the dark corners of the Old Market. Ben himself has fallen for Angela, ripe and willing, or should I say, sexually mature, but the boy Ben is too shy to make any headway. Back in the present, there are wonderful portraits of Ben's two children, and his gentle mother. She radiates an old-fashioned dignity, but has a strong voice of her own, a remarkable memory, and as many gripping stories as her son. One is the sad ghost story she thrills her grandchildren with by telling once again. They know it by heart.

Finally, there is the third story, told through Ben's memory of the letters the orphan girl, now a married woman, writes to him from America. These letters are filled with solitude that stands in stark contrast to Ben's circle of friends and family. He might have suffered, but he could always count on a cushion of support. When he sees Angela going off in a field with a black-bearded soldier, Tom tells him not to worry. He will find another girl. 'From here to China the world's full of them.' With his mother, daughter, and son, and the memory of his father, waving to him as he goes off to college, Ben may be the aging 'widow man,' but he is the centre of a loving family. As 'Down Then by Derry' proceeds, the letters reveal a much bleaker existence. Still, they bring the girl and the woman into the wider circle. Ben has done this even before the trip to Omagh. While living in Georgia he answers and counters her letters with letters of his own. They contain clippings from the newspapers he receives from home. Ben's daughter, taking after her father, prods him to tell the story. He does so, little by little, and the silent voice of the letters is no longer silent. In some ways, the voice is stronger because of the silence. After all, the letters themselves are a defiance of solitude. As a writer, and a reader, Ben would have known this better than most.

Examples of counter-telling abound in Kiely's stories, with variations as numerous as the examples. 'The Weavers at the Mill,' 'A Great God's Angel Standing' and above all 'The Dogs in the Great Glen' are among my favourites. But what about 'A Letter to Peachtree'? I thank you, or Uncle Dewey, for asking. It is about time to head home.

As far as I can determine, 'A Letter to Peachtree' is the last work of fiction Benedict Kiely published. It is a remarkable performance in many ways. For one thing, it rebounds or fights back from the dark vision of depravity and death in *Proxopera* and *Nothing Happens in Carmincross* with a final ode to the joy of living. Living well, when we have the will and the wit, is the best revenge, and living well, for Ben Kiely, demands the human voice and its creative power of warding off dullness, stupidity, and self-importance with poetry, song, story and convivial human contact. No simple summary can do 'A Letter to Peachtree' justice, but we can begin with the title, and go on from there. John Karney is a young graduate student at Harvard University who has come to Ireland to do some research on the writings of Brinsley MacNamara. John is a student at Harvard, but he hails from the Deep South, and is writing a letter home to his girlfriend in

Atlanta. That is all the background we need for John.

The main thrust of the story is propelled not by John but by the group of four Dublin friends, all working for the same newspaper, who invite him on a wild weekend in May into the midlands to see a play, and then back to Dublin. One of the friends is Patrick Lagan, the alter ego of Ben Kiely, who used that very name when he wrote a column for the *Irish Press*. The others are Conall, the cameraman, and Brendan and Niall, both reporters like Patrick. Think of their names: Conall, Brendan, Niall, Patrick, a thundering rollcall of mythical, legendary, or historical Irishness that echoes and resonates all through the story. They take young John under their Irish wings and hustle him off on a train westward. On the way they pick up an unattached young woman referred to as Jodhpurs. She is on her way to the horse race in the Curragh of Kildare, but really out for a lark, and despite her riding boots, footloose and fancy free. Her surname turns out to be Carney too. She joins the others, and that makes six. Two is company, and so is three, or six, as far as Benedict Kiely is concerned.

And here my account of the narrative action must stop. If not, I run the risk of going on forever. To tell you the gospel truth, after each reading, I feel I know less and less. Perhaps only an old Dublin friend of Ben's at the time would recognise all the local allusions and private jokes. And no one but Ben could remember every verse of every poem that the booming voice of Patrick Lagan lavishes on his audience. Apparently, the trip is based on one that Ben himself made, and I suspect the original version of John Karney is now teaching somewhere in the United States, under his real name, probably in the South. What does it matter, as Ben might say, as long as we take the train in the right spirit, and go along for the ride. Anyway, a great deal of liberty has surely been taken with the biographical facts, and the transposed story we read on the page is what counts in the end.

It does help, even in a first reading, to recognise that the main literary reference is to the Samuel Ferguson poem about Conall Carnach, the great Celtic warrior in the Ulster Cycle. 'The Healing of Conall Carnach' is from Ferguson's nineteenth-century collection, *The Lays of the Western Gael*. Commenting on the name of his friend, the cameraman, Patrick Lagan recites the poem, on and off, to young

John, as a baptism into Celtic mythology. Conall, the cameraman, is a champion lady killer, and thus, though not in the same line of work, a man of many conquests like his namesake. He is the source of much of the laughter and misadventure in 'A Letter to Peachtree.' Patrick calls him Conall Carnage. Names seemed to be wrapped up in the story's meaning. Patrick and Conall share the same surname, and so do Jodhpurs and John. Thus there are two Lagans, and two Karneys, and to add to the confusion, the Ulster hero in Ferguson's poem is Conall Carnach, which is not all that different from Karney. Remember the theatrical context of the story. The group has left Dublin to report on a play that has been denounced by the local clergy. It was supposed to be Genet's 'The Balcony,' according to Conall, but 'The Balcony' has been replaced by John Ford's Jacobean revenge tragedy, 'Tis Pity She's a Whore.' With all this role-playing going on, and the duplication of names, we could be tempted into thinking of 'A Letter to Peachtree,' as a comedy of errors, one more genial Irish farce. There are certainly enough confusions, imbroglios, and mistaken identities for more than one.

But the doubling of names might also suggest that the southern scholar and his friends are more like each other than not, despite all the differences of age, culture, and origins. Instead of one more comedy of errors, Ben Kiely gives us a one-of-a-kind comedy of complicity. What drives the story along is the binding nature of friendship, with the group of old friends holding on and helping out each other through hell and high water, and bringing a young stranger from faraway Georgia into their 'mixed and merry throng.' And naturally, being a Ben Kiely story, the binding is done through speaking and the telling of stories. All four friends take their turns. At one point Brendan and Niall go off to Limerick, and come back with a tale of their own adventures, drinking with an old man in the mountains. The only weak voice in the circle is John's, but he is beginning to learn. With a mentor like Patrick Lagan, he cannot fail. At the end of the story, back in Dublin, Lagan has gone to be with his family, after a night of drinking and a sunrise swim off the Bull Wall in honor of James Joyce. But even in his absence John hears Lagan booming away with song and poem. He tries to sleep, but 'rightaway the room is full of voices and above them all the voice of Lagan intoning . . . .'

This is the reason of course, that the voice of Lagan, read Kiely, is heard throughout the letter. What is more natural for an impressionable young man (Lagan calls him the 'embryo scholar') than to be impressed. The words he writes are the ones he has heard, but at least he has listened, and the memories, if not the words, are his own. He can add them to the stories his grandmother from Mayo has told him, and draw on them in the future. There are signs at the end of 'A Letter to Peachtree' that he is beginning to find his own voice. Throughout the story he is determined never to begin a sentence with the letter I. Just before dropping off to sleep in Conall's spare room, he breaks his rule for the first time. He then dreams of writing a poem, and reciting it to a group of Roman citizens. It makes little sense when he wakes up, but he grapples with it until a semblance of meaning emerges. It has something to do with crucifixion, and the essential solitude of the human creature. Solitude and speech, two halves of the same reality. Before leaving Ireland there is a reunion. Conall is wearing the flaming necktie of many colours that John's girlfriend has given him in Atlanta. Conall will keep it, and share it with Lagan, from week to week, so that 'they will never forget me.' The tie that binds. Ireland and Georgia, Georgia and Ireland. He has become part of their memory, and they of his; a new cycle of stories can now begin.

Ben Forkner
(Benedict Kiely Literary Weekend 2008)